P9-DEW-728

# Love Is Red

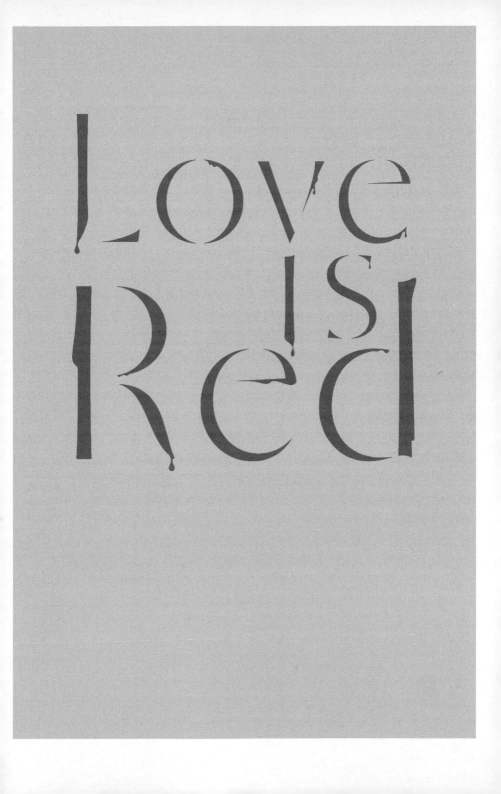

HARPER

*An Imprint of* HarperCollins*Publishers*

# Love Is Red

*A Novel*

SOPHIE JAFF

This book is a work of fiction. The characters, incidents, and dialogue are drawn from the author's imagination and are not to be construed as real. Any resemblance to actual events or persons, living or dead, is entirely coincidental.



Book photograph by Palokha Tetiana/Shutterstock, Inc.

*Designed by Sunil Manchikanti*

ISBN: 978-0-06-234626-1

*For my family;*

MY MOTHER WHO PROOFREAD,

MY SISTER WHO CHALLENGED, *and*

MY FATHER WHO IS STILL PATIENTLY WAITING TO READ A COPY.

*I love you all.*

There is no word or action but has its echo in eternity.

—PYTHAGORAS,
AS QUOTED IN
*Pythagoron:
The Religious,
Moral and
Ethical Teachings of
Pythagoras*,
EDITED BY
HOBART HUSON

O world, I cannot hold thee close enough!

Thy winds, thy wide grey skies!

Thy mists, that roll and rise!

Thy woods, this autumn day, that ache and sag

And all but cry with colour! . . .

—EDNA
ST. VINCENT
MILLAY,
"GOD'S WORLD"

# Part *One*

# 1

You pick her up in a bar. She's not the type who would usually let herself be picked up but that's not a problem for you. She's a beautiful woman but she's lonely. The men she's chosen haven't been kind. They've lied to her and made her feel less than she should. And time is ticking on; she's beautiful but she's not getting any younger. She was sitting at the bar when you got there. She had a book. You've seen that move before. A book, to show that she's cool enough to go to a bar with a book, a book and not some girlfriends, a book and not a man. The book is *The World According to Garp* by John Irving. You appreciate that; it shows she has a certain sense of style, sense of humor. You don't approach her immediately. That would be silly. She clearly has her guard up, the way she's nursing that drink, determinedly reading. Still, the outfit she has on says: *I might be reading but that doesn't mean I'm all mind and no body.*

You admire the display, the long shapely legs with their sheen of black panty hose. There's just enough displayed to give you a sense of the thighs, creamy and smooth under the panty hose. But it's just a hint, a suggestion more than anything. Again, you appreciate it. This woman's no slut. She's got class, maybe even a master's degree. She wears the almost regulation pencil skirt, an innocuous good-quality white blouse. She's drinking a vodka tonic by the looks of it.

The pale glass, the slip of lime, and the beautiful lonely woman pretending to read her book. It makes a pretty picture and you admire it for a moment before you move in. Nothing as crass as "hello," though; you've seen a few others try that approach, even calling her "the librarian." Amateurs.

Instead, you wait till they've left and she's really alone. She's stayed on that page for far too long. Then you send over an eighteen-year-old Macallan, a real drink, a serious drink. It's a drink that you know will take her by surprise with its quality and class. You send it over and you wait. She is annoyed at first and suspicious, although it's highly unlikely that any frat boy or middle-class middle management guy would send over that amber-colored beverage.

Then she sees you.

You're not what she expected. You're attractive, serious. You stare at her just long enough to make her uncomfortable and then you tip her a tiny smile, a mere curl of your lip. That's it. Make it clear there are no strings for this expensive drink. She should drink it and be happy and forget about you. But now she can't; now that she knows that she can walk away, she doesn't. So it is she who indicates that you can sit by her, she who initiates conversation, she who is now worried. She's worried you might have a girlfriend, a wife, might be bored, might leave. And you aren't too encouraging, just enough. You give her just enough space to feel safe. You speak quietly. You are witty. You never touch her, not even to emphasize the good point you just made. She leans in to hear you make another dry, amusing observation. She wants you to touch her.

You don't.

Instead you buy another round and then another one. Nothing garish about the gesture, of course. You just nod your head to the bartender. This shows that although you have class, have style, have money, have power, you never show off. You're well educated, smart, powerful, and ambitious but you're not an asshole.

Now the alcohol is entering her bloodstream.

She grows a little looser. Her hair, the small silken pieces by her ears, begins to rebel and grow soft and loose too. The book is pushed away, forgotten. Elbows on the table, leaning in, laughing, touching you lightly on the arm. When she does this she feels how firm your arm is. You work out. She is sizing you up when she thinks you're not looking. She's wondering where this could go.

Already in her mind she's telling her girlfriends how she met you. In her mind she tries out the phrase "in a bar" and melds it to "about to go, looked up, saw each other, talked the whole night through."

Then the bartender announces last call. You say, "Well?" You smile. You shrug.

Suddenly it seems that all her dreams are about to be blown away. You pause just long enough for her tipsy heart to sink like a stone and then you ask her where she wants to go next. This is the question that opens all the doors. This is the question that's really the "yes."

But maybe she's not quite ready yet to admit where she'd really like to go with you. You, with your strong arms, your wry smile, your warmth, the laughter lines around your eyes, the easy way you listen, your clean expensive clothes, which fit well. She doesn't want to be seen to be easy. She's not one of *those* women. She's educated with a job. She's doing okay. She's a lovely woman. She just needs to be courted, a little more anyway. She's keeping a firm hold on herself even if she's a little unsteady. You remind her to take her book. She blushes. She's charming.

You go on to a little bar you know, filled with candlelight that throws quirky small shadows on the wall. You order for both of you. She loves the Pisco Sour you choose for her. You knew she would. She drinks it too quickly. She thinks you're drunk too because you're so warm, because you seem to know her so well.

The small red booth you chose forces you to sit across from each other. She studies your lean attractive face. She marvels at her luck. She wishes you'd touch her. She suddenly wants you very, very much. If you don't touch her she'll die.

Lust is the color of honey dribbled from a spoon; it smells like other people's popcorn at the movies. It tugs like a wave on the underside of your toes, it clinks like a bracelet on the glass of a display counter, it sounds like two people laughing at a private joke, it feels like slippery linen against your cheek, a wall pressed against your back.

You lean over and kiss her passionately. Your lips are strong and warm and soft. You crush her mouth, your tongue and her tongue. Your mouth is warm and tastes faintly of mint. And you kiss her and you kiss her and you kiss her. It's a wonderful kiss. It's a magnificent kiss. It's a kiss so perfect that it leaves her weak and speechless. She doesn't have any bones left in her body. She's amazed that she's still sitting up. You say that you want to get out of there. She nods. She does too. She wants you, wants you so badly that she doesn't care anymore what you, or anyone, or even she herself thinks of her. She wants to be in bed with you. She wants you to kiss her and that whole kiss to envelop her, as if she could live forever in that kiss. Wants you in her and above her and consuming her.

This time you take the book yourself. You don't want her to forget it again.

You go to her place. She still knows what's safe, still wants to be on home territory. It's pleasant but impersonal, Matisse-like prints on the off-white walls. The apartment of a woman who works long hours, the apartment of a woman who's a professional, the apartment of a woman who doesn't want to assemble furniture all on her own. You had offered yours, but completely accept her choice. She imagines your home to be very beautiful and filled with masculine and elegant things. In time she's sure she'll see for herself. She tells you to help yourself to wine; you do. You pour her another glass too. She is on her long soft couch, longing and longing to be in bed with you. You haven't touched her again yet, though. She keeps thinking of that kiss and all the other kisses to come and the things that will follow. You talk as you pour the drinks. You are funny but not inappropriate. You are never inappropriate, never tasteless. You sit beside her with the wine. She's very drunk now. Still, you urge her to take a further sip. You admire her perfect throat as she swallows. Then she closes her eyes. You slip off her shoes, and she smiles faintly as you massage her feet. You are wonderful. It feels amazing. She moans a little because you are good at what you do and you work quickly. She keeps her eyes closed and that is good because it adds to her experience. She can feel your hands, different sensations and textures and touches. She would think about it but she cannot think. Her head is too hot. Her clothes are too tight.

Tight. You run your hands down her motionless arms and massage them, then her hands. This too feels incredible; her eyes are still closed, trying to take in each experience competing for her senses, soft and firm and stroking. Each finger light and tapering, her wrists, their clever elegant bones. You admire each and every digit while you work, while you prepare her. She sighs and you tell her not to open her eyes yet.

Then you are next to her with your arm around her neck. You pull her in closer.

Closer still.

You lean in, and farther in, and you whisper a little secret into her creamy and curved and vulnerable ear. Exposed like a soft little mouse.

Her eyes widen.

You continue whispering and she tries to sit up. She tries to sit up, to look you in the face. She tries to sit up, to see if you are serious.

But you are very strong.

You have put something in her drink.

And now she will find that you have bound her hands with rope. Thin and nylon, the kind that folds easily into your pocket, the kind of rope that will not fray or break.

You slip your strong hand from the base of her neck to her soft warm mouth. She tries to bite you but you remember that trick well. You put some of your fingers into her mouth, holding her jaw apart so her bites feel like nothing more than a puppy teething. You like the wet dark of her mouth, your fingers in the wet dark, and you give her tongue a little pull. Just a little pull, because puppy must know when not to bite, puppy must learn. She whimpers. Maybe it hurts. But it hurts in a good way. You like that. You know that her adrenaline is fighting against the alcohol and the drugs. The adrenaline is no match for you. With your other hand you move down her body. Because she has other parts that you like. So many parts. Slowly you unbutton each button on her blouse. She is trying to wriggle free but she is still unsure. You are incredibly delicate, despite the wiggling. More so, perhaps, because you like a challenge.

You don't want to ruin her shirt. Her breasts, in her bra, are exposed. You run a delicate hand over them. Her nipples tighten despite, or because of, her fear. You bend your face down and suck through the material. She moans again. She's terrified that you're going to bite her nipples, bite them hard. She thinks this because of the secret that you told her.

*How can anyone truly appreciate life who has not destroyed it?*

She thinks she knows what kind of man you are. But she's in for a surprise. She has no idea. No one does. So you are content to suck and lick her round, creamy breasts. Till her nipples are hard and hot in spite of herself. Still struggling, but she's wearing herself out.

Which is foolish.

You, who bring death, know how fleeting life is. You know because you take it, you break it, you inhale it, blood and breath and bone.

Your one hand is still in her hot, wet pink mouth, expertly holding her tongue, and your other hand is down her pencil skirt, down, down and slow. A firm deliberate stroke and then suddenly up between her legs. Now she tries again to wriggle free and maybe for the first time feels a sudden constriction because you have also bound her legs together. You are feeling up her legs, the slick sheen of the tights against the softness at the crotch.

More layers to go through. What to do now? You like it. It's nice to have choices. Puppy moans and writhes a bit.

"Be good, puppy," you tell her. "Be good."

While you think you make circles against her stockinged crotch with your thumb, wide and then smaller, then stroking back and forth against the tight fabric. She tries to close her legs tight. Silly puppy. This only makes you excited to play. You will have to teach her. Casually you tear a hole through her stockings. A perfect hole.

"Bad puppy," you whisper. "Look what you made me do." You like the way she smells now. Sweaty. A rank snarl of animal fear cutting through her floral perfume. She is wearing pale blue panties despite the lace bra. Not her best underwear. She didn't dream she would actually be getting naked tonight. She didn't plan on meeting you. You are rubbing and rubbing her through her underwear while she is still trying to move away. Her eyes so wide and full of tears. You like the wet. You lick the tears away with your tongue and the salt makes you hard. Very, very hard. You are having so much fun. It's fun to play, after such a long time-out. She's smelling the way you like her to smell. You want to eat the way she smells now. You can smell women like a pig smells truffles. Snuffle, snuffle for the truffle. The wet begins to show. Now you ease down the pale blue panties.

"Is my little puppy wet?"

You want to know.

You place one knuckle on her pink nub and gently rub. Rub-a-dub-dub on the nub. You will make her as hard as you. You give it a tiny pull. She moans. Through your hand, your fingers on her tongue. You are tireless. You are strong.

"You like that?" you ask. Yes. Yes, she must like it. You are sure she does. They always do. Thumb rubbing and circling, your fingers climbing down. The eensy weensy spider. And then they go in. Slowly, slowly up, up into the tight, wet, slick dark. So tight and wet in spite of herself. Two fingers up in dark pink pinkness. From somewhere far away you hear puppy whimpering louder and louder.

"Shut up," you say. "Be a good puppy."

Now you have two hands in her. One in her mouth and one in her cunt. You could spin her like a top. Spin and spin and spin. Maybe you will. But she is squirming and moaning too much. You give her shoulders a little shake. Shake 'n bake.

"Play nice," you say.

You don't say, however, that you will play nice. You will not play nice.

She's your first drink after the drought, your first bite after the famine. Hers are the first streaks, the first leaks of bold and brilliant color. You intend to savor every drop.

In the Beginning you did not hunt; you merely sought out and destroyed.

In the Beginning you were swift and did not linger. You took what you needed, you harvested the Vessel, and you were gone. But as the ages of time passed you began to love the colors humming in your veins and pumping through your heart. Each color brought you closer to life, gave you a deeper understanding of how it is lived, so different from the nothing of nothingness, the great absence.

You began to slow down.

You began to enjoy.

You will tell her more stories. Stories to make her eyes wide and her thighs tighten as she tries to draw backward. That's why it's safer when you tie them up. You learned that long ago. It's for her own good. Otherwise she'll move too much, more than you like, and you'll have to stop her moving. Then she won't last too long. This has happened before. Bad girls don't get playtime.

The pills and wine are really taking effect now. You think that she won't give you much more resistance at this stage. Your joy and their suffering always end too soon. You'll have to show her the knife. That should wake her up, for a little while anyway. You open your elegant Italian leather bag—those Italians really have style—and bring out a few of your favorite things.

You expertly gag her with the soft red silken scarf you keep for just such an occasion. Once she can no longer scream, you hold out your blade for her to see.

You smile. You can tell that this one is going to be a fighter after all.

As you prepare her for your true purpose, you call her the name you've wanted to call her all evening.

You lean over and softly call her Katherine.

She stares up at you blearily, the tears leaking down her face. Wet, wet, wet all over. Woozily she shakes her head. That is not her name, and more amusing still, it has dawned on her that maybe if you realize that you have the wrong woman, you'll let her go.

*Oh, I'm so sorry, I've made a mistake,* you'll say.

This you can't resist.

You ask if she means she is not Katherine Emerson. You allow your forehead to wrinkle charmingly. She violently shakes her head, making as much noise as she can through the gag. Which isn't much. You know how to tie a gag. You ask again if she's positive. Her head turns wildly from side to side and clammy desperate sounds come through the silken scarf. The light grows in her eyes. She might still have a chance of escaping you. You're complete crazy, and maybe this has been the key all along.

She's Kathleen, not Katherine. *Kathleen,* she tries to tell you through the gag, *my name is Kathleen. Kathleeeeen!* But it comes out "Eeem, eeeem!"

"Well, in that case," you say cheerfully and move over her as if to release her bonds. The desperate look of hope and relief in her eyes is truly delightful. Really, she is a lovely woman.

Then you laugh and call her "silly puppy," straighten up and step away. Just for the pleasure of seeing her face turn ashen. You drink it in.

Terror is the color of under the bed, it is the color of bone marrow and the color of chalk, it wails like sirens, it hums like wasps, it thuds like an MRI machine, it tastes of sweat, it tastes of metal, it tastes of rising bile, it feels like the scrape of cement against skin, it thumps like a pounding heart.

You come back to the present with a sigh. As pleasurable as this is, you have a mission.

And she is only a means to the Vessel.
Katherine, who woke you from your darkness.
Katherine, who calls you ever closer.
Katherine, your destiny.
Katherine, the perfect one.
Katherine, the only one.

You turn back to Kathleen, bound and gagged on the couch.

Kathleen, your generous provider, the first woman you will harvest from. Her glorious hues of lust and of terror, confined within her skin, cry out to be unlocked.

"Thank you," you say. You pick up your knife.

After all, it's rude to keep a lady waiting.

# 2

Right now the man wearing the cardboard box is telling me about Mexican food.

He looks me in the face as he tells me all about a restaurant called Agave that I must try. I want to look back but I'm not used to so much eye contact. I'm also not used to barely dressed men earnestly telling me about restaurants. My hindbrain is squeaking at me to look down. I want to see his penis. I do not want to see his penis. I never remember specific penises anyway. I appreciate them but I don't remember them as individuals.

Distracted, distracted, distracted, distracted, distracted, distracted.

Right now the man wearing the cardboard box is telling me about empanadas.

"They're the best I've ever had," he says, "one hundred percent guaranteed organic."

He looks me full in the face as he says this. This is not normal in conversations. In normal conversations the eyes tend to naturally slide away and return. No one maintains this much eye contact unless he is taming a dog, or looking at his infant or at his lover in bed. It's unsettling.

"The place is called Agave because they don't use any sugar, and if you're serious about Mexican food, you have to try it."

Currently I am at an ABC party. "ABC" stands for "Anything But Clothes." I myself am wearing only a curtain. Although theoretically the curtain qualifies as "not clothes," it is, in fact, material and therefore has already created a hostile environment with those who take the theme of this party seriously. The people who take this party seriously are the two plump girls and three small hairy men dancing with them. It's been a thin and grudging spring and everyone is tired of layers.

I don't mind the lack of clothes though I find it strangely decadent given what's happening. They just found another girl. That makes three this month. Three girls found in their own apartments with their throats slit, intricate carvings all over their bodies. No one can talk of anything else.

*They're saying it's a serial killer.*

*They can't work out how he gets in.*

*Shit, it's so scary. And she was only found after a week?*

These days when I go to a party I want to get just a little tipsy on red wine. I want to talk about movies seen and unseen, and a smattering of politics, with people who mostly share my viewpoints. I want to flirt and laugh and maybe even dance to a song like "Love Machine" by the Miracles. Now I'm clutching a plastic cup of punch, wishing I were at a laid-back bar where no one is standing around in items that are anything but clothes, talking about murder victims. This party is the reason I wish I were married. I wish I were in a serious relationship, or even a not-so-serious relationship. This party makes me wish I were watching TV, eating Thai, or Chinese, or Japanese, or something ending with "-ese" takeout. Takeout and my socked feet on someone else's lap.

I was blackmailed into attending by one of my remaining single, gay friends, Colin. "Come," he had said, "to a divine party."

He had asked me way in advance. I had said yes. Single and gay is a windfall. I don't have many of those left. I can't afford to lose him.

Only after I had accepted did he tell me that it was a costume party. The bastard. The worst part is that I could be with David. But I thought it would have been rude to bail on Colin, Colin who now sits too close to the host of the party. And I thought I would play a little hard to get with David. "Don't look too eager," said my friends who have husbands. "Make him work," said my friends who have steady boyfriends and long-term partners.

I made the mistake of listening to people who have forgotten what it's like, and now I'm sitting alone and furious in a curtain, wanting to go home. Scantily clad people are having earnest conversations. I watch their teeth gleaming in the dim light. Some lounge on the couches; others stand in small circles. They move as if underwater. I sit on the couch. I stare at my phone. Nothing.

I am waiting for a text. There's no reason why he should text, but still, I want him to text. I could have been with him tonight. We met just over a week ago and now I sit and wait for a text.

Last week I was waiting at the Morgan Library to meet him. Although it was already almost seven o'clock the lobby was flooded with light. Some museums stay open late on Fridays and I thought it was a classy suggestion for a first date. The shining sweep of wooden floor and the clean architectural lines make you feel that (a) you are getting your money's worth of "culture" and (b) you really should do something about organizing your apartment space. Although I was early I was looking at my watch, a nervous habit I've had since forever, when this guy walked up and asked me:

"Do you know what time the museum closes today?"

I was about to answer when I looked at him properly. He was long and lanky with light brown hair that flopped onto his forehead, round glasses, gray eyes, an oval chin.

"David?"

"Katherine?"

When he smiled he looked even better than he had online.

"I'm so glad it's you," he said.

"Why?"

"Because if you weren't Katherine I was going to have to pretend you were anyway."

"Thanks, I think."

"Shall we go in?" He had bought tickets already.

It was a good time to come; the tourists had largely dissipated to take in an early meal before their Broadway musical, and the evening crowd of locals was only beginning to arrive. We walked through the atrium, all acoustics magnified, past the little café in the center with its small steel chairs and round white tables. A couple of waiters were glaring at two doughy women in sneakers and fanny packs who lingered, deep in conversation, over the remnants of their cooling cappuccinos. I thought that after we saw the exhibition we might come here for a drink. It was a little expensive but worth it for the people-watching.

We had wanted to see the *Little Prince: A New York Story* exhibition, but as we entered the second-floor gallery we heard the tour guide before we saw her. Haggard and authoritarian, with a mass of brittle red hair, she beckoned her charges closer.

"Saint-Exupéry smoked like a chimney," she rasped at the group, who had gathered around her. She sounded judgmental. "Come closer, and you can see where he burned a page."

They did, holding up their phones and wriggling offspring for a better view. David and I looked at each other in unspoken agreement, and we went to check out the woodcut exhibition on the third floor.

Here, in the more traditional hush, bowler-hatted figures printed in black blocky ink hung on the dark red walls. An illustrated copy of *The Works of Geoffrey Chaucer* was open under a glass display case. A stunning young black woman stood guard. She looked like she was dying to tackle anyone to the ground and break their fingers joint by joint if they so much as *thought* of taking a photo.

We didn't take photos. Instead we walked slowly from print to print. David didn't hover over me, nor did he leave me completely alone. We moved more or less in time together, making the little *mmm* noises in the back of our throats that one makes when looking at art. When we got to the end he asked, "So what do you think of them?"

"There's something ominous about the 1920s woodcuts, very foreboding."

"Agreed."

"As for the Chaucer"—I shrugged—"they're like fairy-tale illustrations, aren't they? Sort of dark and inviting."

"That is the perfect description. That's exactly what I was thinking."

I felt absurdly pleased to have gotten it right.

Back on the second floor the tour guide was still droning on, now about fighter planes, so we moved to the permanent collection. The aesthetic abruptly changed to the lavish opulence of a nineteenth-century financier's private rooms. Pink swirls in the marble floor yielded to rich red oriental carpets. A magnificent stone fireplace swelled out of the wood-paneled wall and bronze horses reared up by glowing paintings of sorrowing Madonnas, but the most prominent stars were the books. A symphony of volumes in their gilded and latticed casements soaring to the frescoed ceilings, where cupids and angels floated by and gods and goddesses romped on golden clouds. I stared up, drinking it all in.

"Psst!"

I walked over to him, amused. "Does anyone say 'psst' anymore?"

"Okay, I admit it, I've always wanted to say that, but look." He motioned with his head to the corner, where a door stood ajar.

We strolled over.

Next to the door was a sign that said:

TREASURES FROM THE VAULT:
THE SECULAR SPIRIT OF MEDIEVAL LIFE

I bent down to examine it further and realized the exhibition had ended two days ago.

David smiled. "Shall we go in?"

The guard was well on the other side of the hall. There was no one around. It wasn't what I would normally do but—

The gallery was cooler than elsewhere in the museum and dark apart from the faint light of the glass display cases, although most of the objects had been removed. There was something eerie about these empty, glowing cases, as if the contents had crawled away of their own accord. Like furtive children who have snuck into a circus tent, we walked quietly, stopping to look down at what remained: a piece of jewelry, an illuminated sheet of music. I felt a strange little thrill of satisfaction with each item we encountered in our secret treasure hunt. I was so caught up in this new spirit of living on the edge that I deliberately veered away from David into another anteroom of the gallery.

It was a move I regretted almost immediately. All of the cases in this room seemed empty and there was a feeling about the space that unsettled me. It felt like it was *waiting*. I was about to leave when something in a lit case in the far corner caught my eye.

An illuminated manuscript lay open.

I walked up and leaned in closer to look.

The illustration was an arresting one. It was sunset in the picture, the sky a deep crimson hatched with golden lines. In the last of the dying sun a woman stood in the center and stared back out at her viewer. Her skin was eggshell white, her eyes tiny black ovals, her red mouth neither frowning nor smiling. She wore a deep-green dress, the dark folds of her skirt pooled around her feet. Her chestnut hair lay thick upon her shoulders. In her right palm she cupped an apple; in her left she gripped an ornate silver dagger, four red tears dripping from the blade. Behind her, a forest of densely twisted trunks, pale leaves, and yellow ferns crowded together. A little steam drifted up from a squat iron cauldron set off to one side. I could just make out a slim gray tower of a castle in the distance. But my gaze was drawn again to the woman, in one hand an apple, in the other a dagger. *Make your choice*, her tiny black oval eyes seemed to say. *Make your choice.*

"That's an Ouroboros."

I gave a little "oh" of surprise. It was David. He had come up behind me, and as I laughed, he did too.

"Sorry I startled you." He looked down.

"What did you say?"

"I was pointing out the Ouroboros, the snake devouring its own tail, there."

He pointed to the facing page of the text, Latin executed in curved black strokes. The first letter, an *O*, was indeed in the shape of a huge curled serpent swallowing itself. I marveled at the intricate brushstrokes, the rows upon rows of miniscule scales, a line of red, then blue, then red again, at its golden underbelly. The serpent's eyes were dots of venomous green, and the gleaming white fangs emerging from its scaly lower lip engulfing its own tail with a savage ferocity.

David looked at me. "Not every man's going to be able to use the word 'Ouroboros' so comfortably in a sentence. I hope I get points."

"I assume that's why we're here sneaking around, isn't it?"

"Pretty much. I've been trying to use that word ever since I met you, that and 'psst.' " He peered down at the tag containing the description of the work. " '*The Maiden of Morwyn Castle.*' " He spoke softly enough but his voice carried, emphasizing the silence around us. It made me uneasy. " 'From the private collection of'—" He broke off, then continued, " 'Matthew de Villias.' I'll be damned."

"What is it?"

"That's the same last name as my friend."

"Weird."

"I guess it's not completely weird. The guy comes from an old family, makes the *Mayflower* folk look like gentrifiers." He squinted down again.

We heard the hollow tones of a bell, then:

"LADIES AND GENTLEMEN."

The voice was harsh and loud. We both jumped, and then laughed.

"The museum will be closing in approximately fifteen minutes."

"Guess we need to get going."

"I guess so." I tried to sound reluctant but I was glad. I knew we shouldn't be here.

David started off toward the main door out of the gallery, but despite my growing unease I decided to have one more peek at the manuscript. Chances were I'd never see it again, and there was something about the illustration that both fascinated and unnerved me. It had the creepy allure of a jack-in-the-box. You know that if you turn the handle long enough while the tinky-dinky melody plays, eventually a horrible little jack with a grinning face will pop out at you, but you do it anyway.

Just to see if you can.

The woman still held an apple in her right hand and the dagger in her left. Behind her lay the twisted forest and the tall gray tower. Only something seemed different. I leaned forward. Were the waving grasses bent in the same direction? Was steam rising from the cauldron? It was the woman. She was smiling. *She wasn't before*, I thought. I bent down, as close as I could go, my nose now nearly pressed against the glass. Yes, she was smiling, and was there someone, or something, standing just behind her in the trees?

"Katherine!" David's voice held a note of urgency.

"David?"

He didn't reply.

"David?" I called again, a little louder this time, as I wound my way back between the endless empty display cases. I turned a corner and found myself in a room I'd never been in before, the wrong room. My stomach tightened. "David, where are you?"

"Here."

*Get a grip, Katherine.* I made my way to the sound of his voice. He stood at the door through which we first came in, his back to me.

"What's wrong?"

"It's locked." He kept trying to turn the handle, first one way and then the other.

My stomach clenched further. "Are you serious?"

"Yes." The words were flat.

I fought down a wave of panic. It wasn't just that we would get into trouble, which we would; it was that I realized then I was locked in the darkness with a stranger. I knew nothing about David.

*Samantha Rodriguez.*

"I guess we could call out and get someone's attention." I fought for a casual tone but my voice sounded shaky and shrill.

David had stopped twisting the handle. Now he stood completely still, his shoulders slumped. Oddly emotionless, without raising his head, he said, stating a simple fact, "They're not going to hear you."

*Oh God. Oh God.* My body tensed, either to run or to scream. The name Samantha had come to me because—

Then he laughed and opened the door. "Gotcha!"

I walked out. I didn't say a word. I didn't look at him. My heart was pounding through my ears. "That wasn't funny."

"Sorry, I couldn't resist it." He was still grinning a little, pleased that his stunt had worked so well. When I still didn't respond he grew defensive. "Hey, why so uptight?"

I wheeled around to face him. "You know they found another murdered girl, right? That's the second girl with her throat slit in just two days. So in view of everything that's been going on, I don't think what you did was particularly cool."

His face fell immediately. "Oh shit, I didn't think of that."

"Clearly."

I wouldn't acknowledge him as we made our way to the exit, though I could sense him stealing glances at me. Outside the evening had grown dark and slightly chilly despite it being mid-May.

"Katherine, please, I'm really sorry. Sometimes I have an infantile sense of humor."

I shrugged. A cab went by; somewhere a woman laughed.

"Let me buy you a drink and make it up to you."

"That's okay, thanks."

"Don't be mad with me."

"I'm not, it's just late and—"

"Hey," he said and took my hand.

I was surprised and felt awkward. I tried to pull my hand away, but he kept hold of it. His hand, large and warm, holding my own. I refused to meet his eye.

"I know you think I'm an asshole now and I admit it was a totally stupid thing to do given the circumstances. Please forgive me and let me take you to this amazing wine bar so I can grovel properly and you can yell at me in the comfort you deserve."

I finally looked up at him. He didn't look away, only stood holding my hand.

"Fine," I said, embarrassed. "I guess I'd like to be drinking while you grovel properly."

"I know just the place," he said. I was annoyed to feel a twinge of loss when he let go of my hand.

It was, in fact, a Spanish tapas bar, with chic little stools and framed old photos of decked-out matadors. David was warm and relaxed. I began to unwind. While the fate of those women had been on my mind, it was the manuscript that had triggered me. Something about it had gotten under my skin. I began to feel embarrassed about overreacting. Poor guy! No wonder his harmless joke had shaken me more than I cared to admit. I wondered if I should bring it up and explain, but fortunately, it seemed less and less necessary. As if by unspoken agreement, we didn't refer to it again.

The wine was wonderful, full and red. We sat at the bar and ate delicious, expensive things on small toasts. He talked and I talked and the hours melted into one another until we had talked the place empty and the waitstaff started stacking chairs loudly and looking at us with irritation. It was honestly getting late by then and David wanted to give me money for a cab but I said no so he walked me to the subway.

He texted me to make sure I got home and I texted him back. It was fun and stupid and lovely.

He phoned me the following Tuesday.

"Hey."

He had a good phone voice.

"Hey." I was nervous, happy.

We talked for a little about nothing at all and then he said, "So a friend is having a birthday at a bar Saturday night, nothing major but . . ."

"I can't. I would have loved to but—"

"Crap! You already have plans, don't you?"

"Unfortunately, yes."

"I know I shouldn't have waited those seventy-two hours before asking you to something three days in advance, but I was playing it cool."

"See what being cool gets you?" Flirting with him was fun.

"And now you're going on several amazing hot dates at the same time?"

"Obviously."

"I see." He sounded so woeful that I laughed.

"I promised a friend I would go to this party and I haven't seen him in ages so I really have to go. It's a costume party," I admitted.

"A costume party? Are you sure the friendship is worth it?"

"Not really, but sometimes you have to make the sacrifice."

"Well, next time I'm not going to wait so long."

*So there'll be a next time.* At least that's what I thought, but there weren't any follow-up texts and there was nothing formal arranged, no definite meeting time. I wonder if maybe that was my chance and I blew it.

I check my phone. Nothing. There's something tragic about the saggy bearded man decked in Tupperware dancing with the somber girl clad in glasses and stuffed animals. They're smiling but their eyes aren't smiling. They want to find love outside of this small circle in this darkened room. They want to belong to a club that won't accept them.

Right now I could be with David at some great bar, getting to know his great friends, but I'm here, sitting next to some random guy on the couch, listening to the ghoulish speculation all around me.

*Why only now?*

*That girl, Samantha something, had a jealous boyfriend. They thought he went nuts and stabbed her to death. They didn't connect her to the first girl until they found this new one. Then they realized that there were three girls killed the same way.*

*Shit.*

*I know, scary, right?*

I try to talk about something else. I have to work hard, have to work to be heard above the music, have to lean in. The guy makes no effort to meet my half lean halfway. He smiles but his eyes never leave the dancers. I wonder if he's drunk. I wish I were drunk. It is one of those nights where I will not be able to become drunk. *Fuck you, jerk,* I think about the nonleaner as I stand up. *You wish you could have taken me to see the woodcuts.*

I pass a girl wearing a lampshade and another brave soul sporting a belt of potted plants. It's definitely time to go. I find

Colin in the corner. He is sitting close to the host. They are both beaming with the easy intimacy of something just beginning. I recognize the warmth of the smile. And I said no to David for this. *Thanks again, everyone.* I tell Colin I'm leaving. I say I have to wake up early the next day. He makes all the usual protestations but I know he won't mind now that he's found someone. I debate texting David to find out where the bar is but it's late and I'm far out in Brooklyn.

I go into the host's room to change. The bed is a sea of clothes. The walls are a light shade of gray, soft in the glow of the bedside lamp. I move quickly. I don't want someone to walk in. I want to change and get out of here. Bra hooked, top pulled over and down, jean buttons done, shoes tied, and it is only when I look in the full-length mirror that I see the man sitting in the chair. He has been sitting there the whole time.

I wheel around with a little scream.

The guy sitting there has dark curly hair and a leonine face, hooded sleepy eyes and a wide mouth. He does not apologize. He doesn't even rise from the chair.

"The best part of New York," he drawls, "is the people-watching."

"What are you doing there?" *He was watching me change, and I'm wearing my shitty underwear. Did I scratch myself? Adjust my bra?*

"I thought it was obvious."

"I trust you enjoyed that?"

He pauses in thought. Insult added to injury. "Wasn't terrible." The sides of his lips turn up ever so slightly.

"Aren't you going to apologize?"

"No."

"You should apologize."

"Why? I'm not sorry."

"I don't know how you were raised, but when people do something wrong, it's customary that they apologize."

"Actually, you're wrong. Society pressures people to apologize to satisfy the need for an acknowledgment of wrongdoing. People rarely feel bad for what they have done, only bad that they have been caught." His tone is bored, faintly patronizing.

What an asshole. I think of the most wounding thing I can say. I'm vulnerable. He has seen the backs of my thighs and my ass, and not at flattering angles.

"So, you're a psychopath." My mouth is dry and my cheeks feel hot.

"Meaning that I don't feel guilt?" He thinks about this. "Maybe I'm just honest."

His eyes are so pale green that they're almost yellow. Now they gleam. It's clear that he's having fun. I need to wipe the smirk off his arrogant face.

"You're right. You're not a psychopath. You have no manners. You're classless."

His smirk fades. Bingo.

He looks at me coldly. "So, how many dinners?"

"What?"

"How many dinners would it normally take to see you naked?"

My lips grow numb. My cheeks tingle as though he has slapped me.

"It usually takes the women I date about two," he continues, "sometimes one, depending on the restaurant. And the girl," he adds as an afterthought.

The air solidifies into ice. We stare at each other.

"Get up." My voice is dangerous, soft.

There must be something in my tone. He unfolds from the chair, languorously, like a cat.

"Come here."

He moves toward me.

"Stop."

He does. Now he stands, waiting.

I walk around him to the bedroom door. I turn the key in the lock. Then I walk back to the very chair from which he watched me. I sit down and stare at him. Our tables have turned. "Well?"

"Well?" he echoes. His smile is insolent.

I keep my voice expressionless. "Take off your clothes."

He looks at me for a long time and I wonder if he'll laugh or leave the room. Time thickens. I will never get away with this.

Then, deadpan, not dropping his gaze, his hands start at the buttons of his shirt.

"Slowly." My mouth is dry. I keep my voice calm, as if I often utter instructions of this nature.

Each button is undone.

His shirt.

Eased off.

His shoulders are smooth.

His chest is cream with a dime-sized mole in stark contrast to the rest of him.

Shirtless, he looks at me; again the corners of his mouth twitch up.

*He doesn't think I have the balls for this.*

I swallow. I force myself to meet his gaze. "Take off your jeans."

He's not smiling now.

I don't know what I've started, but I have to continue.

He wouldn't apologize.

He pushes down his jeans and steps out of them.

He stands looking at me, clad only in his boxer briefs, black with white elastic. He remains utterly poised while I look at him.

I allow myself to stare. His body is wonderful. I feel a prickle of sweat start between my breasts, under my arms.

I will finish what I started.

"Those too," I say.

This must be a dream. It is not a dream. It has the languid motion and the strange heaviness of a dream.

A man, broad-shouldered, muscled and lean, stands naked in front of me.

Somehow the gravity in this room has increased in strength. I don't know if my legs will hold me, if they will support my weight. Part of me wonders, *Was it this easy all along, all I had to do was ask?* His face gives nothing away, but I can see. Men's bodies give them away. He is aroused.

I force myself to get up, to walk toward him. As slowly as I told him to undress.

He merely looks at me. He waits to see what my next move is.

I place my hands lightly upon his shoulders.

I go up on my tiptoes.

Standing on tiptoe, I lean in and whisper one word into his ear: "Five."

Then I walk past him toward the door. I turn the key. It clicks and the door opens, letting in the thudding beats of the music, the raucous laughter, the hoarse yelling that passes for banter at 1:35 on a Sunday morning.

I leave. I don't look back.

# 3

The third girl loved this grocery store.

Here in the gourmet grocery store there is warm butter light. Not harsh fluorescence but a soft glow, and shelf upon shelf and row upon row of everything she did not need but wanted.

There's a counter and behind the counter there are people who sometimes smile and sometimes don't. The guy behind the counter who she liked is James. He knew she wouldn't buy anything but he always gave her full samples in those little sample cups, teriyaki chicken salad or wild rice and cranberries, filling them up generously. Maybe he saw in her face that she would have if she could have.

In the gourmet grocery store the vegetables and fruits are bright and beautiful and shining with inner light. These vegetables and fruits are in the prime of their lives, much like the shoppers of the gourmet grocery store.

Here are the milks. There are rice milks and soy milks and coconut milks and almond milks, vanilla and low-fat vanilla, chocolate and low-fat chocolate, and strawberry and original and low-fat original, and whole milk and half-and-half milk, which says "half" but has twice the calories of other kinds of milk, and milk that has vitamin A, and milk that has vitamin D, and milk that has vitamin $B^{12}$, and milk that has extra calcium, and milk that has vitamins A, D, $B^{12}$, and extra calcium added to it. There's organic nonhomogenized milk, ultra-pasteurized milk and enriched low-fat milk, 1% and 2% and nonorganic milk and fat-free milk and hemp milk and creamy nondairy lactose-free beverages that look like milk and taste like milk and are used in place of milk but are not milk.

The third girl wasn't that into milk anyway.

The third girl loved kale chips. They were really expensive but worth it. The vegan cheese kind was her favorite. "Vegan cheese" meant that it wasn't even cheese. She always thought this was funny because she wasn't a vegan. She wasn't even a vegetarian. "I'm not a vegetarian," she used to say, "but sometimes I date them." The vegan cheese kale chips were so good that she thought the vegans must have put something in the chips to convert her. She did once have a vegetarian boyfriend who had first introduced her to the love of kale, also seitan. "Are you Seitan?" she had asked him. It was only half a joke. He hadn't been kind. This was one of the reasons she had fallen in love with him. She had told her friends afterward that although vegetarians might be thoughtful toward animals they are cruel to women. "Look at Hitler," she had said. She had only said this once, though, because that was really a little too dark, and she had a ton of Jewish friends.

Unsalted mixed nuts, salted cashews, unsalted cashews, honey-roasted cashews, natural pine nuts, soy nuts, raisin-and-nut mix, sesame crunch mix, rocky mountain mix, natural berry mix, natural ultimate mix, yogurt deluxe mix, omega-3 mix, healthy chocolate mix, Cajun hot mix, fantastic fruit mix, Turkish apricot mix, yogurt cranberry mix, milk-chocolate-covered peanuts, dark-chocolate-covered peanuts, dark-chocolate-covered almonds, milk chocolate almonds, dried blueberry and strawberry mix, cranberry explosion mix.

On the rare occasions when the third girl actually shopped here she bought a container of dried strawberries. She liked strawberries but she really loved freeze-dried strawberries because they reminded her of the freeze-dried ice cream fad when she was at school. She remembered learning that astronauts ate it, and when she had a piece she imagined herself weightless, floating and gazing down at Earth. It had a forbidden and scientific taste, milky and chalky sweet. Her mother never bought it for her. She remembered her first piece, taken from a friend's packet. Her friend's mother bought more junky kind of snacks. Her friend's parents were divorced. Now the third girl would place each freeze-dried strawberry on her tongue, letting it fizzle and soften and become itself again. She tried to go slow because the bag is never as full as it should be, but often she ended up eating it too quickly, her fingertips pink with powder.

You didn't have a cart the day you met the third girl. You don't have one now. Carts are unwieldy. You can't follow anyone properly. One of the best things about following someone who doesn't know she's being followed is the exquisite feeling of control. It tastes smooth and cool, like sucking a mint during a play, like a secret.

The third girl didn't know she was being watched. She thought she was the one watching you. She watched as you helped a sweet old lady pick a box of tea down from a great height. She watched how you then moved away. She watched you not being solicitous or smug, just efficiently helpful. She watched the way you joked with James behind the counter as he served you a helping of pasta salad with sundried tomatoes, artichokes, and feta cheese.

Cranberry, Cranberry Cocktail, Cranberry Pomegranate, Cranberry Raspberry, Cranberry Blueberry, Cranberry Apple, Cranberry Cherry, Cranberry Strawberry, Cranberry Tangerine, Cranberry Pomegranate Cherry, White Cranberry, Cranberry Lemonade, Cranberry Grape, White Grape, Grape, Mango, Mango Passion, Mango Papaya, Mango Carrot, Mango Orange, Orange, Orange Carrot, Orange Tangerine, Orange Strawberry, Strawberry Kiwi, Strawberry Banana, Strawberry Banana Orange, White Peach, Lemonade, Passion Fruit, Passion of Christ, Fruit Punch, Guava, Pineapple Ginger, Pineapple Guava, Pineapple Coconut, Pomegranate, Tamarind, Pink Grapefruit, Sorrel Ginger, Pear, Blackberry, Raspberry, Cherry, Ruby Pink, Ruby Red, Ruby White, Blueberry Pomegranate, Amen.

Choice is a wonderful thing.

The day you met, the third girl had wanted to say something to you but she had been shy. She wanted to say something to you, but she didn't. So you started talking to her, by the cheese counter. You picked up a piece of Brie and remarked on the price. The third girl could take or leave Brie but she was happy to start a conversation. She also liked the way that, although you raised an eyebrow at the price, you still put it into the red basket that you were carrying with you. You aren't rotten, like the "outside" fruit from the greengrocer's the third girl is sometimes forced to purchase; you have money but you are still aware of prices. She liked the fact that you gave a smile and said, "A necessary luxury?"

You phrased it as if it were a question, as if you wanted her permission, as if, although she was a stranger, her good opinion was somehow important to you. She paused and you started putting the cheese back with a look of dismay and this made her laugh at your expression and your slow-motion placement of the cheese.

"You took too long," you had told the third girl, "so it's an *un*necessary luxury," and she said, "Sorry," but clearly she was not sorry; clearly she was happy. She was happy that you were talking and happy that it was a Thursday with no classes tomorrow and happy because there was an eighties song playing that she loves. The third girl gravitated toward songs in which the verse moves from the initial minor chord to an augmented fourth, then to a sixth, then a seventh, and back to one. She liked her choruses a little more predictable, though, with the chords moving from a first to a fourth, a fifth, and back to one.

She didn't know this, however. She just knew that she loved this song. You confided to her that you love this music but that you thought it was a plot to make you buy things. She stared at you amazed because she was just thinking that, and this made her happy too.

That day the third girl was filled with hope, which is pale green and smells like new buds and tulip shoots and pencil erasers. Hope sparkles like champagne. It rings out like the first chord that the small live band plays at an outdoor wedding.

Hope is a cool green swallow. It is delicious.

If this were a different type of grocery store then there might be a variety of tabloids, like the *New York Post* or the *National Enquirer*, at the front near the cashiers. The majority of people who shop here might ostensibly look down on these papers, but secretly they'd want to read them. Paging through them is easy and comfortable and doesn't require much thought, like gliding.

These papers will be the first to break the news of this girl's death. She will make the front page and also be given a generous two-page interior spread. It makes a change from the baseball games, and neither the politicians nor the celebrities are acting up, and most importantly, she is the third. Accompanying the two lovely, if somewhat blurry, pictures of her graduating from college, and another of her at a party, will be the description of her murder. Half a column will be dedicated to how the dead girl was only discovered after the better part of a week. It's easy to go missing in the city, especially if you live alone. The papers will talk about how her neighbor's terrier wouldn't stop barking when the neighbor returned from her weekend away, and how the police broke down the third girl's door. They'll make much of the thin nylon ropes that tied her, how the sheets were soaked in blood. The third girl was found braless, her jeans still on. Half clothed, she is completely vulnerable. So much better to display your work, your art, your lines of release.

But they'll do no justice to the multitude of curls and swirls that spiral down her arms, the web of fine lace etched in her shoulder, the three delicate waves that tickle her navel. Instead they'll focus on the mark in the center of her chest, what appears to be the eye of a snake within the outline of a leaf. And of course, the long deliberate slash across her throat. These papers don't appreciate the finer subtleties of your work, your infinite skill. Instead they butcher your beauty with:

**WEIRD SEX CARVINGS!**
**TEACHER'S THROAT SLIT**
**GRISLY MURDER SHOCKER!**

Some details will purposefully be left out, at the police's request. It's early days still.

No one takes these papers seriously, although they are the first to link your victims together. They will connect the first two murders you committed to her, the **THIRD MURDERED GIRL FOUND WITHIN WEEKS**. They render the women as flat and lifeless as the thin sheets they're printed on. Once labeled "tragic victims," these women are forever pressed down into the past. *And after all it couldn't possibly happen to us or anyone we know—those deaths would be too good for this tabloid trash.*

But these are the papers that will christen you. At first they will call you "Reaper Man," "The Creeper," or, even more crudely, "The Carver." Eventually they will learn what tool you use to dispatch the girls, and one paper, inspired by the cuts, inspired by your blade, will call you by a name that all will know you by, in time. It's not, of course, your true name, but it's one that pleases you. It's an old name. It's a good name.

In time the third girl will be reduced to one picture, to make room for other dead girls' pictures. As the summer progresses she will shrink until she is merely a thumbnail included in the growing column of dead girls.

There have been others before her and there will be others after her, but she is the one who establishes you and your place in this world. People will remember her as the third girl who made it official, who placed third in the race where the winners are losers.

**SERIAL KILLER AT LARGE!**

It feels right to go back to the place she loved, the place you first met, the place where she spent one of her last hours on earth. The checkout line that you exit from today is the same one that the dead girl exited from, in all senses of the word. The cashier won't remember her, though, not even when she sees her picture in the paper a week later. The third girl was the two hundred and forty-ninth customer she rang up that day. All the cashier wanted to do was to—

*—get off my shift and find out what that son of a bitch who calls himself a man is doing and if he is fucking that bitch like I know he is then—*

You smile at the cashier, and despite her hot fevered thoughts, she smiles back at you. Everyone does. They can't help it. You have such an infectious smile. Infectious, catching, irresistible.

You have a reason to smile. This has proved to be a great place for getting what you want. You with a single goal, closer, closer ever still.

There's nothing like a little shopping to get the party started.

NE NEVER KNEW WHERE THE MAIDEN first came from; some said from the neighboring village and others said by way of another town, but most said she came unbidden into their presence from the woods, without kinsman or clan. And whether the Maiden was fair or not, it could not be agreed upon, for her hair was as dark as a raven's wing and her eyes were as black as a starless night. But since she was a maiden and all alone, the wives offered to take her in. However she refused their charity and let it be known that she would earn her keep. For she claimed to have a wondrous skill for brewing drink, be it ale or wine.

All who heard this would have her make sure of her boast and so they took her to meet the alewife at the tavern there. Then the alewife, as stout as she was fierce, said, "Come, we shall see your skill for all your talk, but if you cannot best me then you shall be silent and work for your keep in some other manner." For she hated on sight the Maiden's youth and loveliness and feared for her business.

Word traveled around the village that such a match was taking place and all the people came, noisy and rough with their bowls to taste the brew. The alewife grew red in the face as she stirred and stirred and sweated over the ladle, but the Maiden kept as gentle as the breeze and as cool as the water and the people remarked how she neither sweated nor strained, but only smiled and crooned a little song:

*Grown from the earth,*
*Golden in worth.*
*Barley and wheat,*
*Belly full sweet.*

She stirred and hummed, and by and by both brews were ready for the tasting. Though the tavern wife's ale was neither bad nor bitter, the Maid was declared the victor, for the people said they could not remember a time when they had tasted such a drink. It held full summer and sweet kisses, bubbling brooks and fresh bread, and made them exceedingly merry and gay, and they clamored for more, using their hands to scoop up the remains, and fell to fighting over the last drops.

# 4

There's somebody coughing in the Rose Main Reading room of the New York Public Library. Deep racking, hacking coughs. You look up. Locate the cougher. He's two tables down from you, a white-haired man in his fifties with an angry expression, earnest, staring deep into his laptop screen. Look down again. Again the cough, again you look up. This time you catch the eye of another disturbed reader as she turns around and then back again. A girl in her twenties, sitting at your table, with shining red shoulder-length hair. You exchange a quick smile, a second at the most. You don't let your eyes linger too long. Otherwise it might be creepy. A minute goes by, another, and then he coughs again. You both look up again, this time she's waiting for you, wanting to connect with you. Connect with the attractive man at her table. Now you can maintain eye contact. A smile. You're in this together as that old selfish asshole coughs and coughs.

Aren't other people hell?

You allow your smile to spread; then you get up and walk over, around to her. You do this quickly. She stiffens. Suddenly she's nervous. She's thinking, *Smile at some guy, and it's a come-on.* She's thinking, *I'll tell him I have a boyfriend.* She's thinking, *A woman was found murdered the other day.* You lean over, her shoulders are tight, she's ready to flee. Flight or fight or not fight, exactly, she'll just scorn you. You lean over and whisper, "Sorry, can you keep an eye on my stuff for just a moment?"

Her shoulders descend. She exhales. Jesus, you made her nervous, but now she's already chastising herself. Look at the way you're dressed—there's no way you could be crazy.

You walk with a quiet confidence out of the silent section of the library. You can feel that she's secretly watching you, taking in all the clues about who you are, your shirt, your pants, your shoes. Her father once told her, "Never trust a man with gray shoes." Your shoes are not gray. They're black. Almost a little old for you but professional. Italian, maybe. Dark pants, white shirt, broad shoulders, slim hips, long legs. You're tall. She's watching the way you walk. She's checking out your ass. And why shouldn't she? Guys watch her all the time. Why shouldn't she be allowed to do the same? So when no one else is looking, she'll stare at you, this attractive man walking away. You smile.

You are gone for a while. She finds herself looking up to see if you've returned. You haven't. She grows irritated with herself. It shouldn't be a big deal either way. Eventually she'll have to go to the bathroom. Eventually she'll have to leave. If you haven't returned, that's your own fault. She continues to check. She wills herself to concentrate on her own work. Now everything becomes annoying—the way that woman is breathing through her mouth, the tap and then another tap of someone's pen across her teeth, a compulsive throat clearer, a sniff.

She looks up again and sees that you're back. You've come back silently. You mouth *Thanks* at her and then, with a nod of your head, you gesture over to the white-haired guy, the one who's been coughing.

She looks over at the cougher. He's fishing a wrapped cough drop out of a packet, then pushing it, crinkling the paper as he does so, into his mouth.

She stares at you in amazement. *You?* she mouths.

You give a little nod, smile, and shrug your shoulders in a winningly apologetic way as if to say, *What else could I do?* Then you give a little wink, not a lascivious one, just enough to say, *It's been taken care of.*

She realizes at this moment that this is what she's been searching for all her life. *It's been taken care of.* Taken care of with humor, taken care of with charm, taken care of with a lightness of touch. She would like to be taken care of.

Maybe you'll oblige.

"I can't believe you did that," she says. You're both standing on the steps outside the library. Right by the lions, their proud, worn faces impassive and resigned in the late afternoon. You turn to look at her; her hair, her face, are particularly beautiful in the last of the dying sun. "I wanted to kill that guy," she continues.

You smile. You wonder what she would say if you told her that he'll be dead soon enough.

After all, he's rank with depression.

You don't say anything, though. You just look at her, as if you can see through the beautiful outside to her beautiful inside. No one ever looks at her like that. You smile.

She wonders if you'll ask for her number. She wants you to ask for her number. You don't ask for her number.

"So . . . ?" she says, and tilts her head, hopefully, nervously, unsure.

You tell her that you hope that next time it's quieter, but you confess that you're glad that guy was coughing; otherwise you wouldn't have had a chance to meet.

She's staring up at you in confusion. If you're glad to have met her, why don't you ask her for some way of contacting her? She's wondering if she should ask for your number or an email address, some way of contacting you, but no, she can't, she can't. She's already scanned your hands and found no ring. You must have a girlfriend. The nice guys always have girlfriends. You see a small flash of frustration in her eyes. She's used to men wanting her. You were her knight in shining armor. Why aren't you following through?

"Nice meeting you," you say and then she has no choice; she must walk away, but before she goes you see the flash again.

You like this flash, this flash of entitled petulance.

Petulance is maroon, it crumbles like stale graham crackers, it smells of carpets stained with apple juice, it sounds like the tap of impatient fingernails, it feels like the scratch of pearls across your teeth, it gives a twist and pinch of salt to the lavender of insecurity.

You hope you get to experience it later.

She walks away quickly down Fifth Avenue, her back straighter than normal, knowing that you're probably watching her, and it's only a minute or so into walking that she relaxes into her normal stance, slowing her pace, her mind going over the events, trying to tell herself that she didn't fail, trying not to blame herself. You were probably a game-playing asshole anyway. Wondering how she failed. Wondering if she'll ever find anybody. She's so intent on not looking back that she doesn't notice when you begin to follow her.

Not hurriedly, but deliberately and with great pleasure.

You interlock your fingers and stretch; you crick your neck from side to side and up and down; a sweet hum rises from your chest, filling your throat; you ease your leather bag farther up over your shoulder before you head off.

It's going to be a wonderful afternoon.

# 5

I'm sitting in a bar. It's Tuesday. There is exposed brick and tufted leather. Golds and reds and browns. The bottles are many and soft in color, their pale greens and creams backlit.

I come here on Tuesdays. Wednesdays are reserved for the serious drinkers, Thursdays are the new Fridays, Fridays are the new Saturdays, Saturdays are intolerable, Sundays are sad, and Monday is too far away from Friday.

I sit alone, cradling my Côtes du Rhône. It's not the prettiest wine but it gets the job done. A worker wine.

It's been a long day and things haven't gone well. They haven't gone badly either. That would be dramatic if nothing else, but today things just limped along, starting with a run around seven a.m. It was already sixty-nine degrees and climbing. Then a shower. Listening to the radio as I got dressed. I heard nothing good. The callers calling with unanswerable questions.

*What are the police doing to protect us?*

*My daughter's going to NYU in the fall—should we be worried?*

Facing the bleak morning crush as I headed to the office where I'm temping for an administrative assistant currently out on maternity leave. Answering phones, taking messages, and replying to emails while working on a review about a postmodern artist whose canvases of white triangles I have less than nothing to say about. Lunch was a slightly gritty salad eaten at my desk. I booked three glamorous flights for other people. My friend Leigh called; she's trying to get pregnant and the fertility consultation prices alone are a nightmare. My heart broke for her but I was in an office so my answers were muted. I got an email about my friend Sasha's birthday party next week and finally I left at six p.m., only to face the same stream of people, dogged and determined to get home so they can sit some more on their couches or sit at a restaurant or sit at a bar, which is what I'm doing now and why I realize that there's nothing to look forward to.

Maybe that's adulthood. A slow recognition that time keeps going whether or not we have things to look forward to or things to dread. It's a week with nothing but more of the same ahead. I have a bottle at my place but Andrea's out and there's something about drinking alone at home that raises a red flag. Now I'm still drinking alone but at least I'm surrounded by other people, witnesses, who see that I'm out and alive.

This is my local bar. Sweet Afton, in the heart of Astoria. They have very good-looking bartenders here. What's even better is that they don't really talk, at least not to me. They're amiable and good-looking and they have a heavy hand when it comes to pouring. And that's fine. It's one of those nights when I feel lonely but I don't want to talk to anyone. I'm tired of drinking alone, but the idea of small talk makes me feel weary. Wrung out and strung out and limp at the bar.

I can't help but hear the conversations going on around me.

How does he get into their apartments?

Gin and tonic.

I'll have two Stellas.

Just a glass of water.

What's your name?

Can I buy you a drink?

I can't tell you, I've never been so happy to have a roommate.

I know, first time I was like "Thank God I'm poor!"

We have a lovely Pinot Grigio for the lady.

Yeah, that's cool, and a pilsner for me.

I think it's a cop.

They think he's a locksmith.

Mike, the bartender, puts down a glass of whiskey in front of me.

I look up.

"From that guy over there," says Mike, aiming his head in the corner's direction.

I turn but I can't see the guy he's referring to. I steel myself to be nice, to be grateful, to make conversation, to talk about the invisible boyfriend I have, to explain why I'm drinking alone, to the "yes, this is my local bar," and the "yes, I'm just thinking," to the inevitable "yes, it has been a long day," but I still can't see who sent me the drink. I raise my glass in the general direction and hope that he'll be satisfied with that.

I take a sip and the sip is golden and burning and lovely. It tastes of peat and wood. It tastes expensive.

"Do you like it?" He is next to me.

"David!"

He grins down at me. "You know, Katherine, you just have to stop stalking me. I mean I'm flattered, but no means no, take the hint."

"Oh, shut up." I punch him lightly on the arm. "What are you doing in the deepest darkest borough of Queens?"

"My friend heard about this place, heard it had a ridiculous selection of beers. We thought we'd risk it, just this once."

*"My friend," huh? Male or female?* "Yeah, this is my local." I give a tired shrug, a little smile. I'm world-weary. I don't care that he's come here with some other woman who might or might not be just a "friend."

David turns to Mike. "She's a local?"

"Yup." Mike moves to take another order.

"He's crazy about me," I tell David.

"Of course." He is straight-faced. "Who wouldn't be? So how have you been?"

"Can't complain. You?"

"Good, but insane with work. Forgive me for not calling sooner."

"No worries, my workload has been insane too." This is a total lie. I desperately need more work. I would kill to have too much work. I'm trying to remember what David does, something to do with technology law, I think. I can never remember that kind of stuff.

"We're actually in the middle of a big project, but we needed a break and so I dragged him here for a drink."

The friend is a "he." Thank God.

"Come join us?"

My heart lifts. He wants me to meet his friends already. That's a good sign. Apparently I don't want to drink alone after all. "Really? I don't want to intrude on your male bonding."

"Male bonding happens on Wednesdays."

"Well, if you're sure . . ."

"Come on."

Holding my whiskey carefully, I follow David, shouldering past the growing crowd to the most desirable tables at the back.

"Hey," he says, "move over, we've got company."

A dark curly-haired man looks up from his phone.

Oh shit.

"Sael, this is Katherine. Katherine, meet Sael."

*Get up.*

"Actually I think we may have met before." His voice is expressionless, polite, but his pale eyes gleam.

"Oh really, where from?"

*Stop.*

Sael stares at me, pretending to think about it.

*Come here.*

Finally, "I think it was Jerry's party."

"What party?"

"It was one of those shitty ABC, no-clothes things."

*Take off your jeans.*

"Hey!" David turns to me. "Is that the costume party you were telling me about on Saturday?"

*Take off your clothes.*

"Yes." My voice is weak. I feel very far away, as if floating and looking down at myself from a great height.

*Slowly.*

David looks horrified. "Jesus, I know Katherine promised a friend she would go, but why the hell where you there?"

"Networking." He's still staring.

I need to say something. Anything. I need to say something. This is the moment. The moment when I say, *You know, it's the funniest thing.*

I try to clear my throat. My mouth is a desert. As if sensing this, Sael partially rises.

"I don't think we met officially," he says, and offers me a hand.

It's like the thirty pieces of silver. If I take his hand, then the time for telling the truth is over. If I let this moment go by, I'll never be able to tell David.

I take his hand.

"Nice to meet you, Katherine."

"Nice to meet you, Saul."

"It's pronounced Sah-El." His tone is casual and friendly. His eyes are not.

I see David patiently standing, waiting for me to move. "Oh, sorry." I sit down.

Then, "Shift over," says David.

I do. "Sael, that's an unusual name."

*Come on, Katherine, nothing like some light conversation.*

"I think it might be Latin in origin. It means 'beyond,' according to the Native Americans."

"Are you Native American?"

David gives a snort of laughter. "His ancestors were total imperialists, probably responsible for slaying entire tribes."

Sael shoots him a cold look. "They were originally English. My name is probably the result of my parents' whimsy, otherwise expressed as excessive drinking and a tragic desire to be original."

David shakes his head. "You're a cheerful little sunbeam, aren't you?" He turns to me. "I'm always telling him, easy on the positive energy."

They are supremely comfortable with each other. They are friends and they have known each other for years. Still, they are so different. David, peering through round glasses, is warm and engaged like the wisecracking friend in a romantic comedy, while Sael's odd, almost yellow eyes remind me of a predatory cat. He sits quietly enough but I feel that at any moment he could spring. I have yet to hear him laugh, or even crack a genuine smile. After a moment of silence I try again. "So a big project, huh?"

Sael says nothing. Only looks at me while David launches into an explanation. It's something to do with the copyright and legality of systems and apps and launching. I'm trying to listen but—

*He is standing in front of me naked,*
*aroused, his face impassive.*

"Oh! That reminds me, the weirdest thing happened the other day."

*"Five," I whisper in his ear.*

"Katherine—"

I am jerked back to the present.

"—and I were at a museum and we came across your name. It was on some sort of ancient manuscript. Very pretentious, fairly nauseating."

Sael shrugs. "De Villias is my family name. There's little I can do about it."

"Life is hard for the one percent," agrees David.

The night is endless. I want to leave but there's nowhere to go. David is sitting next to me and I'm trapped. He and Sael do most of the talking, and I take sips of scotch, hoping it will get easier if I drink enough. The crowd swells, more legs, more jostling, and the volume of the room rises around us. The music is good and cheesy. Hall and Oates warn us about a woman who will only come out at night. I see some people carrying umbrellas in. I don't have one. Well, I'm only two streets away. I'd gladly get soaked if I could slip away now.

"I'll get you another one," David says.

I look down. I'm gripping an empty glass. I have no recollection of finishing it. David is standing up. "The table service is nonexistent at the moment."

"Don't worry about it." *Please don't leave me.*

"It will only take a second."

"No, really," but he's gone.

Sael de Villias wears a gray T-shirt, a thin black sweater. Jeans. I see that he has a copy of the *New Yorker* with him and what I presume is his phone on top of it. Maybe with any luck he'll ignore me and check out at least one of them. He doesn't. Instead he stares at me.

"So," he says.

"So," I say.

"Shall we tell him?"

"Why not?" I'm nonchalant. I'm bluffing.

"Sure?"

I decide I mean it. "Sure." I don't want him holding anything over me. I'm ready to come clean.

"Hey!" David's back with drinks. "It's ridiculous out there—since when did they let in twelve-year-olds? Also why am I being served by sculpted male models? It's depressing."

No, I can't do this. I turn to Sael. "Don't."

Sael narrows his yellow eyes and smiles a little.

"Don't what?" David is carefully putting my drink down.

Sael turns to him. "Katherine didn't want me to tell you—"

"Wait!" *Please God, stop.*

"She thought you'd be pissed but—"

"Tell me what?" David scooches back in beside me, looks at his friend.

Sael pauses, looks at me deliberately. "I took care of the tab."

"What? No!" David is incredulous. "Don't be insane, you only had two drinks. Besides, I have one here for you."

"You have it." He uncoils in one easy motion.

"Leaving?" David gives him a searching look. "Everything okay?"

"Yeah, I just have some things I need to take care of. Nice to meet you, Katherine. Maybe we'll run into each other again."

"That would be cool." *When hell freezes over.*

"Night." He turns and pushes his way into the throng.

David and I face each other.

"Charming, isn't he?"

"Charming," I echo, and find that I can laugh after all.

"He probably went to go meet yet another woman. He's a total player, the worst," but he smiles affectionately as he says this. Then he takes my hand. "Sorry if that was awkward."

"No worries." *Holy crap.*

"I know he can be a bit strange at times—"

*You have no idea.*

"—but we've been friends since college. The guy's a genius. He's like a dark Vulcan."

"That's an amazingly nerdy reference," I say, but I feel better. A tension has been lifted. Things are easy again and natural. We talk, shouting a little to be heard over the shouts and laughter, and David tells stories and I do and we drink and a bluegrass song plays, and after a time David looks at his watch, is reluctant, but—

"Maybe we should be leaving too. After all, it is a school night."

I see with a pang that two hours have gone by. "You're right. I wish we didn't have to." It's true, I like being with him.

"I'll walk you home and protect you from all the bad guys."

I don't protest, even though it's not far. It's nice to be walked home on a dark and rainy night.

We leave the bar and begin to walk. It's been raining on and off and it's beginning again. The sidewalks are a little steamy, turning the night into a cheap film noir. David opens his umbrella. The cars slosh and shush through the wet and shining blackness. There are not many people around. We walk down the street, past squat redbrick buildings on either side, with their tiny gardens and rookeries out front. We walk in companionable silence, past the building with the strange little stone angels guarding the thin black gates, until we're standing in front of my own squat redbrick building.

"Well, this is me."

Still we stand, not moving yet, and the raindrops make little scuttling noises down his umbrella. A drunken couple goes by, laughing, and then they are gone. The noise of the rain increases. We look at each other.

"So, Katherine." David is serious now, more businesslike. Surprisingly, it suits him. "What are you up to this weekend?"

"Not sure." I sound far too easy. But it's late and maybe I've had a little too much scotch.

"Well, this project is nuts so I can't guarantee anything but I would love to see you," he says.

*Relief.* "That would be great."

We stand a moment longer. He looks down at me. I don't know if he's going to kiss me or not. Under the umbrella it's airless, breathless.

He bends down so that his face is near mine; then he laughs.

"What?"

"You have raindrops in your hair." He reaches out with one finger and ever so lightly touches a strand. "Like dewdrops on a spider's web." His finger finds my cheek. His touch is very gentle. I shut my eyes. I feel him draw close, the warmth of his face close to mine, his breath surprisingly sweet; my mouth opens a little and—

"Whoo! Go for it, man!"

Two frat-boy types across the street are calling out their encouragement. I open my eyes. David is looking back, wide-eyed. We laugh. The world exhales and the sound of the cars and the rain slides back.

"Well . . ."

"Yeah."

"I better make a move—it's really about to pour. I'll see you soon."

"Not if I see you first."

"Funny," he deadpans. "You're a funny lady." He winks.

I climb the steps and draw my keys out and open the first of the two doors into a little space too small to be a foyer, more stairs, and then the second door. I don't turn around. Up the four flights of stairs, past the stained-glass window on the second floor that has some Scotch tape in the corner. I think a tenant broke it trying to move a sofa and the landlady never fixed it. The lighting here is old and yellow. Someone was cooking steak tonight. I can smell the onions. Counting the stairs, twenty-five, twenty-six, twenty-seven—I don't love walking up alone at night. But now I think about how we stood outside in the rain. No, don't think about it. Think too much and it will lose its magic. I think about it. I'm here, apartment 4 "G as in Girl," unlock the door, and go in quietly. Andrea and Lucas are long since asleep, of course. It's a school night, a pre-K night at least. Lucas is only four.

Once in my room I turn on the light. I throw my stuff on a chair and examine my face, my raindrop-coated hair, in the mirror.

Maybe there was something in my teeth? I bare them fearfully. Nothing, thank God. My makeup is a little smudged under my eyes but otherwise I look decent. As I open my drawer to take out a large shirt to sleep in, I knock over the lipstick on my dresser. It falls with a little *thunk* and rolls off and across the warped wooden floor into the corner. These floors are the worst. I have to put my scale on the flat tiles of the kitchen; otherwise it tells me I'm two pounds heavier. The boards creak, you can hear them even through closed doors, and I don't want to wake up Lucas or Andrea, so I move quietly, adjusting the weight on my soles, then getting down on all fours, reaching into the corner for the lipstick. That's when I first see them, unobtrusive in the shadows, patiently waiting to be found: four pennies pushed up against the wall.

Lucas must have gotten in here. We've only once had a talk, but normally he's so good. It's really not like him to do this. I give my room a sweeping gaze. It's lucky I don't leave medicine out, or my one pair of sexy panties. I look back at the four pennies. I move to pick them up and then stop. They're all heads up.

*Find a penny, pick it up, and all day long you'll have good luck.*

It would be better to leave them here and bring Lucas tomorrow and show him, remind him about the "always knock" rule. I'll tell Andrea if necessary, but I don't think it will come to that. He's not doing any harm, they're probably a gift or a surprise, but he needs to learn that he can't come in here without asking. Still, it's a sweet gesture. I smile, thinking about sweet gestures as I put my lipstick back on my dresser and wander to the window to look out at the rainy night.

There, at the far corner of the street, in front of the darkened windows of the Colombian coffee shop, a woman stands looking back at me.

She is naked. Her shoulder-length hair looks red, though it's hard to tell in the rainy night. She stands still, staring up at my window. Her face is expressionless. Her eyes are blank. There are strange lines curving down her neck to just above her breasts. More marks down her left side, concentric circles crossed with jagged lines. They aren't tattoos; the lines run red in the rain.

There's a naked, bleeding woman standing in the rain.

Fuck. What do I do? Oh fuck. Should I leave my apartment and go to her? What do I do? What if she's crazy? What if she has a knife? Is it a joke? Or is it a massive stunt to get me outside in the rain? There's a television show called *What Would You Do?* The show puts actors in all sorts of situations, pretending to faint or pretending to mug someone or drug someone's drink, and there are hidden cameras around to film people's reactions.

I have to do something. Jesus. There is no one around. Like when that woman in the 1960s was attacked and although she screamed and screamed no one did anything about it. I could wake Andrea. Andrea is more capable. Andrea is fierce and a single mother and tough. She would know what to do. But of course even I know what to do. I must phone the police.

I can't find it. Where is it, where the hell is my phone?

The woman hasn't moved. Hasn't moved a muscle. Where is everyone?

Catatonic. That's it. That's what the word is, "catatonic." She must have just been attacked. I'll call the police and then I'll go out and help her. I have to do something. I have to.

The woman stares right at me. Her eyes are dead.

I dial. I think I'm going to throw up. The phone rings and then a voice, neutral, bland, competent, asks, "Hello, what is your emergency?"

I try to speak but nothing comes out.

"Hello, what is your emergency?"

My chest forces up something cracked and whispery, a single breath. "Hello?"

"Hello, what is your—"

"There's a woman outside my building." My words come out in an exhaled rush.

"Ma'am, slow down, please."

"She's naked and I think she's bleeding and she's just—" My words pour out in a torrent. There's a ringing in my ears.

"Slow down, ma'am, you say there's a woman outside your building?"

"Yes."

The voice sharpens. "Hello, ma'am? Is she breathing?"

I look outside.

"Hello, ma'am, can you describe the woman?"

There's no one there.

"Ma'am? Hello?"

No one is there. I speak through numb lips. "I'm sorry, I must have made a mistake."

"Ma'am? Hel—"

I hang up.

There is nothing there but the rain and the darkness.

My legs are shaky. I collapse down onto the bed.

I must have imagined it.

I must have imagined it.

I must have ima—

*The woman was naked. Naked, staring straight at me, her red hair hanging in dark wet clumps.*

I probably just need sleep. I wish Andrea were awake. I wish I had someone with me. This is why I don't want to be alone anymore. My vision trembles. My breath catches in my chest.

My phone lights up. I wipe my eyes and look. There's a new message for me. I don't recognize the number but I know whom it's from. He's sent me a message.

It's short, six words. It should be a question but it's not. He knows I'll say yes.

There was no expression in her eyes. Her eyes were blank.

Her eyes were dead.

*Don't be stupid. You've had too much to drink. It's those women you've been hearing about. The ones with their throats slit.*

It's probably a very elaborate prank, a very, very elaborate prank, or it could have been performance art—maybe I'll read about it tomorrow. *Just go to sleep. Don't think about it now. Don't indulge in this.* Think about it tomorrow, like Scarlett O'Hara.

Think about it when it's daytime, when it's light, not raining and dark. Maybe it will make a good scary story, maybe I won't tell anyone ever, maybe I just thought I saw—

A naked woman standing in the rain. Red curving circles on her neck and down her side and above her breasts.

I'm cold. I take half of one of my little white pills. I really need to sleep. "Stop it," I tell myself aloud. My voice sounds small and strained.

I get into bed as quickly as I can. I'm shivering even though it's a warm night.

They were bleeding because they were cuts carved into her skin, just like on the other women they found.

Once in bed, I look at my phone, now charging on the bedside table. I look at the message again, the message from a man who watched me dress, an arrogant man, a man who clearly isn't loyal to his friends. I don't know how he got my number but he did. I think of David saying, "The guy's a genius."

I read his message again.

Sushi tomorrow at Otoro 9:00 pm

No question mark. It's an order, not a question. It's a presumption. Well, there's no need to go. I shut my eyes and wait for the little white pill to work. The rain continues to fall. It falls on the streets, and the cars and the trees. Water streams and pools and whirls into the gutters. The rain continues on, late into the night.

Falling on no one at all.

HEN THE WORD SPREAD OF THE Maiden's wondrous brew, people came from miles around to taste her ale, and they came in such great numbers that she toiled both night and day. And as she stirred she sang a little song with the voice of a lark:

*Now gold may turn beggars to servants,*
*then masters,*
*And honey may sweeten a brew,*
*But I'd rather your kisses than all the king's riches,*
*For there's none so sweet as you.*

And all the men were dazzled and proclaimed themselves to be in love and tried to win her favor, but she would laugh and make no promise to any of them, no matter what they said. The wives of the town grew weary and the young women sore of heart, for their menfolk no longer courted nor worked because they were always to be found at the tavern, giving posies and pretty compliments to the

Maiden, who brewed and sang and looked so well, and then the men would fall, steeped in drink and fighting among themselves, into a noisy heated brawl.

And so the alewife who had been bested by the Maiden gathered the women of the town together and spoke to them, saying, "Perhaps she is a witch, for surely she has bewitched our men and made them her dogs." All the women grew to hate her and wished her far away.

# 6

You have taken to riding public transport.

It is a thing you have not done for a long, long time, but then again you've only just woken up. You've been awakened and you've risen and you're hungry to experience everything, the fumes, the smoke and perfumes, the bright and bitter scents. The taxis, and buses, and subways, the slick passing of the cards in the slots, the streets pulsing with people and their chariots of metal and steel, the meters ticking, the buildings, cathedrals arching and shooting into the sky, and the cups of hastily grabbed coffee, the bottles of water, the phones, the keyboards, and the billboards, and boards that people wear as they stand and hand others small pieces of paper—*please buy, please buy, please buy*—and the endless lights in a multitude of colors, the towering spikes that needle the clouds so that there is no need for stars, the restaurants and the bars and the endless people sitting on endless high seats and menus and waiters and bartenders tending to the girls in heels, business high and then higher at night, the dresses shorter, everyone listening to music or reading or pretending that they are not sitting next to a million strangers in love and out of love and between love and fear and failure and beyond all hope there's hope.

Oh, how you love this city!

You love public transport because anyone can take it and everyone does, from the claustrophobic man with his summer place in the Hamptons to the woman who has nothing but a row of scars up each of her thin arms. You love how, for a brief moment, you are all together traveling to somewhere else. You enjoy the feeling of transitory impermanence. How, in these moments, people make the place that they are occupying, theirs.

You think about when you first met your Ride.

You came in the night. You came in the dark, under the door, through the window. You came to him as he lay in bed, lay in the thin place between wakefulness and sleep. Why him? Why you?

Because. Because the wind blew, because the ancient cogs clicked into place, because the moon covered its face and the spray from the sea turned red and something stirred deep in the dust of the universe.

You drifted in, finer than smoke, thinner than mist. He breathed in, he breathed out. You leaned over, tasted his skin, his drops of sweat, tasted the wine he had drunk, the grease and the salt of the burger he had eaten. You looked at him asleep. An innocent. Your Ride had not known suffering or hunger or thirst or pain.

You studied the bridge of his nose, the tuck of his chin, the nape of his neck exposed, the soft lobe of his ear. The warm, sleeping lines of him. Your Ride, the body that will hold you while you do your work to keep the world safe.

He smelled like umber, the color of a day well done. He sighed a faint scent of toothpaste and the deeper primal wet of his mouth. He sighed and then he inhaled you in.

He breathed you into his diaphragm, into his muscles, his cartilage, ligaments, tendons, soaked you in through his skin—his nerves and blood vessels sang, oil glands and sweat glands rang—into his follicles and his fat, down and deep within his protein filaments, and into his liver and his stomach with its gastric folds and acid juices, bile black, intestines, gallbladder, deeper, deeper into the lobes and creases and jelly of his brain itself, and deeper, still deeper to the core, the very core of him of you—

*—are first an embryo, curled small and pink, the size of a thumb, a seahorse floating in the dark sea of your mother's womb, forming, growing, being born with a wail. The shock of bright sharp light into the world, fat cheeks to be kissed, screaming your parents out of sleep, or laughing with delight, your first uneasy steps growing surer until you run around, fall down, cry, pull yourself up, start again, your fine hair growing darker, your limbs longer. Learning how to ride a bike, a skateboard, to ski, moving fast, talking, drawing, musical instruments, spraying Lego pieces over the floor, taller now. At school, shy at first, then raising your hand, answering a question,* Me, me! *Knock knock. Orange you glad I didn't say knock knock? Ketchup, burgers, Fourth of July, fireworks from the beach, swimming at camp, pillow fights, real fights, making up, reading, weird feelings, wet dreams, daydreams, some pot, first job scooping ice cream, up to the elbow in cold sticky messes. Down by the dock, drinking, drunk, beer, throwing up, your head hurts, a girl's small breasts, fumbling at the strap. Competitive swimming, the sharp smell of the pool, the echoing, pushing through the water, muscles tighten, broad shoulders, good but not great, good enough, September, tests, mostly good, better in class, knowing the answer, hunting with Dad, hard to talk, the smell of turning leaves, Halloween. College pamphlets smooth and shiny, school, the campus*

*benevolent, wide, brick, and friends to talk and sprawl with, the future spread ahead as green as the grass you lie upon, and life inevitably pushing on like the strokes you take in the water—*

—your heart beat, your pulse pulsed, your blood circulated, hormones repaired muscles, testosterone was secreted, neurons gave orders, food was digested, sweat and semen, saliva and swallow, you took control of each beat and tick and pull and flow and stop and start. You became, You become, and . . .

You Are.

Now you ride the bus, which is agonizingly slow. It grunts and heaves and strains and wheezes like an old, old woman trying to get up. Older people ride the bus too, old ladies, old men. They have more time on their old hands; they have more time because they have hardly any time left. They must wonder why an attractive, elegant man like you, a man in his prime, is riding the bus. You look like you could step onto a private jet. You have done so in the past and will do so again if you have a meeting and the fancy takes you.

But right now you're riding the bus because it amuses you. It's relaxing in a strange way. You can think better here.

It's fairly late and the bus is almost empty. It's been raining and you gaze at those hunkering down and walking fast outside, the ones who don't have an umbrella. It's nice to be in the bus, which is warm, and comforting, and sheltered from the rain.

The passengers who remain are also staring out of the rain-streaked windows but they are not as contented as you. They know that when they get home there will still be meals to prepare, and families to deal with, and they are tired, bone tired, and the rain will make everything that much harder. And it's still only Tuesday.

The woman one seat up is dying for a drink. You can see this by the way her shoulders curve and her mouth is set in a grim line and her eyes are so thirsty. She's thinking about the womb-like warmth of her favorite bar. The one she promised her girlfriend she wouldn't go to anymore. The one where nobody knows her name, which is why it's her favorite. She's thinking about what it would be like to get off two stops early just to grab a quick one. Just to get her through the night. She's supposing she might have to have vodka because it doesn't smell as much, but what she really wants is a golden glass of bourbon. Just thinking about it makes her sweat. And you can smell this.

Addiction is metallic; it sounds like a million pinball machines. It tastes like the last crumbs at the bottom of the packet, of salt- and sugar-stained fingers, it smells like a damp shoulder pressed up close in a crowd, it feels like dew-formed droplets sliding down your fingers, it crawls like the itch in the small of your back.

You lean back and close your eyes but the smell is growing fainter; the woman has gotten off the bus, two stops early.

You smile.

There are only three passengers left, a man and two women. They have both seen you, already noticed you. You're noticeable. A handsome, single, no-wedding-ring man on a bus. It's a little unusual but it works. Maybe you just wanted to get out of the rain. Maybe you like to "experience life" and "all the city has to offer."

You do.

The girls are separated by two seats—two seats and twelve

years, you would guess. One is in her early twenties. She is very pretty, like a piece of expensive fruit. Her hair is a glossy nut brown, a chestnut brown, and she wears lipstick, shiny like seeds and pink like the inside of a pomegranate, on her lips, which pout a little. She looks squeaky clean and juicy bright.

She's on the third day of her menses. You can smell it. Old blood filled with old eggs has a darker scent. She's horny, which has a purple note. As she empties, she wants to be filled up. She wants to be fucked without protection.

Her boyfriend will never do such a thing. He's a nice Jewish boy. He would be horrified by the very unclean thought.

She knows you're looking. Her excitement is electric blue. It smells like fresh-cut grass, it soars like the hallelujahs of a gospel choir, it growls like a motorbike.

You smile briefly at the excited, juicy, fruity, squeaky-clean berry of a girl before turning your attention to the other one.

You don't need her color yet.

The other one has already seen you. She saw the pretty girl and saw you and had not allowed herself to hope. All her life she's been the other one, the friend. Not ugly, not unattractive, just the one who always has the slightly prettier friend. Her personality does not sparkle; she is not witty, not funny, not quirky. She is in fact "nice," which is the bell that tolls social death. All her friends are getting married. Her friends are having babies. She's happy for them. She's fine. She stares out the window at the rain and the spreading darkness and thinks about walking the five flights up to her small room. It's less rent for a smaller room. And of dinner, which will be leftovers, and if, hopefully, her roommate is out, she can sprawl a little in front of the television. Watch some complete garbage. Watch people whose lives are so much worse than hers. People she doesn't have to be happy for.

She is very surprised when you smile at her. She sees your reflection in the window. She can't believe you haven't gone for that gorgeous twenty-something. Someone who could get married and have a baby tomorrow, someone with her whole twenty-something life ahead of her, but no, this handsome man is smiling at her. Almost as if he sees past the twenty-something-year-old and is looking for more.

She doesn't look at you again. That would be too much. She doesn't shift, but straightens a little, her mother's voice in her head, *Sit up! Don't hunch over like that!* And then hunching down again because it's too much, sitting up to attention like this.

*Don't blow this*, she's telling herself. *Calm down. He's probably not even looking at you anyway.*

Her hand goes subtly to her hair just to see what she's dealing with—it tends to frizz when the weather is wet.

You love watching her. It's endearing.

Insecurity is lavender. It tastes like eyedrops at the back of your throat. It squeaks like the first notes of a piano recital. It feels like a too-large bra, too-tight pants—*why isn't anyone looking at me, why is everyone looking at me? I don't, I can't, I wish, I'm not, I haven't, I couldn't, I want.*

The bus stops and the twenty-something gets off. She passes you one last long look as if to say, *You don't know what you're missing*, and pushes out into the rain.

She doesn't know what she's missing.

When the man gets off, an old woman gets on. She wears a long dark coat despite the weather, and a multitude of scarves and shawls. It takes this human bundle of wet cloth forever to find her card. She mutters to herself, her hands shake a little, and when her eyes roll like old milky marbles, you see she's blind. Eventually the bus driver has had enough. He tells her harshly but kindly, "It's okay, it's okay," because it's petty change from an old blind lady, and what does he care if it's his last shift anyway?

She rasps something out that might be "thank you" and might be "fuck you"; the voice is ragged and rusted down. She sways and stumbles and totters like an ancient pirate tapping to a seat and drops her head.

Her eyelids twitch and her swollen, liver-spotted hands twist in her lap.

The nice girl looks at her, even though she doesn't want to, then looks away. She thinks what all women secretly think, and fear.

*That could be me.*

If she doesn't find someone, if she doesn't love someone, if someone doesn't hold her in the dark and ask how her day is, if someone doesn't tell her it's going to be okay, she'll turn into this woman, this blind old madwoman with food stains on her endless shawls. Or maybe she'll just shrivel up and die; her chest, hollowed out by loneliness, will cave in.

Suffering is a deep and spoiled black. It smells of unopened rooms; it smells of sour wine. It weeps like a woman in the last stall of the bathroom. It sounds like a tree falling, it echoes in barren parking lots. It tastes of dust. It looks like a single faded sonogram kept in the back of a cupboard.

This is where you come in. Maybe you'll come to one seat nearer, just one seat, though, so as not to invade her space, and lean in. Your eyes will fix on her, and your smile will be one of embarrassed charm as you ask:

"Excuse me, but is this the bus to . . . ?"

You will ask if the bus is going in the opposite direction.

She'll have to tell you apologetically that it's not.

You'll be comically annoyed with yourself. "I can't believe it!" you'll say but your eyes will twinkle and she'll know that you're laughing at yourself.

Because you have a great sense of humor. Because you're easygoing. Because even though it's late on a rainy Tuesday night, you're always ready for an adventure. You're spontaneous like that because you're warm and funny and perfect.

"Killer."

The words come in a slow, thick croak as if from a great toad. The girl gives a little jump and you look up.

The old woman is staring straight at you with her blind eyes. Her face is an ancient wreckage, lost to gravity and the ages. You look around at the nearly empty bus, then at the nice girl. The nice girl seems horrified, so you look back toward the old hag. You're pleasant, if somewhat astonished.

"Ender of Life."

"What?" you ask. "Who, me?"

"Yes. You. Evil. Spirit." That low growl has no business coming from a human throat.

"Hey now," you say, "settle down." You're firm but still good-humored because you're kind and patient. The girl should understand that you don't take the old woman's mad ramblings seriously.

Slowly she raises her cane and points directly to you. "Nobody. Here. Wants. To. Play."

A light goes on and the bus starts to slow. *Stop requested.* The girl has pushed the button. She throws you an apologetic look. It isn't her stop but she wants to get off. She likes you but she has to get off this bus.

You think about following her out. Saying something like *I'm sorry, but what the* . . . and then waiting for her to chime in with *I know, I know!*

Then you would say, *She's totally crazy. It's sad, really, but that was completely nuts*, and then again her saying, *Yeah, the way she pointed at you with her cane* . . .

Then you could awkwardly, hesitatingly, say that you're kind of shaken up and though it may be weird would she mind coming with you if you had a drink somewhere, even just tea with sugar (though it won't be) to calm down, just for like ten minutes or something, of course she probably has plans but you could really use a drink.

It would be the easiest thing in the world for you, but you decide instead to stay.

This will be a rare encounter.

You wait till the nice girl gets off the bus. You give her one more smile as if to say, *I'd join you but it's too far away from my stop. Oh well, nice knowing you*, just to leave her suddenly doubting that she did the right thing, and then the bus is once more slipping slowly through the rain, leaving her lingering on the sidewalk.

You wait. It's just you and the old woman.

Then you casually take a seat next to her. She expresses no alarm or anger. Just stares ahead of her, like a twitching zombie.

"Is this your usual route?" you ask politely.

She says nothing.

"Cat got your tongue?" you try again.

Still nothing.

"Hello, is anyone in there?" Your voice is warm and welcoming to whoever might reply.

Her neck twists suddenly as if a great hand has turned it. She looks up at you with her blind, blank silver eyes. Her old mouth, her lips gone with old age, opens and the inhuman voice of pebbles says:

*"Abi in malam rem fueri vitae!"*

*Be about your business, you Thief of Life!*

Aha, you knew it. Your fellow rider, an Other.

The Others have been around since Time began, and yet, to your considerable understanding, they are as passive as sheep. They may be conduits for the billions of souls passing through the cosmos, but they make no judgment, take no action. They watch silently, as witnesses. That's why the Others often choose the Rides that they do. It's easier to hide in those from whom the world looks away. It's easy to ride in the old, the ugly, the unseen. They exist on the outskirts of awareness. Give them money but look away. Give them money but don't get too close. Give them money and then swat them from your mind. Look away from the homeless, the addicts, the mentally ill, and the ones too poor to bear the title "mentally ill" and are merely "the crazy."

If you want to keep under the radar and not attract undue attention, to go about your business quietly and without incident, these Rides are easy to hitch, especially if you don't mind the thick and gummy filters of old age and insanity.

But you don't want to keep out of the radar. You want to enjoy yourself. You don't want the loose change, the guilty glances, the cold chill and the stink of defeat. You want the firm handshakes. You want eye contact.

You want to be in the heat and the wet and the rough and the thick of it.

You want the good stuff.

The smells and the tastes, the reds and the blues and the salt and the sweet, the smiles and the sweat, the blush and the blood.

You need their colors.

You did not know what life was but then you tasted it. For the first time you felt jealousy. You felt wonder. Each emotion, each strand of life, made you more present, inhaling and exhaling, and you rejoiced and you grieved.

Each color anchors you among the living.

"Nice Ride," you whisper tenderly to this decrepit sagging sack of skin. "What's the mileage?"

Your fellow traveler turns its silver sockets toward you. "I have no business with you."

You allow yourself to become a trifle stern, righteous, about to teach a needed moral lesson. "And yet your words have delayed my purpose—my color has fled."

"While your purpose may be necessary, the suffering you bring is needless."

You began to take pleasure in the hunting and pleasure in the cutting, and all, all too soon it ended. Everything builds up toward Her and each time the prolonging makes the taking more exquisite. The moment of completion is beyond all imagining but it began to come too quickly and then you would return to nothing, not even darkness but the absence of light and color and sound, anything, everything. The planets must be aligned, the stars must fall, for a Vessel to be born and fulfill her destiny. You come back, but never often enough.

You sigh.

The Birth brought catastrophe, brought war. One mother cried out in triumph; then a million more did so in anguish as the blood of their innocent sons and daughters stained the battle-torn earth. No one Child can be allowed to destroy the beautiful brilliance of this world and all its inhabitants, no one Being can have such infinite power, and that is why the Birth brought you.

So you have a purpose, have a mission; you have a point.

An extremely sharp one, in fact.

"But it's fun," you protest. "Shouldn't we enjoy our work?"

Again, nothing.

But you, you're a trouper. You lean over. You smile. Pleasant to the end you say, "Never mind, I forgive you." You pause and then add, smiling, because maybe you're not so pleasant, "After all, there's plenty more out there."

You lean over and press the black strip to request a stop. Then you kiss her mottled cheek softly as the bus grinds to a halt and you step out into the rain. She looks straight ahead.

Who knows what sights she holds within that silver gaze?

Then again, who cares? The night is young and full of possibilities.

# 7

And so I sit in this restaurant.

Sushi, French, Korean, Greek, and now, finally, Italian. One date a week, drawing it out. Taking his time. The audacity of it.

When I asked him how he got my number he told me it was easy enough if one knew where to look. He even added that I should deal with that soon. "You don't want the wrong types getting hold of your personal information."

I could have said no. I could have said all sorts of things. I could have not replied and let my silence speak for itself.

I didn't say no. I didn't even pause. It felt inevitable. As if our encounter had ever increasing momentum, a current carrying me along.

I sit outdoors in the restaurant's private garden, and the waiter comes and fills my glass full of wine. Wrought-iron tables, white tablecloths underneath short white candles cupped in glass. I gaze at the other diners, who are happy to be outside on such a perfect evening. Outside, yet inside such an elusive, exclusive space. It's the dream of all New Yorkers to be among and yet apart. There's the faint scent of jasmine, which grows on trellises against the brick walls, the clink of cutlery, a sudden spray of laughter from a party of four nearby. I envy these comfortable noisy double-daters. They have things to talk about. They have things they *want* to talk about. Unlike Sael and me, who sit in silence in the deepening dusk.

I think back to the first text:

Sushi tomorrow at Otoro 9:00 pm

The impersonal aspect of it attracted me. If no feelings were involved then no one could be blamed, no emotions would be squandered, no friendship betrayed, no hearts broken.

And Otoro is famous for being almost impossible to get into; you have to book months in advance. He had reservations at nine p.m. Of course he did.

My inner voice—murmuring *You're not thinking about it, are you?* and *You can't be serious*—had grown louder throughout the day until it was unbearably shrill. By eight o'clock it was screaming, *Don't do this! You're going to regret it!* as I pulled on my dress and applied my lipstick. In the cab it ordered me to *Text him you're not coming!* Then slyly, *Why even text? Just don't show up, and call a friend, or have dinner by yourself.*

The cab pulled over, stopped. I paid the driver and got out.

*You don't know anything about him.* I paused and it made one final effort. *Think! There's still time to make this into a funny story. One where you're not the bad guy.*

Then I took a deep breath, opened the rusting door that marked the almost hidden entrance, and headed down two flights of stairs.

The ceilings were very low. No decorations. This was the place that fanatics dreamed about. Extremely plain, it only sat ten people at a counter. It was the food that counted.

*Last chance to turn back.* And then I saw him and the voice was silent. He was there. Waiting, reading something, he looked up, showed no surprise to see me.

"Hello," he said.

"Hello," I said.

"How was your day?"

"Good, how was yours?"

"Okay, busy."

There was a pause. We were served a single piece of gleaming Japanese snapper, with uni and osetra caviar. It was beautiful, delicate, perfect. We ate in silence; then, after a long moment, he looked at me and said, "Tell me a story."

"Any story?"

"Any story you choose."

And that is how it began.

I told him how once when I was twelve I visited my father in San Francisco. It was a far cry from the bland suburbs of Silver Spring, Maryland, where I was born. I hadn't seen him in almost two years. My mother and father split up when I was nine. My father was a journalist and he traveled. He did this, he said, because he cared about the issues. "And not about his family," my mother said. I knew this wasn't true; he just didn't care about us as much. My father got by by the "skin of his teeth." I didn't know what it meant. He had kind of crooked teeth, but a nice smile when he really smiled with his eyes.

When I got to San Francisco, my father took me to a diner in the Mission and ordered me a tuna fish sandwich and a roast beef on toasted rye for himself. They both came with toothpicks, a red tassel for him and a yellow tassel for me, but he gave me his toothpick too. I ate my sandwich even though I didn't like it; it tasted kind of funny. That day we walked the streets and I saw more homeless people than I had ever seen before. There was one man slumped against a wall who didn't even have shoes on. I remember how grimy his feet were. He had really dirty, stained clothes and a matted beard and he smelled like old food and sweat and something else sharp and vinegary that made my eyes sting. He was singing a little bit to himself. He had a small patchy white dog that sat sadly and patiently. I felt terrible for the dog because I could see every one of its ribs as it trembled. My father gave me four dollar bills and told me to drop them into the baseball cap on the ground and the man said, "Bless you, sweetheart."

My father said, "There but for the grace of God go I." He laughed but he didn't sound happy. I knew in that moment that he thought he wasn't so different from the homeless man, and that scared me and made me feel a little angry because the homeless man didn't have any family but my father had me.

Later my father snuck me into a bar. And he gave me a sip of his drink, which was colorless like water but burned and didn't taste like water. Someone objected but he said, "It's cool, Lou, she's my kid." And someone else made a joke and they laughed and I felt great. But soon afterward I felt sick—I don't know if it was the drink or the sandwich—and I threw up.

My father took me home and put a cool facecloth on my brow and said, "Tough luck, old lady."

I felt horrible. I told my dad I was sorry.

"You didn't do anything wrong," he told me, but I still felt like I had messed things up. It was the only time I ever came out to visit him. I don't know what happened after that, if my mom stopped it or if he didn't want me there, but I've always blamed myself.

Our next dish of yellowtail fish was as smooth and as creamy as butter.

"Your turn," I said.

He told me how he once stole a toy car from a friend's house. He was going through a stage of pocketing things: ornaments, pens, small soaps from guest bathrooms. One day a maid had seen him taking a toy car and had told the boy's mother and she had called his mother and he had been sent home in disgrace. His parents had asked him over and over why he had done it but he didn't know what to say because he didn't know why he had done it. He only saw the disgusted way that they looked at him. He felt rage and shame, not because he had been stealing but because he had been caught. The woman who caught him was black and middle-aged and wore a blue and white uniform and he could still remember the triumph in her eyes and her grim smile. He was sent away to boarding school soon after that.

At the French restaurant amid cloudy mirrors, gilded menus, and tiled floors, we ate oysters and I told him about Lisa, this girl I was friends with in middle school. Our favorite game was called Pet Shop. We decided that when we were grown up we would open a pet shop together. We drew pictures of it and worked out names for the store and made up stories for all of the animals that lived there. A puppy saved the store from a fire, and the goldfish granted wishes. Lisa was plump and wore her mousy hair in pigtails and would suck on the end of one when she was thinking.

One day at school during break, Tiffany Rush and her friends Jessica and Kelly started taunting Lisa, calling her names like "sweaty pits," "meat breath," and "baby piggy." They made snorting noises like a pig would make. They held their noses whenever they passed her and said she stunk of farts and BO. I never stuck up for her. Even though we had been to each other's houses and even though I liked her, I didn't defend her. I didn't join in, but

I didn't say anything. I would just look away and wait for break to be over. She called me that night but I told my mother I didn't want to talk to her. I didn't want Tiffany and her friends to turn on me. This went on and on and then one day Lisa started crying in class and couldn't stop. She went to the bathroom and she didn't come back. The teacher sent someone to get her but she wouldn't come back.

Next week it was announced that Lisa wouldn't be returning to school. The teacher lectured us and said we were cruel and thoughtless and cowardly. I felt she was speaking directly to me. That day I got home and called Lisa's house but her mother said she wasn't there. Lisa didn't talk to me again and she moved soon after, whether it was to a different school or a different neighborhood I never knew.

On our third date we went to a hole-in-the-wall Korean barbecue place. We drank frosted bottles of beer and watched the beef shrink and sizzle. He told me about the time when he had become homesick at sleepaway camp. He wasn't even sure what he was homesick for, not his parents, nor his sister, nor friends, and yet he was so homesick that he pretended he had appendicitis. Although the camp's nurse couldn't find anything wrong with him they sent him home anyway. Back in Manhattan a stream of doctors couldn't find anything wrong with him either, though there was talk of food allergies.

There was nothing for him to do back at his parents' Upper East Side apartment and he had watched TV for the rest of the summer. He had been lonely and he had been bored. Still, he had never regretted it.

I told him how, the summer I was nine, I swam in a public pool almost every day and there was an amputee who also came every day. I would wait until she and her friend got in the shallow end; then I would dive into the deep end and swim as close to them as I dared. I would hold my breath and I would gaze at her stump underwater until my eyes stung. Her plastic leg remained baking on the blue deck chair, as if it was getting a tan. Staring at that woman's stump felt like the most forbidden thing I had ever done. I loved it.

These stories are delivered without drama or laughter, or horror or recrimination. They are received without judgment, without raised eyebrow or forced laugh or banal comment. It's like throwing pennies down a well and never hearing the splash.

At the Greek restaurant, not in Astoria but not bad, I told him about the thing that had happened with my stepsister. How, when my mother and I had first moved into my stepfather's large faux-Tudor mansion, my stepsister invited me into her pink and silver bedroom. She asked me if I could keep a secret. I said yes and she pointed to a silver-framed picture of a pretty, laughing woman with light brown curly hair. She told me it was her mother, who had died from ovarian cancer. She said that her father had told her and her brother that he would never love anyone again the way he had loved their mother, that their mother was the most beautiful woman he had ever seen. He said that love like that came only once in a lifetime. He said that their mother had made him promise on her deathbed that he would marry again and be happy. He told them that he didn't want to marry anyone else but that he had to honor his promise.

"That's why he married your mom," she told me. "I just thought you should know."

I remember going back to my room and sitting on my bed and thinking about how she smiled at me while she said this. She told me that if I told anyone else they would say it wasn't true, even though it was.

He told me how his older sister used to have her boyfriend come over when his parents were out. How, one night, he hid behind a couch and watched them make out. He had seen the boyfriend undo his sister's top to expose one small white breast. The boyfriend was saying, "You like this, don't you, tell me how much you like this, you slut," and had stroked and sucked on the pink part, the puckered nipple that seemed so dark to him. His sister's eyes were closed and she was breathing fast and making little moaning noises. The boyfriend had seen him crouching behind the chair and, instead of yelling at him, had slowly winked, as if Sael was part of the joke. He had run out of the room as quietly as possible. Afterward, he was angry with his sister and also disgusted and somehow ashamed of her. He never said anything.

These are the stories we tell each other. They are not the funny stories you tell your friends. They are the private stories that you carry in your bones.

I have grown used to these stories, the giving and the receiving. Tonight, I find his silence and the tension unbearable. So I decide I will tell him my favorite story, which happened years ago when my parents were still together. My father would come into my room after the lights are out and sit at the edge of the bed. He would pretend not to see my legs under the covers and try to sit on them while I wiggled and squealed in protest. Then he would laugh and shift over and say, "So, my Katherine of Katherines, what do you want to hear tonight?"

Sometimes he told me Grimm-like fairy tales in which the bear might gobble up the little pig, or something historical about how the pyramids were built, or about how whales nursed their newborn calves but there was always one story I wanted to hear.

"So, my Katherine of Katherines, what do you want to hear tonight?"

And I would say, "Daddy, you *know*!"

He would sigh theatrically but I knew he was teasing me. He loved telling that story too.

I was born two weeks early. My mother went into labor and they had to rush to the hospital. They arrived in the nick of time, and as the nurses were helping my mother get into bed, a doctor had come in and said—here my father would do a deep and powerful voice—

"Everything's going to be fine, Mrs. Emerson."

Apparently, at the moment the doctor said this, the power went out. It was strange, my father said, because there wasn't any storm to knock them out. The lights didn't come back on. Nurses were running around, patients were crying out for help, the doctor was calling out instructions.

Meanwhile my mother was in labor and the nurse asked—here my father would imitate the nurse with a squeaky falsetto—"Don't you want to stand by your wife, Mr. Emerson, and hold her hand?"

My father said that my mother yelled, "No! Keep him away! He's driving me crazy!" My father did a great impression of my mom yelling. Looking back on it, I think that speaks volumes.

So my father went and stood by the window, which oversaw the parking lot. Then he would always ask me, "And what do you think I saw?"

"What?" I always asked, because this was my favorite part.

And my father would say, "Hundreds and hundreds of stars shooting across the sky. I'd never seen anything like it before. I don't even know how long I stood there, but the next thing I heard was a baby crying, and that was you."

Then he would always finish with the line "That's how special you are, Katherine; you came in on a sea of shooting stars."

I have told no one about Sael. They wouldn't understand. *I* don't understand. They would just tell me to stop. They would tell me it's a bad idea. That he sounds like a bad idea. *It will only end in tears*, they would say. They would tell me that *this might even be dangerous*. They would be right. Nobody knows where I am; no one, let alone me, knows what his intentions are.

We have never emailed. We communicate only through texts. Neither of us wants evidence. I deal with this as a spy might; the less I know, the better, the less torture I will have to take.

I wonder what it's like to be a beautiful young man in this city. He is tall and lean. He has dark hair. He has a strong nose, a firm chin. His hands are long, his fingers elegant; he is impeccably dressed. All his moves are intentional, calculated.

I wonder about Sael's other life, his dating life and whom he's seeing, whom he would acknowledge in public. After all, what we're doing isn't dating. For one moment that first night I surprised him, and he's been trying to dissect me ever since. It has a goal; there's an ending. I wonder how many women he's slept with. There must be many. We do not speak of romantic relationships, past or present.

I know now, through his stories, that his parents are dead. He is an orphan, an old-fashioned word in this modern world. They died in a plane crash when he was nineteen. Not a big one, though; they were on one of the private, small ones. "It's amazing," he said, "the ways you can kill yourself when you have money."

He is interested in some art, and not in other art. He is opinionated but contained. He has never raised his voice in my presence. Never given any indication of a temper. I can't tell when he's joking. He has a poker face and he plays poker, mostly with his friends, although he has played in some semiprofessional tournaments and won some serious money. He also plays chess—of course he plays chess; it suits him. Every movement is controlled; every action is part of a larger strategy. But there's something coiled up inside him, something alien and unknown. I guess I must like this.

He pays for everything. I never take out my wallet. It is understood. I could never afford the kind of places he takes me to. This is on his terms. He can afford it. He is young and brilliant, and does well. Technology. Marketing. Design. Dropped out of college, started his own company, now employs many people. I imagine them to be mostly guys, but some edgy women. People who wear jeans and sneakers and are not the most socially adept, but who know how to create worlds. They know how to help those worlds talk with one another

Ironic, I guess.

We both know how a father's breath smells when he's unhappy.

Here are the things I have learned about myself:

I've learned that I like power, that I am attracted to arrogance, that I like anonymity. In a world where you can know everything, where you are constantly updating and informing, there's something wonderful about having a secret. Most of all, I've learned that I can be another Katherine. This Katherine is cool, almost cold. She doesn't laugh much, or smile. This Katherine isn't so nice. She tells the truth, though, even about personal things. She eats expensive food and is always dropped off at her building by a car service. Then she lies awake, staring up at the ceiling. She vows she will stop it. She vows, every time, that it was the last time. She is lying. She is waiting for the fifth dinner.

This knowledge is the bitter gift we give ourselves.

My pasta cools; the evening cools.

"Check, please," he says.

We walk side by side in silence. There are not many people around. We do not walk to the subway, nor does he hail a cab. I understand. He lives in this neighborhood. We are walking toward his apartment. This is it.

Does it count if I barely touched my food?

We stop at a metal black door around the corner of a brick building. Sael takes out a key. "Private entrance," he explains to my raised eyebrow. Inside the building, the walls are brown and flaking, impersonal, giving no clues as to the tenants. An old freight elevator opens and we enter.

Sael turns a key and we begin our creaky ascent. "This used to be a chocolate factory," he says.

Of course it was. Everything's better with chocolate. I bite my lip to keep from laughing, a hysteria rising in me.

The elevator doors part and we're here. I look around, trying to take everything in; the open-plan kitchen, the bookshelves filled with books, a worn-out black leather sofa, an oak coffee table on which sits a cactus in a white pot, glossy prints on the brick walls. I want to go exploring, look at the art, see what books he reads, but—

He closes and locks the door. There is something cold and final about the sound of the lock being turned. *Click.*

"Now," he says. "Don't move."

I don't.

"Lift up your arms," he says.

I do. He pulls off my thin black sweater. He turns it right side out and folds it, placing it carefully upon the arm of the black leather couch. He turns again to where I stand. I am wearing a sleeveless buttoned silk blouse tucked into my skirt. He gives the blouse a gentle tug and releases it. Its two tails hang awkwardly out, unsure and embarrassed. I have forgotten how to breathe. He starts from the top, slowly, deliberately sliding each one of my buttons through its slit.

One.
Two.
Three.
Four.
Five.
Six.

Now my shirt is open. Shirt, then a slash of skin, then shirt. It hangs like curtains framing the window of my chest. He eases the shirt back from my shoulders. He is careful not to touch my skin. I can feel the warmth emanating from his hands through the silk. I want him to touch my skin but he does not.

It's so quiet you can hear the faint *shhh* of material, soft and slippery, in his hands. He turns and walks to one side of the room. I stand watching him. He slides open a closet door and hangs my shirt carefully upon a hanger. I am standing in my skirt, my underwear, my bra. My clothes feel too tight. I am aware of everything. The absence of some clothes highlights the presence of the others. The cool puff of air-conditioning on my arms, my stomach, my shoulders, my legs. I hear the soft hum of the fridge, my own breathing. There is a faint citrus smell, probably from an expensive oil diffuser. He returns and stands in front of me. Then his hands move behind me. I breathe in.

Inch by inch, he unzips my skirt. The purr that the zipper makes is loud, terrifying. He takes his time. He gives the hem a firm but careful tug. My skirt slips down to my ankles and I am forced to step out of it, one foot after the other. I wobble but his hands close on the backs of my thighs briefly to steady me. He does not hang up my skirt, however, but lays it dexterously alongside the sweater. He reaches around me. He is deft. His expression is impossible to read as he undoes the clasp of my bra. He places it carefully upon the growing pile.

I am naked from the waist up, still in my panties and high-heeled shoes. Waiting.

"Close your eyes," he says. His voice is detached.

I close my eyes. Everything intensifies. The cool air on my skin brings out small gooseflesh; the fridge's hum sounds louder. Through his no doubt double-glazed windows, I hear the faintest honks of Friday-night traffic below us. It hits me with full force that I do not know this man. I don't know what he's capable of.

Then I feel his hot breath upon my neck. I hear the sound, and feel the motion, of his hands sliding down my legs as he kneels as if to worship at an altar.

I feel his mouth moving up my leg. Its soft warmth, higher up to just underneath my pelvic bone.

His face is directly opposite my crotch. He runs his nose down the front of my underwear. Plain, black, silky. I feel the ridge of his teeth through the cloth. I stiffen. The fine hairs on the nape of my neck rise. He exhales hot breath upward into me. He places his face against me. I shudder. I can't help it.

"Stand still," he says.

I do.

"Keep your eyes closed," he says.

I do.

I feel the outline of his tongue as he slowly, deliberately begins to lick. From the thick, long movements of his tongue my underwear begins to cling to me. I can feel his tongue and not feel his tongue. It is agony.

He molds and molds the thin fabric to me. It becomes an impenetrable barrier. It's agonizing. I want more; I don't think I can handle more.

I exhale with a small groan.

There is a moment of nothing, a vacancy, an exposure; my underwear is gone. *But how?* I am lifted up. He is strong; he carries me. *He didn't pull it off, so how is it gone?* I am flung down, naked.

My eyes are still shut tight as I lie against the endless expanse of cool, smooth sheet. I hear the sound of the clothing he is pulling off, shoes, a belt, pants hitting the floor—*Where is it?*—keeping my eyes shut tight against the wanting, the shame of wanting him so badly and my own wantonness.

And he is on me, easing my legs apart. "Look at me." His cock is hard, filled with blood.

He pushes into me. I am wet, but still, a part of me protests at the thick brutal length of him. But there is no stopping now. He holds me firmly down as he enters, inch by inch, his full length inside me. Then he begins to move and I must move with him. There is no choice but to move together. He holds me, one arm pulling me close and tight and the other supporting his weight as he thrusts.

"Come," he says.

I look away. It's too intense.

He holds me so that I must look into his face.

I open my eyes.

His eyes are wide and stare back at mine.

It is too intimate.

*Stop please stop.*

He bites my neck. "Come."

*Don't stop don't stop.*

He does not stop but intensifies, gripping my back, my ass, moving inside me, and the feeling builds and builds and builds and builds and builds and I scream as my orgasm breaks—

—and breaks and my body releases and releases. He thrusts on and on, merciless, and then finally he comes, releasing into me on and on and on and then he is still and the full weight of him is upon me.

Silence. I feel him trembling. His breath is rapid. He feels me shifting underneath him.

Instantly he rolls over, alert. "Am I hurting you?"

"No, I need the bathroom, and some water."

"Down the hall."

"Do you want a glass?"

"No, thank you."

In the bathroom, I take my time. I am overwhelmed. I have never come like that before, as if my orgasm was forced from me, as though I had no choice. Should I feel violated? In the mirror my face is flushed, my cheeks have high color, my eyes look dazed. I look beautiful.

*What now?* I silently ask.

My reflection offers no advice.

I have had a handful of lovers in my life, but as I stand here the memory that floats up is the night one of my stepbrother's friends made a halfhearted pass at me. Our parents were away for the weekend and school was almost over, so he threw a party. Blink-182 and the Chemical Brothers played at screaming volume in the living room, but as the night progressed the party gravitated to the backyard, where joints were being lit and make-out sessions were possible. There was no one in the kitchen and "Your Woman" by White Town was playing. It is impossible not to dance to that song, and I did my own sexy shimmy all the way through the darkened kitchen to the fridge, pretending that I was the prettiest girl at the party. I opened the door, grabbed an apple. In the light of the fridge I saw that a guy was in the corner, leaning against the sink, watching me. His name came to me. Brady. He was a friend of my stepbrother's and I had seen him a number of times at the house. I had noticed him—he was a good-looking guy with reddish hair and lean features—but as a senior he was as far removed from me as a Roman god would be from a mere mortal. I had never even thought to say hello.

"Nice moves." He smiled.

I was mortified. I wondered how long he'd been there. I muttered something unintelligible and made to walk past him. He reached out, grabbed my wrist, and pulled me toward him. Up close I could see his high cheekbones and a peppering of pale freckles. Before I could speak he leaned forward and kissed me gently on the lips, then harder. My mouth opened under his. He tasted of beer, and behind that faintly of mint gum. I closed my eyes, feeling a guy's tongue in my mouth for the first time. After a moment he stumbled away to the garden. I stayed, weak and crumpled, in the kitchen. I can still taste that first beery kiss.

I cultivated a passion for him for months afterward. Whole diary entries were dedicated to him. You are more in love when you're fourteen then in any time after.

I fill a glass from the gleaming tap in Sael's spotless kitchen and I'm on my way back to the bedroom when I see it.

It lies next to my crumpled underwear, which is now nothing

more than a thin, damp shred of material. He must have cut my underwear off me as I stood. I look at it. A small pocketknife with a red handle, the gently curved blade so sharp that it cut off my underwear in seconds. No hacking or sawing necessary. I pick it up; it's light; it has a comfortable feel in my palm.

I knew a girl in college whose boyfriend, it was rumored, hit her. She was a well-educated woman. She had long dark hair and a good laugh. She wasn't a close friend, but even I could see that she wore sunglasses when there was no sun. She wore turtlenecks on warm days. Everyone wondered, *Why doesn't she leave him?*

I think she moved to Canada. We lost touch.

"Katherine," Sael calls again, "come to bed."

I stand looking at the knife in my hand.

"Katherine?"

I put the knife down. I turn and walk back into his room, closing the door behind me.

HE WORD SPREAD, AND BY AND BY A noble knight clad in shining armor came to the village upon a great white horse. The horse bore a caparison with a great serpent coiled around a golden sword, the crest of the House of Morwyn.

The knight proclaimed, "I am sent by the Lord of Morwyn Castle, for word has reached him of this Maiden and her heady brews, sweet songs, and dark beauty that have turned men to fools and fighting."

The Maiden was brought forth, and the knight saw that her hair was as black as a starless night, her brow was as white as milk, and her eyes were like glowing embers. He said, "You must come with me, for His Lordship would wish it so."

And so she went with him upon his horse, and the men of the town were sorely vexed to see her go but their wives rejoiced in their hearts.

So the Maiden was brought before Lord August de Villias of Morwyn Castle, who was well pleased with his knight for he saw that she was young and lovely. She curtsied low and smiled sweetly, and he asked if she would do him the honor of brewing for him.

She said it would be but her privilege, and she set to work and sang softly:

*Heart to heart,*
*Bone to bone,*
*Each cup-filled cup*
*Makes thee my own.*

And when it was brewed the lord tasted it then drained it to the dregs. He declared it to be the finest in all the land, and then nothing would do unless she stayed to brew for the castle. His advisers were alarmed and said, "We know naught of where she has come from, and we have heard tales of enchantments and all the village men turned to fools."

But the lord would not heed their words, for he had seen the Maiden's eyes and thought they were as bright jewels. He made her many gifts, a pretty little mare with a bridle of silver, and a fine sparrow hawk. As the season passed she was seen much in his company and he insisted she should be adorned befittingly in silks and satin and the finest of pearls and gems of great value. They went hunting together and stayed away longer than was modest or good.

# 8

It is sunny in Central Park on this Sunday. Hot. Humid. There is tension in the air, fear and sex humming like low voices on the radio. Picnics sprout up like mushrooms. All over the grass, pale skin meets the sun. Hairy men lie determinedly on their stomachs, and a couple of guy friends throw a Frisbee, a little too hard, to one another.

You see couples draped all over the lawn—what better than to be in love and be slightly inappropriate about it? What is the point of affection if not to rub it in everyone else's face? Friends shimmy up a tree. A redhead with generous breasts, her white tummy spilling over her pink jeans, is surprisingly quick; there's a bearded guy and another man who would be good-looking if not for a flush of terrible acne.

You see amazing amounts of food—potato chips and baked pita chips, potato salad, tabouli salad, hummus and a block of cheddar—and there's Brie, homemade cookies, a pan filled with gooey brownies, their surface finger-swiped, plastic knives and plastic forks and the usual surreptitious search for a bottle opener, but that's for the later part of the day; it's still too hot to drink. There's the obligatory fruit salad, watermelon quietly wilting. There's orange juice and lemonade and water in big plastic bottles, even ice, though it's melting. The guy who comes from Colombia bonds with the Frenchman over the stupidity of having to conceal one's alcohol.

There are people in the park passing out pamphlets. One guy holds a sheaf out but he's not looking at you, only gazing at those two girls on the beach towel. He'll make his way over there. The blonde in the pink bikini is particularly fetching.

You take one of the pamphlets from his unresisting hand. The front says "Heaven's True." There's a single tree in the shape of a cross. A solitary leaf grows on the lowest right-hand branch, but the leaf is red and shaped like a drop of blood. Nice touch, you think. Eye-catching.

Inside the pamphlet declares the world has become an evil place, that sin and suffering abound. The pamphlet says that the Antichrist is coming, that soon the Beast will be upon us and all will have to take the mark or die. The pamphlet says that only in the love and the blood of Jesus Christ will all be saved. It speaks not only of love but also of sacrifice, and asks, "What would you sacrifice for the Lord?"

*Yeah, Heaven's something, I don't remember. I've seen a bunch of pamphlets stuck up in the subways. End-times shit, "only a few shall be saved," "the marks he carves are the signs of the Beast" kind of thing. Fucking fanatics, it's probably one of them.*

Thanks to you, faith is questioned and reaffirmed and questioned again. Why does such a thing happen?

*I hope they knew Jesus, I hope they got right with God.*

At least it got one thing right.

You casually make the pamphlet into a paper plane and sail it softly out onto the still air. You lie back down. You shade your eyes with a book. The sun is warm on your face and neck, soaks through your shirt. The air is filled with the shrieks of laughter; the grass is springy under the towel beneath your back; your legs are bent, your toes spread.

A breeze springs up, and so do two policemen. One group of furtive-looking thirty-somethings near you mutters as the police draw closer—*If you have booze put it away, put it away!*—but the policemen are not looking for stray bottles. They are looking for a little boy. *Have you seen him?*

The cops don't ask you; you appear to be sleeping, lying back on the towel with a book over your face. But you never sleep.

*The parents must be going crazy.*

*And that's not the only thing either, what with, what with—*

They don't even want to say your name, as if by mere mention they'll conjure you up.

In a way, that's true. You *are* called; you *are* summoned.

You know exactly where that little boy is. You can smell him. All the way across Sheep Meadow. You think about it and then you slowly get up; you amble over and ask the group if they'll keep an eye on your stuff, your friends haven't arrived yet (roll of the eyes). Want to see if you can spot them. Maybe they're lost.

*Sure, no problem.* You seem nice. Reading the *New York Times* and you have a book, a bottle of water, a little basket. You're like them. Maybe slightly better-looking but a sweet smile; you're shy. They think about asking you to join their Frisbee game when you get back.

You walk away, hesitant at first, still in their vision, and then you veer a little; the cops go one way and you another.

The cops are old, older than most. It's not a hard post, Central Park. Under the midday sun on the weekend no trouble is (was) expected.

You walk deeper into the park; there are balloons, and a large group of children, a birthday party? Even two. The parents young, determinedly cheerful, showing off their parenting skills to other parents, calling their children old-fashioned names. The girl's names start with vowels, Olivia and Elizabeth, Ava and Amelia—*Isabelle, come here!* The boys are biblical, Jacobs and Noahs and Matthews and Elijahs, all stomping and running and crying and laughing, and rolling around in the grass and eating bits of dirt. The parents are exhausted. They long to sleep. They do not see the little boy who is playing a little game in the shadow of a giant gnarled oak. This little kid is good at blending in.

But you see him. He is not like the others. You wonder what he is. You call out to the boy with your mind to see if he can hear you. He turns to you without a sound, away from the other children, and gazes at you with his huge shining eyes. You gaze back. You are enthralled. It is wonderful, like coming across an animal you have not seen before. You hold out your hand.

He comes over, looks but doesn't take it.

You walk together side by side and there is the distraught woman dragging her own bewildered son. She sees the boy with you, shrieks, draws him into an embrace. "Lucas! Oh my God!"

Pure relief is the color of a ripe peach.

Bystanders clap; the heaviness stealing over people's hearts evaporates as the air lifts, the wind wandering elsewhere to stir up trouble. You smile, give half a shrug, *no big deal.*

She turns to you, still hugging him. "Oh my God, thank you. Where did you find him?"

"Just over on the other side of the hill near a children's party. He was fine."

"Bless you." Her shoulders droop. Her relief is now giving way to defensive embarrassment, a smeary shade of puce. "I swear they were just here playing and when I looked again—"

"I totally understand." You are sympathetic, nonjudgmental. "My sister's having a heck of a time with her own."

She smiles at this, blinks back tears. "Well, thank you again, really, from the bottom of my heart."

She turns to the two small boys. Her voice has a wheedling, cheery note. "Well, that was an adventure, wasn't it? I think we've earned ourselves some ice cream!"

*Please, please don't make this into a big deal. Please don't tell your mother.*

You watch as they head off down the slope of grass toward an ice cream cart. Once more, you call silently to the little boy. Again, he looks back at you. You waggle your fingers at him as you whisper, "Bye-bye, Lucas. See you soon."

His thumb finds his mouth as he turns back around.

Your actions have earned the admiration of another woman sitting on the grass, who has taken her headphones off and is shading her eyes to look up at you.

She's ironic, dry, her method of flirting like mustard, a trifle sharp with some bite, but underneath she's impressed.

"Wow. New sheriff in town, huh? Superman?"

You joke back, with a straight face, "Shucks, ma'am, weren't hardly nothin'." You tip an imaginary hat.

She wants to know how you knew. She's impressed with the

way you helped the child to reunite with the adult. How modest you are. And good with children. "Do you have kids? That was awesome."

You say how you heard the cops talking about it; it was sheer dumb luck, good timing. Luck and timing. How true this is for so many things.

The police have drifted over, only to be told that the work is done; you wave and smile. You're already walking back to your towel. There's no question of you taking the child. They saw you sleeping. They give you the thumbs-up, thumbs-up from the police. The law, as necessary as salt. The moment you don't have it, you notice its absence.

You should get back to your friends.

Wave of disappointment. *Typical. Girlfriend, so obvious.*

She jokes with her friends that men smell need. In her heart she knows it's true.

*Why is it always the good ones?*

In this city where it feels like there's a million women for each single man she feels like a fool.

But then, as you turn, you say something to her. And everything changes. Funny how the world tips and spins on a series of syllables.

You feel her eyes upon you as you slowly stroll back to the group of people who were watching your stuff, the ones who will ask you presently to join their Frisbee game. Clearly you're a popular guy with all those friends, no loner, no creep. Not that guy dominating the news, the knife guy, what's his name? Scythe Man? No, it's on the tip of her clever tongue. Anyway. Nothing bad can happen on a Sunday in the sun, not when she's spending the day stretched out, melting like gum and rocked gently by the music in her ears.

Wistfulness is apricot, the color of the rose that your crush wore to the dance and the last patch of the sky above you when you sat alone at a white linen table, pretending to have a good time; it feels like the smallest, tiniest toe of a baby's foot, a baby who isn't yours; it tastes like the fuzzy warmed skin of a summer fruit; it echoes like the tap of a microphone being tested.

She holds what you said close, teases it out like the last bite of brownie, sweet and dark in her mind.

*I might have to come back to check on you. Clearly it's easy to get lost in this park.*

She had smiled. "Just in case I go missing?"

She's right. You'd hate for that to happen. And after all, who knows who's lurking around in this huge and sunlit expanse of green. Who knows?

You know.

At the tree you get ready to join the Frisbee game, and just before you do, you turn and give her a quick thumbs-up. She smiles; she's been waiting, getting a little nervous; she won't have to wait much longer, though.

Thanks to you.

# 9

You love going to the gym, feeling your muscles stretching and straining, the way sweat prickles, gathers underneath your armpits, beads on your forehead, collects and then slides down your flushed skin, your breath filling your lungs with oxygen, the rapid fire of your racing heart, the effort of pushing through the pain, and, finally, relishing the release as the endorphins flood through your nervous system, all in this glorious body. The gym is a great place to feel human.

There's a fat girl at the gym. The fat girl at the gym wears a long gray T-shirt. Even here, she's hiding what she can. She runs doggedly on the treadmill. Her pink cheeks pinker, her mouth pursed with effort. She breathes in. She breathes out.

The fat girl is watching TV. She's watching Susie Ranford get interviewed again. Susie Ranford, who started the organization DWHA (Don't Walk Home Alone) after her sister Emily, "Emmy" to her loved ones, was killed late last month.

Susie Ranford is the kind of person whom the media loves. Susie Ranford, the unofficial spokeswoman for the victims' families. A petite, pretty redhead, she's earnest but not boring; she's been touched by tragedy. And is she thin? Why yes, she is. Thin, thin, thin.

The fat girl tries to envision how in maybe ninety days she will look like that; she will stop being a "well, at least." She has been someone's "well, at least" for as long as she can remember. She'd probably be a "well, at least" to Susie and her now-dead sister Emmy, who probably wouldn't have looked twice at her, or maybe only gratefully for making her appear even more beautiful.

The concerned host, Cynthia—a pretty Asian woman whom the fat girl thinks of as "America's favorite aunt," with her apple-cheeked face, her chic, streaked black bob and tasteful tailored dresses—has asked Susie to explain the concept of DWHA for the benefit of the viewers, although the fat girl already understands that this service is, in fact, reserved for thin, pretty girls who actually have somewhere to go at night.

Susie's doing fairly well. Her face is drawn and her eyes are red but she's still speaking coherently. So far, so good. Her parents are too devastated to give interviews. Her mother is tranquilized up to the gills; her father turned into a ghost overnight. She must be their mouthpiece. She's a sister, not a mother or a father, not a fiancé, and yet the whole world is reaching out to her. And Susie Ranford has reached back. It's given her a reason, a purpose. She'd rather act than sit in that house; she'd rather be doing, doing, doing so she doesn't have to think about how often her big sister had irritated her, how often Emmy had driven them crazy. How Emmy was too needy, too insecure, how Emmy floated, couldn't commit, couldn't settle down, couldn't be happy. How Susie should have reached out, checked in, how she should have been a better sister, a nicer human being.

Susie Ranford sits in a comfortable off-orange armchair, on a set inspired by a middle-American living room, and speaks in a careful, overly controlled voice. She's intent on getting her message through, intent on saving somebody, anybody, maybe herself.

"If a woman knows she's going back to an empty apartment she should contact DWHA. A volunteer, or a group of volunteers, will come and walk her to her door; then they'll wait for her to check that her apartment is safe before leaving her."

Cynthia nods, then leans in, confiding. "Despite the support and praise you've received from starting this, there's also been some criticism." She wrinkles her nose apologetically to indicate that she, Cynthia, would never criticize.

Susie Ranford doesn't rise to the bait. "Yes, that's true."

Cynthia waits but Susie just stares at her so Cynthia will have to gently prod a little further. "Some would say that it creates potentially dangerous situations, that women trying to protect themselves are inviting strangers into their homes."

The fat girl thinks about letting a strange man into her apartment, of any man wanting to stay in her apartment.

You would.

Susie Ranford's lips tighten; her right hand grips the chair arm.

"Look, we can't guarantee your safety one hundred percent. It's not a perfect system, but at least it's something, okay? We try to do the most thorough background checks possible on our volunteers. Ideally there'd be a police officer accompanying every woman in the city"—now she speaks with a hint of sarcasm, perhaps suppressed fury—"but of course that's impossible, so we're doing the best we can. We always try to send a group of people so it's not just one person having to safe-walk. Even police officers on their time off have offered to help out."

" 'Safe-walk'?"

"The word 'escorting' has some negative connotations so we call it safe-walking."

The fat girl is used to euphemisms. The fat girl knows something about political correctness. The fat girl who has a "great personality," who has "beautiful hair."

"We have the volunteer check in with us before and after the woman has arrived at her destination safely. We also check in with the woman who made the call to make sure she's safe. We try and send at least two people on any walk."

Because there's a psychopath on the loose, using women as his human canvases. You carve their skin with the ancient tool of the Harvest, a sickle knife, so they call you the Sickle Man. The forensic pathologists concur: no other blade could render those cuts.

Each one bears an individual symbol: a leaf, a cat's eye, concentric circles, three interlocking triangles, their carvings determined by their colors. But all your victims are marked with the small crescent moon, a half curve in a darker circle (always over their left ovary, but that information has not been given out), and all suffered a final slash across their throats.

The fat girl thinks she's safe. The fat girl is sure you only kill the beautiful ones. Her fat has hidden her once again, padded her against the outside world and your attack. Unlike Emily "Emmy" Ranford, who, like all the others, was found naked on her bed. Amid your bloody Morse code alphabet, her personal letter swirled like a seahorse above her right breast.

She's wrong. You like the fat girl. She sees you using the weights, quiet, efficient, focused. You don't grunt, don't make noise. When you see her, your eyes don't slide away in embarrassment, as if to say, *Really?* You?

She is pink, which is the color of determination, of a bawling infant's face. It tastes of sweat and it smacks and cracks like bubble gum, it shrieks like adolescent laughter, it feels like early mornings, it feels like pushing upward and through, it is a color that pushes back.

"And what do you think of the steps that others are taking? Of the neighborhoods that are enforcing curfews and the groups organizing phone and text check-ins?"

"I think the more people are involved, the more communities come together, the better. We can't just hide in our apartments forever."

*Not forever,* thinks the fat girl, *but you can do it for a long time.*

"Given how the authorities have handled, some might say 'bungled,' the many aspects of this case, and considering all the unfortunate events that have occurred such as the fire in the NYPD forensic laboratory in Queens, the contaminated DNA, do you agree with what some are suggesting, could there be a possible cover-up? There are rumors that the killer might be involved in law enforcement—"

You smile at this. As if a mortal could do what you do. As if you needed others' help. As if you, the Entity that you are, could ever be caught.

Now Susie Ranford loses it. She's had enough. "The idea of a cover-up is total—"

The fat girl likes it when other people get angry. The fat girl would like to get angry but this is not allowed. She is not allowed to be fat and angry because it's her own damn fault. *Say it*, thinks the fat girl. *Say "a fuck load of bullshit."* She ramps up the speed. She breaks into a jog.

"—total insanity. We're working with law enforcement and they want to find this guy as much as we do. They're doing everything in their capacity to bring the killer to justice. This idea of the government being involved is nuts. Since my sister was killed there have been two more murders! That's six women dead! We don't have time to waste on conspiracy theories. People want to think there's a cover-up because they feel helpless and scared and out of control, and want to turn on one another. Well, we can't afford it now, not when this monster is out there!"

Her face is white apart from the spots of bright red in her cheeks; her nostrils flare. Her knuckles have whitened.

Cynthia's flustered. She's pushed too far. Susie is deviating from the script. America's Favorite Aunt can't seem unsympathetic. She murmurs, "Yes, yes, of course," and resumes a safer line of questioning. "So, for those wanting to get involved with DWHA?"

The fat girl slugs back tepid water from her water bottle. Keeps jogging.

Susie Ranford is trying to calm down. She has to get the message out. Then she can bid this bitch farewell, go back to her boyfriend's place, and cry her eyes out for a couple of hours before succumbing to a restless sleep.

"Of course! If you want to volunteer, please check out our website. We're looking for people, men or women, especially if you have some training in law enforcement and in defense or martial art classes. If you don't want to walk people home, you can always help with poster duty."

"There's been a lot of coverage about these posters. Can you tell us more?"

"The posters feature blown-up photos of the victims. Since DWHA was started, over *ten thousand* have been put up all over the city."

"Ten *thousand*?" Cynthia is incredulous, impressed.

"That's right. People can take them down or deface them, but we'll keep putting them up."

"What inspired the posters?"

"We need to remind women that no one is invulnerable, no one is immortal or immune to this. This doesn't just happen to 'other people.' I used to hear terrible stories and think that that would never happen to me, that will never happen to my loved ones. But it happened to my sister. She was smart and she was strong but she was killed just like all the others."

Now her voice softens, her shoulders ease down a little.

"We also want the killer to see the faces of his victims, know they were human beings. That's why we include personal facts about them. These were individual human beings with lives."

But you know this; you know they had dreams and hopes and passions and longings. They were brimming with life. That's why you chose them.

The fat girl thinks about the posters. It's true, the little facts about each victim have stayed with her. Kathleen Walsh was a corporate lawyer who read science fiction books; Jennifer Wegerle was a teaching artist who taught drama up in the Bronx and loved to cook; Melissa Lin, who worked in marketing, was due to be married in less than a month.

"How long will you be putting these posters up?"

"We'll put them up for as long as it takes. As long as it takes to get him."

For a moment the fat girl wishes Susie Ranford were her sister. She only has brothers: popular, callous, and finally strangers.

"Well, it's been an honor to have you here today, given your loss—"

"I'd just like to tell people about the vigil?"

"Of course."

"We'll be holding a candlelight vigil on Thursday the twenty-eighth for the victims and their families, starting at seven p.m. in Union Square."

You know that this will be exactly a month from when they found Emmy.

"People are encouraged to wear white, bring candles."

"Why white?"

"White is the color of mourning in many cultures, but it's also the color of innocence, to remind us of the innocent lives taken from us." Susie gives a watery smile. "Of course, you can wear anything you want to. Your support will be enough."

"On behalf of myself and all of us here at *Wake Up with Cynthia!*, I just want to say that it's been a privilege to have you here today. We want to let you know our hearts and thoughts are with you and with all the victims' families during this terrible time of loss." It's impossible to tell if Cynthia is sincere. The fat girl has seen her show before and knows she's a great crier.

"Thank you."

"Your final words for the viewers, especially for our women viewers watching?"

Susie Ranford turns to the camera, her eyes bright and brimming. "To the single women out there, or the women who live alone: Don't be proud; it's not worth it. This sick psychopath has now taken six innocent lives and destroyed countless others. I thought it couldn't happen to me, or to anyone I loved. Now my sister is dead, brutally murdered." Tears run down her cheeks but she continues to address the camera. "I'm begging you, if you know there's a chance that you'll be coming back to an empty apartment, contact us through our app or our website or call our number. Even if it's during the day—remember that my sister was last seen at a public library in broad daylight. Wait in a well-lit public area, or somewhere with lots of people around, and one of our volunteers will come and find you. You'll be told their name and a numeric code ahead of time to verify that they are who they say they are. Try to be patient, it might take a little time, but it's better to be safe than sorry. Don't be a victim. Stay safe."

She looks like she's about to break down completely. Real grief can be messy. Cynthia hastily turns to the camera and starts to repeat the information about contacting the organization.

The fat girl pushes the plus sign, which steepens the incline, her red face redder, her armpits sweatier; with jiggling flesh she reaches for her chance to be a victim, pushes on toward lean, trim, slim annihilation.

She'll get there sooner than she knows.

# 10

My mother calls.

"How are you?" she asks.

When I was ten my mother met a well-known heart surgeon thirty years her senior, and when I was eleven she married him. His name was Richard but everyone called him Dick. He was a widower with silver hair. He had an expensive house in a swanky suburb of Washington, DC, and two children, but not really children because they were six and four years older than me and didn't take much interest in a gawky eleven-year-old. My stepfather never told me to call him Dad, and I never did. I didn't call him Dick either. I called him Richard.

"So, what's new?"

My mother has silvery blond hair, bright blue eyes, and a tight smile. She smells bright and clean and efficient, like the inside of an expensive bag. Like winter. After her second husband, Richard "call me Dick," died, my mother found happiness in dogs and real estate. She'll call occasionally, or I will. Just to "check in." It's more like stocktaking. Alive? Solvent?

My mother and I are not close. We treat each other like tourists who find each other in a foreign place. We come from the same country, but not the same part of the country. We might have unexpected things in common, but our lives are different, separate, and "other." We are polite and friendly. We stick to neutral topics and are relieved when the time for talking is over.

But now there's panic in the city. People are frightened. Even my mother is calling more often.

"I'm good. And you?"

"How's your roommate?" My mother's manner is like a folding chair. Theoretically you can sit on it, but it will offer you the minimum of comfort or support. She disapproves of Andrea's single-mother status.

"Andrea's fine, Mom."

"And her son? Is it Luther?"

*She's proud she's making the effort.* "Lucas is fine too."

I think of telling her about the pennies. There were seven today. I'm torn. It reminds me of Secret Santa, which we used to have at my school. I always hoped Amir, my long-term crush, would pick my name out of the hat. I guess that's why I haven't stopped this, picked the pennies up.

I decide not to tell my mother. She would be horrified that Lucas would be allowed into my room at all.

My mother does not ask about my love life. This is good. I wouldn't know what to tell her if she did. I'll never tell anyone. It's better this way.

I haven't heard from Sael. I'm not exactly glad but I'm relieved. Without the rules, the framework of five dinners, there was nothing. We were so brutally honest; where could we go from there? Still, to be so right is a little disappointing.

But something good has come from it. I've started to see David again. During the phase with Sael I hardly saw or spoke to him. He asked me out twice but I found reasons to be busy. I felt too guilty. And after that he kept away too, sensing my uncertain, unhappy signal. However, this past Monday the guilt had faded enough and I reached out and called and now we're going on a date.

Sometimes I wonder if I'll get away with it. I wonder if this could be easier than I ever considered. Maybe no one has to get hurt—really hurt, that is. Sael fades away and David comes back, and technically I haven't done anything wrong.

Technically.

David and I are at the movies tonight.

The movies are public. The movies are safe. No one wants to be too isolated these days. He buys the tickets and I buy the popcorn and a Cherry Coke for myself and a Coke for him. You must eat popcorn when watching a movie.

We split up, him to find seats, me to go to the bathroom. When I walk into the theater, he waves to me. He's sitting up high near the back, the seats I like the best.

"Here you go." I hand him his Coke. The popcorn is to share.

"Ah." He settles back. "Popcorn, a Coke, and thou, not a bad combo."

"Not bad at all."

"It's been a while," he says.

"I know," I say.

He takes a swig. "When all is said and done, when the battle's lost and won, Coke cannot be beaten. It's the drink of champions. And you're drinking?"

"Cherry Coke. I'm not a purist like some people."

"No ginger ale, right? It reminds you of being ill."

I think of my dating profile; I flush, ashamed. He remembered. He cares. Then the previews start and we both fall silent.

It's a good film, a thriller. A woman detective pursues a killer, and it gets a little scary. People have questioned it; given what's happening in the city right now, it's not in the best taste. The theater is pretty empty, but we are not alone. For a few of us it's finally an excuse to say, *It's only a movie.*

David's arm and my arm are very close. I feel the warmth of his skin next to mine. Closer.

Then he takes my hand. He hasn't touched me since he walked me home about a month ago. It seems like an eternity. His fingers thread easily through mine. His hand is warm and smooth and large. I didn't remember but now it floods back. His hand over mine. He holds it for a while; then he places it against his chest. It's a strange move, an intimate one, more intimate than many sexual things I have done. I look at the movie screen again. I try and concentrate. I can't. There's a new sensation: his lips are on the back of each finger; soft, firm, soft, he kisses them separately. My insides weaken, melt, and run together. I sneak a glance at him but he doesn't take his eyes from the screen. I look back at the screen, heart thudding. It is endless and not endless and I wish it would never stop. I stare at the screen. I don't see a thing. A breath in my ear, he whispers:

"I love this movie."

It's hard to breathe; the skin of my arms breaks out in goose bumps. Gently his fingers stroke the backs of my fingers. All over, I want to feel this all over and over and over and over. *It's a serious hand job,* I think. I get the giggles. Hysterical laughter rises up in me, but I can't laugh. It would sound crazy. I don't want this movie to end, I don't want this movie to end, I don't want this movie to end.

When the movie ends I go quickly to the bathroom and splash cold water on my face. Pat it dry with a towel. Try to stop grinning like an idiot. It's always the quiet ones, I guess.

He's waiting for me next to a cardboard cutout of some long-ago hero. He takes my hand again and we walk hand in hand and it's lovely, easy, natural. "That was a great movie," he says.

"It was."

"I mean, I have no idea what happened in it, but it was great."

"Someday you'll have to tell me what it was about."

"It might become one of my all-time favorite films."

We go down the escalator and into the night.

"Drink?"

"Sure."

Outside, the sidewalk is empty. David whistles softly through his teeth. "Wow."

"Yeah."

"Well, I always wanted to see what the zombie apocalypse would look like, but without those pesky zombies."

I look around at the quiet summer street, so unlike the usual craziness of the East Village. No long lines for ice cream, or annoying teenagers hanging about, yelling at the top of their lungs. Not even a large tattooed man waiting patiently while his tiny schnoodle urinates on a fire hydrant. I never thought I would be longing for more people in my way. Now I almost even want a slow-moving tourist pausing just in front of me to take a picture of a building. Almost.

"Let's go to a place where they play cheap music and sell loud beer?" David suggests.

We end up at a dive bar on Avenue C. It's not the greatest, but it's nearby. And open. The first two we went to were closed. There seems to be an unofficial curfew. The city has grounded itself. Not that it will do much good. The dead women have taught us that much, at least. If he wants to enter your apartment, he will. Still, this bar has the requisite Fleetwood Mac on the juke, cheap beer. It will do. We talk; it's so easy to talk with him, about this movie, and other movies, and from there . . .

He turns to me. "I'm glad we did this."

"Me too."

"You know, for a while there I kind of felt that maybe you weren't that interested."

"Oh?" *Tell him.*

"I mean I just got that feeling."

*Now is your chance.* "No, it wasn't that . . ." *It was just that I was fucking your friend.* "I just . . ."

*Tell him.* What would I say? What would be acceptable now that we've made it to this place after such a wonderful night? What wouldn't ruin everything?

He laughs. "You look kind of agonized."

"I . . ."

"Well, the important thing is that we're here now." He leans forward and gently but firmly kisses me.

I lean into his kiss.

He holds me tight and nothing exists but this moment. Eventually we both come up for air.

"Wow," he says softly. "I've been wanting to do that forever."

"What took you so long?"

"Well, the first time we had an audience, which somewhat put me off my game, and then, I don't know, work got crazy, you seemed sort of distant . . ."

"I'm sorry."

He grins. "We'll have to work on it."

I grin back.

He settles the tab, though I protest, and we stand outside.

He sighs. "Now I'm sorry we organized this on a Wednesday."

"What would you be doing Friday or Saturday?"

"That depends."

"Hmmm. Would you like to do something this weekend?"

"What do you have in mind?"

I think about the weekend. Restaurants and bars are closing early, clubs too, although we have no interest in them anyway. High, hysterical anxiety is exhaled like carbon dioxide.

I've had a crush on this guy at work, but I don't know, he seems a little off. Usually that's my type but what with this psycho on the loose, I don't know . . . y'know?

So, she told me she might leave the city.

Leave her job? And everything?

Yeah, her parents are going crazy.

I know. My parents are freaking out, especially my mom.

For me it's my dad, I'm a daddy's girl.

It dawns on me.

"What about a home-cooked meal?"

"Cooked by you?"

"None other."

He is delighted and touchingly surprised. "A home-cooked meal sounds amazing."

I grow a little nervous. "Well, I mean, I'd like to check in with Andrea, see what she's up to, if she wants to join. And if so it will be us four. I hope that's not too domestic?"

"Sometimes domestic is awesome."

"Then it's settled."

He smiles. He kisses me again. It's wonderful, and after a long while we pull away, beam at each other.

"You'll tell me what I can bring?"

"Yourself."

"Come on."

"Maybe a bottle of wine."

"Now you're talking."

He puts his arm up and a cab materializes on an otherwise desolate street.

"I can take a subway."

"Nah, take a cab." He's worried about me. These days all news is bad news. "Here." He folds some money into my hand.

I push it back. "I'm an independent woman, mister."

"Okay, okay, duly noted," he says, his tone solemn, his eyes shining.

He kisses me a final time, and I get in. Then he flings some money and something else in through the window and jumps back before I can fling it back at him. I pick up the money and a little bulletlike object, examine it. It couldn't be a sex toy, could it?

"It's pepper spray, not perfume," he calls as we pull away. "Don't spray it on your neck!"

*What?!*

"Text me when you're home safe!"

And we're off into the night.

"Nice guy," says my taxi driver. A small bearded guy, he looks Indian. "Your boyfriend?"

"Not yet." He will be, though, if I have anything to do with it.

"Is not good for woman not to have boyfriend."

I sigh. My feminist friends would kill me for not making this a teachable moment, but— "You're right," I agree.

"Not with this craziness."

"It's true."

"They found another one." He sounds grimly satisfied, as if this proves his point.

"Oh God." It's like a physical blow.

"Yes, in her apartment."

"Terrible."

"You live alone?"

"No." *Why is he asking me?* "I have some big strong guy roommates," I ad-lib. "They work out all the time."

"That's good," he says grimly. "You a pretty woman. You don't wanna live alone right now."

"You're right," I say.

Then he turns on the radio and listens to some sports update while I look out the window for the rest of the ride home. Over the still-hot street the moon bobs in a lukewarm sky. Some NYU-student types brave the night despite the warnings. They're young and underdressed, the girls trilling and shrieking, the guys awkward in pale T-shirts, baseball caps. They are drunk enough not to care, loud and raucous, looking for a fight, brave in a group of friends, enough drinks between them, sweaty and lustful and secretly hopeful.

I conjure up all the good things about the night—the holding hands, his kiss, *I've been wanting to do that forever*—as I get ready for bed. I'm about to text when my phone lights up.

Safe?

Safe!

Good. ☺

I had a wonderful night tonight.

Me too

The movie wasn't bad either ;)

Not bad at all

Okay sweet dreams, see you Sat

Not if I see you first!

:p

I smile. I feel warm inside. Glowing. I get under the sheet. I guess I'm a little sorry that we didn't go back to his place. But I know that taking it slow is a good sign, and we need to build up trust after the last month of distance.

Maybe this will all be okay; maybe this will all work out.

I turn on the radio and hear a late news bulletin. Another woman, Rebecca Lamb, has been discovered, just as my cabdriver told me. I turn off the radio. My closet door is open again. I get up to close it. I'm feeling antsy. It was a beautiful evening. I don't want to ruin it. There is no rain and there is no one standing in the rain.

I can't sleep. Me and the rest of the city. According to one report I heard, the demand for sleeping pills and tranquilizers has risen sky-high. I close my eyes. I breathe in through my nose, out through my mouth. I visualize myself exhaling the tension.

The worst thing is how he gets into the apartments through locked doors and closed windows, how he leaves no signs of breaking and entering. My window used to have security bars, but I think the last tenant took them out. I never worried about it before. I'll have to speak with Andrea.

Mr. Bob, the unofficial mayor of the block, says this guy is nothing compared to the Son of Sam or the Zodiac Killer—of course Ted Bundy was the worst.

*This isn't even really bad. You should have seen this city a few decades ago. That was chaos, madness, the pushers, the tweekers, the whores, crime was rife, everyone so fucking neurotic, pardon my French.*

No, the worst thing is the way their bodies are found afterward.

Think about how he kissed each one of your fingers in the movie. Think about that kiss in the bar. *I've been wanting to do that forever,* he said. He's taking it slow, which means he might take it seriously, unlike . . . Don't think about Sael. There's nothing to think about.

I ask Andrea the next day about dinner. "If it's okay, I mean, if that works for you?"

"Lucas will be thrilled—he loves your cooking." She looks at me, solemn. "Inviting someone round for dinner, I don't think you've ever done that before. It must be serious."

"Well . . ."

"Relax, I'm just jerking your chain." She smiles. "He sounds nice, can't wait to meet him, talk with him, let him know what he's in for."

"Ha, ha."

She's teasing me, but there's truth in it. I'm careful around Lucas. Andrea has never asked me to be but I am, and I know she's grateful.

"It is nice to see you happy, though," she says. "For a while there you seemed a little stressed out."

*Oh yeah, that's when I was fucking around with David's best friend.*

"Then again, we've all been stressed out." She looks tired, worried, and I know she's thinking about Lucas, how these murders are affecting him. He had a bad nightmare last night.

"I was, but I'm better now." I leave it at that. I'm excited to plan: what to wear, get the necessary groceries, even some flowers, sunflowers maybe? I love flowers but I can't ever seem to keep them alive.

On Saturday afternoon, with about an hour to go, David calls. His voice sounds different, without warmth or sweetness.

"Katherine."

I feel cold all over.

"Katherine?"

"Yes?" *He knows.*

"I have something to ask you."

*Oh fuck, he knows.* "Yes, what's up?" I'm trying to be casual.

"You remember my friend Sael?"

"I think so." *Yes, I believe I do.*

"Well, there's something I want to ask you."

*This is it.* "Yes?"

"He called me today and he's going through a bad time, he's kind of low."

"Oh?" *Wait, hold on.*

"I've heard him like this before and it wasn't good. I think it might be about a girl."

"Oh really?" *Oh God.*

"I sort of don't want to leave him on his own. I really hate to ask this, but is there any way I could bring him?"

"Um." *Shit.*

"I would normally never ask this but—"

"No problem." I am trapped, cornered.

"Are you sure? I feel terrible."

*Believe me, you don't know about feeling terrible.* "Why? Andrea and Lucas will be here, it's really casual."

*Sael's coming. They'll both be here at the same time. Shit, shit, shit.*

David's words are all rushing together in apologies and promises. "Katherine, are you sure? I'm so sorry. That would be wonderful."

"Absolutely! The more the merrier." *Like the threesome from hell.*

"I'll bring twice the alcohol."

"Damn straight." *Because we're going to need it.*

"Seriously, a million thanks for this, see you soon!"

And he's gone.

"Fuck my life," I say to no one.

They bring not two but three expensive bottles of wine, so that's good. I haven't seen Sael since the night of the fifth dinner. He looks well, a little thinner maybe, a little more subdued, but in nothing like the desperate state David described.

"Hey," he says to me. He's quiet, his eyes downcast.

"Welcome," I say to David, basically ignoring Sael. "Come on in. Andrea, this is David, this is Sael. David and Sael, this is Andrea."

"And who's this?" David is bending down ready to make friends.

"This is Lucas."

Lucas seems shyer than usual. I guess he's not around many grown men. His thumb finds his mouth. It's a bad sign, the thumb in his mouth. We won't get a peep from him for the rest of the night.

"Thanks for letting me bring Sael." David and I are in the kitchen now, organizing dinner, getting another place ready. I look out toward the living room.

Andrea and Sael are in conversation over sweet and low jazz songs from the throats of long-dead singers. Lucas, who seems to be recovering from his initial wariness, is sitting close to his mother's legs, drawing pictures with his crayons. Sael says something and Andrea laughs, nods her head in agreement.

"Seems like he's doing okay," I hazard.

"I told him that he better be on his best behavior tonight."

"Or?"

"Or I would beat the shit out of him."

"Really?"

"Nah, but I would toss his phone in the river. Then I would run like hell before he caught up to beat the shit outta me."

"Impressive."

"Where can I find another bowl like this?"

"Up on top over there . . . No, on the left, that's right."

"I thought you said right!"

"Very funny, funny man, now pass it to me." I like ordering him around; it feels cozy, domestic. I was terrified about tonight but I didn't need to be. Whether David gave Sael a lecture before coming here or whether Sael is actually subdued by outside events, I can tell that there'll be no scenes, no drama. Both are being pleasant; the evening is going well.

Now David leans forward; he obviously likes the apartment. "This is great." He's surveying the scene through the pass-through counter window: the warped wooden floors, the tall doors with their little glass transom windows, the rocking chair in the living room with the comfortable oversized cushions, in which Sael leans forward, listening attentively as Andrea talks. "Nice place," he says.

"Tell Andrea. She found it, decorated it."

"How long had she been living here before you moved in?"

"Three years, I think, give or take."

"How did you guys meet?"

"A mutual friend introduced us. It was good timing. I needed a place to move into and she was looking for a tenant."

In fact, I was going through the most massive breakup. Two years ago I had a decent job and a steady boyfriend. I'd thought we were heading toward marriage and children, and then less than one month later I learned that just because you plan something doesn't mean it's going to happen. My position was cut and then my boyfriend, a big tech guy, decided to move to San Francisco. By himself.

He loved me, but not enough. He wanted a fresh start. I had less than a month to move.

It's hard to remember that time. For the most part I was numb, dissociated. The pain flattened me out. It was a struggle to get out of bed, to get out of my sweatpants. I tried to look for a new job. I spent the majority of my days crying, often at inappropriate moments, trying the patience of my long-suffering loved ones. Somehow a friend of a friend heard that I needed a place in a hurry, and after about a week I was sitting face-to-face with Andrea, going through an informal kind of "coffee interview." *Whatever happens*, I'd thought, *at least I got out of my sweatpants. That has to mean something.*

Andrea is gorgeous, black, with incredibly high cheekbones and a long slender neck. One look at her and a model would declare defeat and drown herself in cookie-dough ice cream. Luckily for them Andrea is a public defender, which means she is noble as well as good-looking. I could easily hate her, except she is genuinely nice and funny and she needs me almost as much as I need her.

"No one wants to live with a kid," she'd said over coffee. We had already devoured almost all the cookies. "They think they won't be able to smoke crack or binge drink during the day or bring strangers home to have leather-clad sex with."

"And would they?"

"So long as they shared the crack."

She was so deadpan that it took me a moment to realize she was joking. I laughed. My face felt strange when I did so.

Andrea smiled. "I happen to love the little guy, but I guess the 'keeping it down' at bedtime by seven could be seen as a downer if you're trying to have a party. The last girl couldn't take it. I don't blame her. She was in her early twenties, wanted to have a good time. Said she hadn't moved to New York just to live with her mother all over again."

"Wow, that's kind of rude."

"I said, 'Good, because I wasn't looking forward to having a teenager just yet either.' "

"Then you punched her in the boob?" I suggested.

Now Andrea laughed. "That's right, then I punched her in the boob."

"Momma?" A little kid appears. His brown eyes are huge and wondering, and he has tiny soft black curls. He stomps over with that particular little-kid determination. He's holding a faded velveteen pig in one fist. He grasps onto Andrea's leg when he gets there. Examines me.

Andrea puts her arm around her son. "Katherine, this is Lucas; Lucas, this is Katherine. Can you say hello?"

" 'Lo . . ." My name seems to stump him.

"Katherine's a bit of a mouthful. You can call me Kat."

Andrea turns to him. "Honey, did your movie end?"

He shakes his head. His eyes don't leave my face.

"Let's use our words."

"No."

"Then what's up?"

"I heard you."

"Oh, you heard us laughing and decided to see what's so funny?"

"Yes."

"Just grown-ups talking, sweetie. It's kind of boring."

"An-cay he ave-hay a ookie-cay?" I say, raising an eyebrow at Andrea. I don't want to offer the kid an Oreo till I get his mom's permission.

"Yes, I can has a cookie," he informs me.

Andrea and I both burst out laughing.

"You're smart, mister."

"Can my pig have one too?"

"Well, does he eat cookies?"

He looks stricken.

I am merciful. "Well, maybe I'll give you his cookie and you can show him how."

"Okay!" He brightens up. Enchanting through cookie crumbs, he tugs on Andrea's sleeve. "I like her. Can she stay?"

"Oh," I said, embarrassed. "Um, you don't have to—"

Andrea had smiled and looked at me. "Want me to give you the tour?"

It's hard to believe that was almost two years ago.

"Come to the table, baby," Andrea says. "Dinner is ready." And Lucas gets up and we all sit, and we eat.

Mismatched bowls on place mats, the sauce, tomato-based and basic, steaming, pasta and some bread. A good smell, a cheerful smell. There's still a bottle of wine to go. There is candlelight. Talk is easy. I laugh. I feel my shoulders descending. It's a wonderful evening. Four adults and a child, content on a Saturday night. We do not talk of how many women they've found, or Andrea's job. We speak of broad general things, the weather, movies, books, past summers, and memories. David is kind, Sael is attentive, and Andrea is delighting in their company.

And just in this moment I am happy.

After dinner there are strawberries and David insists on pouring a little orange juice over them. "Brings out the sweetness," he says. It's a neat trick, but that's David, cutting the acidity, bringing out the sweetness with his own.

"Bedtime, honey," says Andrea, and Lucas asks:

"Can Kat take me?"

I get up in answer. I'm happy to do it, to let the others bond. I'm happy to let them make her happy. When we are stuffed with cake, we can afford to offer it. I am glutted on relief, on happiness. It's been a while since I've seen Andrea so relaxed; the Sickle Man craziness has really been getting to her.

Lucas offers me his small hand and I take it into my own. We head off to his tiny room, really more of a glorified closet, home to his little bed and his drawings and toys. Meticulously neat: the less space we have, the neater we have to be.

Lucas changes and brushes his teeth with his big-boy toothbrush—or, as he says it, his "toofbruf." I look at all the books; there on the shelves are Dr. Seuss, and *Goodnight Moon*, and *Caps for Sale*, and I think that this will be a good chance to talk about the pennies.

There were more today. I still don't touch them, as if they're art.

I don't want to touch them, to disturb them.

That's what I'm telling myself anyway.

Eight pennies, all of them facing heads up.

Heads up, it's lucky to find a penny heads up, but "heads up" is a message, or a warning. I'd crouched down, peering at the little bronze profiles of a long-dead president.

I wonder how he got them to stay upright, spaced so perfectly?

"Kat?"

It's Lucas, back from brushing his teeth. I jump. "Honey, you startled me."

He just looks at me for a moment with his large brown eyes, as if he can read my thoughts.

"C'mon, get into bed." I pat the cover and he gets in. "Lucas . . . I start.

"Yes?"

"Before I read this, I have a question to ask you."

"Yes?"

He looks scared, but this can't go on.

"I won't get mad, I promise."

He keeps looking at me.

"Have you been going into my room when I'm not there?"

"No!" He has an appalled expression, comical on a four-year-old. "You has to knock! That's the rule."

*And where would we be without the rules?* "You're right. It's just that I've been finding some pennies in my room. Would you know anything about that?"

He shakes his head.

"Sure?"

He nods emphatically.

*And now?* "Okay, well," I say helplessly, "let's remember the rule, okay? Always knock, only go in when I'm there."

He nods.

*Well, that went brilliantly.*

There's a pause. He's unsure how to proceed. I've veered from our comfortable routine.

"Snuggle down," I order, and he does, pleased to be back on course, back to the normal way of things. "Now what book are we reading?"

He hands me his favorite. It was my favorite too.

There are monsters in *Where the Wild Things Are* . . .

**Creatures cavorting, beasts bumbling, and hairy things howling**—*He bites my neck*—The wild things, monsters reveling—*A naked woman standing in the rain*—**But then**—*Don't move*—**They're seduced by magic, by trickery**—*Take off your clothes.*

I wonder why my thoughts have turned this way, turned sour and twisted in a child's room when I am so full of happiness. Why would these harmless monsters make me think of the real monster? But these days the news is full of—

**They crown the little boy as their king**—*It's pepper spray. Don't spray it on your neck!* David made a joke but he's been thinking about it too. It's hard not to think about it.

**—There's mayhem most wild—**

How many women dead? How many posters? It's already high—seven faces now, blown up on posters, reduced to grainy shots; the police are taking heat, the mayor drawling his nasal drawl, "Use caution," "The police are doing everything in their power," "Be sensible. Use your discretion. It's not an official curfew but—"

**"Oh please don't go—we'll eat you up—we love you so!"**

I always loved that line, always understood it, because sometimes you do want to eat something up because you love it. Some younger comedians tenuously trying out their jokes about getting rejected: "It's not you, it's just that I suspect you might be a serial killer." The older ones know better, have lived in this city, know it will get ugly.

**—But the boy grows homesick and sails back through time—**

Steering us back, Lucas is riveted, breathing openmouthed as I turn the pages until Max comes back where someone loves him best of all, surrendering his golden crown for his mother and his dinner, which . . .

**Waits for him.**

"Now, it's time to sleep."

I suddenly want to go to my warm supper too, except it will be a glass of wine, not milk, and the comfort of others waiting for me. Maybe I'll catch David looking at me and smiling. I turn off the bedside lamp but there is still the glow of the night-light. I wouldn't mind one of those. Grown-ups deserve them more. We know what's really in the dark.

"You want me to sing a song? After all, you're getting the full treatment." I feel bad about earlier on. I wouldn't say I was the Spanish Inquisition, but asking him about the pennies made me uncomfortable.

"Uh-huh." He's quiet now, with his green rabbit's foot key chain held under his nose.

"Isn't it hideous?" Andrea had said when I had mentioned it. "It's from one of those prize-filled gumball machines." She'd sighed. "I'll tell you about it later, when I have the strength."

I sing him the only lullaby I know. The one my father used to sing to me. My charming father, who couldn't sing but sang anyway. It's an old song, sad and sweet, which is everything a lullaby should be. All about a man who meets someone in Monterrey—I thought it was "Mountain Ray." The song includes stars, steel guitars, and luscious lips as red as wine. Unfortunately the singer has his heart broken, but then again, as he says, it was a long time ago.

I think he's asleep when—

"Kat?"

"Yes, honey?"

It's hard to hear him, so quiet through his thumb and rabbit's foot. "I drawed you a picture. On the table."

I get up, pick up the picture, and return to sit on the bed. Great, I'm grilling him and he's drawing me pictures. "Thank you, love. It's dark in here but I can't wait to look at it tomorrow."

"She wanted me to give it to you," he says sleepily.

"Who did?"

"The lady."

"Which lady?"

"The one tonight"—his voice is fading—"with the man."

"Oh. I didn't know—" I am unsure of how to proceed in the area of imaginary friends, especially imaginary lady friends. I guess the kid's starting early. It should be funny, sweet, but somehow it seems a little off. Andrea's been worried about Lucas. I'm worried about him too. This is a new development.

"She say you can't see her," he says, matter-of-factly.

*So that's settled*, I think, and as I do he pulls me in close and whispers loudly in my ear, in that stage whisper small children have:

"She doesn't have no shirt on."

I was not expecting this. "Is this lady at school?"

"No!" Lucas sounds almost shocked. "You have to wear clothes at school, and also she a grown-up."

I decide to opt for a light tone. "I hope she wasn't cold."

"I drawed her a shirt," he continues. "I made it pink 'cause she's a girl."

"That was nice of you."

"Kat?"

"Yes?"

"She says he is just pretend." His voice is low.

"Who is?" He's almost asleep. "Lucas? Who's just pretend?"

"The man."

"Which man?"

The last word almost inaudible: "Pretending."

"Who?"

But Lucas is asleep.

I smile, a little ruefully. Usually he never gets to sleep and the adults become desperate, and here I am disappointed he's asleep. I wonder what Andrea will think of her son mentioning topless women. Now that he's sleeping, I wonder how to bring it up, that and the growing line of small change against the wall in my room. Not tonight, when Andrea's laughing, relaxed and happy. I get up slowly and carefully and head out into the hall. I look at the picture.

Hands cover my eyes.

A low voice in my ear. "Hey."

Later I'll reflect that it was only by some heavenly intervention that I didn't cry out, that I didn't scream. I don't scream but my gasp is a painful wedge of breath. I turn sharply and see David.

"Are you all right?"

Wordlessly I hold out the picture.

He exhales through pursed lips, a silent whistle but more forceful. We stare at Lucas's picture together.

The woman is lying on a bed. She is a woman because she has a yellow ponytail. She wears short blue shorts and white sneakers. She is wearing a long-sleeved pink shirt. Pink because she's a girl. Her legs are sticking straight up in the air. The bed is light blue but there are red patches all over it. The woman's face is a round balloon. It's also at an angle that Picasso would be proud of. She looks out at us. Her neck is impossibly broken. The woman's face consists of three circles. Two circles are small and blue. Those are her eyes. The other circle is bigger and black. That's her mouth. It's a black circle because she's screaming. Screaming and screaming. There is a red squiggle coming from her mouth too. The bed faces the closet. There is a voice bubble coming out from the closet. The word in the bubble reads:

**hELo**

"Kids draw the darnedest things, don't they?" His delivery is deadpan.

I try a smile at this. I, meanwhile, am wondering how I didn't wet myself when he came up behind me. It's one of the worst things I have ever seen. Andrea's going to have a fit.

"What do you think it is?" I'm glad that my voice betrays little of my raw panic beneath.

"It must be all this stuff about that killer. Sucks that it's getting to the little kids."

"But Andrea's really strict about TV."

He smiles at me, but not meanly. "It only takes one kid in class with parents who don't give a crap, and think about all the posters—"

"Still—"

"Still," David finishes my sentence, "it's horrible."

We look down at the drawing in my hands. Now I see it as a bomb, a thin, colorful bomb set to decimate our gift of an evening. And on cue from the main room, as if to taunt us, Andrea's laughter rings out. It's a laugh that's brewed in her belly, honest and throaty and real.

*Don't kill the messenger,* I think glumly. I'm frightened and somehow I also feel guilty. "I put him to bed, he drew it for me, the lady told him to—"

"Do you have to show her tonight?"

I'm shocked. "Of course, she needs to see this."

"Well, yeah," he says, a little impatiently now, "I'm not saying keep it from her. I'm asking if it can wait until tomorrow?"

I'm about to say no; no, it can't wait until tomorrow. Andrea has to know, has to see this, and then she laughs again. She's laughed a lot tonight. The guys have been good for her. I think of the lines around Andrea's eyes.

"Tell her tomorrow not tonight."

"Really? You think so?"

"Did the kid seem freaked out?"

"Lucas?"

"That's the one."

I think about it. I answer as honestly as I can. Lucas calmly telling me that he "made it pink 'cause she's a girl."

"Not really. He did say the woman didn't have a top on."

"Advanced."

"That's not funny."

"I know." He puts his arms around me. The unexpected gesture is kind and surprising. "I'm sorry. I would be rattled too. I think I am."

I close my eyes. He is comforting and inside the circle of his arms I feel safe.

Safe, I feel safe.

"You know, I think Sael once told me that his imaginary friend was a woman." His voice vibrates through his chest.

"Really?" I look up at him.

"Yeah, we were talking about it once. Now, me, I had a dragon, a purple dragon called Rufus, because when I imagine something I do it right."

"The thing I love about you is your modesty." *Oh shit, I said "love."*

He smiles. "My modesty," he says lightly, shifting from our hug and taking my hand, "is one of my best attributes, one of my many, many, many wonderful attributes."

*Oh shit, love, the thing I love about you, shit.*

"Come on," he says. "I want to see if there's more ice cream."

I fold the drawing and place it in my pocket without looking at it again. I never want to look at it again.

We are about to go through when he stops.

"Oh, here." He hands me my phone. "It's why I came here in the first place. You have a missed call."

*Love, the thing I love, the thing I love about you, the thing I love about you. . .*

"Thanks." I glance down at it.

"From one of your many unwanted lovers?"

"Must be."

"How many lovers do you have?"

*One you'll never want to know about.* "A million and one."

"Sounds about right." He looks at my face. "What's wrong?"

"I don't get it. I did the whole 'take me off the telemarketer list' thing but I keep getting these phone calls."

"Do people leave messages?"

"No."

"If I was a telemarketer, I would know when I was on to a good thing."

He smiles at me, a warm, embracing smile.

*Fuck. I'm getting in deep.*

"Come on, there's probably not any ice cream left by now."

Back in the living room, the light is soft; Andrea's pleasantly melancholy music is still playing; and there's still a dig of ice cream in the bottom of the carton and still half a bottle of wine to be had. The conversation has drifted to this and to that with soft gaps for silliness; there's talk of a TV show we all love to hate. Sael is making a valiant case for it and Andrea is rolling her eyes, pretending to be disgusted. I ease my way into an easy chair. *The thing I love about you, I love, I love.* Well, I love them all tonight; tonight I'm in love with everyone in the whole world.

And then Sael asks:

"So what took you so long?"

The question, though lightly posed, is jarring. After a moment David answers easily enough. "We got involved in a meaningful discussion about imaginary friends."

"Leaving your real ones back here? Nice."

Again there's the tone of accusation, but Andrea is connecting the dots. "Everything okay?" She means with Lucas.

I can see her biting her lip. David's right; I'll show her the picture later.

"Fine." I smile.

But she's persistent. "So why that conversation?"

"I was reading *Where the Wild Things Are* and it came up."

She relaxes. "Oh, I love that book."

"Me too."

Everybody, it seems, loves that book.

I look at Sael. "David told me that you had an imaginary friend, a woman? That seems unusual." *I'll be the one to ask questions here.*

"Well, I wouldn't have called her a friend; we just 'hung out' a few times."

He is straight-faced and it takes a moment for everyone to get it and start laughing.

"Touché," says David.

Sael grins.

"It sounds like you were very evolved to me," says Andrea.

*Or maybe he had to imagine female figures in his life because his mom was so useless.*

"I don't remember much. It was strange actually."

"Why?"

"I don't know," he answers, pauses to think, and then, "I don't remember her talking. I think she just watched me."

"Watched you? Sounds creepy." Andrea looks at him, interested. "Could it have been an actual person?"

He shakes his head. "I doubt it. I saw her sometimes in the doorway to my room or sometimes on the side of the street. She never came too close. Long dress, long hair." He half smiles. "Sounds like my imaginary friend was an ancient hippie. Now *that's* really terrifying."

"And she just looked at you?"

"Well, I was a very beautiful child, obviously."

We laugh; he does too; the awkward moment is over.

"And you guys? Any imaginary friends?"

Andrea shakes her head. "None to speak of."

I feel that I have to represent the women; we look pretty unimaginative. "No, but when I was a kid a psychic got really excited about me."

Andrea is intrigued. "When did you go to a psychic as a kid? I wouldn't have thought your mother would be into that."

I've only told Andrea snippets about my mother, but even from those she can decipher enough. Mostly she's amused.

"Oh, believe me, she isn't! They came uninvited to her dinner party." Like Sael, I realize. *Mother, for the first time I think I can sympathize with you.*

"What?"

"They came with a friend of my stepfather's. She didn't even tell anyone, just brought in these two Asian guests." I had come downstairs to forage for hors d'oeuvres when I heard my mother and Richard "call me Dick" fighting about it in loud, angry whispers in the kitchen.

"You mean this woman brought two uninvited guests to a dinner party? That's insanely rude." Andrea is outraged on my mother's behalf.

"Yeah, but she was the type, someone people call a 'character.' She had known my stepfather for ages. And I think she came from serious money, so people let her get away with all sorts of crap. She called herself Cherry. She was clearly manic, larger-than-life—you know, the kind of woman who wears turbans and eye-stinging perfume and could eat you like a prawn."

"Turbans are terrifying," says Andrea. "I'll give you that."

"So the psychic?" Sael prods.

"Well, the gist of it was that Cherry had met him at some

retreat and had convinced him to come and stay with her."

"What did he look like? Did he also wear a turban?" David is having fun.

"Hardly. He wore a black suit with one of those mandarin collars and little blue smoky glasses, John Lennon style, so you couldn't see his eyes."

"Weird." Andrea shudders theatrically.

"There was a woman with him who was gorgeous, really tailored dress, perfectly made up."

I still remember her standing so pale and delicate among the white, suburban upper-middle-class guests, like an orchid surrounded by houseplants.

"Wait, who was the woman?" Sael asks.

"His translator."

"Sure she was." David gives an exaggerated wink.

I laugh. "Now that you mention it, I remember that Cherry didn't seem quite so keen on the translator."

Sael is impatient. "So get to the good part already!"

"Okay, okay. I had spotted these smoked oyster things my mother used to serve sitting on a low table in the far corner of the living room. I was heading for them when the man grabbed my arm. Then he turns and says something to his translator. She looks at me and says, 'Mr. Nakamaru feels a great energy coming from you. He would like to know more about the day you were born.' "

"Wow." David seems impressed.

"I know, but I didn't know anything about that other than it was my birthday, so obviously it was the most important day in the whole world."

"Obviously." Andrea nods.

"So?" Sael prompts, refusing to be distracted by the side banter.

"So Cherry gets all excited, and she calls my mother over, who by that point looked like she was ready to kill everyone."

Andrea is still sympathetic. "I'll bet."

"And Cherry asks her if anything unusual had happened on the day I was born." The room had grown quiet waiting for her answer. "My mom said nothing out of the ordinary had happened, but when the translator pressed her she said she thought there might have been a meteor shower that night."

"And?" Sael leans forward, intently.

"And when the translator tells Mr. Nakamaru, he nods as if that explains everything."

"And then what happened?" Sael stares at me and for a moment it's as if he and I are in a little restaurant together, exchanging stories that no one else will ever hear.

Finally his translator turned to me. I remember the strange blank gaze of Mr. Nakamaru's little smoky lenses, his soft voice carrying weight and meaning in the hushed room. It was oddly solemn—perhaps that's why the scene has imprinted itself so clearly on my mind. Perhaps that's why I can remember it, word for word. The translator's voice was light and musical, with only the hint of an accent.

"She said, 'Mr. Nakamaru says that there are many great legends about meteor showers. Some cultures thought they brought great luck and others believed that a shower would bring doom. Some people see in them the hand of God, and others death and evil. One thing, though, is certain. Those born during this auspicious hour are known to bring great change and wield much power.' "

"That's a little abstract," David remarks.

Andrea smiles knowingly. "Weird how he didn't go into specific details."

"So what did everyone say?" Sael asks. I can't read his expression.

"Well, Cherry said I should be honored and that I was a lucky little girl, but I think she was mostly pissed because I was getting all the attention."

"Ugh."

"Pretty much. I was mad because Cherry had called me a little girl in front of all those people and I never managed to get any of the smoked oysters because my mother told me to go to bed."

"The meteor shower does explain one thing," says David.

"What's that?" Andrea and I ask together.

He bats his eyelashes dramatically as he takes my hand and kisses it. "Why you're such a shining star."

"Awwww," Andrea and I say, but when I glance at Sael his eyes are flat and cold.

"That's adorable." Andrea stands. "Now let's clean up."

I try to rise but she pushes me back down gently. "No, no, the shining star made dinner; the shining star gets to finish her wine first."

"All right then," I say, "twist my starry rubber arm." I watch them all get up, groaning theatrically, and move off into the kitchen. Then I lean back and close my eyes. I think of the other part of that story, the part I have never told anybody.

I was on my way back up the stairs, still angry about Cherry calling me a little girl, when the translator stepped into the hallway. She walked to the bottom of the staircase and looked up at me standing three stairs above her. I involuntarily shrank away; I had no idea what she would want with me.

"Sorry if I startled you."

"That's okay," I mumbled. I looked down, embarrassed that I had been so jumpy. I saw she was smiling. She was so pretty and gentle I couldn't help but smile back.

"If I may ask you, what do you know of meteor showers?" She seemed genuinely curious. She spoke to me as if I were a grown-up, not some "lucky little girl."

"They're rocks?" I hazarded. "Smaller rocks from comets?" Recalling Mrs. Wilson's fourth-grade science class, I grew braver. "When they come too close to the earth's atmosphere they burn up."

"That is right"—she nodded—"but our ancestors believed that they were signs from the heavens. They believed that the fallen stones held powerful magic. They built temples where they had landed and they worshipped them."

"Worshipped them?"

Her smile widened. "Does it seem strange to you?"

I had half shrugged. I didn't want to seem rude. "A little?"

Accepting this, she nodded again. "Yes, though I think our ways would have seemed strange to them. What else do you know about the day you were born?"

"My father said—" I stopped, suddenly choked with shyness.

"Yes?"

There was no escape now. "My father said that I was special because I was carried into the world on a sea of stars." My cheeks burned. I waited for her to laugh at me.

"Your father was right." Her expression was grave.

I gaped at her, speechless.

She hesitated for a moment, as if choosing her words with care. "You see, there is a balance. The Greek philosopher Pythagoras described it as a universal harmony, a 'music of the spheres.' " She saw my confusion. "The spheres are the planets."

"Music?"

"Not that you can hear, but yes, a kind of music. The person who is born under this sacred time has the power to change that harmony, some would even say to end it." She looked at me, and I realized that though she was smiling, her eyes were the saddest I had ever seen. "It is true that your line has not been lucky." Her hand floated out to touch my cheek, her fingertips as light as snowflakes. "But as a wise man once said, 'When there is life, there's hope.' "

Then she leaned in and whispered, "*You have a right to know.*"

Before I could respond, she bowed, turned, and walked back into the dining room, where Cherry was shrieking with laughter.

—and I hear further laughing and Sael's voice saying, "Watch it!" I open my eyes and I give myself a mental shake and head to the kitchen, where there's light and people and no old, unsettling memories.

Andrea's starting to yawn. She has a four-year-old so there is some excuse, but it's contagious and soon David and I are standing together in the hallway while Sael and Andrea say their good-byes.

"It was a wonderful meal," he says.

"It wasn't bad, was it?"

He holds me in the safety of his arms. "I kind of wish we were at my place, though."

"Me too."

"Thanks again for handling that curveball so well."

"No problem," I say, and wince inwardly.

"Speaking of, I had better escort this guy home; it's dark out there."

"At least neither of you seems like the Sickle Man's type, not being a single female."

"You haven't seen me with a wig." He looks hurt.

I laugh. We're being ghoulish, but occasionally you have to let go a little.

He gives me a kiss and looks at me. "Will you take care of yourself until I see you again?"

"How can I make any promises until I know when will that be?"

"Tomorrow?"

"I'll try until then."

So this is what happiness feels like.

"It would have been cool."

Andrea has come back into the kitchen. I'm doing a last go-over, making sure things are put away, not wanting to invite roaches. She's in her bathrobe and is pouring a glass of water from our pitcher, her back to me.

"What would have been cool?" I'm fuzzy from the wine.

"If he wanted to stay the night." Her back is still turned.

I've never invited anyone to stay over. Theoretically I could, but I haven't. It always made more sense for me to stay at the guy's place: sleep in his king-sized bed, walk on his wooden floors, shower in his shower while using his soap, his masculine shampoos. I love sleeping at men's apartments. I love being there, feeling clean and newly made and exciting as if I have left all my woes and my mess behind and become a different person, an efficient woman who needs nothing but a toothbrush. The real reason, though, is Lucas. Lucas's large brown eyes watching strange men using the bathroom, sitting at the kitchen table, using a spare towel. It seems weird to bring some man into his home, his world.

Andrea doesn't talk about Lucas's father. "I want that chapter in my life to stay closed," she'd once said.

I have a feeling things got bad, like really bad, like domestic-abuse bad. Things have to be pretty bad to move with a one-year-old, to New York.

It's hard not to see her primarily as a mother, but I sometimes wonder who Andrea was pre-Lucas. Andrea laid-back, drinking beer, Andrea sexy and ready to dance, who gets involved with the wrong kind of man, makes bad choices. Who knows what makes couples couple, what makes the heart flutter, the pulse race? I know more than anyone that stupidity can happen in the moment. I'm the last person to judge anyone on their choices when it comes to love.

I'm more familiar with the Andrea who works hard, Andrea the tired, Andrea the lawyer, Andrea the laugher, Andrea the wise friend, the tough but good single mother. Andrea, whose shoulders and voice grow tighter when she feels judged, as she so often is, by a world that doesn't seem to understand that the heart wants what the heart wants, the world that makes us pay and pay and pay. We weren't born only children, but it feels that way. I have stepsiblings but they don't count, and Andrea has a half sister with what social workers would call "serious substance abuse issues" and she would call "a drug problem." Her parents are Christian, full-on Baptists she'd said, but apparently not the kind of Christians who would accept their unwed daughter or her son. She once told me she gave up on her family. "Nobody's turning the other cheek."

I can relate. In this city we adopt people; our friends become our family.

So I know what it means for Andrea to say this about David, and this is why I ask again. "That would be okay?"

"I said so, didn't I?" Andrea turns now and smiles.

"Think he's a keeper?"

"I do."

"What do you think of Sael?" Andrea has always been a good judge of character.

"Well, he really is amazing-looking," she says. "But—"

"But what?"

"There's something there . . ."

"Yeah?"

"I got the sense that he was holding something back, keeping something in. You get a feeling for that in my line of work."

"Think he's sketchy?"

"It's not exactly sketchy." She pauses, thinking. "He's the

kind of man other people describe as being 'the quiet guy,' or 'I never saw him lose his temper, he always seemed so polite.' The kind of man who makes work colleagues say, 'So-and-so had a long fuse.' "

"So what are you saying?" I think of the first time I saw Sael, watching, poised to strike.

"I'm saying that you don't want to be around him when the fuse burns down." She looks at me for a beat too long. "Anyway, you're with David, so it doesn't matter."

"That's right."

"Well, good, I give my blessing." Then she yawns. "I'm exhausted. Tonight was fun. Lucas and I had a great time."

"We all did," I say.

I can feel the faint outline of the folded drawing in my pocket.

I'm finally in bed. I think about the evening, which could have been so much worse. It could have been a disaster. It turned out great, actually. Even though he brought Sael. Everything seems to be fine now.

I look at my phone, thinking about that missed call from earlier, yet another call from a number I don't recognize, like yesterday's phone call and the one the day before. I don't answer them. Now I listen to the message. A robotic voice greets me.

*"Hello. This is a reminder call for Daniella Zaretti from Dr. DeLuca for an appointment scheduled for Monday, June twenty-seventh, at ten thirty a.m. If you are unable to keep this appointment, please call our office as soon as possible to reschedule, between the hours of nine a.m. and five p.m. Thank you!"*

"Daniella Zaretti?" I'll have to call them on Monday and let them know they have the wrong number. What a pain in the ass.

My phone gives an angry little buzz. I look down.

Let me in

I bolt upright, heart pounding.

I'm at the window

I look up, preparing to run.

Sael stands on the fire escape. I stare at him. He mimes furiously at me to open the window.

I could shake my head and refuse to let him in but I'm terrified he'll fall. The fire escape was built probably a hundred years ago. It's rusted and tiny and looks as treacherous as hell.

I get up, cross my room, and open the window. He bends down and eases himself through as a large cat might, letting in a breath of warm night air.

"What are you doing here? Are you crazy?" I'm whispering despite my fury. I don't want to wake up Andrea or Lucas.

He stares at me. The intensity in his eyes is frightening. His voice, though a whisper, is urgent. "Katherine, I'm sorry, but I had to see you."

"You need to go. This is wrong. You need to go right now."

"Katherine—"

My lips are numb and tingling. "Seriously, you need to—"

"Can I stay here tonight?"

"What? No!"

"Please, not for sex, I promise, just to sleep here."

I've never seen him like this. So pressing, so focused. As if at any moment he could lose control. "No, you can't."

"Katherine—"

"Sael, we're done."

"It's not that, I just need to sleep."

"What?"

"I've been having these nightmares, I can't sleep, I just need to be with someone."

"Sael, you say that David is your best friend."

He recoils as if I've struck him. In a way I guess I have.

"We can't do this to him. It's bad enough what happened before."

"Don't you think I know that?" He practically spits this back at me.

"So why are you here?"

He glares furiously, and for a moment I think he'll leave, but he won't be deterred, no matter what acts of betrayal I throw at him.

"Katherine, please, just this once. I promise if you let me sleep here tonight I'll never bother you again. I won't make a move. I just want to . . . to be here with you."

"*We can't do this.*"

But he senses weakness. "It's only for tonight, no sex, just sleeping, I swear—"

There is a charge between us. I think of the night we spent together, his broad muscled back, his acres of smooth skin under my fingers, moving together, the weight of him.

I hesitate, and then I think of David bringing out the sweetness in the strawberries, with his easy grin, his affectionate laugh.

*The thing I love about you is . . .*

The thing with Sael and me is a poisonous spider bite that grows inflamed and itches and itches, but when you scratch it, it turns septic, oozing.

"No, I'm sorry, I can't do this."

His voice cracks a little. "*Please.*"

"No, you need to leave."

There's a final frozen moment. His eyes burn in his white face. He moves toward me and I think he will take me by force. I open my mouth to call for Andrea when abruptly he turns and climbs back out of the window. I see him shadowlike on the fire escape, and then he's gone.

I sit on the bed, my heart thudding.

I lie back. I wonder what his dreams were, why they're so bad.

I think about his pale face, his feverish eyes.

I can't sleep.

HE LORD'S KNIGHTS WERE MUCH discontented. Their lord had been spending many of his days and all of his nights with the Maiden and they knew that no good could come from it, for it does not become a lord to spend time with a lowly servant. In their hearts they feared that she had too great a hold over him. "Perhaps she bewitches him with the drink she brews," they told one another, "and what is to stop her from poisoning him should they quarrel?"

And so the knights told his council that she did make a mockery of them. His advisers grew alarmed and agreed to rid themselves of her. They sent an invitation to the neighboring baron, who came to call with his daughter. The advisers told the lord, "She is as beautiful as she is good, and of noble birth, a bride who befits a lord such as yourself."

But Lord de Villias would not heed his advisers and went to shun the baron's daughter; then he saw that her tresses were as golden as the sun, her complexion was fairer than the fairest lily, and her eyes were bluer than the bluest pool of water, and he could not speak. When she saw that his eyes were upon her she blushed rose red to her crown and he knew her to be both a good and a gentle lady.

Then Lord de Villias made up his mind upon the instant that he would wed the baron's daughter. So he told his advisers to order the Maiden back to the kitchens where she belonged, before his betrothed set foot over the hearth. When they told her, the Maiden grew as pale as a corpse and wept so bitterly that even a stone would be softened, but the advisers were hard against her. And down in the kitchens the servants tormented her, saying, "This is what comes of holding yourself so high." She was made to sleep on the filthy flagstones and given only the slop and the dregs kept for the pigs.

The Maiden wept and wept. She wept until she had no more tears to shed; she wept until it seemed a serpent had coiled around her heart and had wrung all the tears and love from her. Then the Maiden dried her eyes, no longer red with sorrow, and smiled, and her smile was as cold and as pitiless as a winter night.

# 11

Love is red.

Anticipation is aquamarine, it glistens like grapes and smells of melted pizza, it brushes against your cheek like party streamers, it feels like the hush of a theater as the lights dim and the curtain rises.

You smell it in three people who are waiting for the train, scratching their lottery tickets, and in that little girl standing with her father, who only gets to see her on the weekends and is now taking her to her first Broadway show.

Ambition is orange, the color of a traffic signal. It sizzles like bacon. You smell it in the bartender pretending to listen to what the red-cheeked guy is droning on about, droning on and on, and on and on, and meanwhile the bartender is working out a plot point in her book; meanwhile she's thinking about characters; meanwhile she's planning chapters, making revisions, editing lines.

Anxiety is light blue, the color of varicose veins; it has the old stale-coffee smell of a long flight, the musk of a high school locker room, of the corner the cat urinated in when it found out it was going to the V-E-T.

Here in the subway car, riding down to Union Square, you smell this on passengers almost too numerous to count, on a beautiful woman still wearing her sunglasses and standing next to an older woman who's going to be cleaning her apartment later in the week, hired from a service she found on the Internet and—

*He hasn't called me yet, they never stay past the first two months, and my boss is driving me crazy, how am I supposed to do the intern's work as well as my own? And I'm gaining weight, I'm gaining weight, I shouldn't have eaten those chicken wings last night—*

The older one sits staring off because—

*My sons, one in the army and one who can't seem to make it past high school, both of them trapped—what did I do, what didn't I do?*

Hatred is the color of a dried-up scab. It smells like a bar the morning after. It reeks of menstrual blood. You smell it less, but when you do it's strong. On the elderly woman who stares at a group of too-loud teenagers—

*Fooling around, putting their goddamn feet on the goddamn seats and cursing, being too goddamn loud. They don't care for anyone else. They're like animals—*

She wishes them dead.

On the "not old, but older" woman who stands, leaning against the pole. She was offered a seat. She said no, thanks—

*Am I really that old? I'm really that old. Paul ruined my life. He took all my good years from me, that fucking waste of space. Once I was beautiful and believed in love. Now I'm being offered seats. It's over—*

She holds the pole tight with hatred.

Jealousy is piss yellow, it tastes of old cough syrup, it tastes of cotton candy and of bile. An unhappily married woman whose friend just "met someone"—

*I'm so happy for you. That's awesome. Congratulations. Great, wonderful, good, cool, fantastic news. It couldn't have happened to a nicer person. Well done—*

Contentment is eggshell brown. Contentment smells like the fine hair on an infant's head; it tastes like French bread with a widely spread helping of butter.

You hardly ever smell this.

And you walk up the stairs with the crowd into the summer evening.

Here you stand in Union Square. The humidity is drawing away, unveiling a soft and perfect sky. Up the broad curved brick steps the crowd shifts and murmurs. Some commuters descending the subway stairs give only a passing glance, determined not to be drawn in, but others stop midstare. The park is filled with summer ghosts. Hundreds of people wearing white: white shoes, white shirts, white skirts, white dresses, white tanks, white shorts. The skateboard kids with the hanging pants and the pierced girls with green hair have moved to the benches on the paths under the trees. They respect the crowd and their purpose. Only the old chess sharks fold their arms and lean back on their plastic chairs, their passive, lined faces giving nothing away; they've seen it all before.

You, who are wearing white, close your eyes and breathe in.

Inhale the sorrow, which is the color of a bruise. It smells like Sunday evenings; it tastes like old cucumbers.

Inhale the desire, which is the color of a clean pool. It prickles like the fine hairs on your arm standing up, and smells of the sandy dip in the dunes just before you spot the ocean.

Women are here, mothers, young girls, students. Young men and older men, fathers too with little kids on shoulders, have come to give support. There is little shoving or jostling; people are kinder, muttering sorry when they occasionally step on toes, nudge into others' backs. There are dead girls, dead women, to be remembered and it's important because—

*I was here, I was here, I was here.*

They are pushing a little, though, trying to see the families up on the stage, the families speaking in quiet tones because they are weary unto the bone, trying to hear Susie Ranford talking through a microphone.

Weariness tastes like your mouth does after you brush your teeth when you have a cold; it's the milky gray of a forgotten mug of tea. It whirrs like an old fan.

You also smell a sullen resentment, an itch to hurt, to stir up trouble.

Resentment hums like beehives and stings of smoke and drain cleaner; it sticks like old Band-Aids and the arid stink of jam-packed classrooms.

They are all here because of you. All these beautiful, passionate, sad, frightened, anxious, excited, grieving, lecherous, hopeful, mournful souls, their colors flickering like the flames of the candles they hold. *We will not forget you*, they say to the dead. But they will, they always do, faces fade, lives seep away into anecdotes. As the years pass, change, inexorable, plows through; wheat is reaped, seeds sown, young shoots rise, stalks are grown and then reaped again. The numbers of those who do remember when, and when, and when grow few.

Tonight is an unfolding flower, as perfect and impermanent as each of the women you've taken. You honor all their wonderful colors caught and lashed within you.

The crowd listens as the names are read.

**Kathleen Walsh.**
**Samantha Rodriguez.**

People seeking faith—*My God, My God*—which is a deep blue; it feels like parchment under the fingertips, it smells like hospitals, it dissolves like white icing on the tongue and curls like incense.

You breathe in, ecstatic.

People overcome by hopelessness—*There is no God, no God would let this happen*—hopelessness, which is putrid yellow like moldy cheese, creaks like a child's bedsprings supporting too heavy a weight, snaps like a tarpaulin wetly flapping where a wall used to be.

**Jennifer Wegerle.**

You stand patient in the crowd, waiting while the members of each woman's family stumble forward to call out their child's, their sister's, their niece's name. To say it aloud, to acknowledge that they lived.

**Emily Ranford.**
**Melissa Lin.**

And now you see her. Here she is. The one who is truly responsible for all of this, the one who has brought you here.

**Lauren Cooper.**

Katherine. Her laughter single grains of sugar, her breath warm pink. Her skin, her eyes, her words are water. Her fingers on your arm, their weight.

**Rebecca Lamb.**

Each time you see her, you drink her in. Often you watch her. Watch her in the distance, walking to work. You follow her. Look at the way she resists gravity. The way her skirt moves and shifts over her side, how her shirt pulls up as it strains against the confines of the waistline.

**Daniella Zaretti.**

Then silence. A grief-stricken man clutching a piece of paper totters up.

Katherine and the crowd bow their heads as he begins to read in a faltering voice, "Dear God, we pray you grant us peace . . ."

Peace is the color of the underside of clouds, dove gray, almost pink. Peace is an ancient smell. It's very faint here tonight. Green pears, bay leaves. It tastes like melting snow; it tastes like rice paper that once wrapped sweets.

Love is red. A little green, a little gold, but love—real love, true love, divine love—that love is red. It smells like pavements washed by the rain. It smells like the nape of your lover's neck. It smells like fresh dirt. It sounds like a match being struck, and a jar being opened. It feels like a hand on the swell of your hip. It sounds like a song sung in the dark.

Katherine is not that color yet.

There are shoots of doubt, tendrils of gray and black threaded through the wonder. There is hope. There is lust. There is tenderness. But there is the spotted and mingling green and yellow of mistrust and the lingering blue of uncertainty.

Blood is red. Wombs are red. Hearts are red. Apples are red. Fire is red. The sky is red.

Blood unto blood, womb unto womb, heart unto heart, apple unto apple, fire unto fire, sky unto sky, love unto love unto love unto love.

Katherine. Here she stands. She does not see you. But it is enough for you to watch and think.

Soon the seeds will be sown, and they will bud and flower and twist up and out and through, and the spheres will shift off course, and the Universe shall falter and stammer, it can't end. Danger is red. Courage is red. Pain is red. Love is red.

And so soon now, so, so soon, Katherine will turn red. All the Vessels do, soon enough.

# 12

I sit on this comfortable black couch. I sit in this pleasant neutral office with its pale yellow walls and the box of tissues on the small table. I look at the woman who sits opposite me. I wonder how we will begin. Who makes the first move? We're like two gunslingers having a showdown.

**Q: You seem anxious. Would like you to talk to me about that?**

Where should I begin? What makes the most sense? There are some things that are more tangible. The messages, the drawings, the pennies. No, not the pennies. Maybe I'll start with the little things, the things I see out of the corner of my eyes. Like a woman sitting in a chair, and I'll turn around and there's no one. Movement just sliding on the side of my vision.

Last week I made an appointment with an eye doctor. *Spots?* he asked me. *Floating dots, shimmering?*

Not dots but reflections.

**A: "I'm seeing reflections of things that aren't there, reflections of people who aren't there."**

These are not reflected in the mirror but on the flat and neutral surface of the turned-off television screen or my cell phone. I turn these devices on more often these days, their pictures better than the ones in my mind.

It's early July. I'm here, sitting in this brown leather chair, unwilling to be comforted.

**Q: Can you tell me what you think you saw?**

**A: "I thought I saw—"**

Like the other day on the TV set I thought I saw . . .

**"—a woman lying on a bed with her neck broken. Like in the drawing Lucas made."**

Lucas saying, "I drawed her a shirt, pink 'cause she's a girl."

There on my television screen's blank face was a woman sprawled on the bed, naked. A jagged triangle etched into her chest, red pooling out.

I looked again and there was nothing.

**Q: Who is Lucas?**

**A: "He's my roommate's four-year-old son."**

Andrea is distraught. She was horrified when I showed her the first drawing. Now there are more. Women lying in twisted positions, blood scribbled red, mouths screaming black holes. The voice, an awkward bubble coming from the closet or from under the bed. She called the school, spoke to the teachers. *No, he hasn't been drawing pictures like that or saying anything out of the norm,* but they would keep an eye out. *Hard with the news of course, children have a way of picking things up, ferreting things out.* She thinks maybe he found out too much.

I overheard her talking to Lucas, wanting to know. *How could you have heard about something like this? Have you seen any ladies? What did you mean, "the pretend man"?* She kept her voice low, steady, but there had been tears. He had picked up on her anxiety.

Over and over I heard him, *No, Momma, no.* He promises, promises, promises, *cross my heart,* he'll tell her if he hears anything from the other kids.

Did he see anything on TV? Hear something on the radio? She won't be angry, but *No, Momma, no.*

Last night we sat up, drinking the last of the white wine that the guys had brought. Andrea had needed a drink. I wasn't so far behind. With our feet up on the couch, life seemed more manageable.

*They wanted him to see the school counselor,* she had said.

*Would that be so bad? It's nothing to be ashamed of.*

*It's not that.* She sighed and rubbed her neck. *It's just the counselor is a really creepy guy.*

*He's a man?*

*Yes, you sexist.* She smiled.

*Ugh. Seems weird.*

*I don't care that he's a man but he's got this thinning hair and a soft saggy belly and a wet mouth and he always gets too close when he talks to me at parent-teacher conferences. A real space invader. I'm pretty sure he was trying to look down my top.*

*As I said, ugh.*

*The point is that I wouldn't want him looking after my dog, let alone my son.*

*You don't have a dog.*

*Well, if I had one.*

*Point taken.*

*Anyway, school's almost over. If he can just hang in till next week I can try to look for someone decent, though God knows how I'm going to afford it. I don't think my health care plan covers scared little children.* She sighed again. *I don't know, maybe it's those damn posters. They're everywhere. Kids are asking questions.*

*It's true. I just saw a new one.*

*What do you think? Think he can hold on, or am I being a shitty parent?*

She looked exhausted and stressed out and miserable.

Then I said, *You're a pretty shitty parent, so why not hang on?*

She grinned, poured me the final splash.

**"And then there're the pennies."**

I still haven't told Andrea about Lucas and the pennies.

**Q: The pennies?**

**A: "He's been putting these pennies in my room, pressed up against the wall, in a line."**

These days I avoid looking in the corner. It's ridiculous. I'll tell Andrea; I'll get it dealt with. I go to look at them, forcing myself. There are more of them. Pressed up against the wall. I bend down to look. I crouch down to look. When does he do it? *Why?*

**"But I'm not picking up these pennies because I need to show Andrea what he's doing and besides they're . . ."**

They're art.

**"But the thing is—the other day I decided 'I'm just going to check, to see what dates they have on them.' "**

If I get down close enough I'll see it. The first penny will have the tiny date engraved upon it. And all of them will have it.

All one to three, four, five, six, seven, oh dear God, all nine of them will have the same date.

**Q: Was there a date you were looking for?**

**A: "1981, the year I was born."**

It's hard to look without touching them. My heart is pounding in my ears. This is stupid. I know what I'm going to see. 1981.

1981, 1981, 1981, 1981, 1981, 1981, 1981, 1981, 1981 . . .

I peer but the date is blurred. Am I crying? I think I'm going to pass out. Then I realize what it is. It's sweat. Sweat has rolled from my forehead into my eyes. I rub at my stinging eyes. I peer closer. The date on the first penny is . . .

1979.

1992, 1983, 1986, 1988, 1978, 1989, 1987, and—

There's a sound; it is me, gulping in the air. I'm breathing. Then I start giggling and then I am laughing. I am laughing like the idiot I am. Like the fucking moronic idiot that I am. Laughing like someone who was really frightened and who is now relieved, and what is there to be frightened about? Why am I so relieved when it's only Lucas? Of course it is Lucas. It's been Lucas the whole time.

**Q: And was it there?**

**"I check all the dates and right up to the end there's not one 1981 penny. Random, random dates. Most of them are mid- to late 1980s, some early 1990s."**

The last date is 1996.

*Oh Jesus, how could I have even thought . . .*

**"It doesn't matter and now I know I can clear them away."**

**Q: And have you cleared them away?**

**A: "No . . . but that's because now it seems more sweet than anything else."**

It's a sweet gesture. His way of saying (*helo*) hi.

**"Really, it's cute."**

**Q: Tell me more about Lucas.**

**A: It happened when I picked Lucas up from school because it was a half day and Andrea had to be in court.**

His teacher, an older, plump woman named Mrs. Ryder, had handed me a note asking if Andrea could contact her as soon as possible. She had also given me a sharp look, one I didn't understand.

I think about how, when we got home, he sat on the couch with his rabbit's foot, now a constant attachment, under his nose, watching a kid's show, a friendly show with baby animals bouncing about the screen. He seemed dangerously close to tears. I risked a conversation.

*So, kiddo. How's it going?*

*S'okay.*

*What happened?*

*Mrs. Ryder wants to talk with Momma*

*Do you know what she wants to talk about?*

*The ladies.*

My stomach tightened. *What about them?*

*I drawed them for you like they told me to and Mrs. Ryder saw them and now she want to talk with Momma.*

No wonder Mrs. Ryder was giving me the stink eye. I just assumed she was an evil old bitch. She probably assumes I'm corrupting him. *Do you know why the ladies want you to draw those pictures for me?*

*They trying to tell you . . .*

*Tell me what, honey?* Oh God, I didn't want to know.

*They say it's a secret.*

*Well, you know you can tell me anything at any time. Right?*

*Mmm-hmm.* Dark eyes on the screen, making the rabbit's foot stroke his nose, up and down and up.

*Lucas?*

*Mmm . . .*

I didn't want to scare him, but it had to stop.

*Are the ladies making you put pennies in my room?*

*What pennies?*

*Remember I once asked you about some pennies in my room?*

*You s'posed to knock,* he said, just like the last time.

*You're right, that's the rule.*

Back and forth, tickling his nose with that rabbit's foot.

*Okay, well, I'll be in my room.*

*Kat?*

I turned when I heard him call. He held out his rabbit's foot.

*You want me to hold it? Really?*

*Hold it.*

I knew what an honor this was. No one is allowed to touch the sacred rabbit's foot. From the first moment it's been strictly Lucas's private property. Andrea had told me the story.

*We were waiting in the checkout line at the Associated when he saw some little kids getting some gum from the gumball machines near the exit. Who knows what first made him look over there but it was torture for him, like a fat man on a treadmill watching people eat ice cream. His lower lip was trembling but he knows I don't let him chew gum, especially not that kind of huge hard bubble gum. It's like a choking accident waiting to happen. So I shook my head and he got that hangdog look—you know the one? I felt terrible all the same, really guilty. He'd been so quiet lately and I really wanted to cheer him up. I'd bought him a little bar of chocolate that I planned to give him later, after dinner, but I still felt kind of mean.*

*We finally got everything belted and bagged and I paid, but as we were walking out one of those clear plastic balls literally fell out of the slot of the last gumball machine. It couldn't have been more perfectly timed. We both froze. It was epically creepy, like a movie. So we stood and watched and it rolled by Lucas's feet and he picked it up. I thought,* Well, at least it's not a gumball, *because then we'd have a scene on our hands. He looked up at me with that sad little face again.* Fine, clearly the universe wants my son to get a prize. *So I said, "Want me to open that for you? See if we can keep it?" Trying to keep my options open. Ha. He said, "Yes, please, Momma." So I opened it, it took some squeezing and I almost broke a nail, and suddenly it went* pop! *There was this big bright green fake-ass rabbit's foot on a gold key chain. I've never seen a prize like that. It was the ugliest, most synthetic thing I have ever seen in my life. I wanted to throw it away immediately but he gazed at me with his hand held out. I took a deep breath and I said, "If I ever see you putting it into your mouth I'm taking it away, understand? This is not for eating. Do you understand me?" And he nodded. "Yes. I understand." So I handed it over and he immediately brightened up. And I ended up eating the chocolate. That was that. Which goes to show that I should have just let him chew some damn gum, because now my kid has this weird lucky rabbit's foot key chain up under his nose like a cokehead. It's what they call a "teachable moment." Shit.*

She jokes about it, but I know how much Andrea resents that rabbit's foot. She resents it because it comforts Lucas when she can't; it seems to offer him some sort of safety. It seems to gloat at her, to say a mother's love isn't always going to be enough, to be the first thing that Lucas loves and she does not. The first diversion of their paths, and as small as it may be, it's still a divergence, a difference, a cleaving.

*I hate the way he's started holding on to it during the day and now with the thumb, like a security blanket.* She sighed. *I guess I can't really blame him. It's like his talisman. I could do with one myself.*

Now I tell the therapist what happened when I put out my hand and Lucas placed the fuzzy charm into my palm. How I closed my fingers over it, soft and slippery and cool, its fur feeling almost wet.

**"I swear I felt a tingling, a light and tremulous buzz. Just for a moment I thought I saw . . . something."**

**Q: Can you describe what you saw?**

*Hold it. It's lucky.*

**A: "For a moment I thought I saw someone standing in the corner."**

*I drawed her a shirt, pink 'cause she's a girl.*

I dropped the rabbit's foot and the tingling stopped.

*You see too.* It wasn't a question.

*I* . . . I began and then I paused. I looked down into his face, his round eyes looking back at me solemnly, trusting. *Maybe* . . .

He seemed content with that one useless word and went back to his program again.

**"Of course, I didn't see anything. I didn't see anything, but—"**

**Q: But what?**

**A: "Small, stupid things have me uneasy—"**

**Q: What things?**

**A: "I'm getting calls. Wrong numbers, all the time now. Mostly there are no messages, just ring-and-hang-ups from numbers I don't recognize, or just silence on the other end of the phone."**

**Q: Have you reported this?**

**A: "I have, but the police said a lot of sick people are taking advantage of everything going on. That there's a lot of these kind of pranks and stuff happening at the moment. If anyone actually threatens me, I have to come in and file a report, but until they do, I basically have to sit tight."**

I guess I could call the numbers back, but I think about the doctor's office, about Daniella Zaretti, and I'm scared.

**Q: What else?**

**A: "There's the closet door."**

These days the closet door is always two or three inches open. It never used to be, but even though I know I shut it, every time I come back to my room, it's ajar. Forcing me to look in before I close it. I do, how stupid, but I do, and of course there's nothing there but my clothes, some linen, my two suitcases.

The closet door is always open. It means nothing. But somehow I feel that it does mean something. I've made sure that there are no bags hanging from the door, pulling it wide, no coat caught in its hinges or a suitcase jutting out. There's nothing. I close the closet door, I leave my room, and every time I come back, it's open.

A camp counselor once told me, *You have to close all the closet doors before you sleep or the bogeymen will get you.* A thoughtless, cruel way of keeping us neat. Nevertheless it has stayed with me. It worked. I always kept the closet doors closed. Now they are always open.

**"Not that it means anything, but . . ."**

**Q: It makes you feel anxious?**

**A: "Yes. And then there was what happened last week."**

I'd been out drinking with Sasha and Liz at some pretentious little bar on the Lower East Side—I can't remember the name.

**Q: What happened?**

**A: "It was almost two in the morning, and I was standing on the Fifty-ninth/Lex subway platform, waiting for the train to take me back to Queens."**

I hated waiting there; the air was thick and clammy. I saw a fat rat scampering along the tracks and the escalator was squeaking in anguish.

**"I didn't want to be alone. I saw a young couple farther down, making out, and a woman playing the violin and I went to stand near them."**

It's better to wait around strangers than it is to wait alone. It's better to have witnesses.

**"I didn't want to stand too close to the couple, it was awkward enough, so I stood and watched the woman. She looked to be in her twenties, her head was shaved, and she was covered with tattoos. She wore a black leather bodice laced tight and her jeans were dark with sweat. She bristled with piercings and chains. I had thought she was playing a violin, but her instrument looked a little bit older, rounder and darker. Her eyes were closed and she swayed in time with the music."**

There were a few dollars and some change in the cap by her feet. I like to support musicians when I can, as long as their music isn't intolerable. Besides, she distracted me from the alien atmosphere on the platform and the distant rumblings of other trains. I stooped and put a dollar down, and she stopped, freezing mid-slide of the bow. The shock of silence was so abrupt that even the amorous couple stopped groping each other and looked up, alarmed. With her eyes still closed she began to play another song. There was something terrifyingly magnificent about her focus, her skill, her piercings and leather bodice coupled with the pretty little melody.

**"She opened her eyes and stared straight at me. Then she started singing."**

Her voice was low and surprisingly lovely, but the words she sang sounded old and strange.

*Sing me a song*
*Of the stars and the moon,*
*Sing of the one*
*Who was taken too soon.*

**"It was as if she was singing to me and not singing to me at the same time, maybe singing to someone just behind me. I swung round, but there was no one there."**

My skin crawled and the hair on the back of my neck stood straight up.

**Q: You felt she was singing to you?**

**A: "Yes."**

Only I felt that it wasn't really the girl who was singing. As if something was using her like a marionette, jerking her strings to make her deliver a message.

*A smile in the dark*
*A knife gleaming bright*
*Sing me a song*
*Of the night*

**"And there's the other thing."**

**Q: What other thing?**

**A: "It was the night of the vigil. I had come home and gone into the kitchen for some desperately needed ice cream."**

*Katherine?*

I shrieked.

**"Andrea was sitting at the counter."**

*Jesus, you scared me!*

*I scared* you? *Holy hell!*

*What are you doing up?*

She smiled guiltily. *Sometimes a woman needs to eat cold chicken and read some trash.* There's the *Us Weekly* spread out in front of her, a drumstick in one of her hands.

I agree.

*So, how was the vigil?* Andrea had said she couldn't get out of work, though I privately thought that she couldn't deal with it. I wasn't going to judge.

*Intense, sad, moving.*

She nodded.

*Speaking of that and of everything that's been going on—*

*Yeah?*

*Do you know where Alexis might have put my window guards when she moved out?* I thought briefly of Sael standing on my fire escape, demanding that I let him in. *It's just that my room faces out onto the street and—*

*Well, it's funny you should mention that because I was just on the phone with a guy from the hardware store today.*

**"She told me that she knew I was worried about getting the window guard reinstalled, so she'd called the hardware store."**

*Really?* Relief flooded through me.

*Yeah, they're going to come and install some window bars in about two weeks. I asked for an earlier date but they're booked up until Fourth of July weekend.*

*Still, you managed to get an appointment! That's great!*

She looked a little shame-faced. *I'm just sorry I didn't get it taken care of sooner. I know you've been really worried about it.*

**"I was puzzled. I hadn't mentioned it before."**

*Why do you say so?*

She looked away. If I didn't know her better, I'd think she was embarrassed. Very un-Andrea-like.

**"She said I'd been talking in my sleep."**

*What?*

*Hey, don't look at me like that! I wasn't eavesdropping, I promise!* She sees my expression and sighs. *Okay, it was about one in the morning and I couldn't sleep, so I went and got a nightcap—it sometimes does the trick, y'know?*

I grinned, in spite of myself. Andrea had received this bottle of brandy last Christmas and she was bizarrely defensive about the tiny amounts she doled out to herself on rare occasions. *You lush.*

*Oh, shut up! Anyway. I saw the light on under your door so I thought you were also up and that maybe, just maybe, if you played your cards right, I would be so generous as to offer you a nightcap too. Because that's the kind of generous and incredible person I am.*

*And?*

*And? When I peeped in you were lying in bed with a pillow over your head, sound asleep. No drink for you.*

*But you heard me say something?*

*Yeah, after I closed the door and turned to walk back to the kitchen. Except it didn't really sound like you, that was the weird thing.*

*What did I say?*

She frowned for a moment, recollecting, then she lowered her voice to a dragging drawl. *"He could get in any time he likes. It won't be long now."*

*What the hell?!*

*I know.*

*Are you serious? That's horrifying!*

*You're telling me!*

*Seriously, I said that?*

*Jesus, Kat, people do all sorts of strange shit in their sleep. It's no big deal.*

*I can't believe it!*

She laughs. I think she's relieved to be talking about it. *Okay, how's this, the next time it happens I'll record you on my phone for undeniable proof.*

**Q: What did you feel when she told you that?**

**A: "I felt unsettled, because I have, to my knowledge, never talked in my sleep. I mean no one has ever told me that before. I guess the window situation was really freaking me out after all."**

Andrea gave my arm an affectionate squeeze. *But Katherine, it doesn't matter! What matters is it made me realize that I needed to get going regarding those window bars! I should have done it before.*

I still felt unnerved, but I nodded, letting it go. *So how did you swing such a fast appointment? I know the demand is ridiculous.*

*I might have mentioned I was a lawyer.*

*You told them you were a public defender?*

*I may have insinuated that I was more of the prosecutor type. The type who would sue their asses if they didn't help out some damsels in distress.*

*Awesome.*

*I know, the only thing is that they need someone to be home to supervise and the earliest date they can make it would be next Wednesday from eleven to twelve. Random huh? I thought if maybe you could take an early lunch break, apparently they're super fast—*

She saw my expression.

*Uh-oh, what?*

I hadn't told Andrea yet.

*Actually, I was planning on working through my lunch break so I could go home early.*

*Why? Everything okay?*

*Yeah, uh, it's just that David asked me to the annual fund-raising gala for his fancy-shmancy university—it's so fancy-shmancy that it's in the middle of the week.*

She smiled. *I guess Wednesday is the new Thursday, huh? Well, I'm glad it's going well with you guys. A gala is a big deal!*

*I know, but what about—*

*Oh, that's all right. I'll stay, I mean, it shouldn't take long. I can work from home until they're done.*

*Are you sure?*

*Oh please, it's no biggie.* She brandished the *Us Weekly* at me like a wand. *Cinderella, you SHALL go to the ball!*

**"She's going to stay and wait for the guys to come and put them in. I guess she's really rooting for David."**

**Q: Who is David?**

**A: "This guy I'm seeing."**

The truth is that everything seems to be on the upswing.

**"I mean, I haven't heard from Sael again, that chapter seems to be finally closed, and David is so lovely, but . . ."**

**Q: But?**

**A: "We haven't spent the night together yet, almost another month has gone by, and I'm starting to wonder."**

Most of my friends say it's a good thing.

**"One of my friends suggested that he could be gay . . ."**

**Q: Do you think he could be gay?**

**A: "No, I don't think so. I can tell from the way he looks at me, the way he kisses me."**

**Q: Who's Sael?**

Oops.

**"Sael?"**

I stall for time.

**Q: You mentioned him earlier, said you hadn't heard from him again.**

**A: "There was this guy Sael . . ."**

**Q: That's an interesting name.**

**A: "I know. It's an old name, from the word 'sailor.' "**

There's a silence as the words die in my throat. I can explain the origin of his name, but I'm not sure how to talk about him.

**Q: Do you want to tell me about him?**

**A: "I was involved with him briefly, just for one night, but that's long over."**

It's true. Ever since the night when he climbed up the fire escape, I haven't heard from him. He kept his promise, which I'm glad about. Obviously.

The therapist nods at me as if to say "Continue."

**"He and David are friends, best friends."**

She nods again.

**"David doesn't know about us, though . . . I guess I feel horrible about the whole thing."**

**Q: You feel unresolved about this.**

**A: "Yes."**

**Q: Would you say that the level of your anxiety heightened when you met Sael?**

**A: "No."**

The word is out of my mouth before I can stop it. I don't want to talk about Sael, or anything to do with him.

**Q: You feel it's an intrusion when I ask?**

**A: "No."**

Yes, I do.

**"No, I just don't think there's a connection."**

**Q: Anything else you want to tell me?**

I've been skirting around it the entire session, until we're almost out of time. Not talking about the real reason I'm here, the thing that happened about a week ago.

It's the thing that made me cautiously ask around for a recommendation. Seeing a therapist is nothing to be ashamed of, but still, I don't want to broadcast it. I asked my friend Michelle, who shared a name. Then another three days of sitting with the number, looking at it and not calling, but I have to tell someone. I have to know.

Now I don't look at this woman's pleasant, impassive face, this woman who sits opposite me. I can't. So I focus on the wastepaper basket by the left-hand side of her desk as I tell her what happened that night. It's as if it didn't happen to me at all, as if I am watching it happen to someone else.

**A: "A week ago I was washing the dishes."**

I like the water very soapy. Our building is too old and the landlord is too cheap for a dishwasher, but at least the sink water will be hot and soapy, filled with bubbles. I use too much dishwashing liquid—Andrea has told me so. It's one of the very few things we bump heads over. But I figure it's okay as long as I pay extra. I always get the green-apple-scented kind, or the pink one. The pink dishwashing liquid has a sharp and bright, efficient smell, like chemical flowers. I wear long yellow gloves and I wash with a green scrubbing pad. I like to dry with paper towels, even though I know this also costs extra money. I put a cleaned plate in the rack, and then two and then three.

**"Then I noticed that something was blocking the sink; it wasn't emptying, not draining fast enough. The water was too soapy to see what was stuck, so I stuck my hand in, fumbling to get at whatever what was clogging the drain."**

The drain gets blocked so quickly. Shit, I want a garbage disposal; I hate that we don't have one. I know I should have used a draining plug but it takes too long for the water to go down. It's probably a piece of tomato, or an olive pit, a carrot.

Fingers gripped my wrist.
A hand.

**"It felt like a hand came up from the drain and grabbed my wrist."**

I notice, as if from a great distance, that the hand has blue sparkly nail polish. The polish on the nails is slightly chipped; there's a black smeary club stamp on the back of her hand.

And then the reality of the situation broke through my mad detachment.

**"I screamed and jerked back."**

Knocking a plate, which smashed on the floor. I don't know how long I stood there, the shards of broken plate around my feet. Frozen. Panting. Adrenaline flooding through my system.

***"In a moment,* I thought, *I'll grab my keys, my wallet, my phone. I'll run out the door and get in a cab and go, go, go to the neighbors, to the police, to a friend's house, to anywhere, just away.***

**"I didn't do any of those things, though."**

**Q: What did you do?**

**A: "I just stood in the kitchen. Stood and waited and stared at the sink. There was nothing."**

I waited. I stared at the sink. I picked up a knife that was on the counter. It was a big knife and it sounds corny now, but when I held it, I felt better.

There was nothing there. Nothing at all. I walked to the sink slowly, knife raised. I must have looked ridiculous, but as some wise person once said, there's nobody here but us chickens, us and a hand that's come up from the sink.

**"Nothing. There was nothing there."**

**Q: So what happened then?**

Andrea and Lucas were gone for the weekend, camping upstate with friends for the July Fourth weekend.

**A: "I called David's phone; it went to voice mail and I hung up. I called Liz's phone. It went to voice mail too. I thought about going to a bar, or calling another friend."**

I even thought about calling Sael.

There was nothing in the sink. My heart slowly resumed its beat. There was nothing in the sink. There was nothing in the sink. Nothing.

**"I picked up the pieces of my broken plate. Slept with the bedside light on."**

I was awake for a long, long time.

Now I tear my eyes from the brown leather of the chair and look at this woman, this professional who sits opposite me. Forcing myself to ask the question.

**"Am I losing my mind?"**

I wait to hear the answer.

Forty minutes later I'm drinking coffee at a little diner nearby. Thinking, or "processing," as someone more evolved might say. Mulling over what she said.

*I think the very act of reaching out for help shows you know the difference between fantasy and reality.*

My uncertainty makes all the difference. I realize that if I hadn't said "It felt like a hand . . . ," that might have been an issue.

*In my view, it would be a good idea if we met again.*

But we won't. It's too much money, even with the sliding scale, and maybe there's something else going on. I let myself think back to the question.

*Would you say that the level of your anxiety heightened when you met Sael?*

The question leads to a darker place, a place where I don't want to go.

"I'm fine," I say aloud, and my voice doesn't sound scared or tremulous or batshit crazy. It's the voice of a woman who's perfectly sane and who is absolutely not having a nervous breakdown. "I just have to get my shit together. I'm *fine*."

I'm fine and I'm going to deal with these pennies today.

Back in the apartment, I go to my room and for a change go straight to the corner. I bend down. On hands and knees, leaning forward, I check the last penny.

1996. Right. Good. I knew it.

Except it's not the last penny anymore. It's the second to last.

But he's only killed—

*No, shut up, stop it—*

The media coverage was endless and frenetic, a new eruption of panic because he had broken his pattern.

*She was killed not in her apartment but—*

I had heard it first on the radio a few days ago. Natalie Shapiro was only nineteen years old. So far, she is the youngest victim.

Natalie Shapiro was found dead in a women's bathroom cubicle at Club23 on Fifth Avenue.

"She shouldn't have even been allowed in," Herman Shapiro, Natalie's father, had said. "She was only nineteen years old, for Christ sake! She was a child!"

Her mother had been too stricken to speak. Their baby, naked but for her panties, propped in a stall. She must have been drugged; she couldn't have gone of her own free will. Friends who might have taken something, God knows what drug, and the music being so loud, the scene was pretty intense. *We didn't see her, but we thought it was okay. Natalie liked to party.*

She was supposed to be at a sleepover party at her friend

Chelsea's house. That's the thing these days. Go out, drink in the city, and then back to spend the night in New Jersey, safe and sound.

Jill Blackson, spokeswoman for Club23, had said, "We're doing everything possible to cooperate with the police and the authorities. We have no idea how she would have been let in when our policy regarding those under twenty-one is strictly enforced."

Natalie Shapiro must have had a false ID, the radio reporter had announced.

1996 *was* the last penny. There were nine pennies last time I checked. Now the last one says 1991. There are ten pennies now.

It has to be a coincidence. It *has* to be. The news reporter informs me that a twenty-four-year-old pharmaceutical rep, Stephanie Dabrowski, was found dead and cold early this morning in her apartment.

Maybe I'll deal with them tomorrow.

HE NIGHT BEFORE THE WEDDING, A guard making his appointed rounds on the castle's perimeter heard a strange and eerie singing. He followed the voice through the castle's gardens, past stone walls, until he came upon the Maiden. She was dancing under a massive blossoming hazelnut tree, which had been there since time out of mind and was rumored to hold much power. The Maiden was as naked as the day she had been born and danced in a wild way back and forth. She thrust her cupped palms up to the moon, which was full and brimming red in the sky. As the guard approached he heard the words of her song more clearly.

*Blood to blood,*
*Vein to vein,*
*Keep my love*
*From fire or flame.*

Then the guard was much afraid. He crossed himself and began to say a prayer, for he knew it must be witchcraft, but the Maiden heard his whispers and she turned and looked at him. The guard mustered his courage to come forward to ask what business she had unclothed and singing in such a fashion and at such an hour, but she walked to him brazenly of her own accord.

"Behold," she said, and held out her hand. His eyes grew wide with astonishment, for there, coiled as a serpent and glittering in her palm, lay a wondrous jeweled brooch. The guard opened his mouth to question her further, but she took his hand and smiled upon him and then he saw she was indeed very lovely, lovelier than any lady he had ever known, even the baron's daughter. All his words died upon his lips as she took him by the hand and led him beneath the hazelnut tree.

The guard never did tell about the Maiden, nor about the manner in which he had found her. Indeed, on the morrow he seemed to have forgotten all about it.

# 13

"So drinks tonight? You're in?"

Megan, the office gossip, has stopped by my-but-not-really-my desk. It belongs to Cora, who's on maternity leave. There's a picture of a husband who isn't mine, and a bobbing cow that isn't mine. Still, I put a small Yoda figure there so I guess I'm even with Cora, maybe even the winner. It is Yoda, after all.

"Drinks? What's the occasion?"

She looks at me as if I'd just asked her what my name is. "Are you serious? You don't know?"

"Know what?"

Her little rat eyes gleam in her bony face. I'm a captive audience. "Really?" She can't believe her luck.

"Megan, *what*?"

"They got him!"

"What?"

"The Sickle Man! Where have you been? Under a rock?"

That's Megan in a nutshell. Who else would say "under a rock"? But I'm too stunned to take issue with her out-of-date bitchiness. "Are you serious?"

"Look!" She leans over me, so closely that I can smell sour coffee on her breath, and types "Sickle Man found dead" into the search bar. "There!" She steps back in triumph.

I scan over the words.

Reports are

Police confirmed

Mother sobs in relief,

Crowds to celebrate,

There's a picture of Susie Ranford practically held aloft by two DWHA volunteers on either side of her. Then there is a white sheet, police keeping people back, ER specialists handling a stretcher.

"Wow." I turn to Megan. "Who was he?"

"Some sicko." She shrugs. "This guy just did two tours in the army. Was due to go out there again. Lived on Staten Island."

"How did they find him?"

"His neighbors filed a report, said he was acting weirdly."

"Awful."

Megan smiles, relishing the whole thing. "So the neighbors called the police, who found him hanging from a rod in the closet. Apparently his apartment was filled with the grossest shit, newspaper articles, women's underwear, fucked-up knives. There was even a note confessing—" She sees my expression. "What's wrong?"

"He killed himself?" I think back to the endless analyses from the various criminal experts, the psychologists and psychiatrists. "Doesn't sound like he fits the profile. Didn't the police say he would know how to fit in, be more social, less of a loner?"

She looks annoyed. I'm not a satisfying audience. "Well, I don't know. I mean, all that army training probably meant that he could break into the apartments really easily and he would certainly know how to kill." She shivers dramatically.

"At least it's over," I say lamely. I know I should feel glad, but something in me stays oddly flat.

"So, now that you're brought up to speed, drinks tonight?"

"I can't, I have this gala I have to go to with David." About ten minutes ago, I would have killed for this opportunity to shut Megan up for once. Now her envy and irritation barely register.

"Is that who you're always texting? Your boyfriend?"

That's our Megan, so subtle, with true regard for privacy. "Yeah."

"But *everyone's* going to be going out and partying tonight." She looks at me pityingly. Clearly I've picked the wrong night to attend a gala. She relents. "You can join us later if you want," she says generously. "I hear people have started already. Bars will be packed. It's going to be total insanity."

She says this like it's a good thing.

"Cool," I say. "Thanks."

Finally, after what feels like an eternity, she leaves.

I sit and I wait. I wait to feel relief, or happiness, or exultation. Instead I feel empty. Strange. A sort of numbness. Disbelief. I guess that's normal.

My thoughts are splattered drops.

*They've found him. They've caught the Sickle Man.*

*An ex-army guy. Dead.*

Andrea will be so relieved. Maybe Lucas will stop doing those drawings now. Maybe the ladies will leave. *I mean,* I correct myself, *maybe he'll stop seeing the ladies.*

In my mind I see the pennies.

*The pennies are no longer pressed against the wall. The pennies lie facedown. Facedown. Facedown in the dirt. Tails up. Bad luck.*

"Stop it!" I say aloud.

"Talking to yourself?" Alan says as he passes my-but-not-really-my desk. "Not surprised, it's a sign of insanity." He winks at me as he goes back to his office.

I smile. I like Alan. We've always shared a gentle flirt, talked about cheesy TV shows we like. He's got a bit of a tummy, thinning hair, and, from his photos, a beautiful wife and an adorable two-year-old daughter. I've tried not to hold it against him.

*Put it out of your mind.* I have a gala to go to with David. Our first appearance as a couple, our public announcement of coupledom! I give myself a mental shake and try to focus, try to forget the image.

*Pennies facedown. Dead pennies. Facedown in the dust.*

Think about tonight.

Tonight.

# 14

When it comes to bed vs. closet, it is important to understand the pros and cons of both.

Let us address the obvious first.

Many in this city don't even have an under to their bed. But if they do, under the bed can offer more storage space. However, *getting* under the bed is far more uncomfortable than stepping into the closet. It's a tight squeeze, but the body gives and gives. People are always so amazed at what the body can do; how, given the right circumstances, it can twist and turn and shift. You're not. You know different bodies well. You know what the human body is capable of.

It's also often dirtier under the bed than in the closet. Forgotten socks, limp and mournful; fierce little dust balls; the odd condom wrapper, the odd condom. Hairpins, the extension cord to the hair dryer, underwear, one earring, a candy wrapper, loose change, the obligatory quarter, and a scrunched-up receipt.

You don't mind a little dirt, however.

Bedbugs. You can sense them before smelling their musty,

sweet odor. Even scarier than you, perhaps, although their smears of blood are small and yours, yours tend to be bigger.

If you can stand, or rather lie with, these discomforts, there's nothing like under the bed. The vantage point is wonderful. You go unnoticed for longer. Under-the-bed fears are dealt with in childhood. There are no such things as monsters.

Except when there are.

In bed is where people feel the safest. Which is ironic. In bed is often where people are at their most vulnerable: wear the least amount of clothes and sink, fall, drift into unconsciousness.

Bed is where people allow themselves to become closer to the state of death.

You're here to bridge the gap.

You'll wait until she's asleep before drawing one hand from under the mattress. Aligning your breath to her breath, settling into her rhythm, eyes growing accustomed to, filling up with, the dark. One hand, and then another. Slowly—the best things need to be drawn out. And soon enough she'll wake. With your hands wandering free, you might decide to tug on her toe, a quick tug, so she wakes and looks about but does not see you. You've done this once or twice before. You love it. And probably, if you are delicate enough, she will go back to sleep.

There's something about being under the bed, staring up, a cheek pressed to the underside of the mattress and her body with its faint warmth above you, that never fails to make you smile.

Slowly, infinitely slowly, you slide out. Limb by limb. In the dark, careful not to wake her.

Partially out, you might be able to reach up, stroke her cheek, entwine a lock of her hair around a finger, breathe into her ear, whisper a secret she will never, ever have the chance to tell.

Not yet, not yet.

And then you'll gently lean over to rouse her from her dreams, to pull her up from her subconscious so that she might look you in the face.

There's nothing like that expression of sheer and complete bewilderment, of unbreathing, unbelieving panic. It fizzes on your lips; it's sweet and sharp and cold and lovely.

Panic is neon orange, it wails like sirens and unanswered phones, it tastes of chlorine and blistered tongues, it smells like a wet bed at summer camp, like the bathroom in the airplane, it rocks like turbulence.

Then again, there's always the closet. The closet is more comfortable, of course. But it's also much more obvious. It's been appropriated and been made coarse by the tales of the bogeyman.

It's actually a wonderful place. Warm and womblike, your own little cave. You stand. You wait for the coat hangers to settle down, to stop their jangling. Closets tell so much. There's wood and there are slats, an intimate smell. Sometimes coats for snow and boots for rain, suitcases, fans. Stuffed animals with sad glass eyes. In the one you're thinking of, the one you visited most recently, there were many shoe boxes filled with photos and paper cutouts and unused postcards. And the quiet pale fluttering of moths. Clothes carry the smells of the city. The scents are ghosts. Cigarettes, of course, falafel from the sidewalk, the pinkest hint of sprayed perfume or lingering deodorant. The pockets still have lip balm for the lips that will widen later, ready to scream. Some closets have files, books, badly folded sheets and blankets, a box of sock puppets, strange but wonderful. Two kinds of hats, one a baseball cap, one furry, and hanging bags that she should throw out but doesn't. Hers has a mirror posted on the back.

There's nothing like when she opens a closet and finds you there. It's a whole different kind of beverage. Whereas under the bed there is a gradual surfacing from sleep to wakefulness, now you watch her eyes as she realizes in an instant that her worst nightmare is true.

Shock is the color of the spots before the migraine, blue and black and floating. It tastes of sugar water, it tastes of rubber, it stings like a slap, burns like a cheek pressed against the floor.

You stand there and you grin. "Hello."

Once or twice you've had the door slammed shut, as if hiding your grinning, grinning face will erase all of you. You wait. They can run, try to dial for help, but you, you are unnaturally fast and you know where their phones are, what they mean to do, the tumblers of the locks upon the doors. And how are you there, with the window closed and the door locked? And yet, somehow you're through and in and—

"Hello."

You have a light and pleasant voice.

You have a lovely smile.

She has seen it before.

Only now she doesn't smile back.

You think about this as you stand waiting to be served at the open bar. An open bar always means a line. Oh, Katherine. She'll be showering quickly, worried that she's running late. You move up a little farther; a woman in front of you wants your attention.

Her husband is growing plump; sweat patches will form under his arms when he dances.

*Yes, he has money but no one told me it would be this lonely.*

She just wants to be noticed again, wants to be told she looks beautiful and have the person mean it.

She's very lovely and well preserved but you choose not to pay attention to her yet. Katherine will be coming through to her room from the bathroom by now, pink and perfect, bare wet feet back and forth to the closet. You saw her dress too. When you looked in her closet all those hours before. You'll compliment her on it. Did she know it was your favorite color?

You wonder if she'll be listening to the radio with its amusing little bulletins on the man they think is you.

You imagine that as she applies her makeup, leaning forward, concentrating on not smudging her eyeliner, opening her lips, she'll be giving herself a little talk, a warning to not have so many expectations, to not get her hopes up. She will anyway.

You're finally at the bar. You ask for a scotch and then turn to the lovely, well-preserved woman next to you and ask her what she'll have. It's a neat trick. Here she was thinking that no one noticed her anymore, and then you did. She is surprised; she blushes as she tells you.

She has a million questions already, but right now she's heady with relief. She's still beautiful. She's still got what it takes.

Katherine will be heading out soon, leaving the apartment that you finally left several hours ago.

"Hello," you had said to the woman you surprised earlier that afternoon.

As the bartender pours the drinks you asked for, you remember how the woman looked trussed up and gagged on her bed. How she wet herself.

"Don't feel bad," you told her. This happens quite often; it's nothing to feel ashamed about. You tell her you'll clean her up. You're good at clearing up messes. You're neat.

Rage is white, it burns like ice, it cracks like lightning, it tastes of tarmac, it tastes of iron, it feels like fingers gripping the fleshy part of your upper arm, it sounds like tires squealing, it feels like splinters, it hisses like gas, it reeks like a cage in the zoo.

You remember the look in her wide brown eyes as you informed her that it wouldn't take too long. After all, you have a gala to attend.

"Here you go, sir," the bartender says as he puts the glasses down in front of you. You hand one to the eager woman by your side.

"Cheers," you say as you lift your glass. She wants to know what you're toasting to.

You pause, pretending to think, and then you say: "Let's drink to the night ahead, and all that it may bring."

"Do you think it will be a good one?" she asks kittenishly for your benefit. She thinks the night includes her. It will not, lucky little kitten. You smile.

"I think it will be a memorable one," you say, and gently clink your glass against hers. "Please excuse me," you say and her face falls in a ruin of disappointment as you walk back toward the crowd. You don't want to keep your real date waiting.

# 15

Every woman has the right to one red dress.

Every woman has the right to be born, to be loved, to learn, to vote, and to run for office. Every woman has the right to be the head of a major corporation. Every woman has the right to be a stay-at-home mom. Every woman has the right to be treated with respect. Every woman has the right to be taken seriously. Every woman has the right to say no. Every woman has the right to say yes. Every woman has the right to one red dress. A little number she hasn't been eating for, at least not eating anything that gives her pleasure. I am a woman and I have exercised that right.

The dress is strapless, with a pleated bodice. The dress is long, and made of silk. It slides effortlessly against my skin like a perfect compliment given by a stranger. The dress is a bright and deep vermillion red. The dress says, *Well, hey there*, in a starlet's husky voice. The dress makes a statement. It says, *I am here*, and I will be there, tonight.

Now I sit in the cab, and the driver and I listen to the radio announcer rehash the miraculous news.

We are informed that Michael John Hanley, referred to by the media as the Sickle Man, was discovered dead in his apartment after he had been reported missing for forty-eight hours. Neighbors concerned by his recent behavior had contacted police, who had searched Hanley's apartment.

As Megan had so gleefully told me, they had found him hanging in his closet. He was pronounced dead at the scene.

It seems that Hanley had written a crazy, rambling note confessing to the crimes. Although it has yet to be confirmed, reliable sources say that the letter contained details only the killer would know.

I listen for anything new but there's nothing that I haven't already heard or read. Michael John Hanley, thirty-four, had completed two tours in Afghanistan and come back with full honors. Known to his friends as Jack because of his love of Jack Daniel's, Hanley was a quiet guy who enjoyed strumming on a guitar and playing football with friends. He was shy but by all accounts friendly and warm.

"He was really funny when you got to know him," says his friend and fellow soldier Jeff Lloyd, a note of amazed disbelief in his voice.

His family had noticed a difference when he returned from his most recent tour. He was withdrawn and seemed distant. They grew alarmed and urged him to seek help, suspecting that he might be suffering from PTSD.

Eliza Clare, a criminologist, says it makes sense: "He was clearly under a great deal of strain." His military training would have allowed him to access people's homes in a way not many civilians could.

Tonight New Yorkers are taking to the streets in celebration. Megan's probably crawling up some guy's leg by now.

"We've all been living in terror," says Staten Island café owner Tony Assetti. Whoever Tony Assetti is, he has the thickest accent

I've heard in a while. It makes me smile and crave meatballs. "Tonight I'll finally sleep well."

There will be more vigils and prayers for many of the victims, but for their friends and families Hanley's death brings little comfort.

"My sister's still dead. That monster destroyed my family, he's destroyed my life. He's broken my parents' hearts," says Daniel Shapiro, the brother of Natalie Shapiro, Hanley's youngest victim.

"The killer, known as the Sick—"

The driver turns it off. I'm glad.

I look out of the window at people congregating on the sidewalks. The air hangs low and close, like sodden sponges. The evening has that thick yellow feel that comes just before a storm. A storm would blow away the summer stink of garbage, at least for a little while, and force the hordes off the streets, where they're milling around, just waiting to do something, acting for all the world like marchers waiting to take part in a parade.

Two young guys strut around bare-chested, puffed up tight with bravado; someone holds up a handmade sign which screams WE GOT HIM! in large angry red letters; a group of friends spills out from a bar and stands in a gesticulating clump on the street. A woman sits on a sidewalk curb. She wears normal summer office attire and her shoulders are shaking as she weeps—with joy or sorrow, it's impossible to say.

She's not the only one. A man braces himself against a wall, tears running down his face, as a shriek of young girls runs past him. The city is triumphant but angry. It calls for piñatas, any excuse to beat something hard with a stick.

I slip back into my fantasy. I will enter Cipriani's foyer and the crowd will part like the Red Sea. They will part for the lovely woman in her red, red dress. My fantasy is taken from the romantic comedies I publically scorn and privately adore, and in it I will walk up to David, who stands resplendent in a tuxedo. I will shake him out of his usual wisecracking state and render him speechless with my beauty.

The taxi stops. I'm here at Cipriani on 42nd Street. The night is warm and humid; I pay in damp bills. I'm nervous, excited and careful in my high heels on the stairs.

*Say a prayer and here we go.*

Walking into the lobby of the Cipriani is like stepping back in time. It was built in the 1920s and I can easily imagine Scott Fitzgerald or Dorothy Parker being witty over gin fizzes while being elbowed by flappers. Then I remember it used to be a bank, so maybe not. There are arched doorways and massive Corinthian columns; the pink brick walls and mosaic floors make a lethal acoustic combination, a hellish empty swimming pool magnifying each and every screeching salutation and laugh of the upper echelon greeting one another.

Dear one!

Darling!

Julia! How long has it been?

Too long!

It makes me uneasy. I look for David. I can't find him in the crush of people. *Where is he? Why didn't we pick a meeting place?* I need a drink. A drink will either anchor me or allow me to float up and not care.

I don't feel like standing here anymore like a moron. I go over to check out the table seating. It's indexed alphabetically and I search for my name. *Katherine Emerson, Katherine Emerson, Katherine Emerson.*

Table nineteen.

Clutching my clutch, I make my way into the ballroom. Immediately a waiter steps forward as if he has heard my thoughts. The color of the drink on his tray is a light pink.

"Sorry, what is this?"

"Pink passion bellini." Clearly he's been answering this question for a while.

It's a ridiculous name, but it tastes wonderful. I look around again, absorbing my surroundings, which, like the inside of a Victorian music box, are rosy plush and bathed in golden light. The massive columns are lit up at the top like birthday candles and the marble walls are softened, draped with rose velvet. In this ocean of gold and rose, round tables bob to the surface, laden under wineglasses, glinting silverware, and bouquets of huge white peonies. The flames of slim white candles flicker below while high in the dusky heavens chandeliers glitter.

Like the music box ballerinas, the guests are on display in bold summer colors; turquoise, pinks and greens and blues and whites. The younger women are radiant in chiffon and lace dresses. They are flushed with youth and beauty, their hair falls in long shining tresses. The older women are well put together, with impeccably messy coifs or tailored bobs. At the age where they can afford to make a statement and have a little more fun, they wear linen shifts with beaded necklines and embroidered jackets in Japanese silk. Large stones set in silver ring their fingers and lie against their tucked throats. The men all seem impossibly handsome, in their perfectly cut black-tie jackets. The younger ones, grinning white grins, lend supporting arms to their teetering dates; the older men with their salt-and-pepper hair bestow charming, weary smiles. They form a wall of moving elegance, setting off their colorful partners: "And what can I get you to drink?"

*Table nineteen, table nineteen, table nineteen.* I wind my way over in between other tables, where people are already beginning to sit.

I see him before I see anyone else.

His black jacket and white shirt, his black hair. His arrogant, elegant profile. He's turning and laughing, more relaxed and at ease than I have ever seen him. This is because the most enchanting girl in the world has just whispered something hilarious into his ear.

She wears a tawny, glittering sleeveless dress with a high neck, made from almost-transparent chiffon with intricate golden beading that is just different enough to set her apart. It clings to every lithe part of her. Her long chestnut hair is gathered into a single full braid that hangs down her one bare shoulder. Her eyes are thickly lashed and her mouth is wide and red. She laughs and her smile is perfect too; there is a miniscule gap between her front two teeth, just enough to be interesting, to give her character.

She can't be more than twenty-five.

There's a hand on my arm. "Hey there, beautiful."

I whirl around and it's David smiling back at me. "Where did you go? I looked everywhere for you."

"I couldn't find you, so I thought I'd see if you were at the table."

"Well, here I am."

He's so lovely, so handsome, so kind. He is better than my fantasy. His hand takes mine. Holds it firm. "Let's go face the firing squad."

I don't want to go near that table but there's no choice. I will have to deal with Sael and his lovely, luminous girl.

"Hey, everyone," he says easily and naturally, "this is Katherine."

Faces turn.

"Hey!" "Hi!" Everyone is warm, pleasant.

"Looks like I got here late."

"Not at all," says a pretty blonde, "we just got here early."

"To catch up—"

"Really to make a start at the bar," adds an amiable-looking curly-haired guy whose friendly face resembles that of a golden retriever.

"Let me make the introductions," says David. "Katherine, this is—" He goes round saying everyone's names. I don't hear anything because I am watching Sael whispering back to the most delicious girl in the world who grins and—

"—and you have the pleasure of knowing Sael already." David rolls his eyes. "And this is . . . Hailey?"

"Margot," says the luminous girl. "Close enough, though." She smiles at us. "Sorry about that antisocial display, but Sael was just being—" She starts laughing helplessly.

"Hey, Katherine," Sael says, with such an obvious lack of interest it's amazing to me that he even remembered my name, and then they're both giggling.

"Come now, children," says David, almost annoyed. "Pull it together." He pulls out my chair and I sit down, though what I *want* to do is run out of the room, down the stairs, and out into the night.

The waiter comes and fills my glass with wine. The candle flames flicker, magnified, through a sea of silverware, an ocean of glass.

Plates are set down in front of us; people eat, people drink, people talk, people laugh, people make conversation. They're all accomplished, good-looking, successful.

I'm in hell.

"So Katherine, what do you do?" a sleek-looking Asian guy is asking me. I think his name is Mark. I can't be sure.

The beautiful girl is looking at me; Sael puts one broad hand over her slender one.

David leaps to my rescue. "Katherine's a writer."

"What kind?"

I try to recover. So like David to make me sound more interesting than I am. "Sorry, um, freelance, mostly art criticism."

"That's cool." Margot has joined the conversation. Apparently she's not just beautiful but is a team player. "Have you seen . . ."

She mentions a forthcoming exhibition of miniature portraiture at the Whitney. I've heard about it, but it hasn't opened to the public yet.

"Actually, I didn't know that was open yet."

"Oh yeah, I think it might have been a private showing." She wrinkles her perfect nose apologetically. "My bad."

Bitch.

"Margot's also a writer." This is from Sael, dreamer of bad dreams, teller of tales. He glances at me for a moment with what appears to be a kind of pity before returning to beam at Margot, who lowers her lashes and dimples.

*Please let me sleep here, just for tonight.*

"What do you write?"

"Oh, nothing much—"

"Oh right, she's only a staff writer at the *New Yorker.*" Sael is a real praise-singer. Margot is modest.

"Nice," I say.

"That must be amazing!" This is from the pretty blonde, like an all-American cheerleader. And she means it; she isn't jealous.

"It has its moments." Clearly meaning, *It's the most incredible job in the world.*

"Weren't you telling me how you interviewed Laurence Underhouse?" Sael prompts her.

"He's famous for his nudes, isn't he?"

"I didn't know he was still alive," says another girl, a brunette, Rebecca or something.

"Well, something's up and kicking because he wanted to paint Margot's picture." Sael is still on the bemused boyfriend kick.

There are exclamations round the table.

"What!"

"Really?"

"Well"—Margot is leaning forward conspiratorially—"I shouldn't tell this story, it's terrible—"

So of course everyone begs her to do so, and of course she does, and it's hysterical and witty and involves waxed vaginas as a punch line.

There is a steel vise around my forehead. "Excuse me," I mutter to David.

"Everything all right?"

"Bathroom break, back in a moment," I reply as the vise grip tightens.

The bathroom is right off the foyer. It's huge and cream and lined with art deco tiles in seashell colors and it smells faintly of vanilla and other expensive scents, the way bathrooms in these kinds of places do, and I'm in the stall with my burning face in my hands and the tears come.

*Can I stay here tonight?*

*Tell me a story.*

I'm so stupid, I'm so stupid. He was just fucking with me. Fucking with me. God, I'm so unhappy, what if I hadn't sent him away?

I hear laughter; I recognize some of the voices from the table; they've followed me. I freeze. The voices get louder just outside my stall, at the sink.

"Hang on! Whoa . . . why didn't you tell me I was so smeary? What kind of friend are you?" This comes from the blonde.

"Bitch, please, you look fine." Now it's the brunette.

"Yes, if you like killer clowns. You have some concealer?"

"When am I ever without concealer?"

"Pass it over."

There's the rattle of a thousand cosmetics being scrunched around, a companionable silence, then—

"So Margot, huh?"

"Do you know who her father is?"

"He's that big producer, right?"

"Apparently. I guess Sael's really lucked out this time."

"Oh please, it will never last."

"Really? Why not?"

"I've seen this before. She'll be with him a few weeks at best."

"Oh . . ." There's a pause. The voice gets a little lower. "You mean it's about Sara?"

"It will always be Sara for him."

"Wow, that's so tragic."

"He's never gotten over her. I don't think he ever will. In all the time I've known him, he's never dated anyone else seriously, let alone lived with anyone after her."

"So sad."

"It really was. They were so perfect for each other."

"Wasn't it just before their wedding?"

"Like three weeks."

"Terrible. How many years has it been now since she died?"

"Three."

"It's crazy where the time has gone."

"I know."

There's the kind of pause people might take to honor the dead while trying to apply lipstick at the same time. The clatter of cosmetics, a sound of a zip, and then—

"Ready when you are."

"I'm ready."

*He's never gotten over her.*
*I don't think he ever will.*

*Tragic.*

*Wasn't it just before their wedding?*

I want to stay in here forever but I can't. I make my way out of the stall to the sink. I stare at my stricken face. Not pretty. Out of the corner of my eye I see someone sitting in the far corner. It's the bathroom attendant. Sleeping. I'm glad she's sleeping. I always feel terrible for these women. I'm not sure why we still have bathroom attendants. They never seem to be white. They always look so unhappy. Flocks of spoiled bitches coming in, either complaining or falsely complimenting one another and plastering on makeup while she sits on a small folding chair and waits to see if they tip her a dollar. This woman, in her fifties or sixties, looks foreign. That is to say, her skin is the color of sand and etched with wrinkles. She wears black pants and a white shirt, which I guess is suitable attire, but over this she wears an unzipped light gray hoodie. I wonder what the management would say about that. The hood obscures most of her face but it's clear she's asleep. The kind of sleep reserved for the truly bone-tired. Her head is a little back, propped against the tiles. There's a small paper sign above her head that says:

THANK YOU FOR YOUR DONATION.

It's a little askew, a little grubby. It looks like it was stuck up in a hurry.

I grin despite myself. I like the defiance of the sign and her apparel. I hope the woman sleeps on. I hope no one complains about having to get her own paper towels. It's the sleeping bathroom attendant and me against the world.

I just want the evening to be over. I want to go home. I want to go to bed. I want to crawl under the covers and never come out.

As I'm gearing up to leave, another woman comes out of the stall next to the one I was in. She gives me a start. I'd thought I was alone in here, apart from the sleeping attendant.

She moves silently up to the sink. She stares at herself in the mirror with an odd curiosity but she applies no makeup. Her blond hair is drawn back from her forehead in a tight ponytail. Her skin is the pale skin that real blondes often have, the kind that burns, not tans. Her eyes are a forget-me-not blue.

She's not dressed for the gala. She wears a good-quality, if innocuous, white blouse and a thin gray pencil skirt. She's dressed as if she came from work, not as if she's at a black-tie event. Maybe she's running this thing. It doesn't matter. The phrases continue to ring in my ears.

*It will always be Sara.*

I take out my lipstick from my poor abused clutch. *Pour yourself a drink, put on some lipstick, and pull yourself together.* Isn't that what Elizabeth Taylor said?

"She's dead."

Startled, I look at the woman next to me, but she didn't speak. She's still gazing at her face in the mirror. Not with vanity, it seems, but with a detached curiosity. Her eyes are without light or interest.

It was the bathroom attendant. She is sitting up a little now and looking at me.

"What?"

"It's red," she says, and points to my red-lipped reflection. She speaks conversationally, with no change of tone. I could have sworn she was out for the count. It just goes to show. Clearly I know nothing.

"Thank you." I need something to say, even though I know it was not a compliment but an observation. I'm thrown.

The bathroom attendant leans back once more and closes her eyes.

*How many years since she died?*

I smile at the staring woman next to me, hoping to share a moment, hoping to reassure myself that yes, that exchange with the bathroom attendant was a little odd.

She does not smile back. She turns and for a moment I think I see an infinite look of sorrow in her blue eyes. Then she walks out of the bathroom.

Nice.

The attendant seems to be asleep again. She snores gently. Maybe she's having a nightmare and I'm in it, but that's a kind of trippy, upside-down, shroom-ingesting *Alice in Wonderland* thinking, and it hasn't been so wonderful tonight. Not wonderful at all.

I move toward the sleeping attendant and help myself to some paper towels from the dispenser. Closer up, the THANK YOU FOR YOUR DONATION sign seems even more grimy, its sentiment strangely aggressive. I look down at the contents of the plastic bowl to see if anyone has deserved the thanks.

There appears to be a large dead mouse.

I half shriek and take an involuntary step backward. I look up guiltily but the bathroom attendant hasn't stirred.

I look down again. There, curled sleepily in the center of the bowl, is a single green rabbit's foot key chain. Is it the attendant's, or did some tipsy guest drop it in for a joke? My arms are pricked with gooseflesh, but it's only a rabbit's foot. Just like Lucas's.

Hours later I'll wake in the terrible, endless darkness, and the realization pitiless and cold and clear, will be:

*That wasn't* like *Lucas's rabbit's foot. That* was *Lucas's rabbit's foot.*

But that thought is still far in the future. Now I merely feel uneasy. The beat of my pulse is *Sara, Sara, Sara*.

The world outside the bathroom is darker and louder. The speeches are over. I hear music and see that couples are starting to dance. I push past the people who are determined to get their worth of drinks while the open bar is still open. "Excuse me," I chant to a mass of endless shoulders and breasts and backs. "Excuse me, ex—"

David turns to me. "Katherine! I was just about to send out a—" He takes one look at my face and the words die in his throat. "Hey, what's wr—"

I bend down a little, trying to speak quietly. "David, I'm so sorry but I think I have to go home."

"Oh my God, food poisoning?" Despite my low tone, someone at the table hears me. I wonder if I look as terrible as I feel. I don't spare a glance for Sael and Margot, whom fifteen minutes ago I hated. Now I almost feel sorry for her.

*It will never last. It will always be Sara for him.*

"Migraine." I look at David. "Would you hate me if I went home?"

"Of course not! I'll go too—"

"No! You need to stay, enjoy yourself." I sound a little harsh. His face falls. I modify my tone. "I'm not going to be any fun tonight."

"You're always fun, even when you're no fun."

I try to smile. "Really, I think I'll be better off with some sleep and some aspirin. I'm so sorry."

"At least let me get you a cab."

"That would be wonderful."

David guides me through the laughing, jostling crowd yelling at one another to be heard. My skull is made of glass and it could shatter at any moment. A woman gives a tittering scream, and I wince. Even the dim light is too bright. My head will explode.

But finally we're outside under the large stone arch of the entrance and the rain is falling, steady and growing heavier. I can hear the pavement almost hissing with relief, the rain falling on the remains of my night like reality drenching us all.

"Taxi!" David calls, and somehow, he gets one, but then again he always does and I can't even question how he manages this on a rainy weekday night before I'm inside and he's at the window, getting wet, the window already misting up.

"Text me when you get home."

"David, I'm so sorry." Now I'm near tears again. *Don't you cry, don't you dare cry. Hold it in.*

"It's not your fault."

"I'm a terrible person."

"That's true." He smiles. "But promise you'll text me."

"I will, I promise."

The taxi driver is playing an old pop song. Something about birds appearing every time the subject is within close proximity. Every song about love either taunts or teases. It's agony. I rub my hand against the fogged glass and look out of the small portal I have created.

In the torrential pouring wet, New Yorkers have abandoned their umbrellas and are rejoicing in the rain. Two women, in sodden business clothes, have crossed hands to swing around in a joyful circle, like young girls. A middle-aged man, his once-white shirt transparently sticking to him, has his head back, his arms wide, eyes closed, as the rain drives into his face. He seems oblivious of his leather suitcase and leather shoes, which grow darker by the moment. Several couples are slow-dancing. A young handsome man holds a hysterically laughing little boy as he jumps into an enormous puddle. This father-and-son team splashes a woman in her fifties, her graying hair plastered to her forehead, oblivious and twirling around like a fairy princess.

People are pouring out of bars, some staring, some joining in. Another young guy, clearly an actor, does an excellent Gene Kelly impersonation, singing his heart out in the rain, one hand hooked around a lamppost, the other holding his now broken umbrella. Cars honk joyfully. A group under a restaurant's dripping canvas cheers.

"People gone crazy!" The driver is utterly incredulous.

"Yes, I believe they have," I say. *How wonderful.* I'm still beaming as we near my street, until I see a circling whirl of red and blue and red and blue, there are police cars, one, two—

*There's been a fire,* I think. *There's been a fire, or a gas leak, or someone has gotten into a fight, had too much to drink, had a heart attack.*

"Sorry, road close," says the driver. "Something happen."

"That's fine, I'll get out here." I pay him but I'm looking ahead and then I'm out and running up the wet street, the rain soaking my silk dress but I don't care, and there are not just police cars but also loops of yellow tape and men and women in uniforms, and an ambulance, the yellow tape, the yellow tape—

I'm stopped by a burly policeman. "You can't go in there, ma'am—"

"But I *live* there! My roommate is there, her son—"

"You can't go in there. It's the scene of a crime."

"What happened? What's going on? I live there, I—"

My words are overheard by another officer, who makes a "bring her over" gesture. Now I'm faced with two cops and two other people, a man and a woman dressed in civilian clothes.

"Excuse me, ma'am, you say you live here?"

Then come the questions.

"Yes, my name is Katherine Emerson."

"Yes, I live in that building, apartment 4G."

"No, I haven't checked my phone. I had switched it off." I had done so just for the evening, for my magical evening, for my wonderful, beautiful evening that I wanted so badly. I needed to take a break from the calls, now coming almost every other day. "Just for the evening, though, just for tonight—"

The one night I needed my phone. *The one night.* Now I turn it on, and sure enough, my mailbox is filled with messages; it's full, full, full. It's Lucy's parents—Lucy is a friend of Lucas—and—

*"We're trying to get in touch with Andrea, and Lucas gave us this number. She's not answering her cell phone and it's now eight. Could you call us back please as soon as—"*

*"Hello, Ms. Emerson, this is Detective LaFontaine from the 114th precinct calling you. We're trying to get hold of you. Please contact us immediately at—"*

I turn to one of the officers. "Where is Lucas?! Where is he?"

"He's safe with Lucy's parents for tonight." Then the cop relents. "Apparently he's been asking for you. We've been trying to contact you for some hours now. We're trying to contact *any* family members."

*No comment*, I hear Andrea's voice say in my head. *No comment*, I think, and so say nothing.

"We'll need you to answer some questions."

The hours are measured in bad cups of coffee drunk under the harsh, deadening lights specific to police stations, the patient way they take me through "did you?" and "did you know?" and "did you know where?" and "how?" and "when?" but there are so many things I don't know. Andrea was a very private person. We are great friends—we *were* great friends—but there were still many doors she didn't open. The smaller the space, the neater you have to be. That's the way you survive in the city. You keep some private rooms for yourself. But they're trying to do their best and I'm not officially being interrogated, I'm not a suspect even, though they—

They found her in the apartment. They found her in her bedroom. In our apartment. Andrea, dead in the apartment. Andrea tied and gagged and murdered on her bed while I—

I would have been home, home and showering and getting ready. The police don't say it, but I work it out. He was in the apartment. When Andrea came home to meet the window-guard guys—

*I'll wait for them, you enjoy your gala, you deserve it.*

—the Sickle Man was waiting for her in the apartment.

"Excuse me," I say, "but where is . . . ?"

They point, I'm off and running, and in the small fluorescent acid-yellow bathroom I throw up and up and up. I can't stop shaking. He was in the apartment. He was in the apartment. I was getting ready, listening to the radio, while Andrea was dead. Andrea's dead and I'm alive. It's like a bad urban legend. While I'm fantasizing about my evening ahead, my roommate lies dead, tied up on her own bed, and I never suspect a thing. *Fuck.* It's a bad movie. It's bullshit. It's a joke. It can't be real. It can't be real. It is real.

Finally I emerge, shaken, gray.

More questions and more and *where will you be staying?* The officer wants to know. *Which friend will you call?* It's now 3:14 in the morning.

The pennies, I should have counted the pennies.

"With me," says a man's familiar voice. "She'll be staying with me."

It's David.

"How did you, when did you?"

"Hold on." He turns to the officer. "You don't need to question her anymore tonight? No? Let me give you my information where you can reach me."

They have mine already and will be in touch within twenty-four hours and then we're left and right down the hallways and out the door; it feels like an escape, but not for Andrea.

I can't, I can't deal, but I turn to David, who is supporting me, and is a miracle. "How?"

"I had a bad feeling about letting you go by yourself and then when you didn't text me . . . You looked so terrible, and anyway, I just thought I'd swing by and that's when I found out . . ." His voice trails away but the rest is clear. *When I found out that Andrea was dead.*

I have no sense of time anymore. It seems to me that no sooner do we get into a cab than we get out because we're here.

David's place is cozy but still elegant. I knew it would be. His bookshelves are overflowing. There are nice touches: little throw rugs on the wooden floors, a black-and-white print of a Parisian café. There are lush plants that, astonishingly, seem to be green and thriving. I have but to look at a houseplant and it withers and dies.

His bedroom is massive. A king-sized bed in the corner, sheets a masculine metallic blue-gray. There's an antique-looking desk and chair in the corner, carved from a dark wood.

"It's Shaker," he says when I ask. Anything to make small talk. "Okay, I'll take the couch," he continues. He actually looks apologetic. "It was a two-bedroom but I made the extra room into kind of an office." He is thorough. "Clean sheets on the bed." A large T-shirt to sleep in, boxers, an extra toothbrush.

My teeth are chattering, but I'm not cold.

"You're in shock. We'll fix that in a minute."

He makes me some tea with honey and lemon and a massive shot of whiskey. We don't talk. I'm grateful. Next to my bed he has placed a glass of water and two white pills. "Take them if necessary."

"Thank you."

"Need anything else? I'll be in the other room." As if I am a child who is scared of the dark.

I'm not scared.

*I'm fucking terrified.*

"David?" He waits in the doorway. I look at him. It was David who ID'd her body. I couldn't do it. I thought I would be able to but I wasn't. Now he stands in the doorway and I try to form the words I need to tell him. "Thank you for this, for this and for everything."

"Don't you dare thank me," he says. He is serious for once. It's strange. "If you need anything, just call. I'm a light sleeper." He leaves the door open, letting in a wedge of hall light. Again I'm grateful, but this time I don't thank him. I wait in the dark till I hear him go to bed.

I lie in the darkness, staring up at the ceiling, the one beam of light stretched across the bed. My thoughts move in barbed-wire circles, and each point is pain.

*He was in the apartment.*

*They found Andrea tied up and gagged in her own bed.*

*This time he made a call.*

*He called the police.*

*A call from our apartment.*

*Lucas is safe with friends.*

*We've tried to reach her family.*

Andrea's answer to any awkward questions was always tight, bright, hard: "It's just us." Never failed to shut people up.

My friends had thought I was crazy: "Why would you willingly live with a kid who's not your own?" "What are you going to do about guys?" "How will you bring them home?" "How will you drink?" "Why would you do *that*?" "What were you thinking? It's going to ruin your life!"

But moving in with Andrea and Lucas didn't ruin my life. Having a kid around made me grow up. I couldn't have wild parties till three a.m. or smoke massive amounts of pot, but then again I never had wild parties till three a.m. and pot just made me hungry and exhausted.

I'd liked Andrea almost immediately. She was smart, tough, and funny. She didn't mince words and you knew where you stood with her. She paid our rent on time, was neat but not obsessively so, and respected my boundaries. But the real truth was that I had fallen in love with Lucas. The moment he looked at me with his large soulful eyes and said, "Yes, I can has a cookie," I was a goner.

He isn't obnoxious or whiny. He doesn't run around the house screaming or crying or throwing temper tantrums. He is a shy, sweet kid. His favorite thing was, still is, to draw—give him some paper and crayons and he will be happy for hours. Andrea is a good mom; she makes it look easy and I know it isn't.

*Andrea*, I think now as I lie in a strange bed, and my mind is flooded.

"Hey, mister," she would say to Lucas, "come over here and pick this up!" Andrea the straight shooter, telling it like it was, but not meanly, never mean. Andrea, who worked hard, Andrea with her back straight and determined. Andrea, who wasn't going to give up. I remember a Sunday night soon after I moved in. I had been watching TV and feeling increasingly melancholy. Andrea had put Lucas to bed and had come through, ostensibly tidying up, but eventually she drifted to the couch and then sat down. Some incredibly bad romantic comedy was playing and I began misting up when the "I loved you the whole time, only I never realized it until you were gone" speech began. I glanced over to make sure Andrea hadn't seen me, and there she was, tears streaming down her cheeks. We both became hysterical and threw cushions at each other, laughing and weeping, and laughing again. Then Andrea had gotten us some ice cream and we had talked until one a.m.

The memory is bright and warm and it had held us together, that and so many other memories, the conversations over glasses of wine and cups of coffee and mugs of tea and bowls of almonds and during picnics and while walking, and most of all it's Lucas I now think of. Lucas's face when he looked up at Andrea, his squealing laughter when she tickled him, his shy delight when she praised his drawings. Lucas, Andrea's heart of hearts. Lucas, who is somewhere in the city now without her, without his fierce loving mother who fought all fires, her strength and her pride lying somewhere in the morgue.

I reach over and take the two white pills, and lie back. It doesn't matter. I won't be able to sleep. I will never sleep again. Here in the dark I'll admit it. I want Sael. I want his warm broad back, the length of him pressed against me. I want him holding me through this terrible night. He came to me when he had bad dreams. I sent him away. I told him we were over and I meant it.

Once again my mind goes back to Andrea. I lie in a strange bed in a strange apartment, waiting for the darkness to overcome me, waiting for the few hours when I will not have to think about Andrea . . .

*I'm going up the stairs in my stepfather's house. There are gales of laughter coming from the living room. Now I have the smoked oysters on a plate—I got some at least. Cherry called me a little girl in front of everyone. She's a bitch, and then Andrea comes toward me wearing a long black dress. She has curved cuts on her arms; there are four in the shape of leaves, with snowflakes in each center. She's wearing small smoky-blue glasses. I can't see her eyes, but she is smiling.*

*"Katherine," she says. She speaks softly. I don't know why her teeth are stained red. I look at her red teeth. "Mr. Nakamaru wanted me to tell you three things. They are very important. The first is that . . ." But as she begins to tell me her voice dissolves into a hissing sound, like radio static.*

*"I can't hear you," I try to tell Andrea. "I can't hear you. Tell me again."*

*She opens her mouth but the static is louder this time and she's moving her lips but I can't hear any words, the static fills my head, white pain will break my eardrums, it's filling my head, Andrea's lips are moving and moving.*

*"I can't hear you!" I scream. "I can't hear you, I can't—"*

"Katherine?" It's David; he's come through and now he turns on the bedside lamp.

I am freezing. I am covered in sweat. *Where am I?* I am in David's bed. *Why?* Because Andrea is dead. Andrea is dead.

"You were calling out," he said.

*I'm fine,* I try to answer, but all that comes out is a watery noise.

"Hey," he says, "hey." He sits down on the bed and he draws me in and against his shoulder and then finally, finally the hot stone in my chest liquefies and the tears come. I sob and sob and sob against his clean warm shirt and he holds me. He doesn't tell me it will be all right; he doesn't try to comfort me; he just holds me as I weep and weep and weep until my eyes are hot pinpricks, until I am a mess of weeping, an ugly mottled thing of grief. I don't want him to stop holding me. Let the world consist of this, please, his arms around me. I look up and he's looking down at me and then, just for a moment in the silence, we both reach across the endless distance and I close my eyes, I feel the warmth of him, his breath and just for a moment his lips, and then he breathes my name. "Katherine."

I can feel the wetness against his cheeks. I peer up at him through my swollen eyes. "You're crying too?"

"Yes," he says. He doesn't make a joke or excuses.

"David?"

"Yes?"

"I slept with Sael."

I have said it. This confession falls from me without effort or weight. My heart is gone; it has spilled out through all the crying. I want nothing in me now. I will not hold anything back or from him. Nothing matters and I want nothing. I am empty. There is nothing now.

I wait for the pressure of his arms to lessen, for him to leave me. Maybe I want his fury, his rage, to feel something other than this grief, this hatred of myself.

"I know."

I turn to him, surprised despite everything. "You knew?"

"Yes."

"How?"

"Well, I've known Sael for a long time now. I know what he's like, what his patterns are. I had hoped at one stage that it was over. You seemed more yourself, but then tonight, when I saw your face as you were looking at him, I knew."

"Why didn't you say anything?"

He looks at me, half smiles, rueful. "Why didn't you?"

Apparently I am *not* yet empty, not yet poured out. More tears leak out of my eyes, my ever-weeping eyes.

"I'm sorry." I mean it with every fiber of my being.

"I know. It's okay." He does not rage or show disgust. He is very gentle with me and this makes it worse. There is no retribution. Only "It's okay."

But it isn't okay. Nothing is okay. Nothing can ever be okay again. And he holds me. I cry; his arms are wet under my face. After an eternity I am all cried out. There are no tears left. I'm as flat as the sheet I lie on.

"David?"

"Yes?"

"Please." It's all I say.

*Please what?*

*Please don't hate me. Please forgive me. Please don't be angry. Please don't leave me tonight.* I want to say all those things but I only get to the "please." I don't have any more words, just "please."

He looks at me and very slowly he turns out the light.

And in the dark he's there. His arms are around me, and for a while I don't have to think about friends, about murder, about death or little boys who must live without their mothers; for just in this moment and place in the dark, for just a little while, I don't have to think about Andrea Bowers, the eleventh victim of the Sickle Man.

HE WEDDING DAY DAWNED ON A bright and shining midsummer morning, and the lady wore a silver mantle laden with pearls sewn with silver thread and wildflowers woven into her golden hair. Upon seeing her, Lord de Villias fell to his knees and said, "My Lady, you outshine the very sun. No damsel in the land can compare with thee." His Lordship was himself decked in the finest array of silken hose and damasks and velvets, and on his heavy ermine-trimmed cloak he wore a brilliant silver and jeweled coiled brooch that glittered and gleamed both in the sunshine and then in the candlelight. There was great celebration, feasting and music made with pipe and with whistle, and golden goblets were raised and raised again and white cake served upon silver plates, and all alike drank deep and well of the ale and wine, which flowed without end.

# 16

It takes ten days for them to return the items they took from the apartment. They were looking for evidence: prints, DNA. I guess they didn't find anything because they're finally giving me back Andrea's stuff in a Ziploc bag.

I am staying at my friend Leigh's place. I'm passed around carefully, like a ticking bomb. I could have remained at David's but I thought that I had trespassed enough. Leigh is away for two weeks with her husband, so this works out. I don't have to make conversation, act like a human being.

I sit on their bed and let the contents of the Ziploc bag fall out. Here on the duvet covers are Andrea's bracelet, Andrea's ring, Andrea's phone. Her bracelet is gold, a charm bracelet, although I guess if we're talking about being charmed it's defunct. Her ring is thin and silver. She always wore it on the middle finger of her left hand. I never asked her about it. Now I'll never know. And finally, the thing that defines all of us, the thing we can't live without, her phone. She had a work phone but this was her personal phone. It has a small crack on the screen but she wouldn't get a new one.

"It still works!" she had protested. "It has character. It will be around forever."

At any rate it outlasted her. I turn it over and see the stickers on the back. It's been decorated by Lucas. There's a small yellow smiley face and a purple monster, also smiling. No wonder she didn't want to throw it away. It does have character and—since they charged it, presumably to search her messages and address book—a full battery life.

There are many messages that she'll never hear. I don't want to listen to those. There's a chance I'll hear my own voice, which always sounds higher than I think it's going to be. I don't want to hear myself talking to a dead woman, don't want to hear myself asking my murdered friend if she'll pick up some household cleaner, or wondering if I should cook dinner for all of us tonight.

But I do want to hear her voice again. I want to hear her laugh.

Andrea had the best laugh I've ever heard. One of those laughs that make the tellers believe that the tales they are telling are hilarious, even if they aren't. I crave her laugh as other people crave drugs or drink.

I see the voice memos app. She was always using it—a habit from law school, perhaps. I'll settle for this; at least this way I'll get to hear her voice, if not her laugh.

There are only five voice memos. The first two are brief, legal stuff, something about some documents, check the McKlean deposition, call Alicia at Vonex Corporation.

The third voice memo turns out to be a shopping list. "Milk," she says, "cottage cheese, dishwashing liquid, apples, toilet paper." There's a pause, then, "Sex toys, whips, chains," but I can hear the smile in her voice. The fourth is another legal note, and then there's the fifth. This one is longer than the others; it's one minute and four seconds rather than the usual thirty seconds. I press play, and Andrea says:

"Katherine?"

I scream and drop the phone on the bed.

The voice is muffled on the recording, but it continues:

"Okay, missy, you wanted me to prove—"

I reach out and press pause. I stare at the phone, at the crack on the front screen. I feel the stickers beneath my fingers. Eternity passes. I take a deep breath in. I let it out. The silence is deafening. Her phone lies on the duvet, waiting, waiting.

*C'mon, you chickenshit,* I think to myself, *c'mon.* I summon up all my will. I hit play.

"Katherine? Okay, missy, you wanted me to prove that you talk in your sleep. Here it is."

Her voice is low; she sounds amused.

"Date: Saturday the ninth. Time: 12:15 a.m. Location: outside your bedroom: Why? Because a certain someone said that she never talked in her sleep and then a certain other person had to go to the bathroom and realized it was an opportune moment." She snorts, pauses, then, "Okay, back to the business at hand. Listen closely."

In the darkness of Leigh's bedroom, I close my eyes and listen.

There's a voice, a female voice. It's very faint. I can barely hear it. It must be coming from behind my closed door and now through this machine back to me. I hold the phone, press it tightly against my ear. Then I hear it.

"Thanks, I'm just waiting for my date."

Pause.

"Well, okay then . . . not too strong."

Another pause, I think it's over, and then, shockingly, giggles. It's a light flirtatious sound.

" . . . I bet you say that to all the girls."

A long silence, then it's Andrea again. She is trying to keep her voice down, but it's hard to whisper triumphantly. "You owe me a drink. Case closed!"

There's another pause and I think she's turned it off when she says, more to herself than to me, "Jesus, I really need to get laid."

And finally, the sound I've been craving: a brief, rueful, honest laugh.

*Click.*

The recording is over.

I lie in the dark. It's a warm night but I am cold. I press play and listen again to the whole thing. Then I try to fast-forward it, but my thumb slips and I go too far.

" . . . because other people have to go to the bathroom . . ."

I rewind and there it is:

" . . . Date: Saturday the ninth. Time: 12:15 a.m. Location . . ."

I pause it. *Saturday the ninth around midnight. Saturday the ninth* . . . I snap upright. I throw back the covers.

I run but barely make it to the toilet.

Finally I press my cheek against the cool floor. *Saturday the ninth. Time: 12:15 a.m.* My head throbs and throbs; bile burns my throat. I want to lie here forever. I don't want to get up. *Saturday the ninth at 12:15 a.m.* Maybe I will never get up. How can I ever go home?

On Saturday the ninth at 12:15 a.m., I wasn't in my bedroom.

I was at Liz's bachelorette party. I think about that poor male stripper she hired and all of us, drunk and raucous. The guy barely made it out of there in one piece. Liz laughed so hard I thought she was going to wet herself.

Whatever voice Andrea heard in my bedroom, whatever voice she recorded, whatever voice that was speaking . . .

It wasn't mine.

# 17

The Sotriakis Funeral Home is a pale gray brick square with a low, flat roof. Apparently the circle of life stops here. Maybe circles are too confusing. With flat lines and angles you know there's an ending; you know what you're getting.

You get out of the taxi and walk through the small but serviceable parking lot. The funeral home offers the only private parking lot in the area and Greg Sotriakis is proud of this. He's also proud that it's been in the family for three generations. Both of these important facts are on his website, which his nephew made. Still, it's not enough, not bringing in traffic, and his business is, as most people would say, "dying." (Greg Sotriakis wouldn't say this, though, because he hates puns, the death ones especially.) It's impossible to fight against these corporations. That's why he was so excited to get the call. A victim from the Sickle Man—of course God knows it's terrible, especially because everyone thought the whole business was behind them, but still. Andrea Bowers, the Sickle Man's newest victim, and a mother too.

Greg is planning on a crowd, has told Janet, his long-suffering wife, to put in extra seats in the blue room. He could understand not having an open casket but had to swallow his disappointment.

Well, yes. Although Maria had done her best after the forensic department. Now he's preparing for the deceased's friends, the curious, the onlookers, and a few reporters. Just needs some decent shots of the place, a reporter standing outside with his home in the background, maybe even an interview.

*It's a Tragic Day*, they'll say, *here at the Sotriakis Funeral Home* . . . with him looking respectful, somber, shaking his head. *A terrible loss.* And then there will be a flawless service so that people can say it was a beautiful tribute to her memory, and think about their own aging parents, think how, yes, this is a day that counts. So he's standing in the doorway, gazing at the half-filled parking lot and wondering why there aren't more people, more trucks, more reporters.

Katherine has asked for a private funeral, "out of respect for the family's wishes." By "family" she means Lucas; she can only imagine how reporters and flashing lights and cameras might further affect him. The hungry stares of onlookers, the gawking, the comments, the needless attention. And so she begged for privacy, and people listened.

They listened because this time it was a single mother. They obeyed because they are beaten. They had thought it was over; they had thought you were dead. They ran rejoicing through the rain, dancing and singing, and woke up hungover to the headlines.

A public defender. A single mother. A four-year-old son.

Andrea Bowers was thirty-five; she had a child. She didn't fit the profile. The mayor will have to resign over this one; the police cannot be trusted. There is talk of rioting, of marches. It is advisable to leave town. No one can be trusted. Everyone is alone. Everyone is vulnerable. The rain is over. And the heat is rising again. The humidity is off the charts.

You have broken the pattern of your hunt and now there is nothing to hold on to, no rules, no guarantees. All the voyeuristic exhilaration, the sick excitement that might have come in the beginning deep in the darkest heart, has turned, because this is not a movie. There will be no happy ending. The city is sick of this sickness. It wants to cut the cancer out. It is weary and defeated and done. It will listen to Katherine's plea for mercy because it longs for mercy too.

Today the living wear white ribbons—white, a symbol of peace, a symbol of hope, and the people need hope.

If only they knew your true purpose, that these women are not victims but martyrs. That each one sacrificed saves millions. They will never know.

You walk up to where Greg Sotriakis is standing. "Terrible loss" you murmur, echoing the words of his fantasy interview.

Greg must swallow hard, swallow his disappointment, and agree, "Yes, yes, it is," because you're a good-looking man in a dark Armani suit and maybe you'll still have grandparents or at least one, if not two living parents, and you look like you have money and could afford to spring for the Copper Deluxe.

If he only knew that you've sent him some business already.

You enter the family-run funeral home. You spend so little time in places of the dead. You are a creature of the living, and of life. Still, you intend to enjoy it, now that you're here.

The funeral home's carpeting is tan and its walls are beige. Low ceilings, low chairs, air freshener. It even smells neutral. In the main waiting room, friends and family sit on couches with slippery cushions. Some check their phones; some stare into space. They stare at vague prints of barns and fields. The tepid watercolors are the opposite of suffering. There is no pain here, no emotion of any kind.

On a nondescript couch is parked a nondescript woman, solid, squat, and knitting. A little boy in a too-big suit is planted next to her, legs swaying, kicking.

The living do not often think about the dead. The memories of their loved ones come at unexpected moments: driving, washing vegetables, seeing an advertisement. *Oh yes! Oh yes.* Now they think about themselves, their own mortality, their own loved ones, their parents.

*Jesus, Mom's getting old. I'm getting old. When did I get so old?*

*I'd rather go fast, maybe a brain aneurysm, than lie about, suffering, shitting myself. The smell of hospitals, nurses being patient, I don't think I could take it.*

*I want to go home and fuck and fuck and fuck. I want to feel alive.*

*I wonder how much a funeral director makes?*

Anxiety, sadness, arousal. Their colors blaze up, and you inhale. Delicious.

"Kat! Kat!" The little boy in the too-big suit is on his feet and calling. The squashed woman next to him drops a stitch in her knitting. She puts out a restraining hand, opens her mouth to admonish, but she is too late.

He runs toward your darling, your beloved, who has entered the room. She's dropped to her knees, her arms spread wide, and he rushes into them and for the first time in days and days and days he knows that he is safe.

She has lost even more weight in this last week and wears a thin black dress, low-heeled shoes. Her eyes though red-rimmed were dry, but now once again the tears are coming. She squeezes her lids tight but the tears come anyway, running into his hair.

"Oh, Lucas, oh, honey, oh, honey, oh, hon," she murmurs, crumbling words of comfort into his curls.

Comfort is a warm brown, the color of a nest, it feels like a faded leather couch, a cool hand on your feverish forehead, it melts like mashed potatoes, it simmers like chicken soup, it sounds like the rain when you are under a tent of blankets and safe, safe, safe indoors.

They are caught and safe and sound in this moment, sheltered in each other's arms. The squat woman has risen to come and stand nearby. Now she coughs dryly, indicating that this embrace has gone on long enough. Katherine peers up, blinking, as if coming out of a dream. She fumbles for a smile; the woman returns it briefly.

Since Lucas is not ready to leave the safety of her arms, Katherine hoists him up. His weight snugly tucked into her hip, as if she'd been doing this for years.

She's giving her credentials. "I'm Katherine Emerson, Andrea's roommate and friend."

"Cheryl Kaskow. I'm from social services, and Lucas's assigned temporary guardian throughout this stage of the process. Nice to meet you," Mrs. Kaskow adds, although from her expression, it clearly isn't.

"The process." Katherine tries not to wince.

You know that they cannot find Andrea's will. It's unbelievable yet true. Hours online and on the phone and it all comes down to "during our recent move it must have been misplaced." The state has had to step in to appoint a guardian, a person willing to take on the responsibility of a bewildered four-year-old.

Katherine, still carrying Lucas, follows Mrs. Kaskow to the slippery noncommittal chairs, the unwelcoming shiny sateen. She sits, with him in her lap. He turns and snuggles up as best he can, presses his face into her neck, her chest. Mrs. Kaskow's lips tighten but she says nothing.

As Kat talks he can feel the rumble of her voice coming through her chest. It makes her real and safe.

You whisper his name without using your voice.

He twists around, looks up, sees you standing there. Near the other man, by the doorway. This alerts Katherine and Mrs. Kaskow, who look in your direction. They have seen you both, tall, good-looking men, nice suits, standing respectful and quiet. They wait for both of you to approach. Katherine's jaw clenches; a tiny vein throbs. She smells of apprehension, which clanks of empty ovens and roars like a plane preparing for takeoff. Only you notice.

"Lucas, do you remember my friends?"

Lucas, staring, barely nods.

Mrs. Kaskow has taken note of the word "friends," and is forming her own opinions about the flighty nature of young women these days.

You both step forward, a half step really. You murmur something and partially retreat. You do not speak to the other man, nor he to you. There's nothing left to say.

Lucas watches you across the room. Or rather, he is looking at the space just behind you. Looking at the specters who surround you like clouds of moths rising up after long-stored clothes have been shaken out. Insubstantial and fluttering, unable to do any harm.

They are shadows. They will remain here as long as you remain here because you now possess their souls. Once you take a sacred color, she is bound to you. It's a necessary evil, part of the job, just as a tailor might be covered with the threads and shreds of the fabric he snips and tears and cuts. Not many realize that mortality is a gift.

They hate you but they have no substance, no weight; they are less irritating than mosquitoes because they cannot draw blood; they have no way to seek revenge. You have grown so used to their presence that you often forget them, just as in time their mortal selves will be forgotten completely.

But not by Lucas, who watches, who listens. You idly wonder if he can see his mother too. You wonder if she's here today.

Her death was really his fault. You knew it the moment you met him in the park. His cryptic little messages and notes and strange behavior were causing concern, and a good mother watches, a good mother listens, a good mother knows. She was smart. She was putting two and two together. What if she had said something to your beloved? Your beloved couldn't be disturbed just when she's on the cusp, when she is so close to turning red. It's a pity that she must lose her friend, but it had to happen. *Sometimes to make an omelet*... Isn't that how the saying goes?

You knew that once the mother was gone, the son would go too. You told her as much the day you harvested her rage. And he will be kept away from your darling heart, because material things in this material world have a way of working out in your favor. Documents disappear, names are forgotten, pens run dry, fires spark, electricity dies, lights blow fans still, wires wear thin, lines go dead, calls are dropped, glass breaks, ice thaws, hell freezes over.

Odd how this always happens when you're around; then again you find it's the little things that matter. Like the little boy who stares up at you now. He's been watching you as you watched him. Watching you and the other man too. Watching as you both stare at Katherine with hunger, but the other man's hunger is mortal and yours is not. One of these things is not like the other.

You give Lucas a very special smile, one that only he can see. *I can see you too.*

Katherine notices his thumb in his mouth. "Honey, where's your rabbit's foot?" He gives no reply.

She turns and looks at the older woman. "He has a rabbit's foot key chain. Bright green?" She's trying to keep her voice calm, trying not to accuse, just making an observation.

"Oh?" Mrs. Kaskow gives a halfhearted shrug, a cold smile. She hasn't seen it.

Mrs. Kaskow is well intentioned, but she lacks imagination. That is a dangerous combination. She has seen kids come and she has seen kids go and they will never be hers and that's fine because she never wanted her own. It's best not to get too attached because then you get hurt and she knows how not to get hurt because she's had a lot of practice over the years.

Repression is a steel gray, the color of filing cabinets, it smells like an unaired apartment, it smells like souring milk, it creaks like a door opening slowly in the night, it sounds like a key being turned in a lock, it tastes like blood from a bitten lip.

There, down by her uncle's pool a million years ago, Mrs. Kaskow lost the taste for imagination or empathy or joy. So she is content to be of use, and be practical and purposeful, and the decor here suits her, right down to the tan carpeted ground underneath her sensible-heeled feet. She goes by the book. She plays by the rules.

Katherine begins to say something and stops. Not wishing to make trouble, she turns the conversation back to a safer place.

And now Greg Sotriakis, having assessed with some disgust that "yes, this is it, this is the showing," asks all the visitors if they would like to follow him to the adjoining room for the service. Everyone gets up quickly, happy to be moving, to be doing something before sitting again. No one wants to be alone with their thoughts for too long.

Mrs. Kaskow and Lucas and Katherine get up too. He's off Katherine's lap but still determinedly holding her hand. The warmth of her hand gives him a small modicum of strength, and as they leave he looks back, and since there's no one else in the room you show your real self for just a moment, just in case he decides to try and tell Katherine anything else.

Just so he knows that you're around.

It's the self his mother saw on the day you came to visit her. And then you fold it away, put the mask on once again.

He turns fast, stumbles, and grips her hand.

*Two nights ago he wakes up and Momma is sitting on the bed, looking at him. Mrs. Kaskow tells him Momma is past, but she is not past, she is here, because she is sitting on his bed, looking at him with so much love in her eyes that he wants to cry out—*

MOMMA!

*—but she shakes her head and puts her finger to her lips, be quiet, so he will not wake Mrs. Kaskow, so he asks in a soft whisper voice if she is hurted and she shakes her head, no, and he asks if she is still dead like*

*the Halloween ladies and she nods her head, yes, and he wants her to hug him—why doesn't she hug him?*

*But she shakes her head and she is pointing and he knows what she wants, what she is pointing to, and he is sad and he doesn't want to but Momma looks at him and looks at him and he knows it is important, so very slowly he puts it down next to the bed and he lies back and closes his eyes and his cheeks are wet but he isn't crying, because he is a big boy and big boys don't cry so he isn't crying, and then he feels Momma lean over him, he feels her soft lips on his cheek in a kiss like she always kisses him good night, and he feels not so sad and he keeps his eyes closed.*

*And when they open it is morning and he looks and his lucky green rabbit foot is gone, but he never tells no one because it is a secret.*

# 18

Hours later in the dark, we lie in a sweating, panting heap.

Then I tell him to get off me.

"Katherine."

"Now." I give him a shove and maneuver myself, lying as far away from him as I can along the side of the bed. I can sense him lying there, not saying anything. I can hear him breathing. I hate him, almost more than I hate myself.

It was seeing Lucas go. Walking away with that woman, his small hand engulfed in her shovel-like one. Trying to turn around. His eyes wide, wondering why he was walking in the wrong direction, getting into the wrong car, instead of coming with me.

And Sael is there, and all it takes is a nod. A nod and we go back to Leigh's place.

Once inside, he follows me to my room. The guest room, gray and white and minimal—there's nothing personal. Which suits me.

I turn out the light. I don't want to see him. In the darkness we take off our clothes, not seductively but businesslike, as I do when I'm alone, and then I drag him down onto the bed.

And briefly Lucas's eyes are not in my mind.

Now I tell this man on the side of the bed, breathing, "Please go."

"Katherine."

"I mean it."

"I will," he says, "but I need to tell you something."

"I don't want to hear it."

"It's a final story."

"No."

"One last story, and then I swear you'll never have to see me again."

I don't say anything. I close my eyes and wait for him to tell it and be done and get out.

He takes a huge breath, like he's about to dive into a swimming pool. "I met Sara in college. It was through David—I mean David was sort of hanging out with this girl Rebecca, and she and Sara were friends. That's how I met her."

So it's about Sara. I'm disappointed; it's going to be a "the thing about my wife" kind of story. How clichéd.

"Anyway, we hooked up at a party, and pretty much started going out soon afterward. It was easy; she was beautiful and smart and we had the same group of friends. I guess the relationship kind of fell into my lap. A no-brainer. Everyone expected us to get married after she graduated.

He pauses now. "Only thing was that there was this little voice in my head. And it would say: *You don't love her.* I would sort of push this voice down but occasionally I'd hear it, at odd moments, sometimes I'd be running or at the computer or just grabbing a cup of coffee and the voice would say: *You don't love her.*

"But time was passing, she graduated, my business was beginning to take off, and the summers became filled with weddings and everyone started looking at us. I know women have it worse. I can't imagine what they might have said to her."

*I'll bet*, I think, but I don't say it. I'm listening now.

"I remember this one horrible bitch at some drink party at her law firm saying, 'So when *are* you getting married?' As if it was any of her damned business. But Sara was pretty feisty. She'd said, 'I don't know. When was the last orgasm you had with your husband?' "

I can hear his grin in the dark. Against my will I start to like her, his feisty dead fiancée.

"But it got me thinking. So I organized this weekend in San Francisco and at this restaurant overlooking the harbor—you know, one of the ones with Chinese lanterns and waiters who tell you every detail about your meal, that kind of thing. I took out a ring and got down on one knee and Sara started to cry."

He falls silent for so long that I think it's the end of the story. I turn over, and take a breath to say, *Thank you, that was lovely, now please get out—*

When he says, low, "She didn't stop crying. She was crying so hard that she couldn't even talk. Eventually I had to get up and pay really fast and get her out. The worst thing about it, looking back, is how embarrassed I was. That I cared more about what people thought than why Sara was crying so much. Maybe that should have been a red flag.

"We got back to the hotel we were staying at and eventually she calmed down enough to talk. I was furious. I was yelling. 'What the hell is wrong with you?' She didn't answer so I said, 'I thought that's what you wanted.' She turned to me and she said, 'Yes, but—' "

My voice startles us both. " 'But it's not what *you* want.' "

Sael sounds rueful. "Yeah, that's pretty much exactly what she said." Then he sighs. "That would have been the moment to talk about it. Right then and there. That was the moment. But I didn't. I guess I have to live with knowing that for the rest of my life."

I don't like the sound of this. Not just what he's saying, but the way his voice is regretful yet just like he's stating the facts. Somehow it's worse than if he were being dramatic.

Sael takes a deep breath and continues. He's strained but making an effort now. "Of course, I wouldn't take no for an answer."

"Wow. Really?" He ignores my sarcasm. Just as well. I'm shaken. I don't really mean it but I'm scared to hear what he might tell me.

"So I went about convincing her. It took a year and a half but I wore her down. She'd been doing it for me, after all, I guess. The next time I proposed she said yes and that was that.

"Everyone was thrilled. Everyone said, *It's about time!* Fuck, people are stupid. At least Sara was happy, though. She was happy. I had convinced her and she really loved me." He says this without self-consciousness. "She was up to her ears in wedding plans and I was content to let her do everything. I was working hard, building a business. I had a million excuses. Of course, I was hiding out."

Hiding out. I take a moment to look around the room. I guess I can relate.

"It was the vows that got me. Sara had a thing about those stupid vows. I can see her now, hair up in a pony, big T-shirt, looking at me, saying, 'I don't want to bug you, babe, but how's it going with the vows? Have you started your vows yet? How are they coming along?' "

I roll back to look at him. His voice is rising but I don't think he's aware of this.

"Finally I had to. We were going to practice with David the next day. He was going to officiate.

"So I sat down. I couldn't think of what to say. I was staring at a blank screen. Writer's block. So I thought, *I'll start by writing about how we met.* So I did that. Then it got a little easier and

I kept writing, and I wrote and I wrote and I wrote. I had gotten into a kind of zone, I guess, and I couldn't stop. It was like coding. Then my phone rang and I looked up. I had been sitting there for three hours."

Even now, three years later, telling this story in a dark bedroom, he sounds genuinely amazed.

"I got up and took the call; then I ran out, went to the gym, picked up some milk, that type of shit. When I got back I saw there was a blue Post-it note from Sara on my computer screen."

Now he's slowed down. Against my will, I'm listening.

"She loved those damned Post-its. She was using them to coordinate the wedding. They were all over the apartment like insane neon butterflies. So I read it. It was only three words."

"What does it say?" I'm thinking *"I love you."*

" 'We should talk.' "

I don't say anything but I grimace.

Sael seems to sense this because he answers just as if I had said something.

"Yeah, it's the universal way of saying, 'You're in deep shit.' So I plopped down at my computer to read over my vow essay. It starts well, but as I keep reading . . ."

"It was bad?"

"Worse. It was honest, but brutally honest. Like, how I loved her but I wasn't in love with her and how I felt like a fraud and a shit and I didn't know what to do. The ultimate Dear John. And you want to know what the worst thing was?"

Why do I always end up feeling sorry for Sael's women? "There's a *worse* thing?"

I can feel the bed rock. His shoulders are shaking. He's weeping. But then his head goes up. And I see that he's laughing now.

"She had fucking corrected it!"

"What?"

"Yeah, she had edited it, put in punctuation, everything. The man she's going to marry in under three weeks has just written a long, insanely cruel letter saying that he doesn't love her, and she corrects his punctuation and his grammar."

There is something so fantastically ballsy and classy about this that despite everything we are briefly united in mutual admiration. "She sounds amazing."

"She was."

"What did you do?"

"I went in there and talked with her."

"You did?"

He laughs. The sound of his self-disgust is awful. "Of course not. I went right back out and got shit-faced at a dive bar."

"Oh."

"Yeah," he says matter-of-factly and with some relish. "This is the story where you find out that I'm a useless, cowardly, pathetic, sack-of-shit excuse for a human being." He pauses. "Well, you think that anyway, but this is the proof.

"I can't remember how I got home. I passed out on the couch. When I woke it was morning. I went to our bedroom, feeling like death, but she wasn't there. For a moment I thought, *Well, that's it, she's left me.* Then I realized that day was her early-morning yoga class. I'd dodged another bullet.

"I spent most of the morning throwing up. The curse of cheap beer, crappy vodka. Lay on the bed with my eyes closed, going in and out of sleep. Waiting for Sara, waiting for her to come home.

"My phone rang at about quarter to twelve."

He falls quiet.

I wait.

Finally he says, so low that I barely hear him, "Do you know what my first thought was when they told me that Sara had been hit by a car?"

I don't think I want to hear this. I say nothing. It doesn't matter. He's going to tell me.

"I thought, *Thank God.*" His voice is horribly flat. "I thought, *Thank God*, because, Katherine, I dodged a bullet. *Thank God* that my fiancée was dead. *Thank God* because we wouldn't be having 'the talk' after all."

From outside I can hear the clank of a truck driving over a pothole. The air conditioner humming.

"Her mother wouldn't stop hugging me. Her father was crying and crying. He said, 'No matter what happens, Sael, you'll always be a son to me.'"

I turn to him, to Sael. In the fuzzy light of this New York bedroom I can see that tears are streaming down his cheeks. He makes no move to wipe them away.

After a moment he coughs, sniffs. "I decided then that I would never, ever let myself be in a serious relationship again. Sex was fine. *Flings* were fine. But love, or marriage? That was done. I thought maybe I was emotionally dead. There had to be something wrong with me. I think women felt it too. Most of them knew what the deal was—they didn't push."

I think of Andrea talking about this kind of man. *You don't want to be around him when the fuse burns down.*

"Then I met you. Jesus. I was so pissed with you for pulling that stunt . . ." His voice trails off. "But I was intrigued. I felt awake somehow for the first time in years.

"Anyway, when David introduced you as a girl he was seeing, I thought, *Well, that's that.* I was determined to walk away, to have nothing more to do with you. You know how well that turned out."

I say nothing. I don't know what to say.

"And after we slept together, I thought I'd gotten you out of my system. That it was all about the chase. But it wasn't.

"When I found out that David was seeing you again I wanted

to kill him. I couldn't sleep. I couldn't eat. And you wouldn't see me. I guess I went a little crazy."

I think of him standing on the fire escape. The glow of my phone.

Let me in

"I wanted to hurt you as badly as you had hurt me. I invited Margot to the gala—I knew you'd be there. It was stupid. When I saw you I knew it wasn't going to work. Then when you left I felt worse and worse. Then when I found out—" His voice breaks, cracks. "Oh God. When I found out that that fucking monster was in your apartment. He killed Andrea. I thought, *Oh my God, he could have killed Katherine.*

He swallows. "I thought, *She would have never known.*" He takes a breath "I thought, *I would have never have gotten to tell her.*"

He turns to face me fully. For the first time he looks at me, really looks at me and I see that his struggle is over. There is no anguish, doubt, or uncertainty in his eyes. His voice is calm and quiet.

"Katherine, I love you. I loved you from the first moment I saw you. I love you. I will always love you."

Then he reaches out to me. He reaches out through the dark to me and I think that maybe this is what love is. This hope, this belief, this reaching out, reaching understanding that the other person might never reach back.

But I do.

FTER THE CELEBRATIONS HAD GONE on for a great while, Sir August's new bride said she would retire. It was her wedding night, and she alone wished to prepare for it so although her ladies protested she bade them all a good night and made her way up to the chamber. And there, placed upon a table and covered in a silken cloth, was a golden goblet inlaid with ruby and pearl, and the bride knew this for a sign.

She thought back to a day not long ago when she and some of her retinue had been picnicking in a forest clearing. They had been laughing and braiding posies in one another's hair when an old hag clothed in pitiful rags, with a lame gait and a stiff clawed hand, had slowly approached them. The hag called out in a cracked, high voice, "May I see the one among you who is to be married to the lord? For I have heard many tales of her beauty and honor, and wish to pay my respects."

The lady's maids were much afraid of the hag, for she was spotted with age and bent and ugly, but the lady herself was brave and true of heart and so she bade her come near. The hag praised both her beauty and gentle ways, and said, "I wish to speak with you, my sweet. May I beg for a private audience?"

Some of the maids protested, fearing for their mistress's safety, but the lady believed only in the goodness of others and so gathered her gown and arose, and they walked a little until they reached a shadowed place where the trees had grown thick together. Then the old woman said, "I would like to give you a gift for your wedding day, which I hear is close at hand."

The lady blushed and made protest but the crone smiled and handed her a small parcel of grubby cloth secured with string saying, "When you are quite alone upon your wedding night, mix these herbs into your cup and say the words I am about to give you, and then drink. You will bear three sons directly, handsome of visage and noble of deed. Only tell no one for this must be done in secret. Men do not always understand such things, and if Lord de Villias should find out, he might claim that it is witchcraft."

The hag whispered the words into the lady's ear, three times so that she would remember. Then the lady thanked her kindly for her gift, and the old woman turned and disappeared into the depths of the forest. The lady hid the small parcel in the band of her skirts and, as bidden, told no one of what had passed.

# Part *Two*

# 19

For you, refrigerators are places where small leftovers go to die. You wonder how long mayonnaise can last, or a half jar of Dijon mustard. You love a good mustard, a condiment that bites back, that puts up a fight. There's the seventh girl's hot sauce. You took that from her fridge. She liked her food hot and spicy. That was one of the lines she had used on you. She had read somewhere in a magazine that men will take a subliminal hint, believing that if a woman says "spicy" she will be good in bed. *I love it so much I even put it on my Greek yogurt in the mornings.*

Somehow these small bottles make the fridge look more human. You smile. More human—oh, you are hilarious.

You pour the rest of the milk down the sink. There is something amazingly decadent about this. The milk had another three days and then some, but you'll be gone and you won't be coming back. At least not for a while, and not to this place. Or, in fact, this time.

You make sure all the dishes are clean and put away. Stacks of dirty dishes are so clichéd. There is no need to attract roaches. Not that you mind them, but others might. You are the sensitive type. You appreciate others' needs.

You move through to the bathroom to pack your toiletries. Humans are so productive even in their dullest moments: their sweat, their plaque, their filth. Many are ashamed of their uncooperative bodies, their smells and wastes, but it is all life and so it should be celebrated. To pack your toiletries and to unpack the last of your souvenirs, taking and spreading as you go.

Here in the bathroom you place a candle. Light pink, it was given out at a baby shower. The woman's sister said she would call when she was getting labor pains and everyone should light them and send her good vibes. The candle is light pink because her sister was pregnant with a little girl. *To each her own*, the fifth girl supposed, and she kept it ready to light when she got the call.

Judgment is navy blue, it has the faint punch of mothballs, it feels like the lapel of a blazer, it sounds like the tear of thin plastic around a packet of papers, it tingles like mint dental floss.

The call came two days after her body was found. Snuffed out. The daughter will be given the dead woman's name. A burden as heavy as a gravestone. The little girl will grow to love her mother's murdered sister, to consider her the best aunt of all. Fantasize about how she could have gone and stayed at her aunt's apartment in the city, about what would have been.

You take a toothbrush. The toothbrush is white with a green strip down the handle. It feels good in your hand. You keep her toothbrush in the little cupboard above the sink behind the moisturizers and the pill bottles. The eighth girl had a thing about people's breath. She said most men had meaty breath. You didn't. It was one of the many things that she liked about you. She had a toothbrush at home and a toothbrush at her office. Ironically, gum made her feel a little nauseated and also she hated the sound of it being chewed. She remembered reading about misophonia for the first time and feeling triumphant that there were others who hated these noises as she hated them. You told her you had it too. You bonded over this.

She also liked to have her hair pulled. She liked sex but hated the noises of sex. The thick sound of a tongue in her ear and a man's heavy panting drove her crazy with disgust.

Obsession is neon lime, it niggles like a popcorn kernel stuck in your back molar, it whines like a mosquito in the dark, it flakes like gnawed cuticles, it smells like hand sanitizer.

You've seeded this apartment with their items. You let the stories grow. The single wineglass that stands apart; the mug bearing the name of a city you never visited, that someone else chipped; a button on the desk; a box of ancient peppermints; a ticket stub for a movie you never saw in your wallet. Once you threaded other laces into your own sneakers. Women's laces and men's laces look much the same in this regard.

These things are flourishing in their new environment. It becomes a game. To write with a pen that was never yours on Post-its originally bought for another's desk. You open the freezer to see the bag of stolen frozen raspberries at the very back, behind the frozen peas. You've stirred a pot with a wooden spoon well worn from stirring the Bolognese another dead girl loved to make.

You feed books to the bookshelf. From a slim volume of unread poetry to a well-thumbed romance, a secret favorite of the tough and funny feminist producer from Chicago. You wonder if her friends ever knew she read such things. Now they'll never know.

There are the more obvious things, a pair of woman's socks in the sock drawer, an earring amid the this and the that. Who will adopt your plants? Will they notice the bracelet winking at the bottom of the fleshy leaves, or the tiny china ornament that belonged to a dead girl's grandmother tucked into the soil? The grandmother and her granddaughter now both dead, leaving only her mother behind to curse at the sunny, sunny days ahead of her in her bitterly long life.

It is a treasure hunt but in reverse, a multitude of hints and glints and gleams. Each object, used often but hardly thought about, certainly never intended as a symbolic beacon shining out to a uniformed authority. The tiny pillow of lavender, by now almost scentless, at the very back of your drawer. An umbrella hanging behind the door. It has been a challenge slipping these little objets d'art, the opposite of talking points, into this apartment so bright and clean, wood and cream. They are hiding points. They are relics of the dead used as a living tribute, if you think about it in a certain light.

You do.

Quantity over quality is often how men pack. Not you. You pack with care, although you will not be coming back. Still, it's nice to fold and see what fits where. There is something lovely and sad about folding clothes into a suitcase. Jeans and shorts, T-shirts, one or two nice shirts, swimming trunks, boxer briefs, and two pairs of socks, for hiking perhaps.

You'll leave the air conditioner on. It's expensive but you know the people who will eventually enter this place will appreciate it. After all, your Ride probably won't be paying the bill, and it's the little things that count. People don't appreciate the little things enough until they're gone. The cool air, the clean dishes neatly stacked. It will take some time for them to find the objects, if they ever do find all of them. Luckily, you have left them little notes, cryptic clues. That will give them days and weeks and months of argument and analysis but still, possibly, no answers.

The suitcase packed. The appliances unplugged. The fridge basically empty. The floors swept. The dishes put away. The mail on hold. The lights turned out.

On your way out the door you turn back for one last look. This apartment, it had a nice view. You took pride in your decorating skills. You hope Katherine appreciated them when she was here.

And then you close the door.

For a time, you ate the world. For a time you took the city's heart. You held it hot and close against your own.

Well, the countryside will be nice too.

# 20

I'm listening to the *brr, brr* of the telephone.

*Brr, brr.*

*Brr, brr.*

"Hello?"

"Hi, Cheryl, it's Katherine speaking. How are you?"

"Hi, Katherine." She's wary.

"Could I speak with Lucas?"

"Lucas is out right now."

"Oh," I say. I wait for her to tell me where he is or when he'll be back but she doesn't.

"Is there something you were calling about? Some message I can give him?"

I clear my throat. *None of your business.* This feels strange. "I was just calling to tell him that I'll be going away for two weeks and not to worry, that I'll call him as soon as I get there."

"You're leaving?"

*Is she relieved?* "Just for two weeks."

"I think that will be good for you, given the circumstances."

"Well, I—"

"Actually, I think this might be a good thing for everyone."

"I'm sorry?"

"I didn't know how to mention it, but I was growing a little concerned with these calls."

"Concerned?" *Oh no.*

"I've been worried about the effect they're having on Lucas."

"What effect?"

"He gets very quiet afterward, won't eat, won't talk. It can take hours for him to calm down."

"I see." *Oh my God.*

"I hope you don't mind me telling you this—"

"Not at all."

"I'm sure we all just want what's best for him."

*Sure you do.* "Of course . . ."

"Why don't you call in a couple days, once you settle in? Just give him a little break."

*It's not you, it's me.* "Oh okay." My voice is faint.

"So where are you off to?" She's determinedly cheerful now that the uncomfortable problem of Lucas's dead mother's friend has been dealt with.

"Vermont."

"I hear Vermont is beautiful this time of year." She's all sweetness and light. I say nothing, so she continues. "Will you be going by yourself?

"I'm going with a friend."

"Well, that's nice. The city can be so terrible in summer, and especially now, what with . . ."

"Yes."

"Well, I'll be sure to tell Lucas you called to say good-bye."

*You'd like it if I said good-bye forever.* "Thank you," I say, "and—"

"You take care now, enjoy your vacation!" *Click.*

"—tell him I send my love," I say to no one.

We have decided to go for two weeks. Two weeks away from the media and the police and the public, the intrigue and speculation and conspiracy theories and burning curiosity, because there's something stigmatizing about my story, something sordid, the headlines, and most of all the memories. Two weeks away from the city frying, the sun soaking through and sizzling the cement. The city has turned ugly now, snarling. Before we were all together, united against something, but then a mistake was made, it was the wrong guy, another woman is dead, and things fell apart.

Now we realize the nightmare is not over; it will never be over; no one is safe, no one, no one. The police have lost our trust and then some. It could be anyone. Everyone is suspect, a suspect.

Two weeks. I asked for leave from my temp job. They gave it. I was only filling in anyway. They found someone else. They understand that I have to get away from

**THE GIRL WHO GOT AWAY.**

Two weeks spared from

**SPARED FROM THE SICKLE MAN.**

"Are you going to sell your story?" Only Megan is brave enough, awful enough, to ask me. She sighs when I tell her no. It isn't my story, it's Andrea's story, and Andrea is dead and my story is only an experience steeped in her blood.

Now people are leaving, fleeing, flying, running. We're two of them.

*We need to be able to contact you*, say the police. *As long as we can contact you.*

"Sounds like a good idea," says Sasha. "I'd leave too if I could."

"Wait, who is this guy? What's his story?" Liz wants to know. "I thought you were with David."

David and I went for coffee. It was early in the afternoon. Around four, a strange time, we couldn't find a place that suited so we settled on a diner and ordered coffee. We sat and made a little small talk. Then, at last, I told him. I choked over the words but I got them out somehow. I couldn't look at him while I said it. Then at last I looked up.

He was silent for a long time, his face a mask. Some music played, something from the sixties.

"I know that Sael told you but I wanted to tell you myself and to tell you how sorry I am."

"That's all you have to say?"

"Yes."

"Okay. In that case, here's what I have to say," he said, and his voice was gentle, and quiet and utterly deliberate. "Please understand that I don't want to see you or hear from you or be contacted by either one of you ever again." He looked at me unsmiling and calm. "Do I make myself clear?"

I was trembling. "Yes," I said.

He quietly stood up, put some money on the table, and walked out.

I sat there. Songs played. Beads of water formed and fell down the side of the glass.

"Will that be all?" asked the waiter.

"Yes," I told him, "I think that will be all."

It's been harder for Sael. I haven't asked him what was said; I haven't dared. It is the one thing we don't talk about.

Now I say, "It feels like we're running away."

And Sael says, "We are."

Everyone wants me gone, and not just Cheryl Kaskow. Grief is a burden. It's embarrassing, dirty somehow. People are happy to hear that I'm taking a break.

"It's post-traumatic stress disorder," everyone says.

"It's going to take time," everyone says.

"So, Sael, that's an unusual name." My mother says "unusual," but she's asking, *Is he like us? White and middle class?* "Well, darling, getting away for a while *does* make sense after what happened."

That's Andrea's murder, as in "what happened," as in "after what happened."

"Call me if you need anything," says my mother. We both know I won't. She has yet to mention Andrea's name, to ask after Lucas.

Lucas, oh, Lucas.

Lucas may as well be a piece of luggage lost somewhere within the system. The "temporary" feels permanent. I call Andrea's office, I call a law firm that Sael recommended, I call social services, I write emails to *everyone*, and each time I run into the brick wall of:

"Without knowing the wishes of the deceased parent, we cannot proceed."

The lawyer's couched language:

"It's been temporarily misplaced, but we're doing everything in our power to address the situation."

But the situation is a little boy who has no mother. An orphaned four-year-old, his life sentence in some lost manila folder. Not that I can help much; I too am adrift.

Sael came with me when I needed to pack my stuff. I won't go back there by myself. We said little. I moved as quickly as possible. Places soak up the people who live in them. She's gone, but the apartment is sodden with memories. I walk past Andrea's room and realize that I'm holding my breath. Like I do when driving past a graveyard. I take my jewelry, most of my clothes. I don't look in the corner of my bedroom. I don't look to see if I can see the pennies.

*What pennies? There are no pennies.*

Afterward I get pretty drunk. I get drunk and I cry and cry and cry and Sael holds me. I wonder if I will ever stop crying.

"Oh, fuck it," says Sael. "Let's get the hell out of here."

"Okay," I say. "Okay."

"Go for it," says Michelle. "You need the time off, but stay in touch."

"Night or day, you can call me, you know that, right?" Liz says.

I do. These are my two-in-the-morning friends; these are my girls.

I haven't heard from my father. I wonder if he's still alive. If he cares that I am.

It can't hurt to leave; it can't hurt to get away from the streets that have become the Sickle Man's grisly playground, through which he runs rampant like a rabid dog, where no one is safe out of the apartment or *in* the apartment. If he wants you, he'll get you.

They found another girl today. Ashley Miller. Dead on her bed in a Carroll Gardens studio apartment, still wearing her retro glasses frames when they found her.

Meanwhile, I check under the bed. Meanwhile, I check the inside of the closet. The dreams are the worst. I wake up bathed in sweat, shaking. Sael is always there. Rocking me back to sleep. Holding me till my eyelids grow heavy again.

I can't remember my dreams, but I know somehow that I soon will.

Two weeks, somewhere new. Somewhere with trees. Somewhere far from here, somewhere I can breathe. So we get in a car and we drive and drive and drive.

Now we are here.

I love it.

The air smells sweeter and the breeze is cooler. My food tastes better. The steaks are more steak-y, the tomatoes more tomato-y. We drink some wine and we drink more beer and we drink gallons of iced tea and lemonade and we combine the two. Sael jokes that we should market this drink; we'd make a fortune.

"Ha, ha," I say.

We play endless card games, sometimes together, sometimes solitaire. There is no connection to the outside world apart from an old TV set, which sulks in the corner, unwatched. We read books. Sometimes I read passages aloud. Sometimes I don't.

We lie on beach chairs on the wooden deck outside the bedroom. We sprawl on threadbare towels on the dark sand by the lake. We rock on the rocking swing on the downstairs porch. We collapse on old green-and-yellow couches, which squeak in protest.

We take walks; sometimes only gentle hikes, close to home and through bits of wood, and sometimes more ambitious, climbing toward a goal. We swim, suits in the day, skinny-dipping at night under a sky alight with stars, the water cool and lapping. It feels illicit, silkier, siltier.

In the twilight we cover ourselves with bug spray. We light large citronella candles and hope, more than trust, that the mosquitoes will be deterred. They whine but we ignore them—ignore them and they'll go away. There are fireflies to be seen, sparks in the dark, and once or twice a bat wheeling and circling in the sky. I squeak and cover my hair and Sael laughs.

Down below is the little town, complete with small and homey restaurants, a dark and woody bar with antlers and little signs with hair-raising homilies and a pool table. Some tourist traps, but some real spots. We find a great coffee shop with wonderful coffee. Sael goes there to work.

There's a farmer's market too, if you like that sort of thing, and I do, although Sael could take it or leave it. There seems to be a thriving community, at least in the summer, and some concerts and art fairs not far away. Just in case we get bored, I collect pamphlets, and there are a million little things to do, provided we want to. We don't, though. We aren't bored. We have taken two weeks to get away, to laze about, to heal.

I cook. Easy things: salads, burgers, cold soups. Sometimes I join Sael at the coffee shop and linger over an iced mocha but mostly I stay up at the cabin. I never feel scared in the cabin. I'm not lonely. I am calm. I am safe. I sleep, I take small walks, I wade into the lake. Sael calls it the fishing hole. I read. I hum old pop songs under my breath. Little is required of me. Sael and I are the only two people on earth.

It is beginning to work.

Slowly, slowly, it is beginning to work. I have a little bottle of white pills. I am ready to take them, to do anything to stop the late-night memories or the dreams. I still can't remember them but they leave me sweaty and wrung out. On the first night I took one, and on the second night, but then on the third I forgot and slept deeply. It's a miracle. I don't question it.

The cell phone reception is not good here in the woods and the mountains. There are pockets on the path near the lake, at certain other spots, but on the whole it's more off than on. I don't miss it: the endless calls from the media, my well-meaning friends, the gossip-hungry acquaintances. Except here I am a week and two days in. Pacing, back and forth, kicking up the gravel, feeling the sun on my arms and the back of my neck.

*Please, God, let it be Lucas who answers.*

If it's her I'll just say, *Hi, Cheryl. It's been just over a week*—see, see I'm being good, I'm staying away, I'm enjoying the Vermont sunshine—*and I thought I would just check in.*

Keep it light, keep it light.

*Hi, Cheryl, how are you doing?* I'll pause for her answer and then I'll say, *It's been almost two weeks, so I just thought I'd see how Lucas was doing . . .*

*Let me speak with Lucas, you bitch.*

The receiver is picked up.

"Hello?"

I launch in. "Hi, Cheryl, how are you—"

"Kat?"

I'm thrown.

"Kat?"

"Lucas!" *Thank you, God, thank you.* "Hey, honey! How are you?"

"Okay." His voice is low, upset.

I shift gears. "What's wrong?"

"You didn't call me for so long."

"Oh, honey." *Fuck this stupid woman. Fuck her.* "Oh, honey, I called, didn't Mrs. Kaskow tell you I was traveling?"

"No."

"Well, when I called she said you were out . . . having fun," I add lamely.

There's a silence on the other end.

"Where is she now, love?"

"She's taking a nap."

*Thank God.* "Excellent! I get to talk to you all by yourself on the phone!" I sound fake, too bright.

"Yes . . ." He is doubtful.

"How are you? What did you do today?"

"Nothing."

*I don't like the way he sounds.* "Nothing?"

. . .

*Lucas, talk to me.* "That doesn't sound like too much fun."

"Kat?"

"Yes, baby?"

"When are you coming to see me?"

*Oh God.* "Oh, babes . . ." I hear her voice in my head: *It can take hours for him to calm down.*

*If she finds out about this I'll never be able to speak with him. What do I say? Oh God, what do I say?*

"Why can't you come now?" He's close to tears.

*How do I answer this? What do I say? What do I do?* "Lucas, I'll come to see you as soon as I'm back in the city, okay?" *Screw Mrs. Kaskow, she'll have to deal with it.*

I hear it, down the phone a tiny sigh. It's heartbreaking that a four-year-old has a reason to sigh like that. "Okay."

"Sweetie, can I ask you a question?" I don't want to ask, but I need to know.

"Yes?"

"How are the ladies, have you seen them around?"

"No." He sounds genuinely surprised now. I'm actually relieved that my question has taken him away from the sadness, just for a moment.

"Well, that's good, right?" I hazard.

"No." He hesitates. "It's because the ladies is with you now."

"Oh." My voice is normal, but my veins carry chips of ice; the hair is standing up on my arms. “Why do you think that is?” I have a sudden desire to look behind me. *What would I see if I did?*

“They want to take care of you.”

“Well, that’s nice.” *Take care of me, like for good?*

“Kat?”

“Yes, hon?”

“I miss her. I miss Momma.”

“Oh, Lucas.” My throat tightens, my eyes prick, I swallow hard. “I know you do. I miss her too.” I would give anything to be able to hug him, but he can’t cry, so I think hard for a moment and then say, “Knock knock!”

“Who’s there?”

“Boo.”

“Boo who?”

“Don’t cry, it’s just me!”

. . .

“Sael’s been teaching me,” I explain in the silence that follows this. “Want to hear another one?”

“Okay.”

“Okay, knock knock!”

“Who’s there?”

“Canoe.”

“Canoe who?”

“Canoe help me with my homework?”

“You don’t *have* any homework.” He is almost reproachful. “You a grown-up.”

“Now you tell me! Why have I been doing all these math problems all night long?” And amazingly I hear a weak, waterlogged giggle. I close my eyes, blinking back tears. “That’s better, that’s what I like to hear.”

“Kat?”

“Yes, hon?”

"You promise you'll come and see me soon?"

There's a lump in my throat. *This kid is killing me.* "I promise."

"Okay."

"Honey, you should probably go." *Before she wakes up and I never get to speak with you again.*

"She's still sleeping."

"What?"

"Mrs. Kaskow."

*How did he know that?* "Well . . ."

"But she'll wake up soon."

"Lucas?"

"Yes?"

"Maybe don't tell anyone we spoke today." *That's good, Katherine, encourage deception.*

"It's a secret?"

"That's right, it's our secret." *Jesus, I sound gross.*

"Kat?"

"Yes?"

"Can you tell me one more?"

"Just one, here goes. Knock knock!"

"Who's there?"

"Noah."

"Noah who?"

"Noah a good place where I can get something to eat around here?"

He laughs. "You're silly, Kat."

"I noah, I noah."

He laughs again.

"I love you, Lucas."

"Love you, Kat."

And he's gone.

Sael is coming down the path toward me. He opens his arms. I walk into them.

We stand for a long time not saying anything, then, "Not so good, huh?"

"No." My face is against his shoulder, my voice muffled.

"I'm sorry."

"I don't know what to do. I can't help him. I mean, he's asking me when I'm coming to see him. She didn't even tell him that I called. I hate that he's with that woman!"

"Boy"—he sighs—"I can't believe they haven't found it yet."

"I know. It's insane."

We have discussed options for hours, trying to be practical, trying to keep calm, yet each time we speak of it my rage and incredulity flares up again.

"Any other family members found?"

"Andrea's half sister, supposedly."

"She wasn't at the funeral was she? I don't remember meeting her.

"Came forward a week later. Apparently high as a kite. Turns out she's a total junkie, clearly hoping to look after Lucas for money."

"Jesus."

"Yeah, it was horrible."

He waits for a moment and then, "Knock knock," he says.

I smile wetly. "Who's there?"

"Olive."

"Olive who?"

"Olive you, Kat."

"Olive you too," I say.

I do. I love this Sael, this Sael who is tender, who is loving, this Sael who holds me in the dark. He lets me cry. He does not roll his eyes or sigh when I check again under the bed, again in the closet. He does not make me feel like I'm crazy, or a burden. Something hard and icy inside him has melted. We are still honest but now we are kind.

"Ice cream?" he asks.

"Ice cream," I say.

As on the other nights we sit on the upper deck and eat our ice cream while the citronella candles flicker and the moths flutter. Then we lean back in our sloping mismatched beach chairs, drink our wine. The temperature falls and under old blankets we stare up into the skies. Sael names the stars and I pretend to listen. I like to hear his voice. I know I won't remember any of the names given for these uncomprehending stars. The names are only for us humans anyway.

Then Sael speaks, pulling me back from the edge of sleep.

"Katherine?" I can tell by his hesitant tone that there's something on his mind.

"Yes, what is it?"

He bends over and sits up. He is holding a box. It's a small wooden box, hand carved, a soft grain in a deep hue, a perfect thing within itself. I take it. It's smooth against my skin.

"It's gorgeous. What kind of wood?"

"Rosewood, now open it."

My heart halts midbeat.

What's inside the box lies shining within. In the night's darkness it seems to float. At first I see a circle, but my fingertips decipher a designed roughness, a pattern of scales. I trace over them. The pin looks like a tiny sword. The metal gleams, as if it were used to moonlight, used to candlelight. A spider-thin silver chain snakes and curls around it.

"You can hold it." Sael's usually confident voice has a slight tremble.

I pick it up. It's hard to breathe as I look at this shining scaled serpent, its mouth consuming its tail. What's the name for that again? I can't remember. It will come to me. I turn it over in my fingers, feeling its grooves. It is small but it has heft. There are five stones set along the snake's sinuous tail and one more brilliant gem for its eye. In the darkness they sparkle black and I cannot tell what they are. It's a thing of perfection and it rests within my palm.

"It's—"

*"That's an Ouroboros."*

*I am standing in a dimly lit room in the Morgan Library, staring at a manuscript as David leans over my shoulder.*

"—a ring brooch. The Romans used it as a clothes fastener. They used the pin"—he taps on the little sword—"to push through the cloth and hold up their cloaks."

"How old is it?" I cannot tear my eyes away.

"Oh . . ." He smiles but I can hear him growing self-conscious. "Pretty ancient. It's been in my family for generations. But not the chain," he adds proudly. "I had a chain made for it."

I can see this. The delicate links shine as only new silver can, unlike the ring brooch, which could be older than Christ himself. Thousands of years cupped within my hand, touching my skin.

Will the chain bear the weight of the circle? Carefully, I let the ring brooch fall, swinging back and forth. The chain is thin but strong. Sael takes my free hand. He kneels before me. He's like a knight wearing jeans and a sweater. It should feel ridiculous, but somehow, it's right.

"The Ouroboros is said to represent infinity, things beginning anew." And then, "Katherine, will you wear this?"

We are so rarely aware of the acts that truly shape our lives. I am still raw and recovering but I can see for a moment, as the doors swing open, everything: what has been, bed and betrayal, and Sael outside at the window, asking to be let in. I think of my underwear on the floor, and first hearing of Sara from the mouths of others. David's face pale and calm, Margot whispering something into Sael's ear and the bitterness of the games we played. But then I think of the lazy days we've had, the nights, the sweetness, my feet on his legs, his head in my lap, how a room feels empty without him, his arms around me, both of us reading with fingers entwined, curled up in the dark, the terror of loss, and gaining back life, and all that might be in the future. The laughing, eating, arguing, remonstrations, car trips, fights, furies, broken hearts, reunifications, reminders, private jokes, walking together, apart, lingering, and maybe, maybe, maybe the future of a family, children, a child we would make, us and our and we, a family, and his mouth is solemn, his eyes are serious at the finality of the question, but they are filled with hope, with light.

"Will you wear this, now and forever and always?"

The lake, the insects, the man who kneels before me—the whole world holds its breath and waits, waits in the gathering silence for my answer.

EN THE NEW BRIDE SAW THE GOLDEN cup, she remembered the words of the old woman she had met in the forest, as she truly did wish to be a good and gentle wife and give Lord de Villias many sons. So she took the small parcel she had been hiding amid her garments for this very day and emptied the grainy powder into the cup of wine. Then she said the words as she had been bidden.

*Song to song,*
*Skin to skin,*
*Lip to cup,*
*Heart to wing*
*Bone to bone,*
*Day to night,*
*Blood to blood,*
*Wish take flight.*

And drank them down.

# 21

You sit in the dimness of an ill-lit bar. The small streaked windows defy the very day. The jukebox plays a sad, sweet country song. A woman sings about her man, how he loves her good but treats her bad. A time to drink and a time to think and now it is time for a toast.

You always like to toast your Ride before the Final Hunt. Afterward there will be no time.

Before you arrived, the problems that he had faced were by comparison as insignificant as a speck of dust in an infant's eye. Your Ride had not known suffering or hunger or thirst or pain.

You were grateful that this Ride, in particular, was a good one. In the prime of his life, good-looking and strong. Fair faces beget fair fortune and life is easier for the lovely.

You think back to the Rides of your past, who lived in darker days, who bore the brunt of wars and famine, hardship and brutality. This Ride has been so favored by his time and place, so educated and clever, at the pinnacle of health and happiness and success. He made your work so easy.

And oh, how you loved his city.

You who have run on stony roads and ridden horses over

dung-smeared cobbles, who have tossed upon turbulent seas and sweated through burning deserts, here you sauntered down the shining streets, the smooth pavements stretching out for miles. How you will miss his world, this now of nows, this present, this time where numbers one and zero allow everything to flow. To travel and to talk, to write, everyone knows, so everyone can know.

Oh, what an age, this beautiful twenty-first century, bright and brilliant and terrible and true and yours for the taking.

So yes, you are grateful and possibly a little sentimental. Good-byes are always sad, and after you depart he will not last long. For when you leave them your Rides inevitably plunge into madness, their ears harboring the endless screams, their memories unblinking witness to the endless upturned faces begging, cursing, pleading, the cutting and the bleeding. Rides have put out their eyes, sliced off their ears, hacked off their hands, and still the mind holds them close; still they see and hear in endless repetition your bloody acts caught in an endless bloody groove. Your Rides must be innocent in order for you to possess them. There must be no vestiges of evil, no foul or murderous thoughts or desire for harm. They must be clean tools with which you can do your work. You have turned them inside out and remade them, and they cannot be comfortable in their stained skins.

You, who are immortal, drink to the great and wasteful and delicious and terrifying gift of mortality as your Rides take their own lives, candles desperate to be snuffed. They leap from high places; they drown in dark waters; they take knives and let their own lives pour out while you, in your righteousness, thrive.

Your Rides do not understand the blood that must be spilled, the many colors that must be consumed. They do not delight, as you do, in every drip and drop. They do not understand that there is truth in all fluids, that there is beauty in putridity; they do not rejoice in blood. For they cannot know the mission they allowed you to fulfill, your purpose, the reason for your being. It is better for them this way.

Of course, a few of your Rides were caught before they could end themselves. After you left they moved too slowly, stunned with horror, sickened and shocked. If a mob ended them, so much the better, but now there is modern medicine and trained professionals who ask *why*.

It makes as much sense to question a straw man, to berate a husk, to smash an empty jug upon the floor.

And each Ride speaks the terrible truth when he says, "I do not know."

So you are grateful to your Ride, and grateful to the women who gave you their colors. Each cut you made was a dedication to them, each cry they gave a poem, each sacrifice a song. Their endless, endless hues, their bright blooming colors, allowed you to stay and seek the Vessel out.

And finally, a toast to the Vessel. To Katherine, Katherine who brought you out of nothing and who will send you back with her passing. From all the many, many you have had, she has been the hardest one to wait for. Still, the grape must ripen on the vine; the vintage cannot be rushed. You will have your drink.

And now you sing a little song, to Katherine.

*Katherine, oh, my Katherine,*
*I loved you best of all.*
*Your heart is red, as red as red,*
*And I must heed the call.*

*Katherine, oh, my Katherine,*
*I have loved you so.*
*Drink up and fill my cup again,*
*For soon I'll have to go.*

*So come and fill my cup again,*
*For soon I'll have to go.*

# 22

I wake with a start. I have no idea how long I have slept. Waking in the afternoon, especially from a vivid dream, is always strange. I'm sweating. The dream, so rich, so real, has already begun to recede, great swaths of it dissolving in the afternoon light. I can feel the sweat cooling on my body. I can hear the birds sing. I will have a swim.

It's not surprising I've been napping. Early this morning I had woken for the express purpose of gloating. *He's mine. His dark hair and his eyes. His earlobes and his nose, his eyelashes. Mine and mine and mine.* I gloat over his smooth back and I gloat over each round cheek of his ass. I gloat over his chest, which contains his heart; this too is mine and every beat a declaration, *I love, I love, I love, I love*. I gloat over the lean length of him, and his penis, curled and soft and sleeping, too *is mine*; his arms that hold me, and each finger and thumb, and his cheekbones and the place between his shoulder and his neck in which I nestle *are mine*. His navel, his chin. His skin, his breath. My heart creaks and groans with the enormity of everything I have. It is too much to bear. I try to rise but his arms, *which are mine*, tighten around me. I can feel him stir and harden against me and wordlessly he is on and then inside me and we are moving together.

Now Sael has gone down into the town—for errands, he said, but I'm pretty sure that he'll have a beer down at the Deer's Head. He likes the jukebox, which plays old-timey tunes; he likes the drinkers with their hound-dog faces. Maybe he wants to casually, or not so casually, mention our engagement. *The ol' ball and chain finally got me. The prison sentence is starting soon. I got life.* Maybe someone will offer to buy him a round, or more likely he'll buy everyone a round, and that will be good because free beer always tastes better. He'll be a man in the company of men.

Again there it is, the cool weight of the ring brooch between my breasts. I have been worried that its pin will prick my skin, but it hasn't yet. I will have to be careful with such an ancient piece of jewelry, with the burden of Sael's heritage.

I could call a friend and share the news but I plan to wait for a day or two. I want to be selfish with this; I want to hold this as my secret gift, and scratching around in the place where I don't want to look, I think I know why this little voice is telling me to wait. When Andrea was **NEW VICTIM BRUTALLY MURDERED!** killed, my life **ROOMMATE WAS IN THE HOUSE!** became public property. My online photos, flattering and unflattering, were now in other people's hands. I took down pictures and links, tried to erase myself, but not in time. Some information couldn't be removed. Some things I had said were taken out of context before I learned to say "no comment." That's why the little voice says wait, because this news is special. It's my news and his news but not anyone else's news. I don't doubt that I'll be seen as callous, getting engaged so soon after Andrea's **GRISLY SLAUGHTER!** death. At the very least eyebrows will be raised; people will be polite instead of happy. So I'll hold on to this private joy for a while longer before releasing it into the world, where it will get kicked around like a soccer ball, growing grubby and worn.

I think there will be time enough to tell everyone. I think there is nothing but time, the way people in love do.

I am wrong. This is in fact the last day, for so many things.

But I don't know this yet. I only know that it's still pretty hot for the late afternoon and that a swim would be nice.

I crunch down the gravel path, wearing an old black bikini and little white shorts, toward the lake with the woods on either side. In my small cotton bag are the following items: a threadbare towel, an Agatha Christie paperback, a plum, a paper napkin, and my phone. I hope Sael will remember to pick up more plums. We both love them. I know William Carlos Williams wrote the whole "Forgive me" icebox thing, but frankly that's a bullshit apology if ever I heard one. I bring my phone because there's a good patch of reception near the edge of the lake and I might as well check my messages.

On either side of the gravel path long fields teem with insects, the *shhh* and hiss of them creating the obligatory sound of a sleepy country afternoon, a living static. Behind the grasses stretch the woods. *The woods are lovely, dark and deep.* I learned that poem in school. My teacher told us it was a metaphor for death, but I always thought it was sexy. *Lovely, dark and deep.*

I am brimming with poetry today. It's probably the "love" thing.

To get to the lake you have to veer slightly left off the path and duck down beneath some small low branches. Then there it is, with a tiny strip of firm wet sand and the huge mossy trunk of a fallen tree to sit on. This is where we lodge the old canoe, which has provided a good workout for my arms. I step into the water and it's cold and then it's wonderful. There's nothing better than to swim in the late afternoon with the last of the sun beating down, pushing through the cold and warm pockets of water, and then to stretch on a towel, eat a plum, and read Agatha Christie. I do this until the shadows are a great deal longer and it's starting to grow chilly.

I heave myself up and begin to walk up to the path again. By the side of the road I hear my phone ringing. I've come to the good patch of reception. Sael and I call it treasure hunting.

"Hello?"

"Katherine!" David's voice sounds strange, and almost to himself he says, "Thank God."

*"Thank God"?* "David, I—"

"Shut up, there's no time, is Sael around?"

*"Shut up"? Something is very wrong.* "No, he—"

"Where is he?"

"He went shopping, he's probably having a beer down at the Deer's Head. Why? Do you need to speak with him?" *Will you be friends again?*

"No," he says, so quickly that he startles me. My heart speeds up. I hear him take a breath. "Katherine, I need you to listen."

It is definitely colder now. The afternoon has taken the turn toward evening. Night will soon be here.

"David, what is it?"

"*Listen.*" His voice is not mean, but it's impatient. "I'm on my way to you now."

"Here?"

"I left as soon as they called me."

"As who called you? David—"

"The police."

My heart stops.

"The police called me. They want to speak with Sael."

"What? Why?"

"They want to talk with him in connection to Andrea's murder."

"Why would they want to talk with *Sael*?" I should have brought a sweater, or an extra towel. Something for cover, for warmth.

"Listen to me! I don't have much battery left."

I will myself to be quiet, to concentrate.

"They called me because they couldn't get in touch with him and they couldn't get in touch with you." Now he sounds angry.

"We told everyone where we were going. I gave them the cabin's address, you've been here before, you know what the reception here is like! And anyway, *you* said you never wanted to hear from us again."

Fear has made me spiteful, irrational, but David doesn't rise to it, like he's determined to control himself. Somehow this is scarier, as if becoming angry would waste too much time. "The police say they've been trying to call him, that it just goes to voice mail."

Is this true? I'm trying to think but panic is beginning to buzz like a swarm of bees. "But he has his phone, I've seen him take calls."

"Katherine"—his voice grows quiet—"I'm telling you what they told me. The police have been trying for at least two days to get hold of him. They may have found some prints that matched."

It's hard to swallow. "*Prints?*"

He's quiet and then, every word an effort, "It might not mean anything."

But it means something. David would not have called unless it meant something.

My knees grow loose; the bees hum louder. I sit down on the side of the path. The gravel is cold and pricking the undersides of my legs and there are ants. I don't care.

"Listen," he says, again. It's unnecessary now, though, to tell me to listen.

I have never listened harder in my life.

In fact I cannot remember a time when I wasn't sitting on a gravel road, clutching my phone to my ear.

"I'm on my way now, the moment I heard I rented a car—"

"You think . . ." I find I cannot finish the sentence. "You think . . ."

This isn't happening, this isn't happening. This can't be happening.

He is silent for a moment and then faintly, as if he's not talking to me now but to himself, "I can't let it happen again, not after Sara . . ."

"Sara?" My voice is not my own. It is a stranger's voice, completely disembodied. "What has *Sara* got to do with this?"

"Katherine," he says, and his forced calm control makes me want to scream. I will scream in a moment. "Katherine, what did Sael tell you about Sara?"

"He said she was hit by a car."

On the other end there is only silence.

"David? . . . Hello? . . . *Hello?* . . ."

Into the void.

"Oh my God." He is almost inaudible but I can hear his incredulity. "Is that what he told you?" There's a sickening hint of hope in David's voice. *Please*, it begs, *please tell me that Sael didn't tell you this. Please take it back.*

Now it's my turn to answer his question with a question.

"What happened to Sara?" There is silence, so I ask it again. "David, *what happened to Sara?*"

After he tells me, he says again that he will be here soon. He will be here and the police will be here. I must keep calm. I have to keep calm.

The laughter bubbles up. Keep calm. What a fucking joke. He mustn't know, he mustn't suspect. Sael my lover, Sael my new fiancé, Sael the Sic—

I laugh and laugh and laugh and—

"Stop it!" David barks, shocking me into silence.

"What do I do?"

"You have to keep calm," he says again. "You have to act natural."

No. I cannot do this. My cheeks are wet and that's how I know I'm crying. Tears leaking out of my eyes, running down my chin. I shake my head as I sit on the cold small stones in the last of the dying sun. I shake my head. *No.*

"Yes," says David, as if he can see me. As if he can see me shaking my head. "Yes, you can. *I believe in you.*"

"I can't."

"I believe in you," he says. "You have to, for me. I know you can do this."

"I don't think I can."

"You will. You will."

"David." I cannot speak above a whisper. "Hurry."

"I am." There's a pause and then he says it.

Says it and it's all I can hold on to.

"I love you," he says, and is gone.

I am unaware of the stones that cut me, or the ants that trickle around my legs. I don't hear the miniscule drill of the mosquitoes or the birds as they sing good night.

Spots, black and shimmering.

*Please keep in touch.*

*Let's run away.*

*Let us know how we can contact you.*

Hands are numb.

*Just you and me.*

Breathe.

*Who had access to your apartment?*

Breathe.

*Was she involved with anyone?*

Breathe.

*She was found dead in her bed, dead in her bed,*
*dead in her bed, dead in her—*

A wave of gray.

*I thought maybe I was emotionally dead.*

Spots.

*He's a keeper.*

Black spots.

*Who had access to your apartment?*

Shimmering.

*What did Sael tell you about Sara?*

Folded over,

*There had to be something wrong with me.*

knees in the dirt,

*The body count has reached twelve.*

a searing pain in my gut,

*Come to bed, Katherine.*

the bitter taste surges up.

*Just to sleep.*

*I guess I went a little crazy.*

A hot wave rises,

*I couldn't sleep. I couldn't eat.*

all the delicious breakfast, the plums,

*They may have found some prints that matched.*

the dark-skinned plums. I will never eat plums again.

*Let's get out of here.*

*They've been trying to get hold of him for at least two days.*

*I think women felt it too.*

Splattering the gravel,

*The police say they've been trying him,*
*that it just goes to voice mail.*

behind the tree trunk, on all fours,

*We strongly advise that you stay in touch at all times.*

up and up,

*Will you wear this, now and forever and always?*

retching, shaking and shaking and retching until

*Just you and me.*

nothing is left in my body, there's nothing left to be sick with.

*You and your roommate, it doesn't fit his pattern.*

The stink and misery of it all. Kneeling in the dirt, head down and pounding.

"Sara was murdered," David had said. "She was found dead in their apartment, and her killer was never caught."

Hours, maybe years, later, I stand up, wiping my mouth clean as best I can. I rub my eyes. I'm freezing. Night has descended while I was here. Already the stars are prickling out at the edges of the sky. The crickets are loud. I round the bend in the path and, as if from a great distance, see the lights in the cabin windows. I see the lights and I know.

He's home.

Y AND BY, SIR AUGUST CAME TO THEIR chamber, eager to join his new bride upon their wedding night, but he found no bride, no one at all, only a pile of white feathers upon the floor and an empty cup with the remnants of thin blue dregs. He thought of the Maiden and her brews, and cried, "There is witchery and treachery here!"

And as he opened his mouth to raise the alarm, so the peal of bells rang out over the servants' calls of "Fire!"

The terrible flames roared through the halls of the castle. And it was said the fire was a brilliant green, and blue and black, and that the very flames reared back and hissed like snakes and slithered and raged among the ramparts and would not be doused. Knights and servants ran to and fro as the fire consumed all in its way, but most of the wedding party were burned to death for they could not be awakened, no matter how they were shaken or beseeched. But not a hair upon the lord's head was harmed and he believed it to be because the brooch that he wore was blessed and that it had protected him, and from thenceforth swore he would never take it off. And as dawn broke the fire died down and smoldered, at last, to an end. Then the lord decreed that all must search for his bride in every chamber of Morwyn Castle and in every neighboring house till she was discovered, and that the Maiden must be brought to him in iron chains to answer for her wickedness.

Alas, the Maiden had disappeared along with the bride and neither was ever seen again.

# Part *Three*

# 23

Live in the moment. Live in the now. Live each day as though it were your last. There is no day like today. Feel the fear and do it anyway. Today is the first day of the rest of your life. Life is a journey, not a destination. Forever is composed of nows.

You do not rush to joyful red. Instead you let each moment linger there upon your tongue before you swallow, each bead of caviar complete, each throatful of oyster sweet.

She sits, holding his hand. You do not hurry. Under a blanket of stars her scent fills your nose, the warm damp cave of nostril, the waving cilia, nerve cells unlocking tiny keys within the brain; her warm skin, with an unseen sheen of mosquito repellent, sweat, the miniscule splattering of drops of the tomato sauce she made. Her nails caught some of the stony gray gravel dust of the path when she fell to her knees. The deep animal scent of her hair, the dark rich *herness* closest to her skull.

Finally, finally, she blazes red. The dandelion is delicate within its fragile fullness; you pause before you purse your lips to blow. You take your time before you step into the darkness.

She sits, holding his hand. Then she sees you standing still. Oh, beloved, oh, my Katherine. She thinks that you have not seen her, you are so quiet.

"Here!" she whispers. It's a stage whisper, stretched and tight, one word carrying the weight of a thousand cries, strained to breaking point.

As if you could not smell her a mile away. As if you could not see her, your chosen one, in the dark. As if she did not flame as red as the core of the earth. There is doubt and fear and horror but they do not sway her as they once did; still, she burns bright. Still, she is red.

"Here," and she waves with a wild gesture. It is a wave of a sailor on a sinking ship in a storm-tossed sea, although it is the height of a summer night and there is not even the littlest breeze to lift a strand of her hair.

She does not call loudly. She is fearful of waking him. She is fearful of not waking him.

"Here," she says and she calls to you, calls what she thinks is your name.

She wonders why you are not running, not frantic.

You smile in the dark as you start up the wooden stairs to the little deck. The corners of your lips, where the muscles pull, cradle the knowledge that soon she will know you by your real name. Your lips are full, are filled with kisses kept for her, and the ends of your lips curl again because finally you see her, and because finally it is time.

Because you are ready, you take your time in climbing up the steps. It does no good to rush.

Now you have reached the top of the stairs and you see him stretched out, even in sleep grasping her hand. It is strange to her that you do not fall to your knees at once to help her. It is strange, your measured walk, your air of calm.

Yes, this is love. Her touch, touching. You bend down to examine him. The man whose hand she holds.

"Thank God," she says. "Thank God you're here."

The irony is unbearably lovely.

"I didn't know what to do." She is defensive. "I drugged him with my pills. Some that I take, for anxiety and to sleep." She reels off the names. "I'm scared that I gave him too much. Oh my God"—now pleading—"what are we going to do?"

We. We, and now you are a *we*. Despite everything that has passed, she thinks you are bonded together by fear and necessity.

"I didn't know what to do." She's crying. She's trying to hold on to what is real. Safety in patterns, perhaps she feels there is more truth in repetition.

"You did the right thing."

"You think so?"

"Absolutely."

"Yes?"

It is beautiful to be honest with her, and truly she did do what was right, for you. You stand up and look out over the railing. "It's so peaceful here," you say.

She wonders why you are admiring the scenery when your greatest friend, outed as a monster, lies drugged and the police are on their way. She doesn't understand. She will, though.

"What are you talking about?" she says. Her voice is growing louder with panic. "What do we do? Where are the police?"

You do not answer.

"David, you said the police were on their way!"

You did say that.

"David?" She walks up to you, grabs your arm.

You turn around slowly to face her. "Katherine."

"David!" She thinks she has your attention again. As if she had ever lost it. "David, *what do we do*?"

"Come here," you say.

You pull her in. You hug her tight.

For a moment she allows herself to relax. You are tall and firm; you smell warm and clean and sure. You know her so well. You're strong and there; you'll know what to do.

You do.

You wish time could freeze like this: the night, the moon cool and watchful over the lake, the lover sleeping, your beloved's face pressed just underneath your collarbone. The perfect place for weeping.

"Katherine?" you ask as you rock her gently, gently.

"Yes?" She sniffs.

"Can I tell you a secret?"

She's unsure but willing to be comforted. "Yes, David?"

You bend forward and, savoring each syllable, tell her, "That is not my name."

"What?" She pulls a little apart, still in your arms, to look up into your face. She hasn't heard you. She's exhausted, emotionally spent, worn and ragged. She didn't hear you.

You smile down, down into her tear-streaked face. Your voice is low and loving and a little regretful. Saying good-bye is hard, but greeting the new is joyful. "I have not been David for a while now."

"David, what are you talking about?"

This time there is a tiny spark, the copper taste, a dawning. Blinking up through her tears, she tries to focus on you. You, the man she knows as David Balan, so calm, so kind, so faithful coming to her aid even after her betrayal, who loves her still.

You lean over and whisper who you are. You bend down and gently form the words with your lips against the cup of her ear, the name she'll know you by.

The name you have been given, an ancient name, a heavy and splattered cloak hemmed with red, encrusted. You name yourself.

It is not disappointing, this moment. The moment of knowledge.

*And Eve took of the fruit and ate it and knew of her nakedness.*

The moment of understanding. Not full and true understanding, not yet, but the first realization of who you are. And before she can stiffen or draw breath to cry out, your hands press on those very special and sensitive places on her neck, an ancient technique from the East that has served you well throughout the centuries. No drugs for her, no dregs of wine or chemicals to alter, disturb, or corrupt and

her eyes roll back to whites,
her eyelids close, the red velvet curtain
sweeping down over
the first tumultuous act. You hold
the full weight of her lolling,
boneless.
You hold her.

Your love. Your life. Your beginning, your end, now finally in your arms.

You sigh. You wish you could stand here longer, but you have promises to keep and miles before you go to sleep.

After all, there is much to be done.

# 24

Head.

Head hurts.

My head really hurts.

My head really hurts and I'm cold. I pull up the blanket.

There is no blanket. I'm on the floor, naked on the floor.

My eyelids are heavy.

Light hurts my eyes.

Blinks.

Red blurs.

Blinks.

Red toenail polish.

Bare toes.

Feet.

There's a young woman crouching next to me, staring down. Strands of her long black hair are matted against her forehead and against her cheek; thin gold hoops dangle from her ears. She wears a mint-green dress, sleeveless and marbled with blood; a strap has been cut to reveal one full striated breast hanging splattered, bare and heavy.

I open my mouth.
The young woman puts one finger to her flaking blue lips.

*Shhh.*

Cocks her head toward the sliding glass door where the moonlight is shining in.

*Downstairs.*

I sit up.
I can't.
My head is full of jagged glass and stones.
I try to sit up.
Slowly.
Where are my clothes?

She beckons with her finger; her nail polish is red.

*Come.*

My legs are shaky,
Trembling.
I reach,
Push on the couch, push myself up.
Standing naked.
Strands of rope fall down.

She crooks her finger.

*Come.*

I follow her toward the door. She is quiet. I stare at the shape carved into the pale brown skin of her shoulder, two wavy vertical lines enclosed in a half-moon. Its crusty contours are mesmerizing, oozing black trails down her back.

She points out through the sliding door leading to the deck.

She dissolves through the glass, stands on the other side. Beckons.

*Come!*

The glass is solid against my palms.

I pull at the sliding door. I pull and pull but there is no strength in my hands; my fingertips slip and slide with sweat. The girl is looking through the glass, eyes widening, opening her hands in the universal gesture of

*Hurry up!*

With all my strength I pull but I can only manage a thin crack. I close my eyes and pull; then it's a wedge. Not enough room to squeeze through but she's desperate now, her mouth open in silent call:

*Come!*

I have to.

One leg.

Ass.

Torso, breast.

Shoulder.

Neck, face, cheek scraped.

Head.

Other leg.

Scraping the side of the door.

Pain, burning.

Through.

Outside on the deck.

It's cold.

Breeze against bare skin.

Cold.

Sael lies motionless.

I move toward him.

A figure sitting next to him looks up.

Her plump face seems familiar, although it's drained of color and almost yellow. Something that looks like it was once blue sweatpants clings darkly to her thighs. Her gray sports bra is stiff and dark with greenish flecks of vomit or bile, and one lace in her splattered sneaker is untied. A thick black gash runs across her throat. Around the folds of her navel is a crusted triangle, each of its points enclosed by a smaller circle.

Her eyes are pinpricks in blue shadows. She raises her hand, palm facing out; there's a cut there too.

*Stop!*

She points down to Sael, then brings her palms together under her head.

*Sleeping.*

She hugs herself.

*Safe!*

Then she indicates herself before pointing to me with her right hand and drawing the index finger of her left along the thick black incision in her neck. She points back inside the house. The indication is clear. Sael will be all right, I'm the one who'll be

*Dead!*

She tilts her head toward the wooden steps.

*Go down!*

Another woman stands at the bottom of the staircase. In her late thirties, wearing cargo pants, a black top, her short hair framing her face, its left side a mass of deeply etched spiraling grooves.

She beckons back and forth frantically.

*Come!*

I put my bare foot on the first step. It creaks. The woman violently covers her mouth with both her hands, terrified at the noise.

*Quiet!*

I descend as slowly and quietly as possible, trying to place my weight silently. Holding on to the wooden rail to lessen the pressure on the stairs.

Down, down, down.

The woman gestures, frantically.

*Hurry!*

My unprotected soles are needled and scratched on the stony path. I need to get to the car, but another girl, a redhead, is waiting in front of the driver's door. She also looks so familiar in her denim shorts, her button-down shirt slashed open. I move toward her.

She shakes her head, her palms out and moving back and forth.

*No!*

Then she lifts one arm and points around to the back of the cabin. I sprint across the gravel, wincing at the pain and at the sharp scratching sounds of the stones. I duck down around the side.

Squatted low is a young woman, her hair dyed a pretty purple, wearing large tortoiseshell frames and a white dress dotted with tiny strawberries. As she crouches the hem rucks up above her thigh, revealing the scabbed outline of a cone enclosing an eye.

*You too!*

I crouch. She points toward the black tangle of the woods, a black woolen tangle of darkness.

*Go!*

I don't move. Out there it's only woods in the night.

Again toward the trees.

*Go!*

I am frozen. There's a ringing in my ears. My heart pounds. My chest aches with suppressed panting. I can't move. I can't.

Her one finger is raised toward the woods. A single way, a single line.

*Go!*

The sliding door to the deck rasps open above me.

Light spills out.

I hear the deliberate squeak and creak of his footsteps as he walks across the planks to the top of the staircase.

I can't move. I can't move. It's all going black, there's a buzzing in my ears.

*Go!*
*Go!*
*Go!*

I turn and run.

# 25

You know how to bind. You know the overhand, the half hitch, the clove hitch and the lark's head, the square, often called the reef knot, and the bow line, the anchor hitch and the alpine butterfly, the double fisherman, the double overhand, the figure eight, the figure nine, the handcuff knot, the girth hitch, the blood knot and the Blake's hitch, the masthead knot and the crown, the highwayman hitch and the slipknot, bunny's ears and the monkey's fist, the butcher's knot and the child's swing and the sliding splice and the Solomon Bar.

But as you stood over her you decided to make it last just a little longer. After all, she was your favorite. After all, this was a glorious Ride and it seems such a shame to end it so soon.

There's nowhere for her to go. You've disabled the cars. No one around for miles and miles. But let her run, a desperate hope, pale to darker green, shards of jade adding infinite sweetness to the taste. Let her adrenaline rush through you; let her think she has a chance of escape before you end her and end your Ride, who's carried you so faithfully for your journey.

The Hunt, the glorious Hunt!

There has been only one through all the ages who died by her own hand. This is rare. There must be something within the Vessel that understands the potential she possesses, that wants to live. It is possible that she saw you coming, and it is possible that she knew why. After all, the world is filled with possibilities. But this time you will not be denied the pleasure of the Hunt, the thrill, the joy of delaying the inevitable for just a little while longer.

Ash and Alabaster, Fuchsia and Fluorescent, Bronze and Brass, Mauve and Mahogany, Champagne, Chartreuse, Sienna, Chestnut, Chocolate, Cocoa, and Copper, and Cobalt. Despair and Delirium, Delight and Disgust, Smugness and Solidarity, Apathy and Acceptance, Breathlessness, Vivaciousness, Competence, Nostalgia, Indulgence, Security, and Confidence, and Ardor.

You harvested each one and each one anchored you and gave you strength to walk upon the earth, to breathe, to live, to achieve your quest so that others too might live.

And so you listened, smiling, as above you your Katherine tried to move as silently as possible through the sliding glass door. She was trying to be quiet, trying to move quickly. She must be cold without her clothes, in shock, drenched in sweat.

Slowly you stand up, stretch, crick your neck one way and then the other, sighing with pleasure. You go upstairs to the bedroom and walk onto the deck and look out upon the wood and think of all that waits for you. The sky is lush with stars. They float in the thin pond of the night, stretched out, brimming purple and soft. A thousand insects, the katydids with clicks and cricks, the crickets, a full, sweet chorus trilling *hush, hush, hush,* the frogs a lower *brack* and *brock* down by the water in the dark mass of trees. Now a faint breeze rises up, lifts and combs its fingers through the grass. She's started now, her final run; you hope she enjoys it and the summer all around her although you doubt she's taking much in. What a pity.

With easy, deliberate steps, you head down the wooden staircase into the glorious, pitiless night.

# 26

I run and I run and I run.

It's black and the air is cold and I run.

I follow the moving shape of faint ashy light through the trees. I crash and crack and push and blunder. The thin branches sting and scratch and tear at my skin, but the other woman running makes no noise, moves no branches. I'm gasping. I'm panting.

*I have to get to the canoe.*

I have to. I'll row, I'll row, I'll row to the other side of the lake to find help, away from here, away, far away. Stumbling and thrashing through the undergrowth, more falling than running, and now there's a bright needle of pain in my side, a sharp, agonizing stitch, and I scramble through a tangle of low-hanging vines, ducking under, and finally, finally, I am through to the clearing of the tiny cove.

*There is no canoe.*

Where is the canoe? Where is the canoe? Why is the canoe not upside down, pulled up along the sand, and where and where and where is it? I look left, I look right, and there on my right-hand side is . . .

*The canoe, upright, its hull half in the water.*

*Thank God.*

I move toward it. And in the moonlight reflecting on the water I see something. A figure sitting in the far end. I stop. I turn back, but the woman by my side runs on toward the canoe and its occupant. Turns to me, eyes burning.

*Go!*

I turn again and slowly approach. The blood in my ears muffling all sounds but a high-pitched hum of panic.

The shadow inside the boat doesn't stir. There is only the gentle lapping of the water against the sand.

I walk up to the canoe. My feet wade through the air, thick and dense, one in front of the other. Moving forward I see that the figure is slumped and still within its hooded shroud. My limbs are leaden.

It makes no move. As terrible as this specter seems, it must be better than what will be behind me. I try to raise one foot and put it inside the hull, but my legs tremble uncontrollably. I try again, concentrating, clenching, using all my might to raise one foot to step in. My leg is still shaking, but this time I'm able to do it, to lift one foot, *one foot*, up and into the boat.

Then the shrouded thing slowly unfolds, slowly stands. I freeze. One sleeve extends, fabric cloaking the hand. It grips one of the wooden oars, thrusting it outward and barring me from getting into the canoe. I peer up into the hooded face. There is only blackness.

The irony is bitter. A moment ago it took all my strength to get one foot into the boat, and now barred, I am desperate to get on. "Please help me." I do not recognize this weak and cracked voice, like a wheeze. I think it's mine. "Please, he's coming, *please*, he'll kill me, I have to get on!"

Its other hand, skin gray, almost blue, the nails thick and black and ragged, slowly emerges from deep within the robe's folds, holding something out. It is a bowl that gleams bone white in the moon's glow, like mother-of-pearl or ivory.

There is a small sign taped to the side of the bowl, a little askew and slightly soiled. Its edges are torn, as if the piece of paper was ripped from a notebook.

THANK YOU FOR YOUR DONATION.

I bend down to peer at the contents. The light glinting off the water isn't much; still from the shadows I can make out a wallet and what looks like an empty perfume bottle, a tiny brush with a mirror on its handle, a pocket notebook, a cell phone. They glisten. An open lipstick, a key ring, a pair of sunglasses, a lip balm, a champagne cork, a creamy business card, a computer plug, a paper napkin with a number written on it, a silver charm bracelet, a red leather glove, a sleek pair of pink headphones. Shimmering. I stumble back and fall down onto the hard, damp sand with a little cry. The bowl is teeming and teeming with maggots. Maggots crawling over the wallet, maggots squirming through the key ring, maggots oozing across the fingers of the leather glove, clustering on the lip balm and curling around the coins.

From far away, I hear whistling.

*I have to go.* I have to get on, but the oar blocks my way. "Please, he'll kill me, he's coming!"

The blade of the oar jabs wet, slick, hard against my sternum.

I look down.

The ring brooch hangs around my neck from its delicate chain.

*Katherine, will you wear this, now and forever?*

"This?"

The cloth of the hood moves a little; it's the faintest of nods.

*Good enough.* I put my trembling hands behind my neck to undo the clasp.

*Katherine, will you wear this, now and forever?*

I don't care. I have to get into the canoe. It's my only chance.

With a loud, dry snap, a branch breaks behind me.

Instinctively I swing around, expecting that he'll be there, but she's standing next to the tree, the one we call the towel tree, close to the entrance of the cove. It must have been struck by lightning long ago. There's a blackened streak running through it, and one of its branches hangs down at a forty-five-degree angle, the perfect branch for hanging towels.

Now she stands by this branch, half turned toward the lake, her face in shadow. But I'd know that slim silhouette anywhere.

"*Andrea?!*" I stagger toward her.

She turns to me. I moan. She'd had a closed casket, even though I had asked to see her. "Too much damage," said the coroner, "too disturbing for her loved ones."

But she's here, she's here, and I stumble forward. She stares at me and then slowly she turns and gazes at the branch where Sael and I hang our towels.

There it dangles. Small, neon green, it swings from its beaded metal chain. I reach out and pull it off the branch. Furry, soft, and slippery.

As my fingers curl around it, I remember.

*Reading in the park's late-afternoon sun, Lucas has fallen asleep on my lap. Looking down at his little curled eyelashes, I know.*

*"I love this kid."*

I look up into her ruined face. I wonder at the cost of love.

"I promise, I'll come back for him."

I hold the rabbit's foot tightly in my hand.

The whistling is louder.

*Hold it. It's lucky.*

I run back toward the canoe, scuffing through the wet sand. The beach is small but the canoe seems an endless distance away.

*I have to come back.* I have to return to Lucas. I have to come back.

The bowl is offered to me again.

Still, I hesitate.

The whistling grows closer.

And now I can hear the *snap* and *crack* as twigs break and branches bend. He's almost here.

I give the rabbit's foot one final squeeze, one last squeeze for Lucas, and then I drop it into the bowl. There is a beat; then it begins to radiate with light. The world and I hold our breath as the rabbit's foot is sucked down, sucked down among the wallets and the key rings and the notebooks and the glasses, like a helpless animal in quicksand.

The bowl flickers even brighter for a moment and then it is extinguished as it is withdrawn into the folds of the figure's garments.

Whistling.

Branches splintering as someone walks toward the little cove.

With all my remaining strength I heave myself up onto the canoe.

The figure lowers the oar and pushes it into the sand and the boat shifts a little from side to side but stays firm. We aren't moving. *Oh God. Oh God.* I look around me and there is a woman now, tall and slender in what once must have been a pretty white sundress with shoulder straps and blue flowers, only now it's stained with blood; a massive stain has seeped through above her breasts. A delicate webbing beads bright, drops down her arms and thighs, still fresh, and she bends down, straining to push us off the sand.

But still we do not move.

He's moving faster.

Another woman runs down the cove toward us, her brown hair thatched with blood, topless above her smeared denim skirt, the bloody rents on her back shining wetly. She too bends down and I see a tattoo of an orange lily growing from a cluster of shooting stars there on her left shoulder; now there are two more women, one in a short, tight black dress and large gold hoop earrings and the other in white shorts, now stained pink, and a yellow tank top with a black smiley face, a beautiful girl—I can see how tanned she is even in the moonlight—and as she runs her hair flies up, exposing a cheek crisscrossed with bloody grooves. Each takes a side of the canoe and both strain to push.

Four dead women pushing a light canoe. The boat barely moves, only rocks maddeningly.

And then through the trees I see—

*Please, please*

—another woman running up. I haven't seen her face before; she is naked except for a river of scars cascading down her breasts. Then another with full thighs and short curly hair, one side of her open shirt stuck to her wounds, and another one, all bending down, shoulders shaking. And more and more women running out of the woods and up the little stretch of beach; some are heavyset while others are slim, one wears the last vestiges of soft khaki shorts and another is draped in what looks like the remains of a toga. There's a woman clad in only her pink lacy bra, the left cup soaked a deep red, her softness jiggling as she runs. There is no self-consciousness, no attempts to cover nipples or shield pubic hair; shame is for the living. They only come, hands gripping the sides of the boat; some wade into the water but make no splash, raise no drop; they surround the bow and pull and pull, no ripples marking their movement.

I stare. On my left side a woman's shoulder blade contracts with effort, pulling black cuts raised on her brown skin; on my right a girl's high blond ponytail swings above her red-caked forehead, which wrinkles as she strains. Behind me a woman in the shreds of a long coarse dress—the fabric looks like burlap, torn and flapping—sets her broken blue lips, and all as one they push and it's working, it's working, the boat is slowly scraping over the last of the damp sand with a slopping noise, sliding into—

He's here.

David's body smashes through the fringe of the forest. Now in the clearing, walking out from underneath the trees.

Coming toward us.

He is smiling. He glances around. His nostrils are twitching, flaring. Then he stops abruptly, like a fisherman with a taut line. He's caught the scent. He turns and then he sees me. He sees me sitting in the canoe, the draped silhouette standing. He sees the women surrounding us, pushing and pulling to set us adrift.

He stops smiling. Now he's leaping toward us, faster than any human should be able to move, and although we're in the water now we're not far enough away from the shore and the lake is so shallow.

Now five feet, now four feet, now three.

He lunges, hands reaching out. I shriek and then, just as abruptly, he stops. Right on the lake's edge. He draws back. He emits a guttural hiss, completely inhuman; his tongue presses against his teeth, as if the water were toxic.

I look back at him on the lakeshore, growling and hissing, unable to touch the water. All the women are gone. As if they were never here.

A mist is drifting off the water, white and floating. It's harder to see now but I know he's there, waiting.

The voice rises out of the curtain of mist. The voice floats over the water. It has shreds of its prior humanity, David's voice with a grating metallic edge, the drone of a wasp, the rasp of a saw.

"You have an hour, and then I promise you, he'll suffer."

# 27

Pale tendrils coil around us as we stroke through the lake. All is silent but for the *gloosh* of the oar pulling through the water. I think of the words, the voice buzzing out in the white.

*You have an hour, and then I promise you, he'll suffer.*

I drugged him. I left him alone and defenseless. I did that. Because I had to get away. I had to get away from that thing and I have, for the moment, but now I am as helpless as Sael.

*You have an hour.*

I don't have a watch. With no means of knowing the time, minutes or hours could have passed. It isn't a big lake. We should soon be on the other side. The moment we reach land I can run, find someone with a phone, get help.

It's like we're pushing through the clouds. Maybe we're in the clouds, we're sailing through the clouds, we're floating in the sky, we're skimming in the sky, we're drifting over the moon, we're—

I realize that the canoe has stopped. "We're here?"

There is no answer swirling in the dense bank of fog and mist. But it's the silence that scares me. A country night is not silent. There's a chorus of crickets and frogs and nightjars, the whisper of the rustled leaves, all adding to the rich, full night hymn. Not this utter silence.

"Where are we?"

A shrouded arm is slowly extended, and emerging comes a waxen blue finger with its thick black nail. It points an unremitting needle of a compass, outward.

"Do I get off?"

Nothing.

"Where do I go for help?"

In my head, I hear it.

*You have an hour.*

I feel a wetness on my face and realize that I'm crying.

*Sael, I will find help. I promise.*

I cannot see the small stones and pebbles under my naked feet but I feel no pain, as if the earth is covered by a thin veil of cloth. Blind in the drifting, dreaming white, my senses smothered, I spin around helpless and lost.

Then it happens.

A tug.

I gasp but my gasp is silent. I am voiceless in this voiceless world. The ring brooch is rising up, out. It strains against the silver chain like a dog strains against its leash, pulling me forward.

There is nothing to do but follow.

I cannot see anything. I cannot hear anything. I cannot feel anything except the pull and so I yield, one step in front of the other into the cloud of soft nothingness.

I do not know how long I walk like this but at last the mist begins to dissipate. I peer into the gloom, desperate for something real and solid, desperate for anything at all, and as the tendrils thin I see it.

It looms up before me. I gape.

An ancient castle. Huge and dark and monstrous. The walls

of rough stone rise endless and impenetrable. I look upwards. If I squint I can just make out crumbling turrets, jagged like an ogre's rotten teeth, impossibly high, the very tops of the towers are lost in the mist.

It is insane. It is mad. It is a place built for death.

I don't know how long I stand there staring but gradually I become aware of a thin, stinging pain tight at the back of my neck; the chain digs into my skin. The ring brooch is pulling me onward. I clutch at it, trying to pull it off, but my hands jerk away. The ring brooch is freezing, so freezing that it burns. I cannot take it off.

*Please*, I beg it, *please don't make me go in there*, but it is merciless.

I stumble on the path, but the brooch drags me forward, through the arched stone doorway onto the cobbled stone of an empty courtyard and farther still into the forgotten and desolate darkness.

There is no clop of horses' hooves, no clank of cauldrons or men's voices calling to one another. There is no warmth of cooking fires, or women's laughter. This place is empty of even its own past life. I am led on and on across a great and silent stone hall and down the dim dusk of a smaller passage and some worn steps finely carved at first but more roughly hewn the lower I descend. Down and down, the light growing fainter and fainter, through massive arches, past thick stone columns, underneath sightless angels and crumbling gargoyles grinning through dust. It's a cavernous vault crisscrossed with stone beams. There are torches high up emitting a blue glow, no real warmth or brightness, and then I am pulled past one and then another; these cold stone beds have lain silent for hundreds of years, waiting.

I know what this place must be. I am yanked, in horror and in terror, tripping, stumbling, on through the crypt.

Abruptly the ring brooch slackens against my chest. And I stop. I double over, sucking in great gulps of airless air. At first I focus only on breathing, and then it slowly dawns on me. There should be some smell here of dank stone, of rot; I should be cold down here in the catacombs or hot because no fresh air circulates. With every breath I take I should be choking on mouthfuls of dust. But there is nothing. No heat, or cold, or taste, or smell. Then I look up to see where I have been led. In the faint blue light, I see my destination.

*God. Please. No.*

It waits as the others did. Pale gray, almost white, the lid is slightly open, a lip of darkness.

"No!" I scream aloud.

"No!" I scream, but I make no noise—is no one in this lost, dead place to hear me?

The chain tautens again as the brooch pulls me again toward the open coffin. I trip over my feet and fall forward.

"No, please no, please, please, please no, I can't, I can't, no!"

I am on my knees but the searing chain drags me along. I fall facedown but still I am dragged. My cheek scrapes against the black packed earth of the crypt floor. I open my mouth in pain and my teeth rasp against the coffin's stone edge as it begins to haul me up against the side. I am going to be hauled in headfirst.

"Okay!" I sob. "*Enough!*"

My throat burns in agony, yet for a moment the brooch stops pulling. I clamber to my feet, leaning against the coffin, my bruised face smeared with dirt and dust.

My chest heaves. *I'll do it.* I surrender soundlessly to the possessed thing around my neck, the thing that is determined to bury me alive.

Weeping, I put one trembling leg inside the coffin and then

the other, perching on the edge as if I were easing myself into a pool for a swim. I can feel something give way, crumbling and crunching under the pressure of my toes and heels. For the first time I am grateful that there is no scent or sound. I crouch and slowly lower myself, feeling the small bits and pieces break under my weight. I take one final look around knowing this forgotten tomb will probably be the last thing I ever see. Then I ease backward into the coffin.

I lie back. My shoulders and arms are constricted by its narrow sides. I can feel the grit of scraps of cloth and mealy fragments underneath my bare skin. I stare upwards. The lid begins to slide silently shut, darkness slipping over like an eclipse. Sealing me off.

*I have to get out—*

Involuntarily I jerk up, bumping my head hard against the stone.

I fall back into bright spots and pain. There is no room to move. This space was not built for a living body. I try to touch my forehead, feeling for the damage in the claustrophobic darkness. My fingers come away wet. A warm drop of blood trickles down my nose, my cheek. I push my hands against the lid, pushing for all my worth, for my life.

Nothing.

The darkness is total. I will die in this coffin.

I will die here, I will die here, I will die here, I will die here, I will die . . .

My chest heaves and heaves and then a voice in my head, clear and cold, says:

*You don't want to use up all your air hyperventilating. Breathe slowly.*

I force myself to breathe slowly.

*Breathe in.*

I inhale.

*Breathe out.*

I exhale.

Then I wait for further instructions but there is only silence. I close my eyes.

Then there is a memory, bright and strange.

*We have gone out early to look for mushrooms*—look, Maggie—*Maggie and I look and Mother is pointing and there are the mushrooms, small, dark, deep in the grass. I jump up and down clapping my hands and Mother laughs and*—

I open my eyes to total blackness. I don't know what that was. I don't know who that was. I close them and I'm—

*—hiding along the monastery wall where the long grass tickles my feet, hiding because I must wait till the boys are gone until I can come inside and learn my letters, it must be a secret because I am only a girl, only a girl, but the priest says I can read as well as any scholar and I—*

I'm dying.

*—walking through the market square, they are watching me, the villagers, with their hateful eyes, muttering and murmuring, they hear the stories and they spread them, poisonous as belladonna, and the words will grow into actions, but not yet because the worst has not been said aloud, but it is only a matter of time before they call me a—*

Trapped.

*—in the belly of the kitchen where I labor over the great cast-iron pot, my hair drawn back under the cloth, my cheeks shiny with sweat, waiting for tonight, when I will silently climb the stairs, my heart is pounding, and there is the candle that he has placed for me on the sev-*

*enth step, leading me on and up, my beloved waits for me at the top of the tower, no longer a lord nor I a servant but lovers together, he has said so and—*

Hard to breathe.

*"Take care of him, Katherine. I give him to you."*

Lucas.

My eyes spring open.

*Remember Lucas.* I have to stay awake. *I can't give in.* I must wake myself up. I will shock myself awake.

I force my hand to close over the ring brooch. It will burn me and the pain will keep me awake, but now it is only warm so I push the pad of my thumb into the tip of the little spearlike clasp and the stabbing, sharp and clear and—

*He keeps it in his chamber in the little gilded vault. I remember it fastened on his cloak, his beautiful woolen cloak now puddled upon the floor.* It has been in my family for time out of mind, it is from a Celtic tribe and very old—*he told me this when I lay with him in the dark, high in the highest tower, before he covered my body with his.*

*Now I hold it up. It shines in the light of the moon, and here in the sweet night air of the garden it will serve my purpose well before I replace it. Then I take the knife. I say the ancient words over it and slide the blade against my wrists, savoring the pain—*

The circle of metal grows almost hot in my palm, I must be dying, must be dying, my mind is slipping away and *Oh God I don't want to die I don't want to die I—*

*—am walking past the great hall. The feast still rages. They are all sodden with drink. The wooden table drenched with spilled mead. Bones on the floor amid the rushes, the dogs snarling, the nobility unraveling. The music is bawdy, the revelers raucous. No one sees me. Hooded, silent. They would not see me anyway. They do not see servants. Even ones who leave a thin trail of red behind them. I do not hurry.* A toast! *someone cries. The words are stones. They hail against my back. I halt.* A toast! *The ones who still can raise their chalices do. They have been toasting all night. They look toward the lord and lady. The lord's face is flushed. His eyes shine. He laughs. He takes his lady's hand. He is soaked with mead and triumph. He kisses his lady's hand. A great shout from the guests.* A toast! *I walk on. Still I can hear the words:* May you bear many sons! *I smile.*

But my eyelids are so heavy, if I could just rest for a moment and I'll wake up from this, I'll—

*—go down to the crypt. It is quiet here in the place of the dead. There is no warmth. There is no noise. A few torches flicker high above me in their iron brackets. I walk past the great stone coffins; I walk underneath the angels with their dead stone eyes. I walk toward the thing that waits for me in the farthest corner, my own stone bed. It will serve me well. It houses another but I know she will not mind.*

*I push against the lid. The grating sound of stone across stone, giant's teeth grinding together. I push until there is just enough room to slide in. I shed my garments, but my wrists remain wreathed in red.* From dust have ye come, and to dust ye shall return. *Easing in, limb by limb, first one leg and then the other. Down into the fetid dark. There are bones in here. I know the previous owner will not protest. I am only a servant and not a person, after all. Lying on my back in my final bed, I use almost all of my remaining strength to pull the lid back across. My will has been seeping out from my veins, leaving a line of life, leaving my mark. My fingers slip and scrape on the stone. I bite at my lip, my fingers are bloody bits, my arms scream protest, and finally, finally with a snarl of grit, the lid slowly begins to give till there is only a lip of air, my breaths are few and shallow, the knife did its work well, the ring brooch is safe back in his chamber and soon I shall pass, they shall not find me once the fire has started.* I cannot breathe, I cannot breathe . . .

I am I am *I am*

# 28

The woman opens her eyes.

Her eyes are open in the darkness. It is too dark in here. There is not enough air.

Her arms stretch up as her palms press against the stone. The woman begins to push, to exert pressure. The lid is heavy and it should not be possible for someone on her back to move it, and yet, and yet it is moving slowly up and back.

And then one hand emerges from its enclosure, its fingers gripping the side of the lid, and the other continues to push against and out and—

The woman slowly sits up, one vertebrae stacking up upon another until she is still and sitting, and then she pushes farther, exerting her weight. One foot down upon the floor and then the other. Muscles, tendons, tissues, fibers, bones. She moves as if she has not moved for a very long time.

Under the burning torches, rays of light reflected. Rays of light pass through her corneas, her pupils. The iris widens, shrinks, widens again and regulates. The light is malleable; it bends back and back it flies to where it is scooped up and processed by millions upon millions upon millions of cones and rods, rods and cones carrying colors, fine details, shapes in the dim and the dark, primary and secondary and peripheral and straight, and all, all, all is sensed, all is converted into impulses sent up to her mind, her mind where an image is produced.

The woman takes one step. She takes another and now another. Her feet in front of each other. Faster and now she is striding and now she is running.

Up the stone stairs and through the passageway to the great hall, looking neither to the left nor to the right. There is nothing left to see, no lords or ladies in their fine clothes, no servants running errands, no fires burning in the hearths, no tapestries against the walls or rushes upon the floor. And through and out of the arched doorway the woman feels the air against her nakedness and there is a breeze that blows against her skin. The breeze is light, a breath of night. Each cell reacts; each miniscule hair stiffens with joy. She breathes in, aware. Air into her lungs, air that carries all that is good and nourishing to her blood; her blood is rich and bright with all the good things from the air. Her back, her breasts, all exposed to the full, dark world. And life.

She shivers, and delights in her body making its objections known. Her skin is chilled by her own cooling drops of sweat. She marvels at the smallest prickle upon her flesh. Flesh, soft and sensitive. Naked in the night. The stars, icy points above her, and the pull of the earth holding her in one place. Her feet, bare. She hears with ears that cup the sound of the wind through the trees, of the things that wake after dark. Beyond that she hears more and knows that out there she will find what she has been waiting for.

The woman begins to run toward the dark water, toward the small boat, half pulled up upon the sand, sure in her purpose and ready.

# 29

You are waiting for your love. You watched her white face float away; she looked back as you told her the time you expected her to return.

*You have an hour.*

But the moon is rapidly sinking and there's no sight of your beloved. Her hour is almost up. Where is she? There's nowhere for her to go, and anyway, you would have sensed it, you are so connected with her now. You know what she's thinking, what she's feeling, you know her fears and hopes and secrets, her dreams and delights, you would know if she had gone too far, she's close, you're sure. Still, a promise is a promise and Katherine should know you mean what you say. It's important to be true to your word. You look at this man who lies sleeping. You sigh; you nod.

You select a long slim blade from the knife block in the kitchen—there is no need to use your knife yet, which waits for you up on the deck. You're saving it for your special someone, your darling. Happy knife, happy wife, and Katherine is soon to be your bride in blood, in death, in red, a consummation and a marriage of fate. You'll baptize her among the remains of her mortal lover.

You walk up the stairs, outside to the deck to where he lies motionless. You take a moment to inhale the night air, to see the stars shine, the moon swimming pale in the sky. Look over toward where he sleeps. Your heart of hearts did well. It was so thoughtful of her and made your task so much easier. Your Ride loved this man. As for you, he has merely served his purpose. And so you pick up the knife.

"Thank you," you say to the man. Sleeping oblivious below its point, he cannot hear you but it's the thought that counts. *Thank you.*

Then—

—you, who are never surprised, you who know the desires and fantasies and all and everything, the darkest perversions and highest ideals, all the wonderful, brilliant thoughts—

—you don't see her waiting in the dark.

You don't sense her at all, don't smell her redness or sense her many fine and distinctive parts, the cloud of love and doubt and fear and joy and guilt and anxiety and confidence and hope and a thousand other things that make Katherine *Katherine*, make her *her*.

She grips your sacred knife, the knife of the infinite, the knife of the harvest, the knife that only you should ever wield, the knife that you left upon the deck. You who read minds, hear thoughts, consume emotions, who bend an ear to the intimate secrets of the world, you who see in the blackness and who listen to the high, sweet, crystal music of the stars, you did not sense her, at all. Now, for the first time in your existence, you feel the prickle of alarm.

"Katherine," you say, "Katherine, my heart."

But she does not respond, just looks at you, her body quivering, her lips drawing back, her teeth bared in a rictus grin, and a low growl starts up from her chest and you see that she is not Katherine at all but someone else, someone completely different, an alien thing gripping your own blade, naked and feral, her skin pale and cold, her eyes red and swimming with something that isn't *Katherine*, and now you feel more than alarm; your breath quickens and your heart beats and now for the first time you feel fear.

She growls low in her throat, and springs.

And then she is in your arms. But not warm and pliant, now fierce and intent and she is strong, she is hellishly strong, and she is going for your throat, clawing at your eyes, biting and scratching and growling like a rabid dog.

Still, you could finish this.

*And then something deep within you rises up.*
*And then something deep within you rises up.*
*And then something deep within you rises up.*

You know and are aware, and see what happened to the time you thought you'd lost.

The night she had stayed with you and called out in her nightmares and you had come.

"Please," she had said. "Please."

He had heard her deep in the deepest darkness, had risen up from deep within the prison of his own flesh, beneath and behind the wall, the small and secret shining sliver left true, the real him had risen up and up and it was he who had taken her into his arms and it was he who was with her, together merely man and woman, and taken her not in lust or hatred or lechery but in love and in sweetness and in all that is good and right and true, because he had loved her with his human and real and true and tender heart, and in reaching out for that one moment deep in the night he had been himself. He had found himself before the nightmare began again, amid the frenzy and sickness and the terror and despair, the misery and the torture of the innocent, the defilement and debasement and destruction and the ruination of lives, spreading out in a congealed mass, a poisonous web of death that he would know and live with intimately forever and forever. The screams, the pleas, the split flesh and despair.

And now Katherine was in his arms, *his* arms, they were his again, and he knew the endless pain and remorse and suffering and fury and hatred and anguish that would follow if he did not, and so he spoke to the Katherine, to the Katherine he loved deep, deep down. He knew that the woman who hissed and growled and spat and went for his eyes was not her but he believed, he believed that somewhere Katherine was holding on too, and he knew that there was no other course, and so in faith and in love he held out his own body, which was finally his own body again, he opened his arms to her, and with a full and honest heart he gave her back her word.

"Please," David Balan said.

The woman screamed in unholy triumph and sank the knife in deep up to the brim. And the scream pulled the man on the wooden deck back up into the terrible world, and he saw and screamed too and then Katherine was there and she saw how David Balan's eyes rolled up in his head and how he fell back through the wooden rails to the earth below, his eyes still fixed on some point in the sky that he would never see.

*Suffer it to be so now, for thus it becomes us to fulfill all righteousness.*

# *In the Beginning*

He did not see them at first. He had come outside to breathe in the night air and to clear his head. He had stood in the overcrowded warmth, watching as the people came, one after another, to pay tribute or to kneel at her feet. He did not know how the word had spread, only that it had. He was forgotten in the shadows, his heart swollen with misery and loneliness till he could not stay but had come to gaze at the stars that shone down without mercy or pity or judgment.

He stared upward and remembered when he had first laid eyes upon her.

She was small and dark and not without a little prettiness. She had seemed modest. Her parents had needed to coax her forward to greet him. He had gazed down upon her lowered head and upon her dark hair. The marriage was arranged.

Then she had come to him two days after that meeting, alone to his workplace. She stood in the dusty shafts of light, amid the splintered chips and curls of wood. Her eyes were bright and her voice was hard. "Hosanna," she had said and had spoken of visions and angels and the will of the One Most High. She had stood with her eyes shining and her voice rising, and he saw suddenly that she was beautiful, and that her beauty was not for him.

He hit her.

He hit her with the flat of his hand. His hand came sailing out of its own accord and hit her cheek and she stopped talking and the silence was terrible.

He could see the white print of his palm against her cheek and a thin line of red ran from one nostril where the meaty part of his hand had struck her face. She neither shrank nor wept nor begged his forgiveness but instead looked at him with pity and with a terrible tenderness.

He had ordered her to leave him, and then it was he who wept. For he knew that she was beautiful and that he loved her and that she would never be his.

That night he lay tossing in the dark. He would never find the man or men who had taken her innocence from her. Whether she was sly, or whether the loss of her innocence had driven her mad, he did not know, but she would not be swayed from her belief that her visions were true.

When he confided to his family, they urged him to leave her, whether he chose publicly or privately. He told them he would not. His mother wept and his father called him a fool to raise another's child, for he would be known as a cuckold and would bring shame upon their name. He thought only of her face and of the thin red trickle and he knew that he could not.

The next morning he had told her that he too had been visited by the Angel and that the Angel had given his blessing. Weeping, she had embraced him, and her tears fell wet and warm against his chest. It was the first time she had touched him of her own accord. He saw then how he might win some small part of her for himself and was resolved.

And so they had gone out into the world. Not driven out by the whispers or the looks, the small slights that he alone seemed to feel, but because she said that they would not be safe if they stayed. When he pressed her for further explanation she gave none, but only said that they must go. He looked in her eyes and saw the fear and knew that it was true. Though there had been no ceremony, in his heart he was wedded to her and he could not let her go alone.

On the first night of their journey as they had lain under the rough-spun blankets he had reached out in the dark, hoping to find comfort. She did not flinch or protest, but had stayed passive and removed. Her eyes fixed somewhere far above, her body inert as rock. His hand fell away and he did not touch her again, neither in hatred nor in tenderness.

And so they traveled, plodding up and down the stony hills. The sun beat down in the day and the nights were cold and filled with stinging wind. They did not see many others and for long stretches they did not talk. The only sound was the tinny clang of the donkey's bell as it swayed under her growing weight.

He had a shameful, secret hope that in journeying she might lose the babe but she showed no signs of weakness. Her youth and strength and single-mindedness terrified him. He was weary unto the bone but he could never leave her. They were cleaved together with bitter clay.

Finally they could go no farther for her time had come, and so they took the shelter where they could find it.

It had been a hard birth and a long birth, but she had only screamed once, as the infant's head crowned through a cap of blood. The man had thought that this moment would bring them closer, but it was not to be. She had gripped his hand as the sweat broke upon her skin, she had borne down, but even then she was as regal as a queen, and as proud, and showed no sign of needing him. Then the child gave a wail and she screamed out in triumph and in power and in joy.

Long afterward he stood outside in the night, away from her and the silent flock of people who had come to see her and her child, and it was only then that he noticed them.

Three figures stood in the darkness. There were very tall, far taller than any men he had ever seen, with broad shoulders and powerfully built. The rich material of their robes hung in heavy folds, dark against the starlit sky. Their heads were swathed in reams of cloth and he could not see their faces for their backs were turned. He approached them silently, and they did not see him. They stood like statues and did not speak but looked toward the mean little dwelling.

Then out of the silence he heard, "So it has happened."

The voice was low and dark, as if the speaker's throat was filled with earth.

A second speaker answered him light and high, like a wind through the reeds. "We studied the skies, the signs were clear—"

"A Vessel will be born when the spheres align under fiery skies, and she will bear a child who will change the Song." The low voice was impatient. "But how can any child born of a mortal bear such power? He'll be the fire that consumes us all."

Now there was a new voice, scarce above a whisper. It was a voice of endless deserts and white twisted roots, the oldest that the man had ever heard.

"Though the Song will be forever altered, we are but witnesses. The sky may catch alight and burn, or the sun blacken and be snuffed out, but we cannot amend or change the Music. Do not forget that we watch, we bear witness and that is all."

Then there was silence and the man thought the exchange was over. But at last the low voice said, almost hesitantly, "Yet see already what this child's birth has wrought."

"You speak of the one who bears the Scythe?"

"The One who Harvests, who brings untold suffering unto the daughters of Eve," replied the low voice.

"An Ender of Life so that more shall live." The ancient whisper was inexorable. "He comes to preserve the Harmony."

There was silence and then the low voice muttered, "Let us pay our respects and leave this place. The night shall soon fade and the journey back is long."

The three figures began to move toward the stable and those it sheltered. At that moment the stars seemed to flare with an awesome and terrible brightness and he could see them clearly. Their robes were dark plum, burnished copper, and deep blue embroidered with glints of gold and silver thread. He saw that each of them carried an object. The first held a small wooden chest with a delicate golden lattice, the second carried a casket woven of pale cream reeds, and the third cupped a jar burnished with a purplish glaze. Their faces remained shadowed by the folds of fabric, but he saw by their hands that their skin was the color of sand and their fingers, curled around their offerings, seemed unusually long and slender. As the man stood watching them, the last figure turned and looked at him, just for a moment, before turning back to follow his companions.

Then the man stood for a long while, alone in the dark.

Years would pass, enough years for a good life, though the man himself would not last another thirty seasons. What days were his he used profitably; his nights were for the most part calm and tranquil. But sometimes, and without warning, the memory would come to him. He would be taken there again. Standing and watching the three figures moving slowly toward the humble shelter where the woman and the child slept, where the people came to pay homage.

He would remember how the last figure turned and stared. Then the man would grow cold. His teeth would clench and his eyes would shut tight, but still he would see it clear, what no man was meant to see.

The silver eyes, the alien gaze.

# SICKLE MAN FOUND DEAD

## "It was like the Devil was on his side"

THE NOTORIOUS SERIAL KILLER RESPONSIBLE for the deaths of twelve women has now been identified as David Balan, a 35-year-old lawyer at Jacob and Rivera.

According to authorities, police discovered Balan's body early Sunday morning in Waterville, Vt., after they received a letter written by Balan. The document stated where his body was to be found.

Balan had suffered a broken neck along with significant chest wounds, and it's believed he fell backward from a two-story wooden balcony after being fatally stabbed by Katherine Emerson during a struggle.

An anonymous tipster informed police that Balan had left for Vermont, intending to kill Katherine Emerson, the girlfriend of Sael de Villias. One of Balan's closest friends, de Villias is CEO of RuBu Enterprises.

Balan came to be known as the Sickle Man because he used a sickle blade to mutilate his victims' bodies in a series of murders that baffled New York City police. He held the city under a siege of terror for over four months. His victims—women between the ages of 20 and 37—were found in their own locked apartments, undressed and bound on their beds.

Though many of the victims had security cameras in their buildings, and at least seven of them had doormen, Balan was never caught on camera. The doormen and security guards never identified him. Nor could any eyewitnesses place him with the victims.

"He was like a ghost," said Nick Gusti, a chief detective for the New York City Police Department, during a press conference Sunday afternoon. "He seemed to come and go as he pleased."

Balan was meticulous and left little DNA evidence or fingerprints, despite undressing his victims and sometimes spending a significant amount of time in their apartments. Experts can't account for this phenomenon, which is unprecedented.

"It was uncanny," said Sandra Haddon, a forensic analyst at the facility. "I've been working at this lab for 14 years and I've never seen anything like it."

During a search of Balan's apartment, police found a journal documenting some of the killings. Items belonging to the victims were also found.

"He had these things hidden all over the apartment. It was a truly disturbing scene," said William Heinreich, an NYPD spokesman.

Eliza Clare, an FBI criminologist and psychiatrist, believes that Balan was obsessed with Emerson from early on, but that his true target was de Villias. "Killing Andrea Bowers and then planning to kill Katherine Emerson was his way of achieving intimacy," Clare said. The ritualistic markings indicate that every kill was highly planned, building up to a final kill.

Several of Balan's friends and family members refuse to believe that he was the Sickle Man. His mother, Sierra Balan, believes that her son was framed.

"David would never commit such atrocities. He's innocent," she said in an interview. "I'll never accept it."

"I'm in total shock," added Jeanette Castelli, a colleague and friend, who said she had known Balan since they were freshman at Haywood along with de Villias. "I never knew him to treat a woman disrespectfully, let alone be capable of such brutality."

De Villias and Emerson repeatedly declined to comment.

Balan, described by those who knew him as personable, attractive, and a "nice guy," has been likened to Ted Bundy, the infamous serial killer who confessed to 28 murders, and who may have caused the deaths of many more.

"The comparison to Bundy makes sense," said Clare. "Both men were attractive, white, upper middle class, and well educated. They used their charm, looks, and education to lure and prey upon single women."

Most of the victims' family members expressed relief that Balan was found dead. "While his death won't bring my sister back, at least we know it's over," said Susie Ranford, who founded the organization DWHA (Don't

Walk Home Alone) as a safe way to escort single women back to their apartments in honor of her sister, 29-year-old Emily "Emmy" Ranford, the fourth victim of the Sickle Man.

But many remain outraged and grief-stricken.

"I wish I could have killed him myself," said Miguel Rodriguez, father of Balan's second victim, 23-year-old Samantha Rodriguez.

"We'll never know why he did it. He's ruined countless lives," said Anthony Goldmark, fiancé of the fifth victim, 27-year-old Melissa Lin.

Gusti also expressed frustration at Balan's death. "We wanted to question him and discover his methods to prevent this from ever happening again," he said. "There are many unanswered questions."

Balan's body was claimed by his parents, Martin and Sierra Balan. A private funeral will be held in Evergreens, Conn., and his body will be buried in an undisclosed location.

"Our prayers and thoughts are with the victims' family and friends," New York City mayor Donald McMeel said in a statement. "The city grieves with them over their tragic loss. They are gone but will never be forgotten."

# 30

Every night it's the same dream.

In his dream everything is white. The canvas tent is white and the tablecloths are white. There are huge arrangements of summer flowers: lavender, lupines, rosemary, also summer roses. A breeze comes through the entrances to the tent. In this dream everyone is happy, everyone is laughing. Guests sit at small round tables. There are little candles on the tables, lit in preparation for the evening. He and Katherine are sitting at the main table facing the guests. In front of them is a cake. The cake is tall with multiple tiers and stiff white frosting. In his dream he knows that it's a carrot cake, which is his favorite. In his dream he knows that he must give a speech, and that he and Katherine must cut the cake. He hears the light clinking of a fork upon a glass, another and another.

"Speech, speech!" somebody calls and everyone starts chanting together. He rises and Katherine rises too.

He says, "I just want to say that I love all of you. Each and every one of you. Thank you for being a part of my life, for your love, support, friendship, and wisdom." In his dream he turns to Katherine and says, "Wherever you are, that place is home."

In his dream they kiss. A sweet soft kiss where everyone claps and laughs and says, "*Awww.*"

That is the good part of the dream.

Then he picks up the knife. It's a normal cake knife, silver, curved, and flat. As he takes it, it turns in his hands as if it were alive. It moves like a small animal; it shifts. He looks down and sees that it's changed. It's older and larger. The blade is sharp on both sides. The hilt is curved. It's rusty with age, almost reddish.

This is the part where he begins to be frightened.

The clapping and cheering grow louder.

Someone calls, "Cut the cake!" Everyone takes up the chant: "Cut the cake! Cut the cake!"

He does not want to cut the cake with this knife. This knife is wrong. Katherine puts her hand over his. Katherine does not notice that the knife has changed, that it is no longer a cake knife, that it is something else. He tries to tell her that it is not the same knife, that there is something wrong. He doesn't want this rusty, strange knife near their wedding cake.

She shakes her head and smiles at him. Her hand pushes down on his hand that holds the knife. It's not a cake knife. It's a dagger.

She smiles tenderly but she is very strong. He is being forced to cut the cake with the dagger. He tries to move away and he looks up at his guests to ask for help and then he sees—

The woman.

The woman stands at the entrance. Long dark hair falls heavy and spreads across her shoulders. Her skin is pale and waxy. She wears a long-sleeved green dress. The dress seems worn and patched and white with mold in parts, but no, *It can't be mold*, he thinks. He peers, trying to see more, but she stands well apart from the crowd. She does not chant or clap or cheer or laugh.

She looks at him, as he remembers she always looked at him. Her eyes are hollowed shadows. She smiles.

"Cut the cake! Cut the cake!"

He looks down again and sees that the knife is hovering over the large white cake.

He tries to cry out, *No!* Because that knife shouldn't touch their cake, their future, their happiness.

But in the dream he cannot stop. In the dream they plunge the knife into the cake.

Dark liquid oozes out on each side of the knife. Dark red liquid pools on the plate.

He looks up and the guests are gone. There's no one except David and Katherine, now sitting at the back of the tent.

They both look at him and start to clap and cheer. He smiles at them but then he sees her, the woman with the long dark hair, moving toward them from the side. She's holding out a plate. On the plate is a piece of the bloody cake. Katherine and David cannot see but behind her back she holds a dagger with a large and ornate handle. She shuffles slowly toward them, her hair obscuring her face.

*No!* He tries to scream, but no sound comes out. He tries to run but the air has thickened and turned to taffy. The woman is at their table and both David and Katherine are looking up and she bends down to speak with them and she is offering a slice and David holds out his plate and says—

*Stop*, he tries to howl. *Stop!*

David holds out his plate and says, "Please."

And the woman takes the knife from behind her back and holds it high above her head and as the knife swings down Katherine doesn't look at the woman or at David but twists her head to look at Sael. She grins and her grin is a bloody smear of red.

And then he wakes up, drenched in sweat, his heart pounding. He lies awake. Lies staring up at the ceiling as the white noise machine says *shhh*. He can see the ceiling because of the crack of light that comes from the bathroom. He can't sleep in total darkness anymore. He lies on his back, staring up at the ceiling. Maybe he'll switch on the TV. Maybe in a moment he'll get up, take a piss. Maybe he'll go to the kitchen, open the fridge, close the fridge again. Maybe he'll think about having a beer. Maybe he'll pour himself another glass of water. Maybe he'll surf the web, maybe he'll do some work. He might do any of these things. He lies awake, stares at the ceiling.

"What does it mean?" he asked a therapist, back when he thought therapy might help him.

*What do you think it means?*

But Sael doesn't want to talk about what it means; he just wants the dream to stop. Therapy doesn't seem to be helping. In the bathroom cupboard there's a small bottle filled with pills. There are prescriptions for Ambien and for Xanax and for Clonazepam. He might go and take one. Once he has the dream sometimes he can sleep afterward, with a little help. Maybe he'll take one. He doesn't.

He lies awake.

God knows how many of the sleeping tablets she had given him. *You could have killed me—you know that, right? Or maybe that was the plan.* He was out of it but he still hears that scream that ripped him up, and still dazed and blinking he saw—

*It was self-defense; he was about to kill us.*

—her stabbing David full in the chest as he stood before her with open arms. David, eyes rolled up to the skies, falling back through the rails, already a broken thing.

*Sael, please believe me.*

But how can he believe anything she says ever again?

*So David told you that I was—*

*Yes.*

*And you believed him?*

*Yes.*

*Why, Katherine?* Why?

*I don't know, I don't know! I guess the time you cut off my underwear, or you came to my window—*

*And that makes me a serial killer—*

I was scared! *And he told me that lie about Sara.*

*I told you about her already. I was honest with you—*

*I was scared* shitless. *I didn't know—*

The irony will kill him. He who betrayed David has now been betrayed. David, the one who brought them together, will be the one who will ultimately and forever keep them apart.

*So you thought I was—*

*It's not like that—*

*You thought I was a serial killer.*

...

*You thought I had killed Sara and all those other women.*

*Sael, I—*

*You thought I was going to kill you.*

...

*Answer me, goddamn you!*

*Yes.*

It's everywhere. Their faces, the story, but not the real story, any version they can get, any rumor they can find. A viral disease, a rash of opinion, speculation; splashed out, debated, discussed, argued, agreed, theorized, and marveled at. He hardly goes out in public these days. When he has to, he wears sunglasses and a hat. It doesn't help.

*The Sickle Man, responsible for the deaths of twelve known victims, a monster that terrified a city, was pronounced dead on—*

People look at him differently. It's not just the police, the incredulous, disbelieving detectives who are suspicious of his motives. *You never had a suspicion, never talked about it? Come on. You were sleeping through the attack? For how long?*

Even close friends no longer seem close, as if he should have known something. Did he know something? Why didn't he know something? Why? Perhaps he was in on it. *You were always so close.* Perhaps he knew deep down that there's a cover-up—there always is. Why didn't he know or say or do something about the man he knew as his best friend, about David, who was squeamish when it came to putting jars over spiders, roaches, refusing to use traps for the mice that overran the dorms?

*But they're so cute! We can tame them, train them to bring us beer, sing in an a cappella group.*

The experts call them trophies, the things they found in David's apartment. Not just the journals and the notes and all the rest, not the underwear, but things like the book, the figurine, the hair clip, and the lipstick. It's the mundane and trivial. There's an earring and a shoe, a toothbrush, a photo, some fish food.

*David calling him, or concerned over beers: "Sael, man, I'm worried about you, talk to me. What's going on?"*

There were many, many objects, each a tribute to the girl he had slaughtered.

*Sael, Sael! Give us a comment! What do you have to say? Sael! Would you be prepared to do an interview? A story? Sael, we'd love to know what really happened, we want to know, we need to hear your side of it.*

"Not David," he said to the police, to the detectives, to anyone who would listen. "Not David, he couldn't have been." There's been a mistake, a terrible mistake, but the letter and what tiny shreds of evidence remained were all saying yes, yes, yes, he was.

*Hi, do you know where Cooper Hall is? I'm totally lost.*
*No problem, I'm going that way myself.*
*Thanks.*
*I'm Sael.*
*I'm David, nice to meet you.*

*Our hearts go out to those who were involved in this tragedy and to their families and friends.*

*Want to grab a drink after class?*
*Sure.*

*Katherine Emerson, age thirty-four, is the sole survivor of the Sickle Man's brutal attacks.*

*This brave and courageous young woman fought to defend not only herself but also her boyfr—*

He had run, groggy and stumbling, down the steps to where David lay. He had screamed at her when she tried to come close. Bloody and dirty like some cliché from a horror movie. Screamed and screamed and sobbed and the words he eventually said were lost in the sirens' howl heard from far away in the country night. They had had to give him a tranquilizer. His voice was hoarse from screaming.

*You crazy bitch, you psycho, you killed him, you killed him, you killed him!*

It's been one month, two weeks, and four days since he last saw her.

*I love you, Sael, please don't do this.*

Maybe he'll get up, put on some running clothes, go for a run.

*Sael, I'm begging you. Please, please let's get through this together.*

He can run along the river. Not many people around. They won't bother him.

*Sael, I need you.*

He'll run and he'll run and he'll run until the thoughts are squeezed from his mind and only the path lies before him; he'll run until all he will hear is the pounding of his heart and all he will feel is the heave in his chest for air, in and out, in and out, driving him on and on and on.

*Sael, you said you loved me. I thought you loved me. I thought you wanted to marry me.*

He'll run until he can no longer think of anything or anyone, until there is nothing but him running.

*The thing is, Katherine, I thought I did too.*

In a moment he'll get up, but for now he lies awake.

# 31

We sit on a park bench and watch the people go by. Some teenagers sit on the grass, all denim and laughter; there is the inevitable guitar but nothing too terrible. For once the Hare Krishnas aren't singing. There are pigeons fighting over half a roll. People stroll. A girl and a guy take pictures with old-fashioned cameras. I turn to my companion.

"How are you holding up, frozen-yogurt-wise?"

His solemn brown eyes regard me for a moment, and then he goes back to meticulously licking round and round the side of his cone to make it even and not drip. He nods.

"It's good?"

"It's good."

"Good." I close my eyes for just a moment, lean back, allow myself to listen to the city around us.

A breeze blows, scuttling the twigs, a paper cup; somewhere a small dog barks; cars honk but sound almost amiable. It's easy to believe in the world at the tail end of a Sunday afternoon while eating frozen yogurt. I open my eyes as a young couple, midtwenties, walk by hand in hand, talking, laughing.

Instinctively I put my hand up and feel the faintest presence underneath my shirt, where it still hangs. *Katherine, will you wear this, now and forever?*

"Kat?"

"Yes, hon?" I sit up, look at him. "What's up?"

"Want a taste?" He proffers his cone.

I know what this means. When I was four years old ice cream was sacred, not to be shared with anyone, or hardly anyone. I must have looked really sad just then.

"Thank you so much!" I take a tiny taste. Still, the amount of sugar is enough to light up a city. "Wow! That's sweet."

"Want another one?"

"I'm okay. Thanks, love."

I yawn. It's been a long day. I was up at seven and on the train. Reading the Sunday paper I saw my story slip to page sixteen. Again I gave silent thanks for the governor who had come so chivalrously into my life to take the brunt of the media.

*Thank you, Governor, for your insatiable appetites, for your penchant for underage girls, for your taste in leather whips, diapers, and cocaine. While I feel terrible for your wife and family, I promise that I will vote for you in the next election. If you're kicked out I'll send you a fruit basket, something to say thank you.*

It is Sunday and the train is on its off-peak schedule, so there was time to go over the documents again, to make sure I've signed all the places I needed to sign. The pages sent by the lawyers, and the New York State Office of Children and Family Services and the courts and the IRS all working it out so Katherine Anne Emerson can become the legal guardian of Lucas Theodore Bowers.

Most single women should take out a life insurance policy, but many don't. I never did. However, nonsmoking, in excellent health and her early thirties, single working mother Andrea Bowers did.

I could have told them, though, that Andrea was always careful, always meticulous when it came to her financial life. Always paid the rent on time, split the utilities, paid her taxes early, saved and was frugal, not cheap, but man, she was careful.

And in this case Lucas will be well provided for.

There is a stipulation that a large portion of the insurance payout must be put away for college, which I am happy with, and the rest is left to the legal guardian's discretion, which turns out to be mine.

In just three weeks the system has become all speed and efficiency; after all it's for the good of the child and honoring the final wishes of the parent. It probably has nothing to do with the fact that when the attractive young woman who defended herself against the infamous killer known as the Sickle Man, and who became the city's and America's and most likely the world's darling, was prevented from being able to care for her murdered friend's adorable orphaned child, she threatened to become vocal on talk shows and in the media, and perhaps she did have the potential to make things extremely uncomfortable for everyone involved.

*Take care of him, Katherine.*

Or maybe it is for the good of the child.

Regardless I was there, ringing the doorbell of this tired-looking suburban house, and I heard him running with a cry of:

"Kat!"

He was finally in my arms and squeezing me tight and tight around the neck.

"Kat! Kat!"

*Andrea, I will.*

On the ride back we were silent, looking out of the window,

lulled by the motion of the train, by the station names receding. It seems somehow that we both want distance between that place and us until we know that we've truly escaped, until we are ready to speak.

And there is so much to talk about and so much to do that I am completely overwhelmed. That's why we're eating frozen yogurt in the park. First things first, one step at a time.

Now, as Lucas concentrates on licking the sides of his cone, I can ask. "So what happened to Mrs. Kaskow? She seemed . . . kind of strange when we said good-bye."

She had been more than that; white-faced, tight-lipped. His bag had been packed, standing ready at the door. "Good-bye, have a good journey," then closing the door fast, clicking the lock.

"She scared. She scared of me when I told her those things." He is matter-of-fact, just stating a truth.

The police were reluctant to tell us, but we eventually we found out.

Mrs. Kaskow was the anonymous tipster who informed first the New York detectives and then the local sheriff's department in Vermont. "She must really care about you," said one cop, shaking his head. "She was *determined* that we send somebody out here." Sael had nodded, grim-faced, but I knew who was really behind it.

Now I have to ask. "What things?"

"Momma and this other girl came."

"Girl, not a lady?"

"No, she was teenager, she had metal bracelets on her teeth." He bares his teeth at me.

"Braces? Okay, go on."

"And they say that I needed to wake her and tell her to call the police to tell them to go find you."

He had stood at the side of her bed. The cabin address had been scrawled in a childish crayoned hand.

"What did she say?"

"She was real mad. She told me to go back to bed if I didn't want a spanking."

"What did you do?"

"They said that if she said no, I had to tell her that her sister Mindy said, 'Remember the summer with Uncle Nicky and the pool.' "

*What the hell does that mean?* "What did she do?"

"She turned on the light and look at me and she got very scared like she seen a monster and shaking and she said, 'It's a joke, how do you know that, you can't know that, no one knows about that, you can't know that, why are you doing this to me?'

"Then I told her that Mindy say, 'Tell Lalabelle that a promise is a promise. Tell her I say she has to call.' "

*So Cheryl Kaskow was a Lalabelle once.* "And she called?"

But now Lucas can't stop; the words tumble out. "Kat, she was crying and crying, she told me to go to bed and called me a bad name." He looks down.

"You felt bad?"

He nods. "She say I was a freak. She screamed at me to get out of her room. 'Get out of here, you freak.' " He looks up. "Why did she say those things? Why was she so mad with me?"

*You killed him, you bitch, you fucking bitch, you killed him, you killed him, you fucking psycho bitch, you killed—*

"Oh, honey, you're not a freak. I'm sorry she called you that. She was just a little scared. Sometimes we sound mad and say mean things, but we're not, we're just scared."

*You psycho, you fucking stabbed him, you stabbed him, why, you bitch, you crazy bitch—*

He nods but doesn't meet my eye. His lip is trembling.

"Hey, look at me."

Finally he looks up.

"I'm sorry you made her scared, but you had to get her to call because I needed help. Your momma and Mindy knew that. You had to help me and I'm very, very proud of you."

"Kat, the pretend man, is he gone now?"

"Yes, babe, he is."

"Good. He was bad."

"Well, it's complicated." I can feel my throat close a little; tears prick at my lids.

"But he hurted the ladies and my momma."

*Can I tell you a secret? I have not been David for a while now.*

"Yes, that part of him was very bad."

"He won't come back?"

"No, babe, he's not coming back."

He looks at me a moment longer and then nods. "Okay."

"So, there's a lot of new things coming up for us."

"Like what?"

I try to sound casual. "I was thinking, how about a new school, how do you feel about that?"

I've been really worried about this. I want him to have the security of a place he knows, but there he'll always be seen as the child of one of the victims. The looks, the talk—he needs a fresh start. Let people draw their own conclusions when they see us. They don't have to know anything.

"Okay."

"Not worried?"

"No. Mrs. Ryder was kind of mean."

"Well, I guess she also got a little scared." I take a breath, plunge on. "Lucas, maybe it's a good idea not to tell people about the ladies."

He smiles, shakes his head. "But the ladies aren't here now."

*That's a mercy at any rate.* "Well, maybe with . . . stuff like that you can tell me first? Okay?"

"Okay."

"And guess what the other new thing is?"

"What?"

"We're going to be moving."

This gets his attention. "With a truck?"

I laugh at this reaction. "There might be a truck involved. Why?"

"My friend Caleb's family moved and he said there was a huge truck bigger than T-Rex!"

"Wow, that's pretty big. I don't know if our truck will be that big. I guess we'll see."

"Where are we going to live?"

"Where do you want to live?"

"Somewhere where I can have my own room."

"I think we can manage that. What else?"

"And my crayons."

"Okay."

"And a fireman's pole."

"Why?"

"So that when we need to go somewhere and you call, 'Lucas, come down and have your breakfast!' I can just slide down the pole!"

"Well, we'll certainly keep it in mind when we're looking. Anything else?"

"Kat?"

"Yeah?"

He looks nervous now. This makes me nervous. I don't want to think about what Lucas is capable of asking me, what I'll be forced to answer.

*Are you sure the pretend man is gone? Why can't we live with my momma? What if the ladies come back?*

I brace myself.

"Can we get a dog?"

"A dog?"

"Yeah, can we?"

The relief makes me feel a little high. Actually a dog would be pretty nice. "Why not?"

"Yay!" He bounces up and down, does a happy dance, singing, wiggling all over, and shaking his little butt. "A dog! A dog! A dog!"

It's completely adorable and hilarious. I start laughing. "I just wish you'd be a *little* more excited."

"Oh!" A sudden thought has just occurred to him. He stops. Looks at me worried again. "Kat?"

"Lucas?"

"Would a dog be bad for the baby?"

I look at him. A car horn blats, the guitar plays, and the teenagers' laughter sounds muted and far away.

"What baby?"

"The baby who's coming, the one you're going to have."

It has only been a feeling. It could have been stress; there could have been a million reasons why I've been late. I haven't even bought the test yet.

I force myself to keep my voice calm, to speak carefully. "The baby that's coming, you know about that, huh?"

"I guess maybe a dog would hurt it."

Already he's preparing himself for disappointment, trying to be a big boy, trying to be strong. I look at him. He looks back, all of four years old, brown eyes anxiously watching me, waiting for my answer.

"No, Lucas," I say at last, "I don't think a dog would hurt the baby."

His anxious look melts away, his whole face lights up with a smile. He puts his small, slightly sticky hand on mine and confides his final secret into my ear in the warm late afternoon.

"I'm going to call him Noodle."

# EPILOGUE

He hadn't even wanted to take the extra course in the first place. "Photography using darkrooms?" he asked. "Really?"

"Every little bit helps," his friend Ian had said. "Try out everything—colleges love that kind of crap."

It hadn't been too bad at that. The instructor, Phil, used to be something of a big deal, took pictures of some pretty famous people back in the day. It was generally understood that as long as you didn't get him started on light because he'd probably come in his pants, he was cool enough.

It was about two weeks into the course that she had sat down next to him and asked if he was wearing his Yankees cap ironically.

"No," he had said, surprised.

"Good," she had said, "irony is so last year," and smiled.

Her name was Lorna. She had one side of her head shaved, though she could put her hair over it, and a small stud in her lip and a gummy bear tattoo on her right upper arm. He thought she was beautiful and unlike anyone he'd ever met, fiercely opinionated and funny. He'd been too terrified to ask her out on a date. She'd probably laugh in his face if he suggested movies and dinner.

He didn't remember who had suggested they go to the small park in Union Square for their assignment, but now they were here. Lorna had wanted to take pictures of the tourists reacting to the Hare Krishnas singing and dancing and tripping out. Only the Hare Krishnas weren't there. "Typical," Lorna said. "Well, let's see what else we can find, now we're here."

There had been a homeless person sitting a few yards away from a wealthy-looking woman with several shopping bags at her elegantly sandaled feet, sunglasses on, talking on her cell phone, but Lorna wasn't having it. "Been done a million times before," she said. However, she had perked up at the sight of the pigeons fighting over a bread roll near a sleeping Rastafarian. "Not bad!" She began to take pictures.

He took a few and then saw them sitting just a few yards over.

He liked the play of light, the way they were sitting together, independent but comfortable. The little kid was downright cute and the woman was striking. She had a familiar quality, *something*—he couldn't put a finger on it.

He nudged Lorna. She took in the scene, the woman and little boy sitting on the bench, underneath the trees, the golden light, the ice cream cone, the sense of peace, and dismissed it with a shake. "*Total* Hallmark." She yawned and went back to the pigeons and the Rastafarian.

He looked again and without thinking, or even adjusting his lens, turned and pressed the button.

*Click.*

Later down in the darkroom, dimly red and chemical-smelling, they took turns fishing at the pictures, and sure enough there was something cool about seeing the image rise and appear, like an old-timey magic trick.

He figured Phil was right. You had to go a little old school to truly understand and appreciate photography.

He was standing, staring at the picture, when Lorna came up behind him.

"What?" she asked. "What is it?" Then she had looked herself.

"Not my kind of thing," she conceded at last, "but I like the way you got the woman with the short hair all kind of glowing and out of focus. How'd you do that?"

"Don't know," he said, still staring. She looked, shrugged, and then started putting the equipment away.

The woman and the little boy sitting on the park bench, eating ice cream, holding hands—all that he remembered. The white chick glowing and smeary in a cool way, as if he had managed to overexpose only her, somehow, but that's not what bothered him. It was the other woman he didn't remember. But there she was, black and thin and attractive, standing a little to the side of the bench, her hand lightly resting on the top.

Lorna called his name. "Some of us are going to Cort's for some beers! Wanna come?"

The woman in the picture was looking down on the two who sat on the bench with a wistful look, half smiling. It was a strange sort of smile, sad and proud all at the same time.

"Mike?"

"Coming," he called as he ran up the stairs.

"Geez, what took you so long?" But she said it with a smile.

"Sorry," he said, returning her smile as they started off down the street.

Ultimately Lorna was right, he decided. Apart from the exposed quality of the woman on the bench, there was nothing really special about the scene after all. But that was okay; there were plenty of other pictures to choose from. He wasn't going to think about it anymore. All that mattered was that he was out with the girl of his dreams and the night was still young.

# *Acknowledgments*

It took me around four years to complete this book, and along the way I was supported and encouraged by a score of amazing people. I can only trust and pray I will be forgiven if I don't mention each and every one of them. There are some, however, that must be thanked for playing such a crucial role. To my phenomenal agent Alexandra Machinist, thank you for believing in me from the first; you are the ultimate reader and doer. To my shining star of an editor Hannah Wood, who has been with me every step of the way; Hannah, without your brilliant insight and passion, this book would not be what it is. You rock. Thank you to everyone at HarperCollins, for their incredible work and commitment. To Dorothy Vincent, for her excellent international representation and board game nights! Thanks to senior trial attorney Richard LaFontaine, for talking with me about lawyers and crime, and to Heather Haddon, for helping me with my article. Thanks to John Vincler and the staff at the Sherman Fairchild Reading Room of the Morgan Library, who provided such inspiring material and made me feel so welcome. Thanks to Mike Javett, for his support during my writing days, and to Fred Wistow, for his help and advice. Thanks to my earliest readers Alex Goldmark, Mariana Elder, and Jean Casetelli, your feedback and thoughts were invaluable. To the Paragraph: Workspace for Writers, for providing me with the perfect space to write this book, and to all the amazing writers I know there, and whom I think of as my writing family. To the Arismans, for their continued love and friendship throughout the years, and to Kathy Tagg, for always raising a glass with me. Thanks also to the late, great Cortland McMeel, who first took a chance on me and published my work. Cort, I miss you and wish you were here. Thanks to Lucy, who has talked me through some of my darkest days back into a lighter place. You helped me become a better writer. To New York and the people who live here, for the endless inspiration. Finally, my deepest thanks to my most beloved Armando. Armando, you keep me anchored in all storms. Wherever you are, that place is home. *Te amo, mi amor.*

# *About the Author*

A native of South Africa, **Sophie Jaff** is an alumna of the Graduate Musical Theatre Writing Program at Tisch School of the Arts, New York University, and a fellow of the Dramatists Guild of America. Her work has been performed at Symphony Space, Lincoln Center, the Duplex, the Gershwin, and Goodspeed Musicals. She lives in New York City.